Praise **W** **OF** **'CTION**

DEATH, T

"[A] sure-shot suc———   —*Fresh Fiction*

"*Death, Taxes and Green Tea Ice Cream* is pure Diane Kelly—witty, remarkable, and ever so entertaining."
                —*Affaire de Coeur*

DEATH, TAXES, AND HOT PINK LEG WARMERS

"[B]e prepared for periodic unpredictable, uncontrollable laughing fits. Wonderful scenarios abound when it comes to Tara going undercover in this novel about tax evasion, drugs and (of course) guns. Good depth of characters and well-developed chapters are essential when casting a humorous series, and Ms. Kelly excels in both departments."   —*Night Owl Reviews*

"Tara's sharp mind, sharp wit, *and* sharp skills are brought to life under the topnotch writing of Diane Kelly."
                —*Romance Reviews Today* (Perfect 10)

DEATH, TAXES, AND PEACH SANGRIA

"Great action, screwball comedy similar to the misfortunes of Stephanie Plum, and relationship dynamics entertain the reader from start to finish."   —*Night Owl Reviews*

"In another laugh-filled book of the Death, Taxes and . . . series, Diane Kelly gives Tara the funniest and the deadliest cases of her career with the IRS."
                —*Single Titles*

"Plenty of action and romantic drama round out this laugh-out-loud novel. Fans of Evanovich's Stephanie Plum series or Pollero's Finley Tanner series will enjoy the fast-paced antics and fruity cocktails of Tara Holloway."

—*RT Book Reviews*

"IRS special agent Tara Holloway is back in another action-packed, laugh-filled adventure that is sure to keep you entertained from beginning to end."

—*Fallen Angel Reviews*

DEATH, TAXES, AND EXTRA-HOLD HAIRSPRAY

"As usual, the pace is quick without being frenetic, and the breezy narrative style is perfection—fun and sexy without being over the top." —*RT Book Reviews*

"This is a rollicking adventure that will have you rooting for the IRS for once—and you won't want to put it down until you find out how Tara will overcome all the obstacles in her way. Keep turning those pages—you'll love every second as you try to find out!" —*Reader to Reader Reviews*

"If you've never read one of Diane Kelly's Tara Holloway novels, I strongly recommend that you rectify the situation immediately. The series has gotten better with every single installment, and I'd be shocked if you didn't see these characters gracing your television screen before too long (USA and HBO, I'm looking in your direction). Get on board now so you can say you knew Tara Holloway when." —*The Season for Romance*

"Diane Kelly knows how to rock the romance, and roll the story right into a delightful mix of high drama with great characters." —*The Reading Reviewer*

DEATH, TAXES, AND A SKINNY NO-WHIP LATTE

"Readers will find Kelly's protagonist a kindred spirit to Stephanie Plum: feisty and tenacious, with a self-deprecating sense of humor. Tara is flung into some unnerving situations, including encounters with hired thugs, would-be muggers, and head lice. The laughs lighten up the scary bits, and the nonstop action and snappy dialogue keep the standard plot moving along at a good pace." —*RT Book Reviews*

"Readers should be prepared for a laugh fest. The writer is first class and there is a lot of humor contained in this series. It is a definite keeper." —*Night Owl Romance*

"A quirky, fun tale that pulls you in with its witty heroine and outlandish situations . . . You'll laugh at Tara's predicaments, and cheer her on as she nearly single-handedly tackles the case." —*Romance Reviews Today*

"It is hard not to notice a sexy CPA with a proclivity for weapons. Kelly's sophomore series title . . . has huge romance crossover appeal." —*Library Journal*

"An exciting, fun new mystery series with quirky characters and a twist . . . Who would have ever guessed IRS investigators could be so cool!" —*Guilty Pleasures Book Reviews*

"Kelly's novel is off to a fast start and never slows down. There is suspense but also laugh out loud moments. If you enjoy Stephanie Plum in the Evanovich novels you will love Tara Holloway!" —*Reader to Reader Reviews*

ST. MARTIN'S PAPERBACKS TITLES BY DIANE KELLY

Paw Enforcement

Paw and Order

THE TARA HOLLOWAY NOVELS

Death, Taxes, and a French Manicure

Death, Taxes, and a Skinny No-Whip Latte

Death, Taxes, and Extra-Hold Hairspray

Death, Taxes, and a Sequined Clutch
(an e-original novella)

Death, Taxes, and Peach Sangria

Death, Taxes, and Hot Pink Leg Warmers

Death, Taxes, and Green Tea Ice Cream

Death, Taxes, and Mistletoe Mayhem
(an e-original novella)

Death, Taxes, and Silver Spurs

PAW
AND ORDER

Diane Kelly

St. Martin's Paperbacks

This is a work of fiction. All of the characters, organizations, and events portrayed in this novel are either products of the author's imagination or are used fictitiously.

PAW AND ORDER

Copyright © 2015 by by Diane Kelly.

For information address St. Martin's Press, 175 Fifth Avenue, New York, NY 10010.

ISBN: 978-1-250-04835-6

Printed in the United States of America

St. Martin's Paperbacks edition / January 2015

St. Martin's Paperbacks are published by St. Martin's Press, 175 Fifth Avenue, New York, NY 10010.

10 9 8 7 6 5 4 3 2 1

To Eileen Marsh—the best next-door neighbor, friend, and dog-sitter a woman could ask for. Thanks for always being there for me, Junior, Reggie, and Turalyon!

ACKNOWLEDGMENTS

A HUGE thanks to my brother-in-law and real-life cowboy, David Parsons. I appreciate all the great information about rodeos. This suburban girl would have been clueless without your help!

Thanks also to Sandra and Sergio Castro for sharing your horse sense with me. You're wonderful friends, even if you do always beat me at spoons!

Thanks to my brilliant editor, Holly Ingraham, for your smart and insightful suggestions. It's always great working with you!

Thanks to Sarah Melnyk, Paul Hochman, and everyone else at St. Martin's who worked to put this book in readers' hands and spread the word about the series. You're a wonderful team!

Thanks to Danielle Fiorella and Jennifer Taylor for the cute and eye-catching covers!

Thanks to my agent, Helen Breitwieser, for your efforts in furthering my career!

Thanks to fellow authors Angela Cavener, Hadley Holt,

Cheryl Hathaway, and Sherrel Lee for your insights on my drafts. You ladies are awesome!

Thanks to Liz Bemis-Hittinger of Bemis Promotions for my great Web site and newsletters. You're a wonderful webmistress!

Thanks to my fellow members of Romance Writers of America, as well as the dedicated and hardworking national office staff. A writer couldn't ask for a better support system!

And finally, thanks to my readers. Connecting with you through the stories is so much fun. Enjoy this new adventure with Megan and Brigit!

ONE
IT'S CONVOLUTED

Fort Worth Police Officer Megan Luz

January 1. A new year full of new resolutions, new possibilities, new opportunities.

I was lucky I'd lived to see it. A mere twelve hours ago I'd been tied to a carousel horse with explosives strapped to my chest. If not for bomb squad officer Seth Rutledge I'd be nothing more than a Hefty bag full of body parts right now. Seth had stayed on task right down to the wire, risking his own life to dismantle the bomb, finishing with a mere three seconds to spare.

What did it say that Seth had remained with me even as those final seconds ticked away, despite the fact that he'd dumped me without explanation only a few weeks before? Did he care so much about me that he'd risked his own life for mine? Was he simply dedicated to his duty as a bomb squad officer? Did he have a death wish?

"I suppose I'm about to find out," I thought aloud, earning me a questioning glance from my fluffy shepherd-mix partner who filled my passenger seat and then some.

I turned my metallic-blue Smart Car into the parking lot of the Ol' South Pancake House on University Drive, dragging a pair of truck nuts behind me. Why was my car sporting a pair of the ridiculous rubber testicles? Because I'd bested my fellow officer and former partner Derek "the Big Dick" Mackey by taking down the bomber. Derek had bet his nuts he'd beat me to it. He hadn't.

Suck on that, Derek.

I pulled into the spot next to Seth's '72 Nova, which sported bright orange flames down the sides and personalized license plates that read KABOOM. The car was basically an oversized Hot Wheels. Sometimes I thought it was goofy. Other times I thought it was badass. My feelings about the car generally mirrored my feelings about Seth. Those feelings had been quite volatile given his drive-by dating style and the aforementioned dumping.

"C'mon, Brigit!" I called, motioning for her to exit the car via the driver's door.

She hopped over and down, her nylon POLICE vest rustling with the movements, her toenails clicking on the asphalt. Forgoing my full uniform when I'd dressed this morning, I sported a Fort Worth PD sweatshirt, blue pants, sneakers, and my holster. Though I was off duty, I figured the restaurant staff was less likely to hassle me about bringing Brigit into the place if I wore some semblance of police attire and weaponry. Call me crazy, but I needed my K-9 partner for emotional support. Though the two of us had gotten off to a rocky start, the enormous beast had somehow become my best friend and confidante since we'd been paired together last summer. She was a good listener and always had my back. She was like a furry, four-footed wing woman.

A poster for the upcoming Fort Worth Stock Show and Rodeo was taped in the restaurant's front window. The annual event, which was scheduled to begin in a couple of weeks, would be held just a quarter mile north of the pancake house at the Will Rogers Memorial Complex. With its animal auctions, competitions, and carnival midway, the show brought in tourists, breeders, 4-H clubs, and livestock dealers from miles around. The beer stand and nightly country-western concerts also pulled in a fair share of rowdy shit-kickers intent on raising hell. Luckily, those hell-raising shit-kickers wouldn't be my problem. My beat, the Western 1 Division, sat just south of Interstate 30, a few blocks shy of the stock show grounds. Thank goodness for small favors, huh?

The aromas of fresh coffee, pancakes, and maple syrup greeted us as we stepped into the restaurant. Also greeting us were the bloodshot eyes, green-hued faces, and droopy expressions of customers who'd stayed out late bringing in the new year, only now making their way back home, and who had taken a detour into the pancake house for a quick breakfast before crashing in bed the rest of the day.

A man sitting alone at a table held up a copy of the *Fort Worth Star-Telegram*. The front-page headline read "FWPD Nets the Tunabomber." An absurd name, one slapped on the bomber after the explosives he'd planted in a mall food court sent up a shower of pizza crusts, Chinese noodles, and tuna salad, some of which had ended up in my hair. Under the headline was a photo of the bomber apparently taken from a high school yearbook. Randy Dunham was definitely *2 crazy 2 be 4gotten!* It was too soon to tell whether he'd *have a great summer!* But it was doubtful given that he'd be spending the season in the state penitentiary.

My eyes found Seth sitting at a booth in the back corner. Like me, he'd dressed casually, but in fire department attire—a long-sleeved tee embossed with the department's logo, along with a pair of cargo pants and black ankle boots.

His bomb-sniffing Labrador, Blast, sat on the seat beside
him. With their square jaws and short blond hair, the pair
looked about as alike as two different species possibly
could.

As Seth's green eyes met mine, my heart squirmed in
my chest like a feral kitten afraid of being held. Every syn-
apse in my brain misfired.

Damn, this guy makes me stupid.

I didn't like feeling stupid.

Forcing myself to appear nonchalant, I weaved my way
through the tables, leading Brigit by her leash. Blast stood
as we approached, his tail wagging vigorously, slapping the
vinyl of the booth with a *whap-whap-whap*.

Seth stood, too, though his tail remained motionless. My
gaze dropped from his eyes and ran down over his soft lips
to the cleft in his chin. The odd urge to reach out and touch
it struck me, just like it always did.

"Thanks for coming," he said softly.

His eyes played over my long dark hair. Though I often
wore it up in a twist or ponytail, I'd left it down this morning. Not because I knew he liked it that way and wanted
to torture him or anything like that . . .

Okay. Maybe that *was* why.

"You saved my life last night," I reminded him. What
kind of woman would refuse to meet with a man who'd
rescued her, even if he'd once cruelly broken her heart?

A dark shadow played across his face. "Is that the only
reason you came?"

No, I thought. I supposed I could lie to Seth, but I'd never
been much good at that. Still, if he thought I was going to
welcome him back with open arms, he had another think
coming. Rather than answer, I gestured for Brigit to hop
up onto the seat and slid in after her.

The waitress appeared with menus. "Coffee?"

"Please," I replied.

Seth merely nodded.

When the waitress left to retrieve mugs and a coffee-pot, I opened my menu and pretended to peruse it, afraid to look directly at Seth lest my eyes betray me. I didn't want him to see how thrilled I was he'd asked to meet me, how bad I hoped he might want to resume our budding relationship and see where it might take us. With Seth, I'd felt a special spark I hadn't with the small handful of other guys I'd dated. Of course I was smart enough to know that not all sparks lead to fire. Some fizzle out quickly with little fanfare, like a cheap Chinese firework. But, given the right conditions, I suspected the spark between me and Seth could develop into a blaze big enough to cause Smokey the Bear significant concern.

"I got you something." Seth slid a small rectangle wrapped in poinsettia-print paper across the table. "I wanted to give it to you for Christmas, but . . ." His voice trailed off and he turned to stare out the window.

I watched him for a moment. He'd bought me a Christmas present? Even though he'd broken things off before Thanksgiving? Obviously that meant he'd been thinking of me, maybe planning on trying to work things out between us before the holiday.

But he hadn't.

I wondered what had stopped him. Given the sentence he'd left unfinished, Seth didn't seem inclined to provide an explanation. Maybe he couldn't. Men weren't exactly known for being in touch with their feelings. I'm not sure they knew why they did anything.

I reached out and slid the wrapped package toward me. There was no bow on it, but men weren't exactly known for their gift-wrapping skills, either. Besides, it was the thought that counts, right? Carefully sliding a finger under the tape at one end, I pulled the paper off.

I'd expected something typical, like perfume or a nice

pair of gloves or jewelry. But instead there was a book inside. The latest offering from David Sedaris in hardback, an autographed copy no less.

No one, not even my parents, had ever bought me a more perfect gift.

How had he known?

My question must have been written on my face.

"I figured you must like his work," Seth said. "I noticed you had a few of his earlier books at your apartment."

Seth had noticed my books? Wow, that was pretty damn flattering. In my experience, guys tended only to notice things like exposed cleavage and neon beer signs.

"You don't have that book already, do you?" he asked. "I can exchange it."

"No, I don't have it." I'd been waiting for the cheaper paperback to come out next year. Rookie cops aren't exactly rolling in dough. "This was very n-nice of you, Seth."

Blurgh. My stutter was rearing its ugly head.

He made a motion with his hand. "There's a card inside."

I opened the book and removed a small white envelope containing a card with a cartoon poodle on the front. Inside Seth had scrawled *I screwed the pooch.*

Hmm. It was more of an acknowledgment than an outright apology, though I supposed the sentiment implied remorse. Still, as nice as it was for him to admit his mistake, I'd hoped for more. Was he simply trying to rid himself of guilt? Is that what this meeting and the book were about? I looked up at him, but he'd turned again to stare out the window. I wasn't sure what to say, so I said nothing.

When he finally spoke, he appeared to be addressing the pickup truck parked outside. "You think maybe we could pick up where we left off?"

I swallowed the lump of raw emotion that had formed

in my throat. "We left off with you telling me it wasn't going to work out."

He hesitated a moment before offering a mirthless chuckle and turning back to look at me. "I meant before that. When we were having fun."

It was my turn to hesitate now, my turn to look out the window. As much as I'd wanted him to come crawling back to me, as much as I'd like to see where things between the two of us might lead, there'd be no sense in setting myself up for more heartache. I'd put up with more from Seth than I should have, having no expectations, making no demands, accepting attention when and if he decided to give it to me. In retrospect, that had been a mistake. A mistake I'd made because I'd sensed something bruised, or perhaps even broken, in him.

Seth had served as an army explosive ordnance disposal specialist in Afghanistan, returning with his skin scarred from metal shrapnel, his heart scarred from emotional shrapnel. Though he'd been back home for two years, he'd enlisted in the reserves and spent one weekend a month on duty. Clearly he was still working through things. Whatever he was suffering, I'd hoped to alleviate his pain through caring and compassion and patience.

Still, though I preferred to consider myself a martyr, it would be wrong to attribute my behavior totally to altruistic reasons. Part of why I'd accepted his sporadic attention was because I'd been desperately lonely, willing to take whatever time he'd give me. But, thanks to my K-9 partner, I wasn't nearly so lonely anymore. Brigit had proven herself to be a loyal friend, always there when I needed her. I no longer felt inclined to put up with a relationship that didn't give me what I needed, to settle for whatever scraps might be tossed my way.

I forced myself to turn back to Seth. He was still watching

me. Though his posture was rigid and his expression stoic, his green eyes seemed to be pleading with me.

What should I do?

The fact that he'd stuck with me last night and carefully selected this book said he harbored some feelings for me, but obviously he stunk at relationships. Did I really want to date someone who blew hot and cold? Who didn't seem to know what he wanted? Who left me feeling confused and frustrated, and more alone and lonely than ever? On the other hand, if I couldn't show him some under-standing, offer forgiveness and reconciliation, what kind of person would that make me? And did I even know what I wanted from him? Was I looking for a serious rela-tionship? Or did I just want to have some fun?

Conflicted, I sighed inwardly. *Why did relationships have to be so difficult?*

"C'mon," he said, his mouth pleading now, too, along with his eyes. "I never got to see you twirl your fire ba-tons."

He'd spotted the batons in my apartment but had yet to see me perform with them. My routine had been a big hit back on the high school football fields years ago.

Before I could respond, the waitress returned with our coffee, plunking two steaming mugs down in front of us. She pulled a pencil from behind her ear and a pad from the pocket of her apron. She looked to me. "Ready to order?"

"I'll have the German pancakes." Starting off the new year with so much sugar was probably not the most auspi-cious beginning, especially for a health-conscious person like me, but after nearly losing my life last night I deserved to live a little, right? I angled my head to indicate Brigit. "My partner will have a side of bacon and a side of sau-sage."

"Links or patties?"

"Both, please."

Seth handed the woman his menu. "Same for us guys."

As soon as the waitress left, Seth picked the conversation back up. This time, he leaned forward across the table and looked straight into my eyes. "Look. I acted like an ass. I know that."

My mind went back to the day in question. When I'd pulled up to his house to see if he wanted to go to lunch, I'd witnessed a disturbing exchange between Seth and the grandfather he lived with, an exchange that concluded with his grandfather calling him a dumb bastard. Seth had clearly been hurt by the words. When I'd later tried to discuss the matter with him, hoping I could learn something about him and maybe soothe his hurt feelings, Seth had shut me down instantly, refusing to let me in, refusing to talk. Instead, he'd turned on me, telling me we were through. No good deed goes unpunished, huh?

Seth stretched a hand across the table as if reaching for me, but he pulled it back when I failed to respond. "I'm sorry, Megan. I should've just . . ."

Again he let his words trail off. But this time I filled in the blank for him.

"Talked to me? Opened up a little? T-trusted me?"

He wrapped both hands around his coffee mug and looked down into it. "Yeah," he said finally. "That's exactly what I should have done."

We were both quiet a moment. He cast furtive, almost desperate, glances at me between sips of steaming coffee. His eyes communicated what he couldn't bring his mouth to say. *He'd missed me. He wanted me back in his life. I was the most intelligent, most gorgeous creature he'd ever seen.* Okay, maybe I'd just wanted to flatter myself with that last part, but he could have been thinking it.

"Look, Seth," I said finally. "I'd be willing to give you a second chance."

His face brightened.

"But it'll have to be on my terms."

He cocked his head, his smile now wary. "Such as?"

"If I ask you questions, you have to give me answers."

It wasn't like I planned to extensively interrogate the guy. After all, he'd been very tight-lipped about his family so far and, other than asking about his grandfather, I hadn't pushed the issue. Having grown up with a stuttering problem, I wasn't much of a talker myself. But if we were going to have any kind of real relationship there would have to be at least a minimum of openness and honesty between us.

He stared at me for a long moment before looking down into his coffee mug again. "Okay."

"Here's question number one." I watched him closely as I tested these new waters. "What's up with your grandfather?"

Seth began to shrug, but slowly lowered his shoulders as if realizing a shrug was not an answer. At least not one I'd be satisfied with. "He's got . . . problems."

"Problems," I repeated. "You mean health problems? Is that why he uses the oxygen tank?" I'd noticed the old man pulling one behind him that day at the house.

"Yes," Seth said. "He's got breathing problems, among other things." Evidently realizing that answer was vague, too, Seth added, "He's belligerent. Withdrawn. Paranoid, sometimes. My grandmother used to tell me that he hadn't always been that way, that he used to be a nice, happy person, but as long as I've known him he's been like this. It got worse after she died."

"Any idea what caused it?"

"Oh, I know exactly what caused it," Seth said.

"What was it?"

"Vietnam."

His gaze locked on mine, his eyes full of pain and grief and knowledge. A knowledge of things no one should ever have to learn. A knowledge of things, once learned, that can never be forgotten, no matter how hard someone might try to forget.

I realized that Seth's grandfather must be suffering from PTSD. Given the ease with which Seth recognized his grandfather's symptoms, Seth likely suffered from it, too. This revelation gave rise to so many more questions in my mind, but I could tell from the expression on Seth's face that he already felt too exposed. I wouldn't push him further now.

As much as my heart ached for Seth, as much as I wanted to be a source of comfort to him, I couldn't put all my eggs in one basket. At least not yet. Seth would have to earn back my trust before I could consider getting serious about him. Besides, before I got in too deep, I wanted to know exactly what I was getting myself into. As attracted as I might be to him, it was clear any relationship with him could be fraught with emotional landmines.

"Let's take things slow," I said. "See how it goes. No obligations, no commitments."

"Agreed," Seth said. But, really, why wouldn't he? A no-strings-attached relationship was every guy's fantasy, right?

I skewered him with a look. "You realize this means no sex, right?"

The two of us had yet to be intimate. Though I found Seth sexy as hell, there was no way I'd consider fooling around outside a meaningful, monogamous relationship.

"No sex?" He threw his head back and groaned. "Why not?"

"Because we're keeping it casual."

"Ever heard of 'casual sex'?" He eyed me, raising a hopeful brow. "It was invented specifically for this type of situation."

I shook my head. "Not my style."

"Catholic guilt?"

"Not entirely, though that's probably part of it."

"I thought the new pope threw all the rules out the window."

"It's not quite that simple."

Another groan, followed by a roguish grin as he began to relax. "I think we should negotiate on this. Like maybe I can touch you over your clothes?"

I shook my head.

"Above the waist only?"

I shook my head again.

"What if I only use one hand? That's a fair compromise."

"Nope."

"What if you bend over to pick something up? Can I at least peek down your shirt?"

I shrugged. "Guess that's fair."

He proceeded to reach out and push my spoon off the table. It hit the floor with a resounding ping. A grin tugged at his lips. "Better get that."

I reached across the table and snatched his spoon instead. "Nah. I'm all set."

"Damn. I'd forgotten how smart you are."

Maybe I should've indulged the poor guy. After all, he was putting himself on the line here and, besides, he wouldn't get much of a glimpse given the sweatshirt I wore.

I sat back against the booth. "That's my offer," I said with more forced nonchalance. "Take it or leave it."

Seth sat back against his booth, too, and tilted his head first one way, then the other as he appeared to be considering. He nailed me with a look so sexy and sensuous I felt naked despite the sweatshirt and pants. "Do I still get to play with your hair?"

A warm flush rushed to my cheeks. "Sure."

He stretched his right hand across the table. "It's a deal."

TWO
MEAT AND GREET

Fort Worth PD K-9 Sergeant Brigit

Brigit lifted her nose to the air, sniffing as the woman who'd brought her partner coffee approached with two loaded platters of bacon and sausage. *Is she bringing it to our table? Dare a dog from the streets hope for such a feast?*

She stood on the vinyl seat, licking her chops as drool pooled in her mouth and drops of saliva fell from her jowls to the tabletop.

The woman stopped at the end of their booth and slid one platter into place in front of Blast, another in front of Brigit.

Score!

THREE
SUGAR DADDY

Robin Hood

She woke with a dry mouth, a pounding headache, and not a stitch of clothing on. All that champagne last night had been a bad idea. But she hadn't been about to turn down a free glass of Dom Pérignon.

Or two.

Or seven.

What a New Year's Eve party it had been! She had never seen anything like it in her twenty-one years on earth. An open bar with bottle after bottle of high-end spirits and liqueurs—none of that cheap, off-brand crap she drank at home—as well as a professional bartender to serve the guests. Waiters circulating through the crowd, bearing silver trays laden with crab puffs, caviar, and diamond-shaped mushroom-polenta hors d'oeuvres topped with roasted red peppers and mascarpone. She had no idea what polenta or mascarpone were, but that hadn't stopped her from sampling several of the delicious appetizers. A dessert table with dozens of tortes, tarts, and pastries, each painstakingly prepared and topped with fancy icing, chocolate shavings, or whipped cream. It was the kind of event she'd only read about in the newspaper society pages.

The house, owned by one of the Lockheed Martin corporate executives, nestled on a lushly landscaped yard in the exclusive River Crest neighborhood west of downtown. A far cry from the trailer park she'd grown up in on the flat, treeless prairieland north of the city.

Applying for an administrative assistant position at the company had been the smartest move she'd ever made, a big step up from her telemarketing job. No more trying to sell solar window screens to people who had no idea what they were, couldn't afford them, or just weren't interested. *A smart homeowner like you won't want to pass up this opportunity. You'll save the planet and cut your cooling bills in half. There's absolutely no downside! We're running a half-price off-season special and can send someone out to measure your windows right away. How does five o'clock look for you?*

Some had politely turned her down. Some had complained that she'd interrupted their nap or their dinner and asked, with varying levels of civility, to be removed from the call list. Others considered her unworthy of a single second of their precious time and simply hung up.

Click.

Click. Click. Click.

Although she knew she shouldn't take it personally, it was hard not to, especially when these cheapskates prevented her from meeting her quota and put her out of the running for an all-expenses-paid trip to Hawaii.

Given that she'd have her own desk and a chair to sit in, she'd thought the telemarketing job would be a step up from the retail sales positions she'd held before. But the job had proved to be just as menial, the clientele just as rude and condescending. After three months, she'd had more than enough and quit.

As she'd hoped, her new position at Lockheed Martin put her in contact with some of the up-and-coming junior executives at the company. The one lying next to her had certainly been both *up* and *coming* last night.

She slipped out of Evan's bed and slunk to his bathroom, opening his medicine cabinet in search of relief. She spotted aspirin. Tylenol. Jock itch ointment. *Ew.* At the back sat a bottle of Excedrin. *Ahh. That's the one.*

She popped two pills into her mouth and washed them down with a glass of water from the faucet. Then she made the mistake of looking in the mirror. *Ugh.* Her eyes were crusty with sleep and mascara, her skin was ruddy, and her platinum-blond hair stuck up in every direction like a disheveled porcupine. No time to do much about all of that, but she couldn't very well hit Evan up for a couple hundred bucks with a raging case of morning breath.

She found a bottle of mint mouthwash under the sink and swished until it no longer felt like her tongue was wearing a sweater. Returning to the bedroom, she slid back into her black lace thong panties and bra. The silky red cocktail dress lay in a wrinkled heap on the floor. She slipped it over her head and shoved her feet back into her silver heels. She'd looked like a million bucks last night. Not too shabby for a girl who didn't have two nickels to rub together. She'd snagged the dress and heels at a five-finger discount on Christmas Eve when the store clerks at Nordstrom had been too busy to keep a close eye on the dressing rooms. She was like a modern-day Robin Hood—or should she say *Robbin'* Hood?—providing a vital public service, taking from the rich and giving to the poor. The fact that *she* was the poor was entirely irrelevant and made her efforts no less virtuous.

Sitting on the edge of the bed next to Evan, she put on her most helpless and beguiling face before gently rubbing his shoulder.

"Evan? You awake?" If he wasn't yet, he soon would be. She rubbed harder, fighting the urge to slap his cheek. Patience might be a virtue, but she'd never claimed to be *that* virtuous. "Evan?"

One eye popped open, eventually seeming to focus on her face.

"Sorry to wake you," she said. "But I need to get going. I promised my mother I'd stop by to see her today."

"Okay," he rasped, his voice gravelly with sleep.

The ass made no move to sit up in bed, let alone offer her breakfast or see her out to her car, a clear sign this relationship had run its course. Fine with her. The sex had been mediocre at best and Evan's conversations tended to focus on his career, his golf swing, or his ex-wife, whom he was clearly still hung up on. That said, the relationship hadn't been totally without benefit. Evan could always be counted on for some quick cash. At thirty-seven years old with a high-level job and no family to drain his wallet, he had far more money than he had time to spend it. Besides, after the things she did for him in bed, she knew he'd feel like a total prick if he didn't toss some spare change her way. The line between sugar daddy and john could be blurry, but she didn't much care. Women had been using their bodies as a bargaining chip since the dawn of time, and she'd always seen their relationship as a business deal anyway.

"I hate to ask." She ducked her head and looked down at her lap as if ashamed to be making the request. "But could you spare a couple hundred dollars? The electric company's threatening to turn off my mother's service unless she pays her past-due bill in full."

"No problem."

He sat up, reached for the pants on the floor next to the bed, and pulled his wallet from the back pocket. Opening it, he fished out ten twenties. She noticed that several bills remained. There'd been a time when he would have offered her everything in his wallet. Looked like that time had passed.

She took the money from him and bent over to place a soft kiss on his cheek. "Thanks. You're so good to me." And good to her mother, who'd been confined to a wheelchair for years, ever since that car wreck. Or had she been hit by a bus? Train? Garbage truck? Oh, well. It didn't much matter anymore.

She stood, folded the bills, and slid them into the inside pocket of her purse. "Bye, Evan."

His only reply was a soft snore.

FOUR
A COUPLE OF STALLIONS

Megan

On a cold but sunny Friday morning in mid-January, Brigit and I were cruising the streets of the Western 1 Division, or W1 for short, when my shoulder-mounted radio crackled to life.

"Officer Luz," came the voice of the dispatcher. "Report to the chief's office at HQ ASAP."

Uh-oh.

Getting called into the police chief's office was rarely a good thing. Last time Chief Garelik had summoned me was after I'd Tasered my former partner in the nards. My Irish temper had gotten the best of me but, hey, it wasn't like the ass hadn't deserved it. That lapse of judgment led the chief to team me up with Brigit. I'd been none too pleased at the time, but the alternative had been to turn in my badge. No way. I'd never make detective if I quit. I'd accepted my fate, partnered with the furry beast, and, well, here we were.

"On my way," I told dispatch, hooking a U-turn in the

specially equipped K-9 cruiser to head downtown. I glanced at my partner in the rearview mirror, our gazes meeting through the built-in metal mesh dog enclosure. "I hope we're not in trouble."

She cast a look in my direction before turning back to the window to scout for squirrels. What did she care? Even if the chief canned me she'd still have a job.

I racked my brain, thinking over my actions the last few days.

Had I made a mistake?

Deviated from protocol?

I'd tossed a bag of Brigit's crap into a yard, but I didn't think anyone had seen me. The yard belonged to Richard Cuthbert, a jackass who'd hassled me when I'd issued him a citation for repeated water-rationing violations. The poop was a little street justice. I'd also caught a couple of thirteen-year-old girls egging a house, but let them go with only a stern warning when one of them began to cry. Four of the confiscated eggs ended up in spinach frittata. I'd scrambled the other two for Brigit. No sense in letting them go to waste, right? Still, using seized property for personal use was against department policy. Would the chief can me for skimming half a dozen eggs? What the cluck?

Fifteen minutes later, I was sitting outside the chief's office in an uncomfortable plastic chair, my K-9 partner lying at my feet.

The chief's administrative assistant, a middle-aged woman with brown hair and a pill-covered pink cardigan, sat at her desk typing on her keyboard. She pushed her intercom button to inform the chief of my arrival, then glanced my way. "You're quite the celebrity, Officer Luz. I've been fielding calls from reporters for days."

After I'd taken down the bomber on New Year's Eve, the chief had contacted me, reminding me not to speak to the press. His admonishment was unnecessary. I knew the drill. The department employed an official public spokesperson who'd been extensively trained on handling the media. Besides, with my unpredictable stutter, I wouldn't take a chance on opening my mouth in front of a television camera. I didn't really want to be in the limelight anyway. I hadn't become a cop for attention. I'd become a cop to make the world a safer, more just, more fair place. Also for the ability to violate traffic laws with impunity.

I pulled my telescoping baton from my belt and flicked it open. *Snap!* Rotating my wrist, I twirled the baton in a basic flat spin. *Swish-swish-swish.* The motion and sound soothed me, leaching nervous tension from my body. Back in high school, I'd twirled with the marching band. Surprisingly, my baton skills came in handy on the beat, too. Who would've thought?

When the woman's intercom buzzed, she picked up her phone. As she listened, her eyes cut to me again. "Yes, sir." She hung up the phone. "The chief's ready for you."

I stood. "Thanks."

Brigit padded along beside me as I stepped to the chief's door. Although he'd summoned me, I rapped twice nonetheless.

"Get in here, Luz!" boomed a voice from the other side.

I slipped inside, closing the door behind me. "Good morning, sir."

The man wasted no time on niceties. "Sit," he barked.

Both Brigit and I sat, Brigit on the floor, me on an imitation-leather wing chair. Brigit lifted her twitching nose, evidently scenting the various animal heads mounted around the room. A mountain lion. A sixteen-point buck. An openmouthed trout that appeared to be either gasping for breath or singing a silent opera. *Rigoletto,* perhaps? Chief Garelik must have spent a small fortune on taxidermy.

As for the man himself, he was bulky and broad, with hair the color of stainless steel. The visible veins at his temple and the purplish cast to his skin evidenced a severe case of high blood pressure and the threat of impending aneurysm. The bulge under his lower lip evidenced a generous pinch of chewing tobacco.

Two Diet Coke cans sat on the chief's desk. He took a sip from one, returned it to the desktop, and retrieved the other, spitting a gooey blob of chewing tobacco into it. *Puhting.*

I fought a disgusted grimace. *Yick.*

"I'm reassigning you," the chief said without fanfare.

"What?" Panic rose in me and instinctively I stood from my seat. "What do you mean?"

"Good God A'mighty, Officer Luz." He frowned and motioned for me to sit back down. "Relax."

Easy for him to say. He knew what was coming. I didn't. Was he planning on taking Brigit from me? He wouldn't do that, would he? I hadn't wanted a K-9 partner at first, but now I couldn't imagine working without her. She was smart and brave, with skills that gave me an edge over criminals. She was my special tool. Taking her from me would be like taking X-ray vision from Superman, the hammer from Thor, or the lasso from Wonder Woman. I would also lose my best friend. It would be like Betty losing Wilma, Thelma losing Louise, or Lucy losing Ethel.

"You and the dog," the chief said, wagging a finger in Brigit's direction. "I'm sending you over to work the rodeo."

I felt a momentary flood of relief, followed by irritation. The Fort Worth Stock Show and Rodeo, which went on for three weeks, was always crowded, loud, and rowdy. The hordes of people would make Brigit nervous, and I wasn't sure I had the patience to deal with a bunch of drunken rednecks. Still, arguing with the chief wouldn't score me any points. But even if I couldn't argue with him, I could still ask for an explanation, right?

I leaned forward in my seat. "May I ask why?"

"You two are famous," he said. "It'll be good PR for the department."

"PR?" What did the chief think we were, some type of police mascots expected to offer the rodeo attendees a cheerful smile, an autograph, and a photo op?

"Exactly. I need you two to make the department look good. The media's been slinging shit at us over that domestic violence issue."

The "domestic violence issue" the chief had referenced involved an officer who'd recently shot his wife in the shoulder with his service revolver. The woman had survived, but only because the officer had been drunk at the time and fallen backward down a flight of stairs before he could get off another shot. Obviously, the screening process for police officers couldn't weed out every violence-prone wacko, but that wouldn't keep the newscasters from placing blame on the department for arming the man.

The chief took another sip of his drink before continuing. "The mayor's been up my ass about the stock show, too. It's a big event, brings lots of money into the city. It needs to go off without a hitch. That's more likely to happen if we have a solid police presence."

I sighed inwardly. The last thing I wanted to do was work the rodeo. But I wanted to make detective in a few years and I'd only get there by doing my job to the best of my ability and keeping my complaints to a minimum. I tried to look on the bright side. At least I'd get a three-week break from the Big Dick, who also worked the W1 Division and was a constant thorn in my ass. "Yes, sir. When do we start?"

"No time like the present." He gestured to his door. "Git."

* * *

Brigit and I drove south on University, the shiny metal dome roof of the Casa Mañana theater looming ahead like an oversized Jiffy Pop pan. We turned right before reaching the theater, pulling into the parking lot of the Will Rogers Center and circling around until locating the parking area reserved for law enforcement vehicles. I pulled my black-and-white cruiser into a spot next to a brown-and-tan pickup bearing the Tarrant County Sheriff's Department logo. Hitched to the pickup was a horse trailer painted to match the truck. I supposed I should count my blessings. Brigit's long hair required constant brushing, but at least I didn't have to pick hooves or muck a stall.

As we climbed out of the car, Old Man Winter blasted us with a cold, blustery wind that carried dust into our eyes and ruffled my bangs and Brigit's fur. *Brrr.* I would've liked to give Old Man Winter a kick in the balls.

Before we could set off on patrol, three yellow school buses pulled into the bus parking area nearby, the air brakes giving off a squeak and a hiss as the drivers brought them to a stop. The doors swung open and a flood of teachers, parent chaperones, and squealing schoolchildren poured from the vehicles.

Brigit glanced over at the kids and looked back at me with an expression of irritation. Though the dog tolerated children, she didn't appreciate them stepping on her paws, tugging on her tail, or shrieking in her ears.

Quickly, I pulled on my jacket, a knit cap, and gloves. "Come on, girl!" I called, my warm breath creating a cloud of steam in the cold air. I took off at a trot, hoping to clear the lot before the inevitable—

"Look!" a little boy cried in a high-pitched voice as he pointed at Brigit. "A police dog!"

Before we could escape, a swarm of students surrounded us like a street gang of gap-toothed dwarfs.

"She's so furry!" hollered a tiny, adorable girl in a puffy

pink coat. She grabbed Brigit around the neck in a bear hug. "I love you, doggie!"

"She's soft!" cried another who pulled off her mitten to run her hand down Brigit's back.

A boy who had yet to grow into either his faded hand-me-down coat or his new front teeth tugged on my sleeve. "Does she poop?"

"Yes," I told him. "And I think she's about to do it so you better step back."

"Ewwww!" The kids squealed and screamed and gave my partner a slightly wider berth.

I bent down, fed Brigit two liver treats, and gave her a pat on the head. "Good girl."

One of the teachers stepped over. "Is that the dog who caught the Tunabomber?"

Technically, I'd been the one to take down the bomber, knocking him out with a strategic hurl of my baton. But Brigit had been right by my side. It was splitting furs, wasn't it? "Yes, she is."

The teacher held her phone aloft. "Can we get a photo of her with the class?"

I supposed I couldn't refuse. After all, the chief had sent Brigit and me to the rodeo for goodwill purposes. We'd been appointed as the department's ambassadors, and so would we be. "Sure."

Brigit and I took several photos with the class and, at the teacher's request, gave them a short primer on K-9s and their special uses in law enforcement. "Dogs can sniff out somebody who's hiding in a building. They can also follow a trail if a suspect has run away. My dog can smell for drugs and catch bad guys in her teeth, too."

A blond girl with light brown freckles crinkled her nose. "Does she eat the bad guys?"

"Only the ones who taste good." I crinkled my nose back at her and gave her a wink.

We begged off then and the children scattered to line up with their assigned chaperones.

Brigit and I spent a half hour circumnavigating the perimeter of the stock show grounds, familiarizing ourselves with the layout. Public parking lots sat to the south and west of the site, flanking the National Cowgirl Museum and Hall of Fame. A row of large swine, sheep, and cattle barns stood on the southern end, along with the equestrian building. The expansive exhibit halls took up the center, with the food vendors and the rides and games of the midway to the north. The stop for the shuttle buses that brought folks from Ridgmar Mall and the historic north side area sat just west of the midway.

Loudspeakers situated here and there played country-western music. Classics from Kenny Rogers, George Straight, the Judds, and Hank Williams, Jr. Contemporary offerings from Miranda Lambert, Tim McGraw, Rascal Flatts, and country's newest and hottest star, bad-boy Brazos Rivers. I found myself getting swept up in the festivities, performing an impromptu polka as I rounded one of the halls.

When the outside temperature grew too chilly to bear, I led my partner into one of the livestock barns. The animals shown at the rodeo ranged from goats to pigs, rabbits to sheep, cows to pigeons. If you could eat it or breed it, its kind was represented here. Brigit glanced into the enclosures, stopping in front of a stall containing a trio of pink pigs. She looked up at me as if to ask, *Can I eat them now or do I have to wait until they're bacon?* The pigs wagged their cute little curly tails and came over to the fence, emitting soft snorts as they stuck their snouts through the slats to check us out.

I gave each of the pigs a scratch on the back. "Just so you know," I told them, "I do not like green eggs and ham."

Jon Hamm, though? I wouldn't mind taking a big bite out of him.

When the pigs wandered back to their water trough, my partner and I proceeded on.

A line of schoolchildren waited at the last pen on the row, their laughter carrying up the hall. I made my way down, stopping to see what held them so rapt.

Inside the pen, a chicken played a game of tic-tac-toe against the little girl who'd hugged Brigit earlier. The Xs and Os were imprinted along with a blank space on rotating tiles housed in a wooden frame. The bird put his head down and pecked at the three-sided rotating tile in the middle of the box—*peck-peck-peck*—turning it to X.

"My turn!" The little girl reached out to turn the upper right tile to O.

The two continued until the chicken had bested the girl with three Xs in a row running diagonally from the upper left to the bottom right. The little girl broke into peals of laughter. No sore losers here.

When Brigit and I had warmed up sufficiently to venture out again into the open air, we headed to the food booths. I chose the healthiest option available, a corn cob on a stick, and bought sliced brisket for Brigit. "No barbecue sauce, please." The dog would only make a mess of it.

We took seats at a picnic table to eat our lunch. As usual, Brigit wolfed down her meal in seconds flat.

"You could stand to learn some manners," I told her.

She gave me her standard kiss-my-fluffy-ass look of indifference.

As I ate my corn, the unmistakable *clop-clop-clop* of horse hooves sounded behind me, growing louder as the horse approached.

"Whoa," came a deep voice from off to my right. The clopping stopped.

My head turned to find a shiny black horse with dark brown eyes stopped a few feet away. The horse was tall and lanky though muscular, built for both work and speed. I had no idea how many hands high the horse stood, but one thing was certain hands down—the sheriff's deputy sitting on his back was the most attractive mounted officer I'd ever seen. Like his horse, the guy was tall and long-limbed, with black hair, brown eyes, and lots of lean muscle. He, too, appeared built for both work and speed.

Part of me supposed I shouldn't be ogling the guy given that Seth and I had just recently reconciled. Another part of me pointed out that the terms of our reconciliation excluded any form of commitment, leaving me free to ogle to my heart's content. The latter part won out and I ogled.

Ogle.

Ogle.

Oooh-gle.

The deputy tipped his cowboy hat at me. "Howdy, ma'am."

Only a guy like him could make those words sound sexy instead of hokey.

"H-hi," I gushed back.

He lifted his chin to indicate Brigit. "That's a beautiful dog you've got there."

"Thanks," I replied. "Your horse is nice-looking, too, and—"

"Well hung?" His lips curved in a roguish grin.

"I was g-going to say tall." I leaned to the side to check out the horse's nards. "But 'well hung' seems to apply, as well."

"Like horse, like rider." He cocked his head, waiting for me to respond.

I rolled my eyes. "That's the worst pickup line I've ever heard."

He stared intently at me. "What makes you think it was a pickup line?"

A hot blush rushed to my cheeks. How presumptuous of me. I'd made a fool of myself, hadn't I?

The deputy slid off the side of his horse and led him over. "No need to blush," he said, quirking his brows. "It *was* a pickup line."

My cheeks cooled, though only slightly. The proximity of this sexy deputy had set my heart galloping in my chest. Up close, I could see his features more clearly. His face was on the long and narrow side, with thick dark brows and lashes that were equally thick and dark. Why had God wasted those lush eyelashes on a man? Despite the fact that it was January, his skin still bore the remnants of a tan. I supposed a mounted deputy spent most of his work hours outside in the sunshine. He had a nice smile, too. The only thing he didn't have was a chin dimple. Instead, he had a shiny silver belt buckle proclaiming him the 2014 Oklahoma Buck-Off Champion.

"Mind if I join you?" he asked.

"Suit yourself," I said. *It would suit me just fine.*

He tied the horse's lead rope to a nearby tree. "I'm going to grab some grub. Keep an eye on my horse till I get back?"

"No problem," I said, though honestly I had no idea how to handle a horse if it misbehaved. What was I supposed to do, put the beast in time-out or threaten to take away his toys? Fortunately, luck was with me. The horse simply bent his head to the ground and grazed peacefully on the dried grass underneath the tree while the deputy stepped over to the barbecue stand to order his food.

A minute later, the deputy returned with a chopped-beef

sandwich and a side of fries in his hands, two coffees tucked between his forearm and chest. He placed the food on the table and set one of the coffees down in front of me. "You look cold. Maybe this will warm you up."

"Thanks."

I circled the cup with my hands, basking in the heat on my palms. *Much better.*

"My name's Clint McCutcheon." He lifted his chin to indicate his horse. "The glue-factory reject is Jack. Short for Jackass. Damn thing's stubborn as a mule."

"He can't be more stubborn than my dog."

As if she knew I was talking smack about her, Brigit cut her eyes my way and gave me another kiss-my-fluffy-ass look.

I extended a hand across the table to the deputy. "I'm Megan Luz."

Clint shook my hand with a warm, firm grip.

Not to be left out, Brigit barked from her seat next to me. *Woof!*

I hiked a thumb at my partner. "This loudmouth is Brigit."

Clint extended his hand toward Brigit and she instinctively held out her paw for a shake. "Nice to meet you, Brigit."

He took a bite of his sandwich and I nibbled at my corn, hoping none was stuck in my teeth. Just in case, I took a big swig of coffee and, as surreptitiously as I could, swished it around in my mouth to clear any kernels.

Clint swallowed his bite and narrowed his eyes at me. "You that cop who caught the bomber?"

"Yeah." I made a fist, blew on it, and pretended to rub it to a shine on the chest of my jacket. "That's me." Of course I hadn't done it for the accolades or notoriety. I'd done it because the bomber had risked the lives and safety of the people on my beat, those I'd sworn to serve and protect. Also because he'd put a screw in my glute and a nail in Brigit's hip. Nothing motivates a woman like some sharp metal in her ass.

"Mighty impressive," Clint said, "taking him down with a baton like you did."

"I'm quite adept at handling a stick." Obvious flirtation with a strong dose of sexual innuendo. *What's gotten into me?* I blamed the caffeine.

He offered a soft chuckle. "Are ya now?"

"Watch this." I stood, pulled my baton from my belt, and extended it with a flick of my wrist *Snap!* As Clint watched, I warmed up with a basic flat spin, then used a thumb toss to send the baton twirling ten feet above us. I caught it easily on its way back down.

He dipped his head. "Not bad."

I gave him a coy smile. "Keep your eyes open, Deputy. I'm just getting started." I threw the baton higher this time, at least a dozen feet over our heads, and spun around twice before catching it behind my back.

Another grin tugged at his lips. "Now you're just showing off."

"If I wanted to show off, I'd break out my flaming batons."

Clint sent me a look that nearly made my knees buckle. "A girl who's not afraid to play with fire. I'm intrigued."

I pushed my baton shut, returned it to my belt, and sat down again lest Clint's smoldering looks send me collapsing to the ground. I took a long swig of my coffee, the heat warming a trail down my esophagus. I wasn't sure how much longer I could stay outside, but I wasn't yet ready to leave Clint. He was a fire I'd like to play with a little more. Then again, if you play with fire, you risk getting burned, right? Still, I wouldn't mind toasting a marshmallow or two over him, maybe making some s'mores.

"Have you always ridden horses?" I asked, attempting to shift the conversation back to a safer, more casual topic.

"Since before I could walk," he said. "I grew up on a ranch in Azle. My parents used to tie me to the saddle so I wouldn't fall off."

"Seriously?" My mouth dropped open. "That sounds dangerous."

He shrugged. "Only if the horse decided to roll."

"Did that ever happen?"

"I wouldn't be sitting here if it had." He crumpled his cup and tossed it into the trash can nearby. "Spent my teen years breaking and training horses."

Breaking horses? Whoa. That sounded almost as dangerous as Seth dismantling bombs in Afghanistan. "That sounds risky and frightening."

"Risky? Sure. But frightening? Hell, no. *Fun* is what it was." He sent me a look that was ten times hotter than my coffee. "There's just nothing like having something wild between your legs and trying to tame it."

Gulp. So much for trying to steer the conversation to safe topics.

The radio at Clint's waist crackled to life. A male voice came through the speaker. "Deputy McCutcheon report to cattle barn three."

Clint grunted in annoyance. "Damn. Just when I was making some time with you." He pulled the radio from his belt, let the dispatcher know he was on his way, and sent a soft smile my way. "See ya 'round, Officer Luz. Maybe next time I'll take you for a ride."

Both his words and expression were full of insinuations, but his teasing tone made him more flirtatious than offensive.

"I'm going to hold you to that," I said. *Seriously, what's gotten into me?* Thanks to my stutter, I'd never been much of a flirt. But there was something about this guy, an easy and natural sensuality, that made it so damn easy.

He untied Jack, swung up onto the horse with the strength

and grace of Mikhail Baryshnikov, and tipped his hat one final time. "Until we meet again, darlin'." With that, he clucked to signal his horse into action and turned away to head to the cattle barn.

FIVE
COUNTING SHEEP

Brigit

She liked the tall man who'd talked to Megan. He'd sneaked her a couple bites of his barbecue beef sandwich when Megan wasn't looking.

His horse was a good-looking steed, too. Then again, Brigit had something going with Blast. It wouldn't be right to start something up with Jack the horse, would it? Besides, he was the wrong species. What would the other farm animals say? No sense rocking the barn with such a scandal. Looked like the two would just have to be friends.

SIX
PRIVILEGES

Robin Hood

She stood in front of the gas pump and inserted her Texaco credit card into the slot, removing it quickly as the screen directed. A moment later the machine declined her card with an accusatory beep.

Damn. She had made only the minimum payments on the card each month, the principal mounting with each bill. Apparently she'd reached her credit limit.

She returned the gas card to her wallet and pulled out her Visa card. She ran it through the slot and waited.

Beep.

The Visa was likewise declined.

"Shit," she muttered.

A sixtyish woman at the adjacent pump glanced over and looked her up and down, a judgmental expression on her face. Robin Hood could tell exactly what the woman was thinking. *Learn to live within your means, young lady.*

She hoped the woman could tell exactly what she was thinking, too. *Mind your own business, you nosy bitch.*

Today was a payday and, though she could have used her debit card, she had earmarked her earnings for much more important things than gasoline. She needed a mani-pedi desperately, as well as an eyebrow wax. And her weekly massage was essential. Plus, there was that great pair of silver earrings she'd seen at the mall.

She checked the cash in her wallet. Three singles. *Ugh.* She opened her car door and leaned in, rounding up what little change she could find in her ashtray and the cup holders. Her efforts garnered her another dollar and seventy-three cents. It wouldn't get her far, but it would at least get her to work. After that, well, she'd have to figure something out.

She slammed the door and went inside to give the coins to the cashier.

An hour later, she pushed a metal cart down the hallway, forcing a polite smile to her lips as she slipped quietly into each of the executives' offices and placed their mail in their in-boxes.

Some greeted her, perhaps even inquired about her well-being. "Good mornin'. How are you today?"

Others gave her a nod or a quick *Thanks* or, if they were talking on their phone, a raised hand.

Some failed to acknowledge her at all, as if she were merely a nameless, faceless apparition.

As if she were unworthy of recognition.

As if I don't even exist.

Her job might seem menial to these latter types, but where would these executives be without the precious contracts, financial statements, and performance reports she delivered to them? They wouldn't be able to function without the information she delivered. They'd be useless. *Worthless.*

Yes, her job was critical to the functioning of the company. Not that her entry-level salary reflected that fact. She was a smart young woman, though. She knew that though her job was important, it took virtually no skill to accomplish. Anyone who could read the names on the envelopes and door plaques and push the mail cart could do it. Hell, she'd been qualified to do this job since second grade.

Given that she walked at least two miles a day up and down the halls of the building, it would have made more sense for her to wear slacks and comfortable loafers, especially since business casual attire was standard. But she'd always heard that a person should dress not for the job she had, but for the job she wanted. So she strolled up and down the hall in a tasteful gray pencil skirt that stopped just above her knees, a sleek white blouse that looked professional yet feminine, a fitted black blazer, and a pair of black stiletto pumps.

Given this classy business attire, did she aspire for a job as an executive assistant? Maybe a management position over the administrative staff?

Oh, hell no.

The position she sought entailed such duties as shoe shopping, choosing restaurants for dinner, and meeting with decorators to furnish a four-bedroom, three-bath home. What position did she seek? *Trophy wife.*

Problem was, the definition of trophy wife seemed to have evolved since she'd been an adolescent. Back then, according to the TV shows she watched, all a successful man wanted was a pretty woman with a nice body to serve as arm candy. Now, though, many prosperous men not only wanted their wives to be physically attractive, but they wanted them to be career women, as well. Educated women with something smart to say. Women who helped bring home the bacon. On her salary, and with her credit cards not only maxed out but also three months past due, the only thing Robin Hood could bring home was a package of nearly expired baloney reduced for quick sale.

Of course she could have attended college if she'd wanted to. With her parents' meager income, she would have qualified for free government grants or need-based scholarships. And she was certainly smart enough. After all, she'd been her elementary school spelling bee champion and had even advanced to the citywide competition, spelling and spelling and spelling her heart out until the only two contestants who remained were her and an Asian-American boy wearing a ridiculous pin-striped three-piece suit.

She remembered that day like it was yesterday. She'd stood on that stage in front of a crowd of hundreds at a local high school, a spotlight shining down on her, warming her face and illuminating her as if she were some type of angel, as if she were somebody, as if she were special.

It was the last time I'd felt like somebody, the last time I'd felt special.

The pink polka-dot dress she had worn was a hand-me-down, having already served her two older sisters, who sat in the third row with her parents. The frock had faded some, but at least her mother had ironed it and tied a pink bow in her mousy brown hair. She'd have preferred a new dress, but she wasn't going to let her secondhand outfit spoil her moment in the spotlight.

She'd stared down at the judge's table, her heart pounding so loudly she feared she wouldn't hear the judge when he assigned her final word.

The judge leaned forward to speak into the microphone on the table before him and looked up at her. "Your word is *privileged*."

Privileged. A word that didn't apply to her at all, yet a word with which she was far too familiar.

Privileged. Those families who hired her mother to clean their enormous, custom-designed homes.

Privileged. Those church ladies who brought her and her sisters donated Christmas gifts, who came after bedtime when the girls were supposed to be asleep rather than staring out the window, dreaming of a better, easier life. On Christmas morning, when she and her sisters opened their presents, Robin Hood had to bite her tongue not to tell her parents she knew the gifts weren't from Santa Claus, that she'd seen the church ladies drive up to her family's rusty singlewide trailer in their sleek, silver Mercedes with a trunk full of wrapped boxes.

Privileged. Those junior high school girls she spotted from the school bus window, the ones who had their hair professionally highlighted, who wore Juicy Couture and carried their M.A.C lip pencils in their Kate Spade purses.

When she had hesitated, the judge again leaned toward his microphone. "Would you like me to use the word in a sentence?"

As if I were so poor I wouldn't even know the word.

"Not," she hissed into her own mic, "necessary." She knew this word. She'd practiced it, multiple times. She took a deep breath and began. "P-R-I."

Uh-oh. Not only was her dress a hand-me-down, but so were her panties. She'd begged her mother for new underwear—*my God, it was the least my parents could give me!*—but her mother had refused.

"There's plenty of life left in these panties," her mom had insisted when she'd pulled them from the dryer. "And I washed them twice so stop your complaining. Don't you know there are kids in India who don't even have underwear?"

On stage, in the bright glow of the spotlight, she felt the waistband loosen as the worn elastic began to give way. "V-I-L."

The panties began to slip down over her backside. She reached down and tried to grab the waistband through the fabric of her dress.

But I was too late.

The panties slid out from under her dress, over her knobby knees, and down her skinny legs, pooling around the scuffed patent-leather Mary Janes her mother had bought at the thrift store.

She continued to spell over the crowd's deafening laughter, the heat on her cheeks now coming not from the spotlight above but from the shame and rage within her.

"E-D-G-E-D."

When she finished, she looked down at the judge's table. One of the judges looked down at his lap, his shoulders shaking with barely contained guffaws. The other male judge, the one who'd assigned her word, had a hand crooked over his mouth to hide his smile. The female judge had bit her lip in an effort to keep her giggles from escaping, but the pity in her eyes was far worse than her amusement.

I didn't want pity.

I wanted my fair share.

When the crowd settled down and the primary judge was finally able to speak, he said, "I am sorry. That is incorrect."

The Asian boy was given a chance to spell the word. He performed perfectly, leaving out the extra *d* she had inadvertently added while distracted by the stiff sensation of the starched cotton fabric of the dress against her bare bottom.

Robin Hood had turned to the boy, shaken his hand, then stepped out of her underwear and walked off the stage, her head held high, her secondhand panties left behind.

The unpleasant memory left her feeling restless and cheated. Her grip tightened on the mail cart, her knuckles turning white as she punished the handle for a crime it had not committed.

She reached Evan's office and peered through the open door. An attractive woman from the accounting department stood next to him. She wore tan zippered boots and a shimmery fitted suit in golden ivory tweed. An Alexander McQueen design, if Robin Hood wasn't mistaken. She'd seen it at the Neiman Marcus store in Ridgmar Mall. The woman bent forward to point out something on the spreadsheet unfolded on his desk.

Though the woman and Evan behaved with perfect professionalism, Robin Hood nonetheless felt a knife of envy slice through her gut. This woman had what Robin Hood wanted. Money. Nice clothes. Security. An engagement ring large enough to choke one of the bulls at the upcoming stock show. Someone who loved her enough to give her that ring . . .

It wasn't right that fate had given this woman so much, yet had given Robin Hood so little. *Is it too much to ask that the fates be fair?*

She grabbed Evan's stack of mail from the cart and slipped into the room. The woman continued to spout off about the numbers on the sheet without so much as a glance in her direction. Evan looked up, guilt darkening his eyes. He'd called her just once since New Year's Day, and then it was only to tell her that he thought they should cool things off for a while, that he wasn't yet over his divorce and didn't feel ready to make a commitment. She'd let him off easy, telling him she understood and that she hoped his heart would heal soon.

As if I give a damn about his heart.

"Thanks," he said softly as she placed his mail in his in-box.

She offered him a polite smile. "My pleasure, Mr. Underhill."

As she made her way back to the door, she spotted Evan's platinum-accented Montblanc pen lying near the edge of his credenza. Those designer pens didn't come cheap. The thing must have cost four or five hundred dollars new. She'd love to have a beautiful pen like that, but she'd probably never make enough money to afford one. Just like she'd never be able to afford a fancy car or a luxurious apartment or any of the other things she was entitled to.

A quick look over her shoulder confirmed that Evan and the accountant were absorbed in their numbers. In a swift, smooth move, she scooped the pen up and into the front pocket of her blazer. *Robin Hood strikes again.*

If fate wouldn't give her what she deserved, she'd just have to take it.

This pen was a nice start . . .

SEVEN
LUNCH AND LIVESTOCK

Megan

Seth phoned late Saturday morning. "How about lunch?"

I glanced at the clock. "It'll have to be somewhere near the rodeo grounds. I go on duty at two."

"How about Dos Gringos?"

"Perfect." Their chalupas were among my favorites.

We met at the restaurant at noon. Seth had left Blast at home today. Brigit seemed disappointed, lying on the floor under the table with her head between her paws. That is, until her chicken fajitas arrived. Then all thoughts of her canine lover were replaced by carnivorous desires.

Seth and I had been like ships in the night since we'd reconciled on New Year's Day, our erratic work schedules preventing us from spending much time together other than quick meet-ups for meals. Nice, but not exactly the fun-filled, romantic evenings a girl dreams about.

Seth dug into his enchiladas, while I took a crunchy bite of my chalupa, savoring the spicy salsa.

When he'd swallowed his bite he asked, "How do you

like working the stock show? Sounds like more fun than street patrol."

I supposed it would to some, but I'd never been big on crowds. Too many people in a confined space gave me a sense of claustrophobia, not to mention the constant aroma of bovine manure. Still, yesterday hadn't been all bad. Meeting Clint had been fun.

At the thought of Clint, my gut rippled with guilt. Ridiculous, since Clint and I had only gone so far as harmless flirtation. I supposed I had no real reason to feel guilty. After all, Seth and I had agreed we could date other people and, for all I knew, Seth could have a dozen girls on the side. Something told me he didn't, though.

Seth took a sip of his soda. "I haven't been to the stock show in years. How about I get a ticket this afternoon? As long as I don't get in your way it won't be a problem, right?"

I took another bite of my chalupa, buying myself time to think through my feelings and come up with a response. Did I want Seth to come to the stock show? Part of me thought it could be a nice way to spend more time together. Another part of me thought I might not get that ride Clint had promised me if Seth were tagging along. Another part of me thought that wanting two men was cheap and wrong. Another part of me thought it might be fun to be cheap and wrong. Another part of me was ashamed I'd had that thought. Another part of me thought too many parts were chiming in and maybe they should all shut up.

"Okay," I told Seth. "Come to the show. But don't blame me if you go home smelling like cow poop."

At half past two that afternoon, I led Brigit into one of the exhibit halls with Seth following along beside me. I'd suggested we go inside mostly to avoid the cold outdoor temperatures but, admittedly, I'd also thought we'd have less chance of crossing paths with Clint if we stayed indoors.

On our way into the building, my eyes spotted a head topped with rust-orange hair cut in a short burr sticking up among the cowboy hats up ahead.

Blurgh. Say it isn't so.

Damn. It was *so*.

Out from the crowd emerged Derek Mackey, who headed toward us, evidently on his way out of the building. He wore his uniform, meaning he was on duty. He also wore his typical condescending, smug expression, meaning he'd experienced no sudden improvement in personality.

As he approached, my thoughts tumbled out of my mouth before I could rein them in. "What are *you* doing here?"

I supposed I shouldn't be so rude. After all, it was Derek who'd discovered me tied to the carousel horse with the bomb on my chest. If he hadn't happened by the mall that evening, I'd be dead. Still, I knew his finding me had been mere coincidence and luck. It's not like he'd set out to rescue me.

Mackey grunted. "*What am I doing here?* What does it look like, Einstein? I'm working." With that, he continued on past us and out the door.

It wasn't too surprising the chief would ask Mackey to work the event. If he wanted to beef up the police presence, what better way to do it than with one of the beefier officers? Derek's biceps and pecs were nearly as big as his ego. Still, his presence here meant I wouldn't be getting the reprieve I'd hoped for.

A sheep show was under way in the hall's arena. Seth and I stopped at the fence and rested our arms on it, watching the goings-on. Breeders paraded Dorper, Dorset, and Rambouillet sheep around a pen. Not that I knew anything about the breeds, but the announcer identified them as such. Judges with clipboards circled the animals, groping them through their woolly coats and feeling up and down their legs like some kind of perverts.

"Cute sheep, huh?" Seth said.

I shrugged. "Honestly, they kind of look like those British barristers to me. You know, the ones that wear those goofy white wigs?"

Seth cut me a glance, an amused twinkle in his eye. "You have an odd way of looking at the world, Megan."

"I'm just perceptive," I argued. "That's a good trait for a cop."

"Point taken," Seth replied. He lowered his voice and leaned his head in to mine. "If you're so perceptive, can you tell how bad I want to get you alone and kiss you?"

Though I was flattered and just as eager to put my lips on his, this was neither the time nor place. I gave him a gentle jab with my elbow. "Hush."

"C'mon, Megan. Nobody would notice if we hid out in one of these empty stalls." He cocked his head to indicate an empty space behind us. "Look. That one's already full of hay. We could go for a roll in it."

Before I could respond, a man and woman with three children in tow stepped up to me. All five wore jeans, boots, and straw cowboy hats. Given that their apparel looked new, they'd probably bought it specifically to wear to the stock show. Only a small percentage of north Texans actually lived on farms or ranches, but at rodeo time every local liked to get their cowboy or cowgirl on.

"Are you the officer who took down the bomber at Billy Bob's?" the wife asked, her eyes gleaming as if she'd just met a big celebrity.

"Yes, that's me." I forced a smile. Frankly, I didn't like being in the proverbial spotlight. It was too much pressure, trying to live up to some glorified, heroic image. I put my pants on one leg at a time just like everyone else. Heck, I often had to wrestle with Brigit to get the pants leg out of her mouth.

"Wow!" the woman gushed. "I can't believe it!" She put a hand to her chest as if to calm her pounding heart.

"Mind if we take a picture?" her husband asked.

I reminded myself that I was here both to perform my usual duties and on a PR mission. "Not at all." If I had a nickel for each person who'd asked to take my photo over the last few days I'd be able to buy one of those overpriced funnel cakes by now.

Seth offered to snap the shot so the entire family could be in the picture. I ordered Brigit to sit at my feet, then turned to look at Seth.

"Everybody say cheese!" he called.

"Cheeeeese!" cried the three kids.

Brigit looked up at them, smacking her jowls.

Flash!

The husband and wife thanked me, rounded up their children, and moved on.

Seth and I continued on, too, leaving the sheep fondlers behind and stepping back outside.

"Walk ahead of me," I said to Seth. "We can't look like we're together out here."

In the crowded exhibit hall, a cop could be expected to be in close quarters with those attending the stock show. But outside it would be best if we maintained some distance so it wouldn't look as if I were goofing off. Of course a secondary benefit was that I wouldn't appear to be with Seth should Clint happen to spot us.

As we strolled across the grounds, a black blur appeared in my peripheral vision. I turned my head to see Clint and Jack trotting past on the main drive. Luckily, the deputy seemed to have a destination in mind and was watching the path ahead of him. He continued on out of sight without noticing me.

In another minute or two, Seth and I reached the noisy

midway. Seth stopped in front of the dart game. "I'm going to win you one of those." He gestured to a stuffed brown dog with a felt tongue hanging out of its mouth and a red bandana around its neck.

He set his money on the counter. The carnie reached under the counter, pulled out three darts, and handed them to Seth.

Seth put the tip of the darts to his finger. "These are dull, buddy. Give me some sharp ones."

The darts may have been dull, but the look the carnie sent Seth was so pointed he could've performed acupuncture with it.

I sent the man an equally pointed look right back. "You're not pulling a fast one, are you?"

"No," the man spat. "These darts are old is all." He reached under a different part of the counter this time and pulled out three different darts, exchanging them for the ones in Seth's hand.

Seth felt the tips. "That's more like it."

Seth raised the first dart and eyed the balloons tacked to the board, picking his air-filled victim. He drew his hand back and sent the dart flying. *Pop!* A pink balloon met its death. He raised the second dart, aimed, and threw it. *Pop!* This time a blue balloon bit the dust. He raised the final dart, eyed the board, and sent it on its way. *Pop!* Stretchy pieces of red balloon exploded into the air.

"Congratulations." The carnie reached up, pulled one of the brown dogs down from the wall, and handed it to Seth.

Seth, in turn, handed it to me. Brigit sniffed the dog, grabbed it by the floppy ear, and yanked it out of my hands, shaking it back and forth as if trying to break its neck.

The carnie snorted. "That dog sure is one vicious bitch."

Couldn't argue with him on that one. I'd seen her in action, seen her tear out after a suspect, grab him with her sharp teeth and refuse to let go. I might be her handler, but I still found her scary sometimes.

We continued on, Brigit carrying her new toy in her mouth as we walked.

Seth consulted the schedule he'd obtained from the ticket booth when we'd arrived. "There's a goat-milking contest in fifteen minutes. We can't miss that."

I followed ten steps behind Seth as he entered the other hall, and paused for a moment inside the door as, up ahead, he scouted a good vantage point for watching the competition. Attendees walked past, some giving me a nod or a "Hello, Officer." Others cut their eyes to Brigit and timidly scurried on as if she were a ferocious beast.

Seth raised his hand and issued a discreet signal, letting me know he'd found a good spot. As casually as I could, I made my way through the horde, glancing left and right to ensure everyone was on good behavior.

Two skinny adolescent boys had climbed halfway up the slats of the enclosure to sit on the fence. There probably wasn't much chance of them getting hurt, even if they accidentally fell into the arena. Goat milking was a rather tame event compared to the bull riding and calf roping that would take place later tonight at the rodeo. Nonetheless it would set a bad precedent. Might as well put them on alert that no rule breaking would be tolerated.

I gave a soft tweet of my whistle to get their attention, motioning with my hand when they turned my way. "Get down, boys! Keep your boots on the ground."

With sullen looks, they dropped to the floor of the hall *Thump, thump.* I gave them a thumbs-up and continued on, slipping into a place at the fence two feet away from Seth. A teenage girl stepped into the space between us, resting her elbows on the fence. Three hefty rednecks stepped up to the fence on my right.

As we watched, the contestants lifted their goats onto

low platforms with a metal frame of bars at the end. Some of the goats were brown, others black, with a single cream-colored one in the bunch. Their horizontal pupils always struck me as odd, but I knew from elementary school field trips to petting zoos that the unusual eyes gave the goats superior peripheral vision, a definite plus when you had to keep an eye out for wolves or coyotes while grazing.

The contestants urged the animals forward until the goats' heads were immobilized between the bars. The goats ready, the contestants slid buckets underneath their udders and positioned themselves on stools or benches alongside their animals.

A woman wearing an official stock show shirt stepped to the head of the group. She raised a bullhorn in one hand, a stopwatch in the other, her index finger poised to hit the start button. "On your mark!" she called.

The contestants leaned toward their goats.

"Get set!"

Two dozen hands reached for two dozen goat udders.

"Go!"

The air filled with cheers from the audience and the tinny sound of pressurized liquid hitting the sides of the metal buckets. For the most part the goats seemed to tolerate the situation, though one doe kept twisting her head, trying to back it out of the bars. The contestants' forearms moved up and down, up and down, their muscles flexing, as they milked their goats. When the time had elapsed, the official hollered, "Stop!"

The participants raised their hands in the air to show their compliance with the order. The official meandered down the row, collecting the buckets for weighing.

"The last time I was entertained by teats," said one of the rednecks, "it was at a bachelor party."

I slid him a look. "Keep the details to yourself. This is a family event."

He raised his palms as if in surrender. "Whatever you say, Officer."

I stepped back from the fence, leading Brigit with me.

Seth followed, pulling his cell phone from his pocket and glancing at the screen. "I better get going. I want to get in a swim at the Y before poker night."

"Poker night?"

"There's always a game at the station on Friday and Saturday nights. I usually lose my shirt but tonight"—he gave me a soft smile—"I'm feeling lucky."

I walked with him to the exit gate outside, strategically keeping Brigit between us.

When we reached the gate, Seth turned to me. "How about I swing by early tomorrow morning? We can grab breakfast at the Busy B Bakery and check out the hot rods. There's a group that meets there every Sunday morning."

I debated my response. I couldn't help but feel cautious. And, to be honest, I felt a little annoyed. I'd met Seth months ago but still knew virtually nothing about him. Though he'd agreed to answer my questions, after asking about his grandfather's issues I'd been hesitant to force open another can of worms. I'd hoped Seth would be more forthcoming on his own, but he hadn't been. Didn't he want to get closer to me? If not, was I just wasting my time with him? Was this relationship worth the trouble? I was beginning to wonder.

"Sunday's the only day I can sleep in," I said. Not that Brigit would let me laze around all day. The darn dog always roused me by six A.M. to let her out to pee.

Seth's eyes darkened with disappointment. "The bakery's got great cinnamon rolls. Good coffee, too."

I looked away for a moment, spotting Clint and Jack near the cattle barns. I turned back to Seth. "What's in it for me?"

He offered a confused smile. "Cinnamon rolls and coffee?"

"I want more than that."

He was the one who seemed cautious now. "What do you want?"

"I want to know about your parents."

Talking about his family seemed to be the last thing Seth wanted to do. And I wanted to know why. *I wanted to know Seth.*

He stared down at me for a moment, before responding. "Okay." He let out a long, resigned breath. "Can we talk about it after we go to the bakery?"

"Deal."

"Good." He turned and began to walk off.

"Hey!" I called after him. "How early is early?"

He turned back around and held up seven fingers.

"Damn," I muttered. "That's *really* early."

EIGHT
BAAAAAD DOG

Brigit

This stock show was nothing but a big disappointment.

All of those people said *cheese,* but then gave her none. Teasing her like that was downright rude. She should've bitten them while she had the chance, taught them a lesson.

She'd been sorely tempted to leap over the fence and help herself to some of that goat milk, maybe even some fresh goat meat. The goats' *baaas* as they lamented their immobilization taunted Brigit. They might as well have been saying, *I can't run away! Come and get me!* But Megan had maintained a tight grip on Brigit's leash, keeping her close. *Grrr.*

Sometimes Brigit wished she could be free, run with a pack of wild dogs in the woods, bay at the moon, and hunt for prey. Then again, she liked sleeping on the soft futon with Megan, enjoyed the liver treats her partner regularly dispensed, had fun chewing on Megan's supple leather shoes. Being domesticated wasn't *all* bad, she supposed. Still, next full moon, she'd be getting her howl on whether Megan liked it or not.

NINE
STALLING FOR TIME

Robin Hood

She climbed the rickety steps to the front door of her parents' trailer. No easy feat in her four-inch stilettos, especially when the metal stairs shook and swayed under the slightest weight. Hell, you'd think there was an earthquake going on.

Saturday night and her two older sisters, Crystal and Heather, were parked on the couch, a bag of potato chips between them, two store-brand grape sodas and a tub of onion dip on the glass-top coffee table in front of them. *White trash food.* She bet her sisters had never had polenta or mascarpone, whatever that was.

How Crystal and Heather could be content to spend the weekend at home in front of the television she would never know. How did they expect to have any fun or meet a man if they didn't ever get off the damn sofa? Did they think Prince Charming would come trolling for his princess at the trailer park?

Of course their chances of meeting Prince Charming

were slim to none, even if they did drag their asses off the couch. While Robin Hood scrimped to have her hair professionally dyed a striking platinum blond, her sisters had left theirs the plain mousy brown all three of them had been born with. While Robin Hood wore the latest fashions by trendy designers, her sisters were content with traditional Levi's and T-shirts. While Robin Hood worked out regularly to keep herself in decent shape, her sisters made no such effort, arguing that their retail jobs and helping their mother clean houses provided more than enough exercise. Though she would never understand how her sisters could be satisfied with their meager, unexceptional lives, a small part of her envied their contentedness. Things would certainly be easier for her if she lacked ambition and taste.

"Hi, honey," called their mother from the kitchen, where she stood on two fully functional legs in front of the open fridge, her arms loaded with bottles of mustard and mayonnaise, packages of processed cheese and salty lunch meat in her hands.

She supposed she should feel guilty for misleading Evan about her mother. But it was his own fault if he'd fallen for her made-up sob story and made no effort to verify her claims. Besides, he had more than enough money to spare. President Obama might have failed to make great strides toward social justice but, without the Tea Party or a burdened conscience standing in her way, Robin Hood had successfully effectuated her own small-scale form of wealth redistribution. Still, though she'd been able to pad her wallet and amass valuable possessions via white lies and petty theft, she had no plans to stop there. Oh, no. Robin Hood could not be satisfied with small amounts of cash and trinkets. She deserved more. *Much more.*

"I'm going to make your sisters a sandwich," her mother called, now pulling a loaf of white bread from the pantry. "Want one?"

"No. Thanks." She didn't want to live like her family. She didn't want to look like them. She didn't even want to *eat* like them.

She retrieved a towel from the bathroom cabinet and returned to the living room. After shooing her mother's mangy mutt from the recliner, she spread the towel over the chair so as not to get dog hair on her designer jeans or leather jacket.

She turned to her sisters, who'd hardly glanced up the entire time she'd been here. Though Robin Hood had come up with a plan to solve her financial dilemma, she needed some Merry Men, or Merry Women, to help. That's where her sisters came in. "Why don't you two clean yourselves up and come to the rodeo with me tonight?"

Heather's brow crimped. "The rodeo? Since when are you into that kind of thing?"

Since I figured out the event could provide some interesting opportunities. Robin Hood lifted a shoulder. "Maybe I figured it was time to expand my entertainment repertoire."

"Repertoire?" Crystal rolled her eyes. "There you go again with your uppity words."

"Yeah," Heather said. "You're such a snob."

It was the same old accusation she'd been hearing for years. When she had begged her mother to sign her up for junior cotillion, her mother had given her a patronizing smile. "Now, honey. Why should we pay someone to teach you how to foxtrot and eat a five-course dinner? You'll never need to know those things."

They acted like it was a crime to want to better yourself, accused her of thinking she was better than the rest of them. They were right about the latter. She did think she was better than them. No, she *knew* she was better. They might be content to live in a tin can and barely scrape by, to scrub other people's floors and toilets, to shop at thrift stores and bag their own groceries at the Save-A-Lot. But she wasn't. She wanted more for herself.

And she was going to get it.

"Come on," Robin Hood said. "It'll be fun."

Crystal gestured at the TV screen. "But *The Bachelorette* is on."

Robin Hood pointed to the DVR. "Record it for later."

"This *is* a recording," Crystal said.

"Then why are you complaining?" Rage and frustration boiled up in her. *Seriously. What is wrong with these people?* She looked away for a moment, doing her best to tamp down her anger. "There will be lots of cute cowboys at the stock show. Wouldn't you rather meet a guy of your own than watch some bimbo on television hook up?"

Crystal and Heather looked her way with vacuous expressions, then looked to each other, shrugging simultaneously.

"I guess we could go," Heather said finally. "We ain't been out in a while."

It's not ain't, she thought. *It's* haven't been. For God's sake, did her sisters have to sound like such hicks? What an embarrassment they were. If not for the fact that they looked so much like her—without her dyed hair and high-end cosmetics, of course—she'd doubt whether they truly shared DNA.

Crystal's face brightened. "I can wear my new boots."

Crystal had recently landed a sales clerk position at the Justin Boots outlet store on west Vickery. Though she paid little attention to the rest of her clothes, she'd always had a minor shoe fetish. It was one of the few things, perhaps the *only* thing, that Robin Hood and Crystal had in common. Given the number of new pairs of boots Crystal had brought home recently, it appeared her sister spent most of each paycheck in the store.

Their mother sauntered into the living room, two paper plates in her hands, the smell of baloney and mustard wafting in with her. "Here you go, girls." She handed one plate to Crystal, the other to Heather.

Her sisters proceeded to eat their sandwiches, much too slowly. The two always moved as if they had all the time in the world, never seeming to experience any sense of urgency. Human sloths.

"Could you two hurry it up?" Robin Hood spat. "If we get there too late all of the good seats will be taken."

Her sisters finally finished eating. They tossed their plates in the garbage can in the kitchen, went to their bedroom for jackets and footwear, then grabbed their purses from the hooks next to the front door.

She let out a long exhale. Heather and Crystal had two and four years on her, respectively, but Robin Hood far surpassed them in experience and intelligence. She seemed to be the only one with detectable brain activity.

Her sisters' stupidity could be irritating at times but, on the other hand, it made them easy to manipulate. Hell, Robin Hood had been doing it for years. Feigning heartbreak over fictitious boyfriends so they'd pity her and do her chores while she wallowed in bed with the latest *People* magazine. Borrowing money from them for specious purposes with promises of repayment that would never come. Convincing them to distract the sales clerk while she pocketed a $15 lip gloss at the Lancôme counter. They were like putty in her hands. *Silly Putty.*

She pulled out her compact to check her makeup. "You both might want to brush your teeth so you don't smell like onion dip," she suggested. "And, Heather, for God's sake! Get that grape soda stain off your upper lip."

Her sisters exchanged looks and laughed.

Crystal waved a hand dismissively. "No need to get your panties in a bunch, Li'l Sis," she said, using the age-old nickname Robin Hood despised. "It's just a rodeo."

But it won't be just a rodeo.

It will be a new business venture.

TEN
A BARREL OF FUN

Megan

Dusk set in, casting the corners and edges in shadow as Brigit and I made our way around the grounds. We strolled through the dark, expansive parking lot behind the barns, passing pickup after pickup and livestock trailer after livestock trailer. A rat scurried across the way in front of us, probably searching for morsels of errant lamb chow.

Brigit's ears perked up and she stopped, turning her head. I followed her line of vision to see three men about my age at the temporary exterior fence that had been erected around the grounds. All three wore boots, jeans, and straw cowboy hats. One held a pair of wire cutters in his hand and put it to the fence while the other two watched.

Snip. A strand of metal curled back.

Looks like these guys are trying to sneak in without buying a ticket.

I hid behind a trailer and, as quietly as I could, radioed dispatch. "Officers needed outside the south fence," I said. "We've got three men t-trying to gain illegal access."

I put my back up against a trailer to make myself less visible, held Brigit close, and slowly slinked toward them.

I counted down.

One.

Two.

Three.

I bent down, unclipped Brigit's leash, and gave the dog the order to charge the fence Just as she bolted forth, I whipped out my Maglite and turned it on the men like a spotlight. Three surprised faces on the other side of the fence blinked against the blinding light.

Brigit leaped at the fence right in front of them, ricocheting off it with a metallic *ching-ching*.

"Shit!" cried one of the men, jumping backward.

"Jesus!" hollered another. "What the fuck was that?"

The one with the wire cutters yelped and fell back on his ass.

"Hold it right there!" I yelled, rushing forward now, too. Not that there was much I could do from this side of the fence other than shoot them, which I had no intention of doing.

They didn't listen, though. Instead of staying put as instructed, they turned and ran smack-dab into two male officers who'd come up behind them.

I turned off my flashlight lest I blind my coworkers. "You got this, boys?" I called.

"Yep," they called. "We got this."

I turned to my partner. "Good job, girl." I held my hand out palm up. Brigit pawed it, giving me a low five.

After a quick dinner at the food booths, Brigit and I headed into the arena to watch the evening rodeo. We passed the pens where men wrangled the rough stock, the untamed bulls and broncs, into pens. No easy task if the number of curses was any indication.

We stopped at a gate spanning a wide, open doorway

that led into the arena. The vantage point would allow me to keep an eye on both the crowd seated inside and the crowd milling around the perimeter.

Frankly, I'd never cared much for rodeos. Some of the equestrian events, like the barrel racing, were fun to watch, but the calf roping, mutton busting, and bull wrestling seemed overly dangerous and somewhat barbaric to me. But Texans were nothing if not traditional, and rodeos had been a way of life in Cowtown for over a century. They wouldn't be stopping any time soon.

The oblong arena was flanked with rows of bleachers, above which hung colorful banners and signs advertising various products. Wrangler jeans. Stetson hats. Ultrashine boot polish. Directly across from me at the far end of the arena, through another open doorway, sat an ambulance. The back doors hung open, a team of paramedics sitting on the bumper. Two more EMTs had stationed themselves near the gate, ready to spring into action if necessary.

The first event was calf roping. Calves were shoved out of pens and into the bright lights and deafening noise of the arena. The startled animals were given a few seconds' head start before a cowboy on horseback launched out of a chute, swinging a lasso over his head as he and his horse pursued the terrified calf. Most cowboys were able to hook the lasso over the calf, yank it to a stop, and leap from their horse to tie the poor calf's legs together. The crowd cheered with each successful toss. As for me, I cheered on the rare occasion when a crafty calf had the smarts to zigzag across the arena and successfully evade the cowboy's rope.

As I stood there, a group of rodeo clowns came out of their nearby dressing room and headed past me to wait at the entrance of the arena. One of them stopped in front of me. Over his red and white checkered shirt and jeans he sported a large wooden barrel, which hung from his shoulders by wide nylon straps.

He reached out and took my hand, pretending to give it a kiss. Then he pointed to me, back at himself, and wagged his brows, which were coated in blue face paint. Though he'd said nothing aloud, his message was clear. *You and me. How about it?*

I gave the clown a smile. "As much as I like a man who sports a lot of wood, I'm going to have to pass. I make it a rule not to date anyone who wears more makeup than I do."

He feigned a frown, stomped a foot in mock indignation, then waved good-bye with a yellow-gloved hand as he turned to follow the other members of his clown troupe into the arena.

The entrance of the clowns could only mean one thing. The bull riders would be up next.

The clowns spent a few minutes entertaining the crowd with silly antics. Pretending to be bucked from broomstick horses. Rolling each other around in the protective plastic barrels situated around the perimeter of the arena. Using oversized shovels to toss plastic poop at each other. When they were done, they gathered up their props and backed away, positioning themselves at even intervals around the oblong arena, ready to perform their duties as needed.

The announcer's voice came over the loudspeaker. "First in our bull-riding competition tonight will be a local favorite, Dusty Moynihan from just down the road in Saginaw, Texas. Ladies and gentlemen, let's give Dusty a big hand!"

The rider stepped onto the platform, decked out in black boots, black jeans, and a red western shirt with black accents. He slid a rubber tooth guard into his mouth and raised his black felt hat, circling it over his head, waving to the crowd with his free hand. The crowd erupted in applause, whistles, and catcalls, fueled by a primitive bloodlust.

I supposed these events weren't entirely unfair; after all,

nobody had forced these cowboys onto the backs of these animals, some of which weighed in at more than a ton. These sporting events weren't much different from boxing tournaments or karate matches or even pro football games. But the thrills came from the risk posed to the riders. Frankly, the whole thing seemed akin to the Roman gladiators of ancient times or, more currently, that *Jackass* television show. But perhaps I was being too judgmental. After all, many people would find the things I was interested in—art films, science museums, psychology, baton twirling—to be boring or stuffy or ridiculous. It took all kinds to make the world go round. Well, that and the physical laws of conservation of angular momentum and inertia. *Wow, Seth was right. I really am a nerd.*

The crowd grew quiet, all eyes on the bucking chute as the rider settled onto the back of the bull trapped inside. The narrow chute prevented the bull from bucking, but once that gate opened, it would be a free-for-all. We held our collective breath.

The bull snorted and tossed his head, his long, pointed horns banging against the metal of the chute. The gate swung open in an instant. *Clang!*

The bull sprang from the chute like a horned jack-in-the-box. He headed in a sideways fashion toward the center of the ring, bucking every few feet in a desperate attempt to rid himself of the rider on his back. When throwing out his hind legs proved futile, he turned his head, his horns nearly gouging the rider's leg as he whipped himself around in a circle, his enormous, pendulous testicles lagging a fraction of a second behind. *My God, those things are the size of bowling balls!*

The size of Moynihan's testicles evidently rivaled the bull's. He hung on, one hand on the rope, the other in the air. After he'd held on for the eight seconds necessary for a qualified ride, he waited for an opportune moment, then leaped from the bull and ran for the perimeter fence, waving his black hat in the air, raising a fist in victory.

Time for the clowns to get to work.

My barrel-suited would-be suitor dashed into the arena from one side, while another clown ran up on the other side of the bull. Now freed from the rider, the bull settled down enough that the clowns were able to steer the beast toward the exit ramp, where he'd be rounded up and returned to a pen.

The next rider wasn't so lucky. He immediately slid to the back of the bull, his hand now between his knees rather than at his crotch where it ought to be.

"Damn!" called a man in the stands nearby. "He's strung out."

In three seconds he was thrown, tossed into the air like a rag doll, landing flat on his back, knocking the wind from his lungs, the consciousness from his mind, and sending up a cloud of dust. The bull continued to buck nearby, his hooves pounding the ground dangerously close to the limp and lifeless man. The crowd gasped as the bull flailed around, the tip of his long, pointed horn missing the man's skull by mere inches.

The clowns rushed forward. The one in the barrel barreled toward the bull, ramming him in the side to force him away from the prone form on the arena floor. This bull would not easily surrender, however. He continued to buck and circle, buck and circle, until one of the clowns roped him and, together, the clowns dragged him toward the exit gate.

As soon as the bull's hindquarters had cleared the threshold, four EMTs rushed forward, scooping the unconscious rider from the ground and onto a gurney, running with him back to the ambulance. They slipped him into the back, slammed the doors closed, and drove away, their lights flashing and siren wailing.

The crowd sat in silence for a few seconds, but after a respectable period, it was business as usual. No sense getting all worked up. After all, the rider knew the risks and had voluntarily taken them on, right? Besides, they'd come here to have a good time and weren't going to let this mishap ruin a fun night out. The announcer called out another name and another rider slipped onto a fresh bull in the chute. This rider had the sense to wear a helmet instead of a cowboy hat.

The gate burst open once again. *Clang!*

After just three seconds, this rider's hand came down to touch the bull's flank. This so-called slap meant his ride was now over as far as judging was concerned.

My radio crackled to life. "Officer needed at the outdoor beer booth."

I pushed the button to activate my mic. "This is Officer Luz and Brigit. We're on it."

The event continued, bull after bull, rider after rider, clang after clang. I tugged on Brigit's leash. "Let's go, girl."

We ventured back out onto the stock show grounds. The wind had picked up now, bringing blasts of icy air with it. Most of the people had gone into the livestock barns to stay warm. The few that remained outside huddled together lest they freeze to death.

I zipped my jacket all the way up and looked down at Brigit. She had her nose in the air, sniffing the various scents carried on the wind, the cold not seeming to bother her at all.

"I wish I had a nice fur coat like you," I told her.

She responded with a tail wag.

I turned and headed to the beer booth with Brigit trotting along beside me. I arrived to find a large man in a sweatshirt bearing the Coors Light logo standing watch over two boys who appeared to be in their late teens. They sat on the ground, outraged expressions on their faces.

I circled the slack in Brigit's leash around my hand to draw her closer in. "What's going on?"

"These two boys tried to buy beer," the man said, "with these."

He handed me two laminated cards purporting to be Canadian military identification cards. The photos on the cards depicted the faces of the two boys sitting on the ground. Though the boys didn't appear to be twenty-one yet, I knew age could be difficult to guess. Some people had baby faces, others aged prematurely. Still, I was with the beer man on this. I thought these boys were trying to pull a fast one.

"Those are real IDs!" said the taller of the two boys. "We're in the Canadian army."

"They certainly look real." I gave the man a discreet wink and looked down at the boys. "You wouldn't lie to a police officer, would you? That could get you in big trouble."

"No," they mumbled, sounding less sure now.

"Where in Canada are you two from?"

"Montreal," said the taller one.

"Yeah," agreed the other. "Montreal."

"Where'd you do your basic training?" I had no idea where the Canadian army held its boot camps, and I suspected these boys had no idea, either.

"At home," the tall boy said. "In Montreal."

Montreal seemed to be the only city in Canada these boys could identify. Americans weren't known for excelling in geography.

"Wait a minute." I narrowed my eyes at the boys. "I've heard that the Canadian army holds its boot camp in Vancouver." I was just making stuff up now, screwing with them a little. Might as well have some fun on the job.

"Vancouver," said the tall one. "Yeah. That's what I meant to say."

Riiight.

"What brings you to Texas?" I asked.

"We're on vacation," said the first.

"Yeah," agreed the second. "Vacation."

"Funny," I said, "you don't seem to speak with French accents. Your military ID cards aren't in French, either."

The two said nothing now, fear gleaming in their eyes.

"If you're from Montreal," I said, "you must speak French. That's the primary language there."

The two exchanged timid glances.

I decided to test their linguistic capabilities by speaking the only French I knew, the chorus of "Lady Marmalade." *"Voulez-vous coucher avec moi ce soir?"*

The two looked from me to each other.

"Jig's up, boys." I held out my hand. "Give me your real IDs."

The two grudgingly reached into their back pockets and pulled out their wallets, handing me their Texas driver's licenses. The tall one had just turned seventeen. The other was only sixteen.

After calling dispatch to run a quick search, I learned that neither had a juvenile record. I decided to cut them some slack. Kids do dumb things sometimes. What was childhood for if not making mistakes and learning from them?

"Call your parents," I told them. "Tell them to come get you."

"But we drove here ourselves," said the taller one. "In my car."

"Either your parents come talk to me here and I'll let you go with a warning, or I can take you two down to the station and they can pick you up there after you're booked for passing false identification with the intent to commit a crime."

Suddenly they couldn't wait to pull out their cell phones to summon mom and dad.

I thanked the beer man and led the boys to the exit, where we waited for their parents. When they arrived, I told them what their sons had been up to and showed them the IDs.

The tall boy's mother put one hand on her hip, and used the other to point a finger in her son's face. "You're grounded for two months! And we're taking away your car, too!"

The shorter boy's father was just as incensed. "Expect a month of hard labor. And no video games until summer!"

As the boys and their parents left, Brigit and I turned to head back inside.

"What do you think, g-girl?" I asked her. "Did we set those boys straight? Save them from a life of crime?"

She wagged her tail with a definite *yes*.

ELEVEN
HORNY

Brigit

Brigit watched the big bucking animal in the arena. She couldn't blame him for trying to ditch the man on his back. She didn't like it when someone tried to ride her, either.

Way back, before she'd managed to escape, she'd lived with a dipshit stoner who'd snatched her from a cardboard box marked FREE PUPPIES in front of Walmart. She'd been the largest of the litter, nearly twice the size of her four siblings. But she'd been the smartest of the bunch, realizing early on that it paid to stay close to their mother and food supply.

The guy hadn't wanted the puppy as a companion. He'd only brought her home because, with those big paws, she was sure to become an enormous beast. She could protect his stash, provide a warning bark if the cops pulled to the curb. Hell, he hadn't even bothered to name her, referring to her only as "dog," "damn dog," or "shithead" as the mood struck him.

One night, when he and his stoner buddies had been particularly drunk and high, he'd climbed onto her back after one of his idiot friends commented that she was as big as a horse. He'd been a skinny guy, but dogs weren't built to carry weight on their backs. She'd crumpled beneath him, her spine feeling as if it had snapped in two. As she lay flattened on the ground he'd kicked her in the ribs, fracturing two of them. Of course they'd been left untreated. Hell, the jackass hadn't even bothered to have her spayed or get her shots. It was a wonder she hadn't died of parvovirus.

She'd wanted to bite the stoner, to rip the guy to shreds. But she knew he was mean enough and stupid enough and messed up enough to kill her if she dared. If she'd had a nice pair of horns like these bulls, though, she would've gone for it, gored the dumbass right through the stomach and tossed him out into the yard like the garbage he was.

Still, she'd exacted a subtle revenge. When he'd been passed out cold the following morning and one of his so-called friends snuck back into the house, she hadn't made a peep. Thanks to Brigit's silence, the intruder got away with untold pounds of marijuana and five hundred dollars in cash the stoner had hid under his mattress. If a dog could laugh, she would have then.

A few weeks later, in the dead of winter, he'd left her outside in the cold with no food or water. She'd managed to dig out of the backyard and was eventually rounded up by an animal control officer. She'd been slated to be euthanized at the city pound, escaping her fate only when a police officer came into the shelter looking for a dog with the potential to be a K-9 officer. Brigit had impressed the cop with her smarts and size and determination, so here she was, working as a cop, getting three square meals a day and overtime paid in belly rubs and chew toys.

Brigit continued to watch the action in the ring. After the bull threw the man off his back, the beast trotted toward the nearby exit, his head held high. Brigit barked in encouragement. *Arf-arf!* They might not be the same species, but any time an animal bested a human it was cause for celebration.

TWELVE
STALLING FOR TIME

Robin Hood

As expected, convincing her sisters to run interference for her had been a snap. She'd given them a sob story, too, delivering it while they sat in her Chevy Spark in the stock show parking lot.

The inexpensive car might not be much, but at least it wasn't a hand-me-down. Sick of secondhand goods, she'd refused to buy a used car. Given her young age and less than stellar credit score, the cheap car had been the only new one she could qualify for. Chevy called the yellowish-beige color "Lemonade," but to Robin Hood it looked more like the color of butterbeans. Regardless, it was all *hers*. She only wished it didn't now smell like the Revlon Fire & Ice perfume her sisters seemed to bathe in. Robin Hood would never wear a scent sold at a drugstore. She bought her Tom Ford Black Orchid perfume at the cosmetics counter at Macy's. Or at least she had when she'd still had a viable credit card.

"I'm pregnant," she told her sisters, blinking her eyes

repeatedly to fight back tears that weren't coming. *Like I'd ever let my twenty-five-dollar mascara run.* "Evan, he wants me to . . . to . . ." She turned her head away, as if unable to let them see her grief. "He wants me to get rid of it!"

Crystal reached out and put a hand on her sister's shoulder. "That asshole!"

Robin Hood turned back to her sisters and gulped back a sob that, like her tears, didn't truly exist. "I don't know how I'm going to afford the medical bills."

Heather frowned. "Don't you have health insurance through your job?"

"Yes," she said. "But there's a three-thousand-dollar deductible plus a hundred-dollar copay for every office visit."

She hoped that sounded reasonable. Honestly she had no idea what her insurance policy covered. She was twenty-one years old and in perfect health. The last time she'd seen a doctor she'd been nineteen and suffering with a genital wart. She'd been unemployed and on county health insurance at the time. The doctor at the clinic had simply burned the thing off, warned her about the dangers of unprotected sex, and sent her on her way.

Her sisters exchanged glances.

"We'd offer to help you out," Crystal said, "but we pooled the last of our money to get the trailer leveled. Our bedroom was a foot lower on the end. If it sank any further we'da fallen out of bed."

Robin Hood eyed her two sisters, opening her lids wide in an expression of hope. "But you would help me? If you could?"

They exchanged glances again.

"Of course," Crystal said. "You're our sister."

"Sure," Heather agreed after a slight hesitation.

Robin Hood explained her plan. "So all you need to do is run a little interference if necessary. Got it?"

Crystal nodded once.

Heather, on the other hand, asked, "What if we get caught?"

"We won't," Robin Hood said, letting a tone of *how-can-you-be-so-stupid?* underscore her words. The fictional Robin Hood had never gotten this kind of shit from his Merry Men. "And even if the police catch me, they can't charge you with anything. It isn't a crime to use a public restroom."

"Oh." Heather's face brightened and she sat up straighter. "Right."

After Robin Hood traded her stilettos for sneakers—*getaway shoes*—they climbed from the car. She popped her trunk open and retrieved a pair of crutches she'd bought for three dollars at a yard sale. She held them out to Crystal. "Here you go."

Crystal took them and slid them under her armpits. They were a little on the short side, but Robin Hood hadn't thought to bring tools to adjust them. They'd have to do. Crystal hunched over and crooked one leg up behind her, feigning a sprained ankle. Robin Hood wasn't as impressed with Crystal's acting skills as she'd been with her own, but they would have to do.

The three bought tickets at the ticket booth and headed inside, making their way to the arena to watch the rodeo. Crystal and Heather seemed to enjoy the show, cheering on the calf ropers and bull riders. Robin Hood, on the other hand, was bored out of her skull. Stinky animals and dust and farmers were so *not* her thing. She was here for one thing and one thing only. To relieve a wealthy tourist of her cold, hard cash.

After enduring the events for an hour or so, she let out a long sigh. "Can we please get moving?" When she realized she'd sounded impatient and thus unsympathetic, she added in a whisper, "It's just hard for me to keep sitting here. I keep thinking about the baby and all."

Murmuring words of support that fell on deaf ears, her sisters followed her down the bleachers, out into the corridor, and down the hall to the ladies' room. As they'd planned back in the car, her sisters positioned themselves at either end of the sinks, Heather washing her hands and Crystal fixing her hair. Robin Hood hovered near the stalls with her oversized Michael Kors tote. She looked down at her cell phone and pretended to be texting, when actually she was using the ruse to hide her face while secretly checking out the women who came in to use the facilities.

Several women came through, but most looked like young mothers or farm folk, not likely to have much cash in their wallets. Finally, in walked a woman with some potential. She was fiftyish, with blond hair styled poofy on top and short on the sides and back, with a longer piece lying stylishly on her cheek in front of each ear, like a blond female Elvis. The woman was dressed in hundred-dollar Miss Me jeans with rhinestones and embroidery on the back pockets. She wore hand-painted boots and carried one of those pricey tooled-leather western-style purses. She also wore the happy, loose expression of someone who'd had a few glasses of wine with dinner before heading to the rodeo.

The perfect victim.

As the woman slid into a stall on the end, Robin Hood slipped into the adjacent stall. She watched the floor. Once the embroidered jeans came down, she climbed up onto the toilet. Keeping her head as far back as she could, she glanced down into the stall. The woman's face was down as she pulled paper from the roll. *Good. She was paying no mind to her purse.* All it took was a quick hand over the top of the stall and the bag was yanked from the hook. Spoils in hand, Robin Hood jumped down from the toilet to the floor.

"Hey!" the woman cried. "You took my purse!"

Oops. Looked like the woman hadn't been quite as inattentive as Robin Hood had thought. She kicked at the toilet knob, hoping the flush would drown out the woman's screams.

Flushhhhh.

"Give it back!" the woman cried. "Give me my purse!"

As the woman yanked up her pants in the stall next door, Robin Hood shoved the purse into her oversized tote, zipped the tote closed, and exited the stall without so much as a glance in her sisters' direction. Five steps later she was out of the bathroom, merging with the bustling crowd, home free. It took everything in her not to throw a victorious fist in the air.

Robin Hood rises again.

THIRTEEN
BUCK-A-ROO

Megan

After sending the boys home with their parents, Brigit and I had returned to the arena.

When the bull-riding was over, the announcer jumped back on his mic. "Keep your seats, buckaroos! Up next will be our bareback riders. You won't want to miss this classic rodeo event!"

I decided to leave the arena at that point. The dust had my eyes feeling gritty and made me sneeze. Besides, the way Brigit kept eyeing the bulls and drooling I feared that if I didn't get her away from that arena she'd try to take one down singlehandedly. Or would that be single*paw*edly?

As I led my partner into the outer hallway, Deputy Mc-Cutcheon strode by with a group of men. He'd ditched his uniform for jeans, chaps, and a burnt-orange western shirt over what appeared to be some type of padded chest protector. Like the other men around him, he now sported spurs and a straw cowboy hat. While these men looked every bit as tough and determined as the bull riders, by and large this group tended to be taller. I supposed having long legs would be a benefit when trying to remain on the back of a horse who was trying to throw you.

Clint spotted me and Brigit and turned our way, spinning to walk backward as he continued on. "You can't leave now!" he called. "I'm riding in ten minutes."

I glanced down at the schedule in my hand. Sure enough, his name was listed third among the bareback riders. *Clinton McCutcheon, Azle, TX.*

"He won't be riding long!" hollered the man walking next to him. He gave Clint a friendly pat on the shoulder before turning back to me. "McCutcheon drew Tornado Loco. Toughest horse in the bunch."

Clint raised his palms in a final invitation before turning back around to watch where he was going.

What is it with the men in my life? First Seth and his bombs and now Clint and his unbroken horses. I wasn't sure if the two had a death wish or just an overabundance of testosterone. Or perhaps this said more about me than them. Was there something about me that scared off normal men, something that said *only men with oversized co-jones need apply?* Either way, I wasn't going to miss Clint's ride.

Brigit and I returned to our place at the gate, pulling rank over a quintet of young female rodeo groupies wearing low-cut tops and jeans so tight it was a wonder they could bend over to put on their boots. "Step back, girls," I said, though they were only a year or two younger than me. "Official police business here."

Riiight. As if stalking a sexy cowboy could in any way be considered part of my duties.

The broadcaster announced the start of the bareback riding event, calling the first rider to the chute. The man slid his right hand into a leather glove, and rubbed it with some rosin from a bag. Ready now, he settled onto the back of the horse immobilized in the chute and slid his hand into the rigging.

The gate clanged open and released the horse, a dark brown stallion with a wild mane. The horse leaped to the left, then right, then bucked three times in quick succession. The rider spurred with perfection, marking to the horse's shoulders with each jump. When the horse seemed to realize his tactics weren't working, he combined a buck with a spin, sending the rider flying off to the side. The man impacted the ground like he'd been slam dunked.

A collective and sympathetic "Oooh!" rose from the crowd. We were all thinking the same thing. *That had to hurt!*

The horse bucked a couple more times for show, then seemed to realize it was a waste of energy since he'd already ditched the cowboy. While the clowns shooed the horse toward the exit, the rider stood, clutching his shoulder. His arm hung limply at his side. He released his arm just long enough to give a wave to the crowd before leaving the arena. Looked like the paramedics would be busy tonight. I only hoped Clint wouldn't need their services.

As we watched, a young man joined the girls' group next to me. He wore a powder-blue shirt with embroidered white roses along with a shiny silver belt buckle featuring a towering oil rig. Far be it from me to stereotype, but something told me he might be more into bulls than heifers.

The second rider's performance was mediocre. He started off well enough, but after four seconds slid sideways on the horse and was thrown forward on a spin.

"Clint's up now!" cried a black-haired girl in the group hanging near me.

The girls and guy pressed forward en masse, squishing themselves up against the gate next to me.

"There he is!" called another, pointing across the arena where Clint was heading toward the chute.

"That is one *fine* cowboy," said another. "I wouldn't mind giving him a ride. Except I hope he'd hang on for more than eight seconds!"

As the girls laughed, my hand reflexively found the baton at my waist. I supposed I had no right to feel jealous. Heck, Clint and I had only spoken for a few minutes yesterday and for a matter of seconds today. It's not like the two of us were dating or anything like that. Still, the thought of them lusting after Clint made my blood simmer. I'd enjoyed his attention, maybe even *needed* it, and I didn't want to share it with anyone else.

"Next up is local favorite Clint McCutcheon!" the announcer called with enthusiasm through the loudspeakers. "McCutcheon is a two-time winner of the Houston rodeo, a three-time winner at the rodeo in Checotah, Oklahoma, and winner of last year's Oklahoma Buck-Off. Clint also placed second last year at the PRCA National Finals in Las Vegas, Nevada. Clint will be riding the notorious Tornado Loco, who's thrown more riders than Nolan Ryan threw home runs. Ladies and gentlemen, let's show Clint some love!"

The girls squealed and clapped and jumped up and down in their hand-painted boots, one even going so far as to put two fingers in her mouth and let out a whistle. *Thweeeee!* The rest of the crowd went wild, too, their applause roaring through the arena as many of them stood. Evidently Clint was a minor celebrity around these parts. *Who knew?* Not me, that's for sure. Then again, the rodeo wasn't my usual scene.

As Clint settled on the horse's back, my heart went still, as if trapped in its own chute. Clint could end up unconscious or hurt, like the earlier riders. Then who would flirt with me, make me feel desirable and witty and interesting?

Clang!

The horse bolted from the enclosure, dashing forward only three steps before bucking so high and hard it was a wonder he didn't flip over. Clint spurred over the horse's shoulders, virtually standing in the air given the horse's extreme angle. The horse bucked a second time with equal force, yet Clint hung on. When he failed to clear Clint with a third forceful buck, Tornado Loco lived up to his name, sending his body into a crazy leaping spin. How Clint was able to fight against the spinning force was a mystery, one that was solved not by Colonel Mustard in the conservatory but by Clint McCutcheon on the abdominal machine in the gym.

Rather than tire out, the horse only seemed to gain momentum as the seconds ticked by. Clint managed to stay on for the requisite eight seconds, defying both the odds and gravity. Finally, the horse effectuated a surprise sideways snap maneuver, bending nearly in half one way then the other to toss Clint. Amazingly, Clint landed on his feet, bouncing to absorb the impact. He stood, took off his hat for a quick bow, and trotted to the side, circling his hat over his head and pumping his fist in victory.

"Men want to be him," the black-haired girl said dreamily, watching Clint, "and women want to be with him."

"I don't know," their male friend said, tilting his head as he checked out the ass framed between Clint's chaps, "I think I'd rather be with him, too."

"Watch out for those spurs," I said as I turned to go. I'd seen, and heard, more than enough. Seemed everyone wanted a piece of Clint. I only wondered whether there was enough of him to go around.

I wandered back outside to patrol. A half hour later, as Brigit and I circumnavigated the perimeter, loud chanting from the parking lot drew my attention. I stepped up to the chest-high fence to see what was going on.

A dozen people stood in the parking lot just outside the

fence, carrying signs. Some of the signs were raised on sticks over their heads, others were scribbled on poster board and carried in their hands.

SPURN THE SPURS!

RODEOS: CRUELTY FOR A BUCK

REAL MEN RIDE BIKES.

THERE'S NO EXCUSE FOR ABUSE!

BUCK THE RODEO!

My eyes landed on two of the protestors, a curly-haired blonde and a thin man with a bushy gray beard. Sherry and Michael Lipsomb. I'd met the two not long ago at the Shoppes at Chisholm Trail, a mall in my usual beat, the place where the Tunabomber had planted his first bomb. The couple had been on site the day the bomb exploded, protesting the mall's fur store. They'd initially been suspects in the bombing, but had later been cleared. Though firmly dedicated to their causes, the two were a pair of relatively harmless hippies.

I stepped to the fence. "Hello, Mr. and Mrs. Lipscomb!" I called, waving a hand.

Sherry turned my way and lifted a hand in acknowledgment. Michael cast a glance in my direction and raised his chin, but didn't smile. The couple probably had mixed feelings about me. Though I'd supported their protest at the mall, telling them to let me know if anyone gave them any hassles, I'd also tagged along with the detective who'd interrogated them about the bombings. Nevertheless, I wanted them to know I was on site. Protesting at a rodeo where beer flowed freely on a Saturday night probably wasn't the safest thing to do. I had no right to send them away and they had every right to speak their minds, but frankly they were asking for trouble. I decided to stick close by.

Minutes later, I noticed Clint heading through the milling crowd toward me. He was back in uniform and back atop Jack. Yet another shiny belt buckle graced his belly, today's selection proclaiming him the bareback champion of the Houston rodeo.

He pulled up perpendicular to me and reined his horse to a stop. He beamed down at me and pulled a blue ribbon from his pocket. "I won first prize. Scored ninety points."

I reached up to pet Jack's snout. "Congratulations. That was quite a ride."

"My best ever!" He pumped a fist in triumph. "If I do well in the final round, I'm gonna think about going out on the circuit."

"Meaning . . . ?"

"The professional rodeo circuit. I'm placing consistently enough now that I could make a go of it."

"Wouldn't that require a lot of travel?" I asked. "What about your job here?"

"Being a professional rodeo cowboy is the chance of a lifetime. I can always come back to law enforcement later." He offered a sound that was part snort, part chuckle. "After all, it's not like people are going to stop committing crimes."

If only.

Behind me, a drunken voice hollered, "Fuckin' hippie . . . fuckers!"

Such eloquence, no?

I turned to see a squat, potbellied redneck pull a plastic tin of Skoal from his back pocket and hurl it at Michael. He ducked in time to avoid the projectile, but the tin continued on its course, flying over the fence and past me to hit Jack in the ass. *Thump!*

With a frightened whinny, the horse reared up onto its hind legs, its front hooves pawing the air mere inches from me and my partner.

"Whoa, boy!" Clint called.

I yanked Brigit back as far as I could, but we were trapped between the horse and the fence. If not for Clint's expert handling, both Brigit and I could have been trampled or crushed.

Once the horse's feet had returned to the ground, Clint pointed a finger at the gaping-mouthed redneck and yelled, "Stay right there!"

Realizing he'd effed up in a major way, a way that could land his sorry, chubby, and drunken ass in jail, the offender took off running.

Knowing a dog could maneuver through the crowd more easily and with less risk than a horse, I raised a palm to Clint. "We got this."

I unclipped Brigit's leash and gave her the command to pursue the idiot. Her nails scrabbled on the asphalt as she took off running. Five seconds later, the guy lay facedown on the asphalt amid flattened drink cups, paper cotton candy cones, and hot dog wrappings, his arms curved protectively over his head and face. Brigit lay spread-eagled across his back, the collar of his shirt gripped firmly in her teeth. She yanked on his collar, jerking his head left and right as he howled in terror.

I headed over, pulling my baton from my belt and extending it with a flick of my wrist. *Snap!* Clint and Jack trailed along behind me.

"Call off your dog!" the guy shrieked as I stepped up.

"I will," I told him calmly, "as soon as you apologize to those people." I used my nightstick to gesture to the protestors at the fence before motioning at Clint and Jack. "And to them."

"I'm sorry!" he cried. "Now get the dog off me!"

I called Brigit off, giving her the order to return to my side. After reattaching her leash, I looked down at the man, who rolled over onto his back and sat up.

Clint slid down off his horse, gathering the reins in his hand. When the guy made a move to stand, Clint said, "Nobody told you to get up."

The guy sat back down on the asphalt, glaring up at Clint.

"*Now* get up," Clint ordered, chuckling.

When the man stood, Clint stepped close to him and took a sniff. "You smell like alcohol."

"I only drank two beers!" The guy looked to the side, a sign that he was lying, intimidated by the tall deputy towering over him, or both.

"Two beers," Clint repeated. "Just two beers? Nothing else?"

The eyes darted around.

Clint motioned with his index finger. "Take off your boots."

"Why?"

Clint bent down and got in the man's face. " 'Cause I told you to."

After casting another glare at the deputy, the guy complied, removing first his left, then his right boot, having to grab the fence to keep from falling over. A crowd had gathered around to watch. He glanced around at the spectators and scooped up the boots, holding them tight to his chest.

"Set your boots down," Clint said.

When the guy failed to move right away, Clint, too, pulled his nightstick from his belt. "I said to *set. Your. Boots. Down.*" Though Clint didn't say it in so many words, his tone said it for him. *This guy could either comply voluntarily or get his ass kicked.*

With a huff of anger and frustration, the guy set his boots on the ground. Clint looked down into them. "Just as I suspected." He kicked one of them over and a metal flask slid out onto the pavement.

Another huff from the redneck.

"Let's see here." Clint rubbed his chin. "Looks like we've got a nice list of charges." He counted them off on his fingers. "Littering. Public intoxication. Drunk and disorderly. Assault on a law enforcement officer—"

"I didn't assault you!" the guy cried.

"You assaulted my horse." Clint's eyes narrowed. "If you'd have hit me, I might have found it in my heart to forgive you. But nobody messes with my horse."

Desperate, the guy said, "I don't think I'm drunk."

Clint snorted and looked my way. "That sounds just like something a drunk would say, don't it?"

"Sure does." I stepped forward now. "We could give him a sobriety test."

Clint raised his palms. "Be my guest, Officer Luz."

I pulled my penlight from my pocket and shined it into the guy's eyes, checking the reaction time of his pupils. Yup. Definitely on the slow side. But might as well be thorough. Might as well give the guy a little payback, too, a little tit for his tat, shit for his shat. "Recite the alphabet."

"A, B, C," he began. "D, E, F."

When he'd successfully recited his ABCs, he said, "See? I'm not drunk."

"Inconclusive," I said. "Fill in the blank. *Once upon a midnight dreary, as I . . .*" I made a circular motion with my finger, inviting him to finish the sentence.

He looked up as if racking his brain for the answer. "Uh . . ."

"Whacked off!" called a male voice from the crowd.

I ran my penlight over the crowd. "Wrong answer."

Another guy in the crowd took a shot. "Tried on my girlfriend's underwear!"

"You're getting closer," I said.

A female voice chimed in now. "Turned into a pumpkin?"

Did nobody in this crowd read the classics? I shook my head. "Sorry. Still wrong."

"Good guesses, though," Clint added, giving the crowd a thumbs-up.

"See?" yelled the redneck. "They don't know the answer either and they're sober!"

I stepped toward him and looked him in the eye. "Did you just admit that you're drunk?"

He looked up as if trying to remember what he'd just said. "Uh . . . no . . . I don't think so."

Clint and I exchanged glances before turning back to the redneck.

"You've failed the cognitive test miserably," Clint said. "But we can't tell if that's because you're drunk or just plain stupid."

The guy's face turned red with rage. "I'm not stupid!"

Clint raised a brow. "So you *are* admitting you're drunk, then?"

"No!" The guy looked from Clint to me. "No, I'm not!"

"Let's try a physical test." I used my baton to gesture at his feet. "To the left."

He took a step to the left.

"Take it back now, y'all."

He took a step back.

"One hop this time."

He hopped once.

"Right foot," I said. "Stomp."

He stomped his right foot.

"Left foot," I said. "Let's stomp."

He stomped again with his other foot.

"Now cha-cha. And do it real smooth."

"Wait." His brows angled in consternation. "Is this 'Cha-Cha Slide'?"

Clint cut his eyes my way and offered a snicker.

Realizing we'd had as much fun with the guy as we could without crossing the line, I returned my baton to my belt, my penlight to my pocket, and retrieved my handcuffs.

"Turn around," I told the guy. "Put your hands behind your back."

"Now wait just a minute." Clint stepped up close, though his towering over me didn't so much intimidate me as excite me. "This collar is mine."

"*My* partner took him down."

"And *my* horse took a hit to the ass."

Our gazes locked in a challenge, his eyes searing into me like lasers. Though I fought to control them, my breaths came hard and fast. But when Clint ran his tongue over his lips in overt seduction, a laugh escaped me and I acquiesced.

"All right." I stepped back to allow Clint to cuff the guy. "If you need this collar that bad you can have him."

The deputy pulled out his cuffs and slipped them onto the guy's wrists. *Click-click.*

Before hauling the guy off, he gave me a sly smile. "Nice doing business with ya'." A wink followed. "Don't think I've forgotten about that ride."

Heck, I hadn't forgotten about it, either.

As Clint headed off with his horse on one side, his prisoner on the other, the crowd dispersed. A dispatcher's voice came over my shoulder-mounted radio. "Officer needed at the arena ladies' room."

The male cops on site quickly deferred to me, their voices coming through loud and clear over the radio.

"Sounds like a job for you, Luz," one said.

"Girl problems," said another. "I'm out."

Derek was even more direct. "Ain't no way in hell I'm going in a ladies' room."

I rolled my eyes and pushed the mic button. "I'm on it."

Minutes later, Brigit and I found a blond, fiftyish woman dressed in upscale western attire standing outside the ladies' room. Her skin bore a light flush, as if she'd had a glass or two of wine. Tipsy, but not drunk.

Brigit snuffled around for a moment on the floor around the woman's feet, then raised her head high, her nose wriggling. She looked off down the hall.

"Somebody stole my purse!" the woman cried. "It was hanging on the hook in the stall and then a hand reached over and"—she threw her hands into the air in a magical *poof* gesture—"it was gone!"

"Did you see the person who took it?"

"Only her hand."

"Was there anything identifiable about her hand or arm that you noticed? A ring maybe? A tattoo or scar? The color of her sleeve?"

The woman squinted in concentration. "I think her sleeve was dark. Leather, maybe? And it seemed like maybe her nails were painted pink. But it happened so fast it's hard to say for sure."

I nodded to let her know I understood. "When you exited the stall, was there anyone else in the bathroom?"

"Two girls," she said. "I told them my purse had been stolen and asked if they'd seen the person who'd come out of the stall next to me. Both said no. They'd been washing their hands and hadn't gotten a good look. I'd called out when I saw the thief take my purse but I guess the girls couldn't hear me hollering over the sound of the running water."

"Any chance one of them could have taken it? Maybe hidden it inside their coat?"

The woman shook her head again. "They were both in jeans and those fitted knit jackets the young ones wear these days. There wouldn't have been anywhere for them to hide my purse."

"These girls," I said. "How old were they? Teens? Younger?"

"No, not that young," the woman said. "I'd say they were in their mid to late twenties."

I supposed that would make them "girls" to a woman her age, though I was in my mid-twenties, too, and considered myself a full-fledged woman. *Hear me roar.* "What did you do then?"

"I tried to run after the thief. Took me a second or two to get around the girl with the crutches. By that time, whoever had taken my purse was long gone."

"One of the girls had a broken leg?"

"I don't think so. There was no cast on her leg. I suppose she just had a sprained ankle or something like that. She had on the cutest pair of boots I've ever seen. Tan on the foot with bright pink on the upper part."

The boots did indeed sound cute. They also sounded irrelevant. Maybe if this woman had paid as much attention to her purse as she had to the girl's boots, she'd still have her bag.

I unzipped my police-issue jacket and pulled my notepad and pen from the breast pocket of my shirt. After jotting down the woman's name—*Catherine Quimby*—and some notes—*Suspect: Pink nails/dark leather jacket. Witnesses: 2 women/ 20s/crutches no cast?/tan & pink boots*—I resumed my questioning. "Were the two women who were in the bathroom there together?"

Catherine's brows tipped inward as she thought. "I don't believe so. They were at opposite ends of the counter. Friends would have likely stood closer together."

Unless they were pretending not to know each other. After all, women often traveled in pairs or groups when going to the restroom. *Hmm . . .*

"What did they look like?"

She looked up, as if trying to visualize them in her mind. "Unremarkable, really. Brown hair. Average height and build. Wearing jeans and jackets and boots, like I said."

Just like virtually every other young woman at the stock show and rodeo tonight.

"What all was in your purse?" I asked.

"Hairbrush. Makeup. Tissue. Gum. My wallet, of course."

"How much cash was in it?"

She looked up in thought. "Forty or fifty dollars maybe? I don't know the exact amount. Oh, and my pills were in my purse, too."

"Pills?"

"My prescription arthritis pills. Vicodin."

Painkillers, a mix of hydrocodone bitartrate and acetaminophen, a type of legal drug sometimes sold illegally on the streets. *Interesting.* "How many pills were in the bottle?"

Again she looked up in thought. "Maybe a hundred and ten pills? It was nearly full. I just had the prescription refilled."

The gears of my mind began to turn. *Was it possible someone had targeted her for the Vicodin?* "When's the last time you took a pill?"

"This afternoon around three," she said, "before I left the house."

"So you haven't taken any here at the rodeo?"

"No."

"Did you take the bottle out of your purse for some other reason while you were here?"

"I took it out and sat it on the counter when I stopped to buy a corn dog. I was digging through the bottom of my purse for change and it was getting in my way."

Someone might have spotted the bottle and targeted her for the pills. Then again, she could just be a random victim, chosen because her outfit and purse indicated she was well off.

I motioned for Catherine to follow me and Brigit into the bathroom. Whipping my baton out once again, I used it to poke around in the trash cans. Nope. No sign of a discarded purse.

I looked back at the woman. "Which stall were you in?"

The woman pointed. "The one on the end."

I stepped over and went inside to take a look around. Brigit took advantage of the opportunity to grab a drink from a toilet. I yanked back on her leash. "Stop it! That's disgusting."

It was bad enough when she did it at home, but a public toilet? *Yick!*

Nothing in the stall provided any clues, though writing on the wall in pink lipstick informed me that *Sophie + Clint McCutcheon = ♥.*

Hmm. I wasn't sure that math worked out. *If a rodeo groupie throws herself at a bareback rider at two hundred miles an hour, how long until their genitals meet?*

I decided not to put any time into answering that word problem. Instead, I radioed my fellow officers. "If anybody sees a young woman in a leather jacket and pink nail polish or one with brown hair on crutches, hold them for questioning."

FOURTEEN
EAU DE TOILET

Brigit

A public bathroom was the canine equivalent of happy hour. So many toilets to drink from!

Brigit got only three laps of water before Megan pulled her back from the commode and issued a cry of disgust. As if Megan were so clean. Right now she had pig poop on her shoe and wasn't even aware of it.

Humans can be so stupid. And their noses were so useless. Brigit's far superior nose picked up all kinds of things. For instance, though she didn't know their names, she could make out the scents of two different colognes. One smelled like flowers, with a hint of those round fruits that Megan cut in half and twisted on her cheap plastic juicer. The other smelled like flowers, too, and vanilla. Why human beings wanted to smell like a garden or a cupcake was beyond Brigit. She much preferred the personal, natural scent of sweat socks discarded after a long run.

FIFTEEN
PAYROLL

Robin Hood

As she waited in the car for her sisters, she fingered through the woman's wallet.

She found photos of two smiling boys, probably the woman's grandchildren.

A coupon for some type of high-fiber cereal. *EW.*

There was $53.87 in cash. *That's all? Damn.* She'd hoped for more.

Robin Hood slid the two twenties into the inside pocket of her jacket. What her sisters didn't know about she wouldn't have to share with them.

She continued to riffle through the purse. Hairbrush. Lipstick. Eyeglasses in a hard-sided case. A prescription bottle of Vicodin. Recently filled, too, not a pill missing that Robin Hood could tell. Surely the pills would be worth far more than the cash. According to the label, the prescription was for a Catherine Quimby, who suffered from arthritis.

I chose my victim well. Of course she'd always been very

careful when she stole things, too. That's why she'd never been caught.

She remembered the first time she'd stolen something. It hadn't been long after that humiliating day at the spelling bee. Her mother had dragged her and her sisters along one Saturday when she went to clean a house in the Colonial Country Club neighborhood. Normally her mother left them at home with their father when she had weekend jobs, but he'd been out that day, forced to paint over graffiti as community service, part of his sentence for passing a bad check at the grocery store. He hadn't meant to rip anyone off. He simply hadn't balanced the checkbook in a while and didn't realize just how dire their financial situation had become. When he'd been unable to repay the funds right away, the manager of the store turned the matter over to the district attorney. Because her father had no prior record, the DA let him plead out and offered him twenty hours of community service in lieu of a fine he couldn't afford.

The family who'd hired their mother to clean had only one daughter, a girl three months younger than Robin Hood. The girl had skin and hair so fair she was virtually colorless. What she lacked in pigment she did *not* make up for in personality. She was quiet and dull and annoyingly well behaved. It took less than three minutes for Robin Hood to decide she hated the girl.

The girl's mother had turned to Robin Hood's mom and said, "Your daughters are welcome to watch TV in the playroom with Hayley. Maybe they'll find some toys in there to keep them occupied while you work."

Robin Hood felt her gut tighten. This little girl not only had a bedroom to herself, but an entire playroom, too? *It wasn't fair.*

When Robin Hood, Crystal, and Heather stepped into Hayley's playroom, they might as well have been stepping into Oz or Willy Wonka's factory. The bright and airy room was lined floor to ceiling with shelves that held every toy and game imaginable. Hayley owned the Barbie Dreamhouse, the pink convertible, even a plastic play camper. She had clay and beads and paints and yarn in a dozen different colors. A large trunk contained clothes for dress-up, including a mermaid costume, a ballerina costume complete with soft pink shoes and a fluffy tutu, and assorted princess attire.

But what impressed Robin Hood most was Hayley's American Girl doll collection. Five of the pristine dolls, still in their original packaging. Robin Hood remembered counting them, memorizing their names. *Julie. Rebecca. Addy. Caroline. Josefina.* She couldn't imagine ignoring the beautiful dolls like this, leaving them in their boxes. Oh, how she'd wanted one for the longest time!

She knew her parents couldn't afford to get her one of the dolls. She'd looked on the Internet on the school library computer and learned that the dolls cost over a hundred dollars each. She'd asked Santa for an American Girl doll when she'd sat on his lap at the mall last December. He hadn't brought her one. Instead he'd filled her stocking with candy and crayons and Play-Doh. She'd decided then and there, on that fateful Christmas morning, that Santa was an asshole.

She'd looked from the dolls to Hayley. "How come you never took these dolls out to play with them?"

Hayley had lifted one shoulder. "I like Barbies better."

Again, it wasn't fair. Why should this girl have all these toys when she didn't even appreciate them?

Crystal found a *Pocahontas* DVD on the shelf and Hayley put it into the player. The two of them curled up on the couch with Heather to watch the movie, paying no attention whatsoever to Robin Hood.

It was the perfect opportunity to exact some social justice.

She'd pulled the prettiest doll off the shelf and slipped out of the room with it, heading to the front door. She supposed she should have felt guilty about stealing the doll, but she didn't. *She was doing a good thing. She was making the world more fair.*

As she sneaked down the hall, she saw her mother on her hands and knees on the kitchen floor, scrubbing the grout, the stiff brush giving off a *scritch-scritch-scritch* as she rubbed it back and forth between the floor tiles. Meanwhile Hayley's mother stood outside on the patio, her back to the windows as she sipped a lemonade and yakked on the cordless telephone. That situation wasn't fair, either.

She quietly tiptoed out the door and stashed the doll under the seat of her mother's battered hatchback. In less than a minute she was back inside, sitting on the couch with her sisters, no one the wiser.

But what she remembered most about that day was the thrill she'd experienced, the sense of power and excitement, the smug sense of satisfaction that she'd evened the score, if only by a little bit. To this day she wondered whether Hayley had ever noticed that the doll was missing.

Her reverie ended when Crystal and Heather returned to the car. Robin Hood jabbed the button on her key chain to pop the trunk open. After Crystal slid the crutches into the trunk, she and Heather climbed into the car.

Crystal raised her brows in anticipation. "How much did we get?"

We, thought Robin Hood. *How cute.* "Thirteen dollars and change."

Heather frowned. "That's . . . what? A little over four bucks each?"

"Shit," Crystal said, frowning now, too. "That's not even enough for a latte at Starbucks."

Robin Hood shrugged. "Everyone uses debit and credit cards now. People don't carry much cash anymore."

"Sucks for us," Crystal said.

"Next time," Robin Hood said, "we'll go for jewelry, too."

Why not? The three of them could easily disable a single victim and relieve her of her earrings, rings, necklaces, and bracelets. They could either take the jewelry to one of those cash-for-gold places or sell the stuff to a pawnshop.

Robin Hood handed four one-dollar bills to Heather and a five-dollar bill to Crystal. "I figured you should get a little more since you had to deal with the crutches. Sound fair?" She looked from one sister to the other.

"Okay," Heather agreed.

Robin Hood tucked the remaining four singles into her tote.

"Hey!" Crystal said. "What about the eighty-seven cents?"

SIXTEEN
AUTO-EROTICA

Megan

Brigit and I made our way around the entire grounds twice, looking for the witnesses who'd been in the bathroom when Catherine Quimby's purse had been snatched. I saw two elderly people on motorized scooters, one disabled person in a wheelchair, and a young boy with his arm in a sling, but no brown-haired woman on crutches. None of the other officers had reported seeing her, either. I peeked in all of the trash cans, using my baton to poke around for the stolen purse, but didn't find it. If the thief had discarded it on site, it had either become buried under other garbage by now or hauled off by the maintenance staff to a larger Dumpster.

The music hall was a flurry of activity when Brigit and I stepped through the door. Couples twirled around the floor, turning this way and that, two-stepping to the rapid tempo of "Georgia on a Fast Train." Texas singing legend Billy Joe Shaver graced the stage, treating the crowd to their favorite songs.

I took a spot along the wall, my eyes scanning the crowd, looking for anyone who might be poised to cause trouble. *Oh, who am I kidding? I was looking for Clint.* I'd noticed Jack had been returned to a stall in one of the barns. Evidently Clint was done dealing with the drunk redneck and had set back out to patrol on foot.

I wasn't a great dancer, but like every self-respecting Texan I could manage a basic two-step, polka, and waltz without embarrassing myself too much. I wouldn't mind scooting my boots with Clint, even if my "boots" were ugly rubber-soled tactical police shoes rather than pretty hand-painted cowgirl boots.

My eyes spotted a blur of Clint's brown and tan uniform as he twirled by on the dance floor with one of the groupies from earlier. She tossed her head back, laughing and smiling up at him as he spun her around. I wondered if she was the Sophie who'd written on the wall in the bathroom. I felt a twinge of envy, though I had no right to, especially given that I had a breakfast date with Seth in a mere nine hours.

Clint raised one arm, and the girl twirled under it, spinning three times before he captured her by the waist again. Clearly the guy knew his way around a dance floor. He also knew how to lead a woman so that her body did exactly what he wanted it to do.

Gulp.

The guy in the baby blue shirt danced past Clint and his partner. The woman in his arms had thirty years and just as many pounds on him, but the two nonetheless made great dance partners, keeping in perfect step as they executed a series of advanced turns and complicated maneuvers in which they repeatedly crossed their arms over each other's head in a weaving pattern.

When the song ended, the band segued into a slow version of "Honky Tonk Heroes." Despite the fact that she hung on to his arm and appeared to voice a protest, Clint backed away from the girl he was dancing with. He tipped his hat to her, then put a hand on the small of her back to escort her off the dance floor.

Everything here seemed under control. Better leave lest Clint catch me stalking him. No sense making a fool of myself.

Brigit and I had just reached the door when Clint slipped past us to block our way.

He looked down at me with those big brown eyes of his. "You're not going to leave without giving me a dance first, are ya? That would be downright cruel."

I hadn't even realized he'd spotted me. The fact that he'd picked me out in a crowded room was flattering. Then again, with a gun at my hip and a dog at my side I didn't exactly blend in.

"Whaddya say?" he asked, moving his head to indicate the dance floor.

At the thought of dancing with Clint, my heart beat a tempo much too fast for the slow song that was playing. I held up Brigit's leash. "I can't leave my partner."

Undeterred, he grabbed my hand. "Then she'll just have to come with us."

He dragged me to the dance floor and gently but firmly pulled me into position, taking my right hand in his and raising my left hand, still clutching Brigit's leash, to his shoulder. He set off in a basic two-step, our feet sliding in the classic pattern—*slow, slow, quick-quick.* I moved stiffly along, keeping track in my head so I wouldn't get off. *Slow. Slow. Quick-quick. Slow. Slow. Quick-quick.*

Clint glanced down at me, evidently noting the look of concentration on my face. "We'll keep it easy," he said, of-fering me a smile. *"For the dog."*

Busted. I narrowed my eyes at him.

We made our way in a circle around the floor, Brigit trotting along next to us in her own four-legged rhythm. Though she mostly kept an eye on the dancers around us, probably to keep her paws safe, she glanced up occasionally with a look that said she didn't enjoy being our four-legged third wheel.

As the song wrapped up, Clint steered me to the edge of the dance floor and released my hand, but not before giving it a soft squeeze. He glanced over at the bar. "Too bad we're on duty. I could really go for a beer."

"There's hot chocolate outside," I suggested, as much to offer an option as to get him out of the dance hall. The girl he'd been dancing with before me was casting daggers at me from her seat at a nearby table. No sense risking her reporting us for unprofessional behavior.

Clint and I left the hall, venturing out in the clear and cool night, aiming for the hot drink stand.

On our way over, I told him about the reported purse snatching. "Any thoughts?" I asked when I'd told him everything I knew.

He shrugged. "Big crowds like this, with people distracted and carrying lots of cash, it's prime hunting grounds for pickpockets and purse snatchers. Odd that the purse was taken from the ladies' room, though. Most petty thieves are male. I can't imagine a guy could've gotten in there without the women throwing a fit, though. Not unless he was in drag and the women didn't notice."

"A guy in drag at a Texas rodeo? I don't see that happening." Not unless he wanted to get his ass kicked. The general public here feared gays more than guns. Texas law allowed citizens to own an arsenal big enough to launch a one-man Armageddon, but prohibited them from marrying their same-sex partner lest Dallas and Fort Worth turn into Sodom and Gomorrah with people fornicating all up and down I-30.

"What about the pills?" I asked. "You think the thief was after the Vicodin?"

"Who knows?" he said. "More than likely they got tossed out somewhere with the purse. These kind of petty thieves are more interested in cash."

Is he right? Or could the pills be an important piece of the puzzle?

Clint and I waited in line for a minute or two, then stepped up to the booth to order our drinks.

"You want marshmallows?" Clint asked.

"It wouldn't be hot chocolate without them." If I was going to blow my healthy diet with a sugary drink, I might as well go all the way, right?

A minute later, our drinks in hand, we set out on foot patrol. I positioned myself on Clint's right, keeping Brigit between us for appearance's sake. By this time of night, the outside crowd had thinned. Virtually the only people who remained were the rodeo's cleanup crew and those responsible for tending to the animals.

As we strolled along, I turned my head to look up at Clint. "I have to ask. What makes a seemingly sane person risk his life climbing onto the back of a wild horse?"

" 'Seemingly sane?' " Clint chuckled. "Looks like I've got you fooled, huh?"

"It wouldn't be the first time." The Tunabomber sure had fooled me. Before I'd figured out he'd been the one to set the explosives, I'd thought he was an odd but harmless guy.

Clint tilted his head. "It's a cultural thing, I suppose. I grew up around horses, cows, rodeos. Besides, this is Texas. If you're a boy, you've either got to play football or ride a horse or bull. Otherwise, you're a sissy."

Not all Texans were quite so narrow-minded. Nevertheless, I understood his point.

When we reached the equestrian barn, Clint cut a glance

my way. "How 'bout I round up Jack and give you that ride I promised?"

My heart performed the squirming-kitten dance again. "Why not?"

I knew *why not*. Because of Seth. Because of the way he made my soul ache when we'd been apart. Because despite the fact that I found Clint to be charming and sexy and intriguing, despite the fact that I enjoyed the attention he gave me, I wasn't sure about him. Part of me thought he could be a stand-up guy. Another part suspected he might be nothing more than a flirt, a cowboy Casanova, a player. A guy I could have some fun with, but nobody I should let myself get too worked up about. Perhaps the knowledge that this little fling, if it could even be called that, would probably go nowhere was precisely why I was so willing to participate. After nearly being killed at the hands of a sociopathic bomber and dealing with the heartbreak Seth had wreaked upon me, didn't I deserve a little fun?

Clint led me into the barn and down a long, wide corridor lined with stalls. Tack hung from pegs and hooks or was stored in plastic tubs in front of the stalls. Saddles sat empty on supports mounted to the walls. Jack's stall was halfway down the row, between a pretty palomino and curious paint horse, who stuck his head over the stall gate to check us out. When he nickered for attention, I gave him a solid scratch under the chin. "Hello, boy."

"Yo, Jack," Clint called as he opened the stall door. His horse looked up briefly from his water trough, drops dripping from his whiskery chin to the hay at his feet, before returning his lips to the water. Clint patted the horse's neck and retrieved Jack's reins. Done drinking now, Jack lifted his head. Clint slid the reins over the horse's head and finagled the bit into his mouth. He didn't bother saddling the horse, just led him out of the stall and closed it behind him.

Clint led the horse over to the other side of the corridor, hooked a boot between the rungs of a stall for leverage, and swung himself up onto the horse's back. Glancing down the row, he called to a cowboy a couple of stalls down. "Little help over here?"

The man stepped over, squatted to the left of Jack's rump, and cupped his hands. "Up you go."

Still holding Brigit's leash, I hooked my hands over the horse's back and went to put my right foot into the improvised stirrup. Clint stopped me, glancing up with amusement in his eyes. "Other foot, city slicker. Unless you want to ride backward."

"Oh. Right." *Duh.*

I put my left foot into the man's hands and pulled with my arms as he hoisted me up. He grunted with the effort.

"Holy cow," Clint said. "Next time you might want to do without the marshmallows."

The grin on his lips told me he was only teasing. Good thing or I might've whacked him upside the head with my baton.

I thanked the man for his help.

"No problem, Officer."

As I settled in, I found myself wondering how I was supposed to hang on. Should I put my hand on Clint's shoulder? At his waist? Wrap it around his abdomen?

Fortunately, Clint solved the dilemma for me. "Scooch forward," he directed, reaching back to take my hand and pulling it around in front of him.

I slid forward, leaving a good six inches between my crotch and his ass.

"A little more," he said.

I scooted again. We were down to four inches.

"More," he said.

Two inches. I didn't dare get any closer. I couldn't trust myself not to bite into the back of Clint's neck. I mean, it was right there in front of me, looking soft and fleshy and delicious.

"You sure are a nervous Nellie." He played with my hand, forcing it out of the fist I'd involuntarily made, and pressing my palm up against his rock-hard belly. "Nice six-pack. Wouldn't you say?"

Hell, yeah! Seth had a nice six-pack himself. Great shoulders, too, from all that swimming. Still, no sense giving Clint a bigger head than he already had. "I've seen better."

Clint made a *tsk-tsk* sound. "Megan Luz, you're a filly who hasn't been broke yet." He tucked his chin and eyed me over his shoulder. "I just may have to see about that."

With that, he made a clucking noise and squeezed Jack with his muscular thighs. The horse started forward, his enormous buttocks moving up and down behind me.

Brigit walked along next to the horse as we rode out of the stable and onto the rodeo grounds. The dog picked up speed as Clint brought the horse to a slow trot along the street. A few seconds later, he reined the horse in, bringing Jack to a quick stop. Momentum carried me forward on the horse's back, my chest bouncing off Clint's back, the two inches that I'd maintained between our nether regions reduced to zero.

"Gotcha," Clint said, his tone tinged with both humor and seduction as he glanced back at me again.

I narrowed my gaze at him. "You're a sneaky snake, Clint McCutcheon."

"Hell, yeah." He tossed me that dark-eyed look again. "You best be careful how you handle me."

My alarm beeped at six A.M, yanking me out of a deep sleep. After the late night we'd had working the stock show and rodeo, even Brigit, who was usually bouncing off the walls by this time, wasn't ready to get up. She opened one eye for a moment, then closed it without moving.

"Ugh," I said to myself and the universe in general. "Why did I agree to this breakfast?"

I knew *why*. Because Seth had agreed to answer some questions about his family. Because maybe, *finally*, whatever was going on between the two of us would make some progress. I knew I'd said I wanted to keep things casual, but I had since realized that if a relationship wasn't moving forward it would either regress or stagnate, turning frothy and green and stinky like a pool of still water. I didn't want Seth and me to become green and stinky.

I climbed out of bed only to find myself barely able to walk. Though I'd been on Jack's back for only twenty minutes the preceding night, my thigh muscles felt as if I'd performed a thousand squats or more. *Talk about saddle sore.* I found myself wondering how my thighs would feel after twenty minutes of riding Clint. Then I found myself blushing for thinking such a naughty thought, even though I was the only one who knew I'd thought it. Or at least I thought I was the only one. Brigit looked up at me with a disgusted expression, as if she'd read my mind. More likely she was annoyed I'd disturbed her sleep.

I made my way to the bathroom, pivoting my hips to move my legs along in a bowlegged waddle. It was less painful that way. That afternoon I'd have to soak in a warm bath.

An hour later, I was fully dressed, though still only half awake, when a single soft knock sounded at my door. Seth stood on the walkway, dressed in tennis shoes, jeans, and a striped green button-down covered by a black wool vest. It appeared to be another of the vests his now-deceased grandmother had sewn long ago for his grandfather. A pocket watch was tucked into the vest pocket. Although

Seth had never come out and said so, I'd read between the lines and surmised that his wearing the vests was a subconscious way for him to maintain a connection to his dead grandmother. She must have meant a lot to him. I wanted to know more about her. I wondered how much Seth would tell me.

"Hey," he said in greeting.

I stifled a yawn. "Those cinnamon rolls better be as good as you promised."

"They will be. Just you wait and see."

I left Brigit with a nylon bone to chew on, a pat on the head, and a vague threat. "If you touch any of my shoes," I warned, pointing a finger in her face, "there will be consequences."

She wagged her tail in an up-down motion, her trademark gesture of sarcasm. *Yeah, yeah,* the tail said. *We both know you're full of crap.*

I headed down the stairs in silence, Seth following. I stopped next to his Nova. He opened my door and even held out a hand to help me in. Once I was seated, he closed my door and rounded the front of the car to climb in on the driver's side. After starting the engine, he turned on the heater, the blast of air fluffing my hair, which I'd left loose. *For him.*

"How's that?" he asked, putting a palm in front of the vent to test the heat.

"Perfect."

The climate now controlled, he jabbed the radio button, tuning it to 90.1, the local NPR affiliate.

My eyes cut his way. Seth normally listened to classic rock. The radio selection this morning was entirely for me. It was a thoughtful gesture.

The *Humankind* show was under way, featuring an Israeli music conductor who had formed an Arab-Israeli orchestra with the help of a close Palestinian friend. If these two men could bring people together, maybe there was hope for the world. Feeling more awake and upbeat now, I clicked my seat belt into place.

Seth backed out of the space and drove out of the apartment lot, turning to head north. "How have things been going at the rodeo? Any problems?"

Other than me getting hot and bothered over a dark-eyed, dark-haired deputy? "We arrested a drunk redneck who threw a can of Skoal at protestors."

Seth grunted. "There's one in every crowd, huh?"

Luckily there'd been *only* the one last night. Drunken assholes sometimes traveled in packs, like wild dogs. "There was also a purse snatching in one of the women's restrooms. The thief reached right over the top of the stall and grabbed the purse off the hook. Can you believe anyone would be that ballsy?"

"Wait. You mean the thief grabbed it while the victim was using the toilet?"

I nodded.

Seth cringed. "Talk about being caught with your pants down."

"No kidding. I poked around in some of the trash cans but there was no sign of it."

He turned onto the freeway entrance ramp. "Sounds like you did what you could."

True. Without hard facts or a description of the alleged purse snatcher, we had nothing to go on. Still, I figured I'd keep a closer eye on the ladies' bathrooms the next few nights in case the purse snatcher returned.

Seth headed north on I-35, then west on I-30, exiting onto Camp Bowie Boulevard and continuing on until he reached the Weatherford traffic circle. He pulled into the parking lot at the Busy B Bakery and parked between a black car that looked like something Bonnie and Clyde would have driven to escape law enforcement and a fifties-era powder-blue bubble-windowed car that looked like it had driven off the set of *Grease*. Several other cars pulled into the lot. An ancient brown pickup truck that sported whitewall tires and sat only an inch or two off the ground. A black-and-gold roadster. A classic '65 Ford Mustang.

I wasn't sure what, if anything, distinguished a hot rod from a muscle car, but it didn't much seem to matter. Everyone here was a classic car enthusiast and that was enough to draw them together.

Seth and I went inside the bakery. The scents of vanilla, yeast, cinnamon, and sugar welcomed us. We stepped into line behind half a dozen other people eager to sink their teeth into something sweet.

Finally, it was our turn at the counter.

"Two coffees and two cinnamon rolls," Seth told the clerk.

"And a bag of sausage rolls," I added. "To go."

We emerged a few minutes later with cinnamon rolls in one hand, coffee in the other, and a bag of sausage rolls tucked into my purse to give to our dogs later. While Seth talked cars with the mostly male crowd, who bragged about the size and power of their motors—*gee, no symbolism there!*—I wandered among the vehicles, admiring them primarily for their aesthetic qualities. The Mustang's cherry-red paint job. The quaint appeal of the low-slung pickup. The heavily padded seats of the Bel-Air, which looked comfortable enough to lie down and take a nap on. Looked like my coffee hadn't quite kicked in yet.

"Ain't she a beauty?" asked the owner of the Bel-Air, a white-haired man of about sixty. "My dad says I was conceived in one just like her."

I nearly choked on my roll but forced a smile. "Yeah, she's a beauty, all right."

I meandered back to where Seth stood alongside a purplish-black car.

Seth glanced my way. "This is a thirty-five Chevy Standard. Nice, isn't it?"

"Very nice," I agreed, though given the size of the engine and the primitive engineering, it probably only got five miles to the gallon.

When the owner stepped away for a moment, Seth locked his gaze on mine and traced his fingers down the hood and over the rounded headlights. The gesture made me wonder what his touch might feel like on *my* headlights, which I suspected from the grin tugging at his lips was exactly his intention.

He stepped close to me, so close I could smell his shampoo.

His soap.

His warm, soft skin.

He spoke softly, his breath feathering across my cheek like an invisible caress. "How about we renegotiate that 'no sex' clause?"

"No." I paused just a moment before punctuating my words with a coy smile and the words, "Not yet." *Gotta give a guy hope if you want him to stick around, right?*

Seth's green eyes flashed and his lips spread in a roguish smile.

After an hour or so, when Seth had gotten both his cinnamon roll and classic car fix, we returned to his Nova. As soon as he pulled out of the lot and onto the street, I reminded him of our deal. "You said you'd tell me more about your family."

He released a long, slow breath. "I hope you're prepared for what you're going to hear. We're pretty screwed up."

"All families are screwed up to some degree in one way or another," I replied. "The ones that claim they're not are in denial."

If I'd learned anything in my time as a cop, it was that human behavior could be odd and unpredictable and that people were prone to conflict. Heck, I supposed I wouldn't have a job otherwise.

I turned sideways on the seat so that I could watch his reactions and body language, knowing they might tell me even more than his words would. "You said your grandfather has breathing issues. Does he have asthma? COPD?"

Seth gave a single shake of his head. "Emphysema."

"Was he a smoker?"

Seth cut his eyes my way. "No, he never smoked. The doctors suspect his lung problems were caused by Agent Orange."

"Was he drafted?"

"Yeah, he was drafted."

I sat quietly for a moment, processing the information. Though I'd been blindsided to hear Seth's grandfather call him a *dumb bastard,* knowing what I knew now it was hard to be too upset with the guy, even if his words were mean and hurtful. He was probably in pain. Lugging a tank of air around behind you couldn't be much fun. And for all of the pain and inconvenience to have been caused by a war in which he hadn't voluntarily participated only added insult to injury.

"Have you always lived with your grandparents?" I asked.

Seth kept his eyes locked on the road, but I detected a slight flex in his jaw. "Mostly. I lived with my mother off and on starting when I was six and ending around the time I turned ten."

"What happened? Why didn't you continue to live with your mom?"

The flex in his jaw was much greater now. "Because she couldn't get her shit together."

I wondered exactly what "shit" it was that she couldn't get together. Was she addicted to drugs or alcohol? Unable to hold a job for some reason? I wanted to know, but wasn't sure I should dig that deep just yet.

"What about your father?" I asked.

He issued a derisive grunt. "If you figure out who he is, let me know."

Whoa. Seth had never known his dad? Why not? Had he run out on Seth's mother? Abandoned them?

I wanted to ask him these questions and more, but I could sense the tension building in him. I wanted to get to know Seth, to understand him, but I didn't want to cause him unnecessary stress, either. He'd given me enough for today. There was no rush. I decided to let things go for now.

Seth cut a glance my way. "You scared off yet?"

"Me? Scared?" I cut him a glance right back. "Never."

SEVENTEEN
DOGGIE BAG

Brigit

The packaging might have promised to provide a dog with months of chewing satisfaction, but it took a mere two hours for Brigit to reduce the nylon bone to smithereens. When she heard a car in the parking lot outside, she stepped to the window and peered out. A young woman backed her small car into a parking space at the back of the lot but didn't get out. Brigit watched her for a few minutes, but the woman just sat there. Bored now, Brigit set her sights on the shoes inside Megan's closet.

After Brigit had easily yanked the hook and eye from the closet door a few weeks ago, Megan had added a sliding bolt just above the lever-style door handle. Though the dog's thoughts came in concepts rather than words, if translated to English they'd read: *Megan thinks she can stop me. How cute.*

Though she wasn't sure exactly how the bolt worked, experience told her that if she pawed at it long enough, gave it a nudge or two with her nose and put her teeth into it, she would likely be successful.

Brigit knew she shouldn't chew up Megan's shoes. But she was a smart dog, an energetic dog, one who needed to live in a house with a big yard where she could run around and chase squirrels and dig rather than a tiny studio apartment with iffy plumbing, an outdated electrical system, and a minor mice infestation. If the dog behaved herself, she'd never convince Megan that it was time to move out of this tiny hellhole.

She set to work and in two minutes flat had slid the mechanism up and over, releasing it. A quick paw to the handle and the closet opened, revealing a veritable smorgasbord of shoes. She'd just begun to make her selection process when she heard footsteps outside the front door. She put her nose in the air and twitched it to capture the new scent.

Sausage rolls!

EIGHTEEN
LET'S MAKE A DEAL

Robin Hood

She didn't personally know any drug dealers. Though she'd been known to get shitfaced now and again (and again and again . . .), she limited her drug use to alcohol. She'd heard that drug dealers sometimes cut drugs with baking soda or powdered sweeteners and even mixed up batches of drugs in sinks or toilets. Though she enjoyed a good buzz as much as the next party girl, no way would she ingest a product manufactured with such a lack of quality control. She had standards, after all.

Despite her lack of personal contacts in the drug world, a quick Internet search with the key words FORT WORTH, DRUG BUST, and APARTMENT led her to identify three apartment complexes that seemed to house a fair share of potential dealers. She decided to aim for the one farthest away from her place, on the east side of town, a place called Eastside Arms. Just the name of it sounded skanky. She could only imagine the types of low-class losers who lived there.

She slid into a hoodie, a pair of jeans, and sneakers, and pulled her hair back into a low ponytail. Though she normally refused to venture outside without a full face of makeup and her hair meticulously styled, she figured there was no point fixing herself up for whatever assorted scumbag might buy the pills. It would be not only a waste of time, but a waste of her pricey cosmetics. With her Visa card out of commission, she needed her makeup to last as long as possible.

Fifteen minutes later, she was at a standstill in her car, stuck in heavy traffic on the street in front of a megachurch. Looked like most of the congregants chose to attend the late service. She crept forward, feeling no sense of guilt whatsoever. She knew the Bible said, *Thou shall not steal,* but it also said that the wealthy should share their worldly riches with the less fortunate, and that a camel could go through the eye of a needle easier than a rich man. Those words didn't seem to stop the so-called one percent from continuing to amass their wealth. Surely the commandments were not meant to be taken at black-and-white face value. Besides, why should she obey orders from a god she wasn't even sure existed? Just as Santa had failed to deliver, so had God, leaving her prayers unanswered. Rather than look to the heavens, she'd take her advice from a real flesh-and-blood man, a smart one who'd discovered electricity and whose face graced the hundred-dollar bill. *God helps those who help themselves.*

So here she was.

Helping myself.

The traffic inched forward. After another minute or two, a police officer tweeted his whistle and raised his hand to wave her through an intersection. *Good to know local law enforcement is tied up this morning.* Fewer cops on patrol lowered her chances of being caught selling the Vicodin.

Four more turns and she pulled into the complex. A trio

of outdated three-story stucco buildings formed a U-shaped perimeter around a small, murky swimming pool. The buildings were painted an odd shade of blue that would have been more appropriate on an ice cream stand, yet the narrow windows and flat roofs gave the place a prisonlike feel. The only saving grace was the bright yellow wicker furniture with sunflower print cushions that sat next to the pool.

Beater cars filled most of the parking spots, oil spots and flattened beer cans and cigarette butts filling the others. Given that it was not yet noon and also cold outside, few people were out and about at the complex. She backed into a spot at the end of the lot, next to one of those goofy-looking Smart Cars that, for some reason, had a pair of rubber truck nuts hanging from the back. *Talk about tacky.*

She turned off her engine and waited. Surely someone would go out for diapers or a pack of cigarettes or meth at some point.

Movement at a window on the second floor of the middle building caught her eye. A huge, furry shepherd-mix dog stood at the glass, watching her intently. No matter. It wasn't like the dog could snitch on her. Besides, the dog probably belonged to a dealer who'd gotten the beast to protect his stash.

She had been sitting for only ten minutes when— *bingo!*—a grizzled white guy with greasy hair and a colorful neck tattoo emerged from a third-floor apartment wearing a pair of dirty, wrinkled jeans and a dingy T-shirt. Seemingly oblivious to the cold, he stepped to the railing, pulled a lighter and a pack of Marlboros from his pocket, and shook one loose.

Before he could light his cigarette, she unrolled her window just far enough to extend her hand and wave to him. When she had his attention, she motioned for him to come to her car.

Before coming down the steps, the man glanced first left, then right, as if looking for potential witnesses. Seeing none, he trotted down the staircase, making hardly a noise in his bare feet.

He came over to the car, crooked his fingers over the open window, and put his face to the open gap, instantly filling her nose with the odors of accumulated BO and sour beer breath. For the first time ever, she found herself wishing for the smell of her sisters' drugstore perfume.

The man smiled a stained-tooth smile and winked at her with a yellowed, bloodshot eye. "Hi, gorgeous."

She fought down her revulsion. *Maybe this was a bad idea.*

He raised a scraggly brow. "You looking to buy something?"

Then again, maybe not.

"Actually, I'm looking to sell." She pulled the bottle of pills from her purse, holding them out of reach in case he pulled a fast one and tried to reach in and grab them from her.

"Whatcha got there?"

"Vicodin."

"What strength?"

Her eyes scanned the bottle for the information. "Five milligrams."

He chuffed. "That's the low dose. How many you got?"

"A hundred and nine." She had carefully counted them on her bed last night, dividing them into small piles of ten pills each. After counting the pills, she'd done some research on the Internet. Though the online sources quoting prices for street drugs were of dubious origin and provided a wide range of prices depending on location, she estimated that here in Fort Worth the street value of the pills would be between $1 to $3 each, which meant the bottle was worth somewhere between $109 to $327. Of course she'd have to discount the price to give the dealer a profit margin when he resold them.

The guy's gaze went from her face to the bottle and back again. "How much you askin'?"

"Two hundred," she said, essentially splitting the difference. "And you have to pay in cash."

He laughed. "You're new at this, ain't ya?"

An embarrassed blush heated her cheeks. She supposed her reference to cash had been naïve and unnecessary. It's not like drug dealers used credit cards or personal checks in their transactions.

"I'll give you a hundred," he countered.

She split the difference again. "One fifty."

"Screw you, bitch," the man spat, stepping back from the car. "You're out of your element, girl. Get your ass back to the suburbs." He turned to walk away.

"Wait!" she cried. "I'll take the hundred." Frankly, as brave as she liked to consider herself, this interaction had her spooked. She'd rather sell the pills now than risk going up against an even meaner, smellier dealer at another complex.

Looking left and right again, he pulled a wad of bills from the front pocket of his jeans. The bills were held together with a silver money clip engraved with a skull and crossbones. He peeled off five twenties and offered them through the window, clenching them tightly in his fingers until she had released the bottle of pills into his other hand.

"Got anything else you'd like to sell?" He looked down at her breasts, leering, before raising his eyes back to her face. He arched a lecherous brow.

The mere thought of this man's hands on her made her stomach squirm. "No!"

He chuckled and stood, backing away from the window. "Nice doing business with ya, sweet cheeks."

Their transaction complete, she started her car, nearly running the man over in her haste to leave the complex. She pulled out of the lot, passing a blue muscle car with flames painted down the sides as it turned in.

Ew, Lord. Three blocks later and she could still smell the man's stench. Despite the cold, she unrolled all of the windows to clear the car, then yanked the lemon air freshener from her rearview mirror, held it to her nose, and inhaled deeply.

Aaah. Much better.

NINETEEN
FAST TALK

Megan

As Seth pulled into the parking lot of my apartment complex, I noted one of my neighbors, a scuzzy parolee named Dwayne Donaldson, backing away from a small yellow boxy car. Dwayne had two prior convictions for selling meth and, from the looks of things, he was back in business.

With a squeal of tires, the car zipped past us at warp speed, the pretty young blonde at the wheel appearing both disgusted and panicked. I looked back just in time to catch the first letter of her license plate before she sped out of view.

T.

"What kind of car was that?" I asked Seth as he pulled into a spot. "Was it a Honda Fit? A Nissan Versa?"

He glanced in the direction the car had gone. "Some kind of Chevy, I think."

I turned my attention back to Dwayne. By this time he'd scurried up to his apartment door and pulled it open.

I threw open the door to Seth's Nova and stepped out. "Dwayne!" I hollered.

The thug pretended not to hear me, closing his door with an emphatic slam. Given that nearly a quarter of the residents at my low-budget apartment complex were ex-cons or on probation for one offense or another, I got the same reaction from many of my neighbors. Brigit and I weren't exactly popular around here.

Seth and I went up to my apartment. "Wait here," I told him as I rounded up Brigit and clipped her leash onto her collar. "I need to go talk to my neighbor."

"That creep who ran up the stairs?"

"That's the one. He's had two convictions for dealing drugs. I think he may have just sold something to that girl who drove out of the lot."

"I'm not letting you go alone."

A small laugh escaped me. "You realize I do this kind of thing every day? It's how I make a living."

"I know," Seth said. "I try not to think about it too much."

I hurried to my bathroom, slipped into a FWPD T-shirt, and strapped on my belt. Armed and in some semblance of a uniform now, I led Brigit down the stairs of my building, stopped to let her take a quick pee on a patch of dirt, and headed up the stairs to Dwayne's unit.

Knock-knock-knock. There was no answer.

Brigit snuffled around the door, her nose twitching as she sniffed along the bottom and up the sides.

I knocked again, this time using the side of my fist instead of my knuckles. *Bam-bam-bam.*

Still no answer. "Dwayne!" I hollered. "Open up. Fort Worth PD!"

Screeeee!

We turned to see Dwayne peeling out of the parking

lot on his Kawasaki motorcycle, no helmet on his greasy head.

"Want to go after him?" Seth asked. "My Nova can do one-sixty."

"And you know that how?" I raised an inquisitive brow.

He raised his palms. "I plead the fifth."

Brigit finished her sniffing and sat, giving a passive alert on Dwayne's door. *So much for having the morning off.*

I pulled my radio from my belt and asked dispatch to have officers keep a lookout for Dwayne. "Looks like he's dealing again."

Meanwhile, I went down to the on-site manager's office to get a key.

Dale Grigsby answered his door wearing only a pair of too-long gray sweatpants that hugged his paunchy, pimply belly and puddled around his pasty ankles. He rubbed his bulbous nose. "What?"

"I need a key to apartment 33A."

"Why?"

"Donaldson's dealing again."

"How do you know?"

"My dog alerted on his door." My partner might chew up my shoes and steal food off my plate when I wasn't looking, but her nose was never wrong.

Grigsby rolled his eyes, reached over into a cabinet, and pulled out a master set of keys. He fingered through them until he found the right one, eased it off the large ring, and handed it to me. "Bring it back when you're done."

Seth waited outside on the walkway while Brigit and I searched the tiny efficiency apartment. Though she sniffed intently at the dresser drawers, the soiled mattress that lay directly on the floor, and the toilet tank cover, she gave no alert. I pulled open the refrigerator door to let her sniff inside. People were known to hide drugs inside things they thought might mask the scent and throw a dog off track. Coffee grounds. Pots of baked beans. Cans of tuna. Though Brigit failed to alert on anything in the fridge, she helped herself to a cold hot dog from an open package on the bottom shelf. I didn't bother to stop her. Heck, she was putting in overtime here, too, and deserved a treat.

As we finished up and headed out the door, Dwayne came trotting up the steps, a smug expression on his face. "Didn't find anything, did ya?"

"Only because you took the drugs with you when you left." Given that my partner had alerted on the door, there had definitely been drugs in the apartment not long before. She must have caught a residual whiff.

Dwayne emitted a sour, beer-scented chuckle. "Prove it."

I couldn't, of course, and he knew it. "Who was the girl?" I asked.

"What girl?"

"You going to play dumb?"

"I don't have to play at that," Dwayne spat. A look of confusion crossed his face a moment later when he realized his blunder.

Seth shook his head and gave me a look that said *Really? This is what you deal with every day?*

"You know exactly who I'm talking about," I said to Dwayne. "The pretty blonde in the yellow car."

"Maybe she's my girlfriend," the thug said, his lip curling up in a stained-teeth grin. "Maybe we spent all morning making sweet, sweet love."

The mere thought had my coffee and cinnamon roll battling to see which would be first to make its way back up my esophagus.

"No way," I said. "She's out of your league." After all,

she looked like she'd showered in the last week and had no visible herpes scab on her lip. I couldn't fault the guy for being an ugly SOB. His DNA was to blame for that. But his personal hygiene failures? Those were all on him.

Dwayne's smug look turned indignant and he crossed his arms over his chest.

I narrowed my eyes at him. "You sold her something, didn't you?"

A nasty grin spread across his lips. "I can honestly say no to that."

Funny thing was, I was pretty sure he was telling me the truth just then.

"I'll be watching you," I told him.

He gave me another nasty grin. "I'll be watching you right back."

I spent my day off on Monday cleaning my apartment and training with Brigit at the K-9 facility. It was important to keep our skills sharp. Though we spent forty hours a week on duty, the vast majority of our time was spent simply cruising in the car or walking around on foot patrol. Regular training was critical to maintain our edge, to make sure that, when the time came that our special skills were needed, we'd be ready.

Monday evening, I decided that merely watching Dwayne wouldn't satisfy me. If he was pushing meth again, I wanted to bust his sorry ass. The drug had ruined too many lives already.

I plopped down on the couch with my FWPD laptop, logged in to the DMV records, and searched for a yellow Honda Fit with a license plate starting with the letter *T*. There was one in the area. It was registered to a Myrna Belvedere who, according to the driver's license records, was eighty-two years old. Definitely not the woman I'd seen driving away from my complex. I searched for Nissan Versas next. There wasn't a single yellow Versa listed in Tarrant County.

I logged on to a Chevy Web site next, trying to figure out what model the girl might have been driving. *Could it have been a Spark?* Possibly. The Spark had a similar boxy design and came in a yellow color.

Brigit hopped onto the couch next to me, draping her head over my thigh and looking up at me with big brown eyes.

"Hey, girl." I ran a hand over her neck and continued to type, hunting and pecking with the fingers of my free hand. Not an efficient process, obviously, but how could I deny my partner some attention when she worked so hard?

I found three yellow Sparks registered to women in Tarrant County.

The first belonged to a thirty-year-old woman named Erica Ryan Spencer. I looked up Erica's driver's license photo. Though she was blond, she looked a little too old to be the woman I'd seen driving by. Then again, the woman in the car had been without makeup. Maybe if Erica's face were bare she'd look younger.

I squinted at the photo, trying to picture the woman without eyeliner, blush, and lipstick. *Hmm* . . . I supposed it was possible the woman had been her.

The second Chevy Spark belonged to a twenty-one-year-old named Amber Lynn Hood. Amber Lynn's driver's license photo showed a pretty young woman with brown hair. *Hmm.* The woman who'd been interacting with Dwayne had been blond. Of course it wasn't that hard to change your hair color. All a person had to do was make a trip to Walgreens for a bottle of Clairol.

I leaned in to take a closer look at the woman in the photo. *Inconclusive.* I hadn't gotten a really good look at her face when she'd driven by, only an impression.

The third yellow Spark belonged to a Gigi Redding, who was in her early fifties. Gigi was definitely too old to be the woman I'd seen, though I supposed it was possible that she or Myrna had loaned their car to a daughter or granddaughter or neighbor or something.

What to do next?

The criminal records database might be able to tell me more. I typed Amber Lynn's name into the system and waited while it churned through the data. Five seconds later, the screen told me that no record was found in her name. Evidently she wasn't the person I'd seen on Sunday or the woman I'd seen didn't have a record. If this Amber Lynn had committed any crimes, she'd gotten away with them so far. But things had a way of catching up with people. Sooner or later, if she was up to no good, somebody would catch her. Heck, maybe it would even be me.

I ran Erica's name next.

Bingo.

Bango.

Erica Ryan had a conviction for possession of marijuana. Evidently she'd been caught with only a small amount, and the conviction was seven years prior, before she'd married. But that didn't mean she'd changed her ways. She'd probably just learned to be more careful. Though Dwayne's convictions were for methamphetamine distribution, that didn't mean he hadn't decided to dabble in other drugs. Or maybe Erica had developed a new drug of choice. Marijuana was a gateway drug, after all.

I glanced at Erica's address. She lived in Kennedale, a small town southeast of Fort Worth and technically outside my jurisdiction. That didn't mean I couldn't pay her a visit, though, ask a few questions. As a courtesy, though, I'd need to run things by the Kennedale PD before dropping in on her.

As long as I was logged on to my computer, I decided to run a search and see if I might be able to identify the person who'd snagged Catherine Quimby's purse. Given that I didn't have a name to run through the criminal records database, I figured I'd have better luck searching the police reports for key words. I typed in *bathroom, purse, drugs,* and *theft.*

The system churned for a few seconds before informing me that 3,784 records included those key words. Looked like I'd have to narrow it down.

I added *female suspect* and hit enter to activate the search function again. The additional words narrowed things down considerably, but still left me with 692 reports to read.

I typed *painkillers,* which cut the list down to twenty-seven reports.

I spent the next couple of hours skimming the reports. In most cases, the word *bathroom* came into play because stolen purses containing painkillers had been found discarded in restroom trash cans. Several of the thefts had occurred in area hospitals or medical clinics. I found only two instances in which women had reported being robbed of their purses and prescription painkillers in a restroom. In one instance, the victim had passed out in the bathroom of a bar and woken to find her purse and Percocet missing. No suspects had ever been arrested. The other report was the one I'd entered after interviewing Catherine Quimby.

Darn. Looked like I'd have to track down this purse snatcher the old-fashioned way.

Tuesday morning, I swung by the station early to pick up my cruiser. I wasn't officially on duty for a few more hours, but I wanted to get down to Kennedale and talk to Erica before too much time passed. No one would ever call me a procrastinator.

I stopped at the Kennedale PD headquarters first, letting Brigit take a quick tinkle in their bushes before going inside.

"Hi," I told the receptionist. "I'm Officer Megan Luz with Fort Worth PD. There's a resident I'd like to speak to in connection with a possible drug offense in Fort Worth. Just wanted to clear it with you all first."

"Just a moment." She pushed a button on an intercom, waited a moment, then explained my situation to someone on the other end. "Okeydoke." She hung up her phone. "Officer Munsen can accompany you. He'll meet you out front."

Brigit and I returned to our cruiser, waiting outside in the crisp air. A moment later a gray-haired officer pulled up in a white cruiser with a large letter *K* and two green stripes down the side.

I stepped up to his car and gave him the address, which was only a mile or so east of the station.

"After you," he said, gesturing with an open palm.

I loaded Brigit into the back of my patrol car and climbed into the front. In less than three minutes, we were at Erica's door. Her house, which was relatively new, sat in a nice, well-maintained subdivision. Not what I'd envisioned exactly, though I knew drugs crossed all socioeconomic lines.

I pushed the doorbell. It played a tone that sounded like a grandfather clock. *Ding-dong ding-dong, ding-ding-ding-dong.*

Twenty seconds later, the door opened. Erica stood there in a green bathrobe that hung open to reveal wrinkled pink pajamas. Though she was definitely the same woman I'd seen in her driver's license photo, today her nose was pink and crusty, her eyes swollen, and her pallor pale and green.

"Miss Ryan?" I said.

She wiped her nose with a tissue and replied in a stuffed-sinus voice, "It's Spencer now."

"Oh. Right. I have some questions I'd like to ask you."

"About what?"

"About Dwayne Donaldson."

Her crusty pink nose scrunched. "Who?"

She seemed genuinely unfamiliar with the name, but I knew she could be acting. Or, perhaps, she didn't know the name of the guy she'd bought drugs from.

"Dwayne Donaldson. He's a convicted methamphetamine dealer."

Her head tilted to the side. "I don't know him."

"Are you sure?"

She wiped her nose again. "Look, I need to sit down. Me and the kids have got the flu. Why don't y'all come in?"

I exchanged a glance with Officer Munsen. Being invited in by a suspect was highly unusual.

Erica led us into her kitchen, where a towheaded toddler sat in a high chair. Several Froot Loops lay on the tray in front of the little girl, while several others were stuck to her cheeks.

Erica took a seat at the kitchen table. I sat next to her, ordering Brigit to lie at my feet. Munsen, evidently fearing he'd catch the flu virus if he came too close, remained standing in the doorway.

"Donaldson lives in the Eastside Arms apartment complex in Fort Worth," I said. "I saw him step away from your car on Saturday before you sped off in it."

Sure, I was overstating the case a bit. After all, I only thought I'd seen her and her car. But I'd learned that suspects were much more likely to admit their bad behavior if they thought law enforcement had definitive evidence.

She shook her head, wincing at the movement. "It wasn't me," she insisted.

The toddler leaned sideways in her high chair to get a better look at Brigit. A Froot Loop fell from the baby's cheek to the floor, where Brigit promptly snatched it up with a loud crunch.

"You have an alibi?" I asked Erica.

The baby picked up a piece of cereal from her tray. She tried to drop it to Brigit but it stuck to her hand. She flung her hand three times but the cereal hung on as if glued to her skin.

Before Erica could answer me, a child's wail came from down the hall. "Mommy! I threw up again! On the floor this time!"

"I'll be right there!" Erica put a hand to her forehead and looked at me with her one exposed eye. "Any chance you could just shoot me? Put me out of my misery?"

"Your alibi?" I reminded her.

She removed her hand. "My car's been in the shop since last Thursday. Some idiot ran a red light and broadsided me. Luckily none of the kids were in the car."

Brigit pushed herself up on her front legs and licked the sticky Froot Loop from the toddler's fingers. *Crunch.* The baby giggled.

"No!" I admonished the dog. Brigit gave me a dirty look and settled back down on the floor. "Sorry," I told Erica.

She blew her nose into the tissue. "A few dog germs are the least of my worries right now."

I told her about the criminal record I'd found. "Do you continue to use marijuana?"

"I didn't even use it then," she said. "I went out with a group of friends one night, and one of them brought some new girl along, someone they didn't know very well, and she had a joint. She smoked it in my car and left the butt in the ashtray. She offered some to the rest of us but we weren't into that kind of thing. I got a flat tire on my way home later that night and a cop pulled over to help me. He saw the end of the joint in the ashtray and busted me for it."

Her story sounded plausible. "Why didn't you fight the conviction?"

"Because the DA said if I'd agree not to fight the charge, all I'd get was probation. It seemed like a quick solution. I was a flight attendant at the time and traveling a lot. Going to court and meeting with attorneys would have been a huge hassle." She blew her nose again. "In hindsight, I should've lawyered up and fought the charge. It's dogged me ever since."

"Mommy!" screamed the child from down the hall.

"Are we done here?" she asked. "If I don't get things cleaned up soon I'll never get the smell out of the carpet."

"We're done." I stood from the table, began to offer her my hand, then thought better of it. No sense picking up flu cooties. "Thanks for talking with me."

"No problem."

Crunch. Crunch. Crunch.

I turned to find Brigit standing on her hind legs, her front paws on the tray of the high chair, licking Froot Loops from the giggling baby's face. I grabbed her collar and pulled her off. "Bad dog!"

There was no sign of Clint at the rodeo on Tuesday or Wednesday. Must have been his days off. I caught a couple brief glimpses of him on Thursday. The first time he was engaged in conversation with a mounted FWPD officer. The second time he was chatting up a curvy redhead who leaned back suggestively against a lightpost, her breasts thrust upward as she gave him a shameless and seductive smile. He'd given her a smile right back, one that looked suspiciously similar to the smiles he'd given me.

As disappointed and disgusted as I felt, I supposed it was just as well, really. When Seth had brought me home last Sunday, I'd invited him in for lunch. After a bowl of pasta marinara, he'd drawn me into his arms and given me a kiss that was better than any dessert could have been, better even than crème brûlée or a lemon tart or chocolate-covered strawberries. When he'd left, I'd felt sexually frustrated but much better about where the two of us stood.

Still, I wasn't sure about things. Seth seemed to have many complex layers, and I wasn't entirely sure what I might discover if I kept digging deeper. Clint, on the other hand, seemed much more simple and straightforward, a what-you-see-is-what-you-get kind of guy.

By Friday afternoon, the purse snatching seemed like a distant memory. Though I'd kept my eyes peeled for a woman in a dark leather jacket with pink fingernails and a young brown-haired woman on crutches, I'd seen neither. The week had been calm and uneventful and boring. *Until now.*

"Well, hello there, filly."

I looked up to see Clint sitting on Jack's back. Lost in my thoughts, I hadn't even noticed the two of them standing watch near the cattle barns. "Hey, Clint." I stepped up and gave Jack a pat on the neck. "Hey, boy."

The horse responded with a friendly nicker and nuzzled my shoulder, which I took as positive signs.

Clint swung his leg over the back of the horse and dismounted. "What say we go watch the cattle auction? Make sure there's no rustlers lying in wait to nab a cow or steer?"

I doubted we'd run into any livestock thieves. Horse and cattle rustlers had pretty much gone the way of pirates. But I knew the suggestion was Clint's not-so-subtle way of saying he'd like to spend some time with me. I wouldn't mind spending some time with him, either. "Okay."

He led his horse by the reins and I led my dog by the leash as we entered the barn. Temporary bleachers had been erected on one side of an open area and provided seating for two dozen cattle ranchers who held numbered paddles in their hands. Next to the bleachers sat three women at a table topped with paperwork, laptop computers, and printers. The accounting staff, evidently. The contrast between the high-tech equipment and the barnyard smells and sounds bordered on amusing.

Clint and I took spots on the second row of bleachers, sitting on the end where Clint could keep hold of Jack's reins. Brigit hopped onto the aluminum seat beside me and lay down sideways, her head resting on my thigh.

A man with a wireless microphone walked into the arena to begin the auction. "Good afternoon, ladies and gentlemen, and welcome to the Fort Worth Stock Show and Rodeo. We hope you all have been enjoying yourselves. In just a moment here we'll be kicking off our livestock auction. But before we do, it is my most sincere pleasure to introduce our celebrity auctioneer."

What? There were celebrity auctioneers? Who knew?

"Let's put our hands together and give a warm welcome to a fast-talking man with a slick tongue, Jimmy Don Robichaux, also known as the Speedy Mouth of the South!"

As the announcer turned and held out his arm in invitation, a bearded man in boots, jeans, and a khaki duster strolled into the arena, one arm crooked over his head in greeting.

"Admit it." Clint nudged me in the ribs with his elbow, a roguish twinkle in his eye. "All that talk about slick tongues and fast mouths has you a little turned on."

I cut him a squinty gaze. "Speak for yourself."

"Okay, I will. *I* am turned on." Chuckling, he leaned back on the seat, resting his elbows on the empty bench behind us. His legs relaxed, his left knee brushing up against my right. Though I pretended not to notice, the touch sent a thrill through me. It's like our knees were kissing. It was a chaste, closed-mouth type of kiss, but exciting nonetheless.

Wasting no time, the auctioneer took the mic and got down to business. "First up on the auction block is a nice Hereford heifer."

A thirtyish man led a huge reddish-brown and white cow into the arena. A numbered plastic tag hung from the cow's ear like a dangly earring. But in her case the tag was not so much a fashion statement as a means of distinguishing this particular cow from dozens of others who looked very similar to her.

After describing the cow, giving her age and weight—details that would have caused a human female to slap his face—the auctioneer began the sale. "We'll start the bidding at sixteen hundred dollars. Who'll give me sixteen hundred?"

A man on the front row raised his paddle. "I'll give ya sixteen."

Warmed up now, the auctioneer began his fast talking, his speech running together as if he were saying one very long, multisyllabic word. "I-see-sixteen-hundred-dollars-who-will-give-me-seventeen? We've-got-seventeen-hundred-from-the-gentleman-on-the-back-row-who-will-give-me-eighteen? Do-I-hear-eighteen?"

His rapid-fire talk was impressive, especially to someone like me who had to enunciate carefully to keep from tripping over her words. I wondered if the guy had ever used his fast talk on women.

The auctioneer continued, taking the bid higher and

higher. At one point, Brigit lifted her paw as if bidding on the beast.

The auctioneer chuckled. "Folks-the-furry-dog-on-the-second-row-has-bid-twenty-two-hundred. Now-are-we-going-to-let-this-dog-take-this-cow-home-or-is-one-of-you-going-to-give-me-twenty-three?"

I scratched the back of Brigit's neck. "Somebody better outbid you, girl. There's no room at our place for a cow."

"Not even in the freezer?" Clint asked.

Now it was *my* elbow in *his* ribs.

A rancher in the back raised his paddle and the bidding continued.

Shortly before seven o'clock, I parted ways with Clint and headed to the midway. My fifteen-year-old sister Gabrielle and her boyfriend T.J. planned to come to the festival tonight, and we'd agreed to meet up by the Tilt-A-Whirl. With my irregular work schedule, getting time with my family was sometimes difficult. At times, I was glad to have work as a convenient excuse to miss family dinners. My mother was a lousy cook and with seven people at the table meals were often loud and chaotic. Though I'd been used to the hectic nature of my family growing up, since I'd lived alone I'd become used to the quiet, relatively controlled sanctuary of my apartment. At other times, though, like when Gabby invited me to go shopping with her and our mother for a dress for the homecoming dance, I lamented the fact that my scheduled shift preventing me from going with them.

As I passed one of the stages, I stopped for a few minutes to listen to the Texas Girls' Choir. They hit each note perfectly, and the tiny girl who belted out a surprisingly soulful solo was good enough to bring many of those passing by to a full stop to listen.

When the choir wrapped up, my partner and I strolled

down the game aisle where Seth had won the dog for me,
the dog that Brigit had promptly ripped to shreds the minute we got home. People threw darts at balloons, baseballs
at milk jugs, and basketballs at orange-netted hoops. At
another booth, a young boy chewed his lip in concentration as he tossed a dingy, once-white rope, attempting to
lasso a painted wooden steer. A group of people aimed
water guns at small targets that sent metal racehorses
moving down a track.

The prizes, displayed overhead and hung along the
sides of the booths, included the usual stuffed animals of
various sizes, though here at the stock show they were
primarily rodeo or farm themed. Small white sheep not
much bigger than a Beanie Baby. Pink pigs the size of a
bowling ball. A yellow long-legged chicken. And the granddaddy of all stock show midway prizes, an enormous
brown and white steer with horns that spanned four feet
across.

Brigit and I reached the Tilt-A-Whirl and waited until
ten minutes after seven, when Gabby and T.J. came running toward us, hand in hand. With her long black hair and
scattered freckles, Gabby looked like a younger, more care-
free version of me. T.J. was a cute kid, clean-cut with gin-
gery brown hair, a slightly upturned nose, and an affable
smile. Under Gabby's free arm was tucked one of the huge
brown and white stuffed steers. Somebody had gotten
lucky.

"Sorry we're late!" Gabby cried. "T.J. was playing the
ring toss and look what he won for me." She wiggled the
animal in her arms as if I might have overlooked it. Fat
chance of that. The thing was nearly as big as Brigit.

I gave Gabby a hug and T.J. a friendly pat on the shoulder. "Good to see you two."

We continued down the row of rides, most of which were
geared toward young children. A car ride that went in

circles. A plane ride that went in circles. A boat ride that went in circles. I was beginning to detect a theme here. At the end of the row was the pony ride, which also went in circles, but at least that particular ride wasn't made of cold steel.

When Gabby saw the Scrambler ride, she squealed. "We have to go on the Scrambler, Megan! Remember that year Dad brought us here and we rode it six times in a row?"

How could I forget? The year before Gabby had been too short to ride, but to her delight she'd grown just enough to clear the height line. To be honest, I'd hated every second of the ride. It slammed me up against the metal side of the bench and gave me a sideways form of whiplash, leaving me with a painful bruise on my hip-bone and a stiff neck the next day. I'd been forced to wear soft sweatpants until my hip healed. But Gabby had been having such a good time, her face beaming with that pure, unadulterated joy reserved for young children. How could I have refused, then? And I wasn't about to spoil her memory now by telling her how awful the experience had been for me.

I turned to T.J. "You mind keeping a hold on Brigit's leash for a few minutes?"

"No problem." He reached out to take the leash from me.

"You have to be firm with her," I warned. "Let her know who's boss."

"Okay."

Gabby likewise ditched her stuffed cow with him.

Minutes later, Gabby and I were seated on the ride, our hands resting on the metal bar in front of us. Given that I outweighed my sister by a good ten pounds, I'd taken the seat on the outside so I wouldn't crush her once the ride got going.

The ride's operator, a gangly man with more enthusiasm than teeth, turned the key to set the machine in motion. He danced a goofy little jig and swung his arm. "Away we go!"

The bench my sister and I sat on slid slowly to the right, then back across to the other side, gently at first, but gaining speed and force with each pass. As the motion began to pull me to the outside, I tightened my grip on the bar in a desperate attempt to stay in place.

Gabby did the same next to me, laughing it up all the while. "Hang on, Megan!"

I imagined this ride had some similarities to riding a wild horse or bull. The same physical forces pulling at the rider. The same sense of disorientation. The same desperate attempt to retain your seat even when your butt seemed to have its own center of gravity.

Finally, the pull became too great and I slid across the seat, my hipbone once again slamming into the metal side of the bench. *Bang!* Damn, that hurt! Looked like it would be yoga pants for the next week or so. Gabby slid over a second later, colliding with me. We laughed and squealed like a couple of children and, for just a few moments—and despite the sore hip—I was able to forget about purse snatchers and drug dealers.

Eventually the ride wound down and slowed to a stop with an earsplitting *screeeeech*. They might want to put some WD-40 on this thing.

The operator made his way from car to car, releasing the locks and lifting the safety bars so the riders could exit. "Have a fun night, folks!"

Gabby and I climbed down from our bench and headed back to T.J., both of us a little wobbly, our brains scrambled. The ride's name was definitely fitting.

I found Brigit finishing off the last of a corn dog. "Did you buy her that corn dog?" I asked, hoping she hadn't snatched it from someone. I wouldn't put it past her. The darn dog had an insatiable appetite.

"I couldn't help it!" T.J. cried. "She pulled me over to the stand and wouldn't stop barking until I bought her one."

I pulled the stick from my partner's mouth before she could eat that, too. "It's okay," I told T.J. "Trust me. I know how persistent she can be."

A pain in the butt is what she was. Still, I couldn't imagine working with another partner.

After a half hour at the midway, most of which I spent on the sidelines holding the stuffed steer while Gabby and T.J. enjoyed the rides, I begged off. "I better get back on patrol. See y'all later."

My sister gave me another hug before I left and ruffled Brigit's ears. "Bye, Briggie Boo!"

My partner and I set off, heading back to the exhibit halls. Although there had been no reports of purse snatchings during the week, the crowds were much thinner on weekdays than they were on the weekends. A thief would have slimmer pickings and run a greater chance of being identified. Though last week's theft might have been a one-time crime of opportunity, there was a chance the thief had held off, waiting until tonight to strike again. The crowd here this evening was even bigger than it had been last weekend. It would be easy to snatch a purse and disappear into the teeming hordes.

It wasn't right for someone to take what wasn't theirs, to steal what someone else had worked hard for. Was it too much to ask for people to be fair?

Yet I wondered about the thief's motives, too. Was this an Aladdin situation, where the thief had to steal to eat? Though robbing another person under such desperate circumstances would be understandable though still wrong,

I doubted that was the case here. After all, the purse hadn't been snatched on the open streets by a homeless person or hungry runaway. Whoever had taken the purse had paid to get into the venue. The culprit couldn't be totally destitute, right?

Hmm . . .

As much as I would have liked to catch the thief, I knew that a big part of my job was acting as a deterrent. Visible law enforcement often prevented crimes from taking place, which was undeniably a good thing. Still, it was difficult to accurately measure when deterrent efforts were a success. But nabbing a criminal? That was a clear victory for justice.

I like it when things are clear.

Unfortunately, they rarely were in law enforcement. The penal code might specify in plain language that a certain action was punishable, but in real life the line between right and wrong wasn't always black and white. There were innumerable shades of gray, not to mention ivory and antique white toward one end of the spectrum, with charcoal and ink at the other.

But I supposed that was enough philosophical contemplation, no? It was time to think tactically.

There were several ladies' rooms scattered around the stock show grounds. Would the purse snatcher target the same restroom again? Given that last week's heist had gone off without a hitch, the thief might attempt a repeat performance. On the other hand, the thief might expect law enforcement to keep a closer eye on that particular bathroom and choose to target a victim in one of the other ladies' rooms. The actions of petty criminals could be hard to predict, because they sometimes did stupid, illogical, irrational things. I tried to think like a criminal, to get into their minds, but it was difficult to think illogically and irrationally. I supposed my best strategy was to patrol a route that would take me past all of the ladies' rooms.

How glamorous. I'm on latrine duty.

TWENTY
SUCKER!

Brigit

The instant the teenage boy had taken her leash Brigit knew he'd be a sucker. He clutched the leash tightly in his fist and stood stiffly, sending an obvious message that he lacked confidence. Brigit knew when she was in charge.

Dragging him over to the corn dog stand and barking until he bought one for her was a cheap move, but she wasn't above such lowly tricks. Not when there were beef byproducts at stake.

TWENTY-ONE
CASHING IN

Robin Hood

While making the rounds with the mail that week, Robin Hood decided to set her sights on Kevin Trang, another young executive. Maybe he'd be interested in a trophy wife, or at least a trophy girlfriend.

The young woman realized some might consider her a gold digger, but she had no problem with that. As far as she was concerned, why would a woman want to work her fingers to the bone when instead she could ride the coat-tails of a successful man? It only made sense to expend the least amount of effort needed to achieve one's goals. If other people couldn't see that, then they were idiots.

While Evan had been a financial type, Kevin was a te-chie with roots in the information technology department. But far from being a geeky computer-guy stereotype, Kevin fell into the hip Asian category. Their eyes had met over their drinks at the New Year's Eve party. When Evan had later introduced them, she'd seen a subtle spark in Kevin's eyes. Kevin's date for the evening had been cute enough, but she laughed like a donkey. *Haw-haw-haw!* Surely that would grow old very soon if it hadn't already.

She'd lingered in Kevin's office after dropping off his mail on Wednesday. "How's . . ." *What is donkey-laugh's name?* "Amanda?"

"It's *Miranda*," Kevin corrected her. "And as far as I know she's fine. I haven't seen her since New Year's."

Good to know.

He'd leaned back in his chair and eyed her intently. "How are you and Evan?"

She shook her head and offered a small smile. "Not meant to be. He's still hung up on his ex. Frankly, it gave me an easy out." She cupped one hand around her mouth and stage-whispered. "I was getting B-O-R-E-D."

Kevin had laughed, but then his phone buzzed, drawing him back to his work. She'd waggled her fingers at him as she left his office. Unfortunately, he'd been away on a business trip the rest of the week and she hadn't seen him again.

Until she could resume Plan A and take down Kevin with her womanly wiles, she might as well keep moonlighting for herself, right? Still, she wasn't about to risk an arrest for a mere $53. Although she'd made another hundred dollars from the Vicodin she'd sold to that stinky, slimy creep, what were the chances she'd be so lucky again as to snatch a purse with such unexpected treasure? Slim to none.

No, tonight she'd decided to use a different strategy. While her sisters hung out in the dance hall, enjoying the music from the live band as they waited for her to contact them, she positioned herself just outside the midway, where she had a clear view of an ATM but passersby would overlook her among the lights and sounds of the rides, games, and carnival barkers.

She waited.

And she watched.

Ding! Someone at the midway had managed to bring the rubber sledgehammer down hard enough to ring the bell. *Pop!* A dart had found its way to a balloon. *Beep-beep! Beep-beep-beep!* Young kids sat in the tiny cars that circled around and around, mashing their tiny hands on the horns, turning the little steering wheels as if they could control the cars. They couldn't, of course. The cars were designed to take a set path and didn't go the way the children wanted them to. Kind of like her life. No matter how hard she tried to rise above her upbringing, it seemed as if she were predestined to live a life of frustration and mediocrity. To go around in circles, having no real control, getting nowhere.

But perhaps she was being too melodramatic. She was only twenty-one years old, just starting out in the world, really. She had lots of time to turn things around. But why did it have to be so much work?

A group of teenage girls stepped up to the ATM. Though girls that age were naïve and thus would be easy targets, Robin Hood knew they probably had paltry bank accounts. Sure enough, the girl who used the machine extracted only a single twenty-dollar bill. Besides, the girls wore cheap costume jewelry. Not worth the trouble.

The next person to use the ATM was a man who had his wife and kid in tow. Best Robin Hood could tell he'd withdrawn sixty dollars. Not that she'd paid all that much attention. After all, she was going for female targets here.

Three women in their thirties sauntered up to the ATM now. Their nice dye jobs, chic haircuts, and designer purses spelled money. Diamond engagement rings twinkled from their ring fingers. Two of them used the machine. The first, a tall woman with auburn hair, withdrew several twenties. The second, a petite woman with rich, dark brown curls, an even thicker stack.

Ka-ching.

As they headed out, Robin Hood followed them through the crowd, glancing this way and that, shifting to the left and right so they wouldn't realize they were being tailed. Probably not necessary given the size of tonight's crowd, but it couldn't hurt to be cautious.

The women headed into the dance hall. Could she be any more lucky? Not only would it be easy to keep an eye on them there, but they were likely to drink a beer or two as they listened to the band. And once those beers processed through their digestive systems and into their bladders, they'd fall right into her lair.

Robin Hood slipped into the dance hall, noting her sisters sat at separate tables near the doors as she'd instructed. She didn't acknowledge them, not wanting to take any risk of people associating the three of them.

She bought a beer and stood along the back wall, sipping from the bottle. A couple of men asked her to dance, but she politely turned them down, telling them she was waiting for her boyfriend.

Sure enough, as she watched, the three women stepped up to the bar, bought beers, and looked around for a free table. They spotted a couple vacating a table near the dance floor and snagged it as the man and woman left.

Fifteen minutes later, when their bottles were empty, one of the women made a second trip to the bar, returning with bottles for all of them. Robin Hood had to fight the urge to raise her fist and chant *Drink! Drink! Drink!* Just because she hadn't gone to college didn't mean she hadn't crashed a frat party or two.

She began to grow impatient when, *finally!,* the two who'd made withdrawals at the ATM got up from the table, leaving their friend behind to save their seats. Robin Hood pulled her phone from the pocket of her jeans and texted her sisters. *Follow me.*

While she trailed after the women, Heather trailed after her. Crystal, in turn, trailed after Heather, *thump-thump-thumping* along on her rubber-tipped crutches, her right leg crooked up behind her.

Just as expected, the women aimed straight for the restroom. Robin Hood glanced around, noted nobody watching, and pulled a hand-lettered sign and a roll of Scotch tape from her purse. She pulled two strips of tape from the roll. *Zip-zip.* She held the sign to the door and slapped one piece on the top of the sign, the other on the bottom.

She smiled at her clever ploy.

OUT OF SERVICE–SEWAGE BACKUP.

That would keep any potential witnesses out of the bathroom for sure. And if anyone didn't see the sign, Crystal would be stationed outside to point it out and direct them to another facility. Crystal would also be outside to slow the victims down when they exited the restroom. A few extra seconds could mean the difference between getting away and getting caught. It never hurt to take extra precautions.

She held her nearly empty tote close to her body as she entered the bathroom. She'd been a little concerned earlier when the security guard checking bags at the gate had peeked inside and noted that there was little in her bag.

"Just you wait," Robin Hood had said, offering him an insincere grin. "I'll be leaving here with one of them cute little stuffed pink pigs in my bag."

The guy had wished her luck. *Ha!* If he only knew. She wasn't about to throw her money away on those games at the midway. Hell, most of them were probably rigged. She had a much better chance of filling her tote with loot from the ladies' room.

There were four stalls in the bathroom, all of them empty. The women aimed for the two in the center. Though a mother stood with her adolescent daughter at the sinks, they were both drying their hands on paper towels and would soon leave. Robin Hood slipped into the end stall next to the tall woman with the auburn hair.

She pulled a pink bandana from her pocket and tied it so that it obscured the bottom half of her face like an old-west bandit. As she watched through the thin vertical space between the stall door and the frame, the woman and the young girl left. Heather sauntered in, taking up a station at the far end of the counter, tying a bandana over the lower half of her face to hide her features, too.

Robin Hood exited the stall and positioned herself just outside the door. Opening her tote, she pulled two black pillowcases and two tubes of lipstick from the inside pocket. She tossed one pillowcase and lipstick to her sister, keeping the other for herself. She pulled a small plastic bag of change from her pocket. She'd washed the coins earlier, scrubbing them with her abrasive kitchen sponge to make sure they'd contain no fingerprints. Given that she had no criminal record, the cops wouldn't be able to match them to a record even if she had left a fingerprint. But why risk ending up in the database?

Flushhhhh.

Looked like the woman with the auburn hair had finished her business. Robin Hood's heart began to thump wildly in her chest. *This is it.* She opened the plastic bag and the end of the pillowcase and held them at the ready.

There was the grinding noise of metal on metal then a click as the woman slid the door latch open. Robin Hood released a barrage of coins that *clink-clink-clinked* to the floor.

As the woman stepped out of the stall, looking down at the coins rolling about, Robin Hood brought the pillowcase down over her head and jerked it back tight around her neck.

"Oh, my God!" The woman shrieked, putting her hands to her neck, struggling to free herself from the darkness.

"Don't move!" Robin Hood hollered, shoving the woman up against the wall and jabbing the tube of lipstick into the woman's side as if it were the barrel of a gun. "Or I'll shoot you dead!"

The woman stopped struggling and instead began to wail. "Take whatever you want! Just please don't hurt me! I have children!"

The other woman rushed out of her stall to meet the same fate at the hands of Heather.

While Heather held the lipsticks to the women's ribs, Robin Hood relieved them of their purses, engagement rings, and wedding rings. It took less than twenty seconds to collect the loot and cram it all into her tote bag.

"Don't move until you've counted to a hundred!" she barked, backing away from the women and jerking her head to indicate Heather should follow her. "We've got people outside who will take you out!"

That latter part was a lie, of course, but she hoped they'd believe it enough to hesitate and give her and Heather time to make a getaway.

Robin Hood tugged the bandana from her face as she left the bathroom. Though she was tempted to run, she knew doing so would only garner unnecessary attention. As she made her way across the lane, cutting a path through the mob, she tugged the clip from the back of her head and shook her hair loose. She spotted a storm sewer drain ahead. *Perfect.* When she reached it, she dropped the bandana and clip and discreetly kicked them through the opening. Finally, just in case either woman had gotten a glimpse of her clothing, she shrugged out of the lightweight black sweater she'd worn over her pink satin blouse and wadded it up, carrying it in the crook of her arm like a football.

She was out the exit gate in less than a minute, rushing

for her car as fast as she dared so as not to attract attention. A glance over her shoulder told her there was no one on her tail.

Good.

She bleeped the door locks as she approached and slipped inside, yanking the door closed. Her heart pounded in her chest, but she felt absolutely exhilarated. *I did it. I did it!* Taken from the rich to give to the poor. She couldn't wait to find out how much the take was tonight.

After scanning the surroundings to make sure nobody was watching, she dropped her tote onto the floorboard on the passenger side and unzipped it, reaching in to open the purses and retrieve the wallets.

Score!

The first wallet had $145 in it, the other $82. Though she was tempted to pocket the $145 for herself, she knew if the payoff was as paltry for her sisters this time as it had been the last, they'd likely bail on her. Instead, she skimmed off a quick eighty dollars, leaving $147 to split three ways. She figured she'd be generous this time, round their shares up $50. With their minimum-wage jobs, those two would have to work nearly a whole day to earn that much once you accounted for taxes and Social Security and what-not. She also pocketed the Starbucks gift card imprinted with the words HAPPY BIRTHDAY!

Robin Hood smiled to herself. "Happy birthday *to me.*"

As an added bonus, the purses themselves were nice, designer bags, ones she would be happy to add to her collection.

She pulled the rings out of the front pocket of her jeans where she'd stashed them. One set was relatively plain, with a solid gold wedding band and matching engagement ring with a large, round-cut diamond. The other set was more ornate, with a platinum setting and a sparkling marquise diamond flanked by a half-dozen baguettes. She slipped the marquise ring onto her finger. It fit perfectly. Maybe she'd keep this one for herself. Just until her own Prince Charming came through, of course.

Ten minutes later, Heather stepped up and climbed into the passenger seat. Crystal followed a couple of minutes behind Heather. But instead of hobbling up on crutches, she walked up normally, the crutches nowhere in sight.

Uh-oh.

Robin Hood was on her the instant she opened the door. "Where are the crutches?"

Crystal plunked herself into the backseat and pulled the door closed. "You said we wouldn't need them after tonight."

"I know what I said." Before they'd headed into the stock show grounds earlier, she'd suggested they find another ploy after tonight's heist. Robin Hood didn't know whether the woman whose purse she'd snatched last week had told the cops she'd seen a woman on crutches in the bathroom. She wasn't sure the women tonight would, either. The victims were unlikely to make the connection on their own, but a cop who asked the right questions might elicit the information. Just in case, it couldn't hurt to mix things up. Still, she'd expected her sister to at least carry through until she returned to the car. "Where are they?"

Crystal waved a dismissive hand. "I ditched them in a trash can. They were digging into my pits."

Robin Hood couldn't believe her sister was dumb enough to leave the crutches behind. They were evidence, damn it! And they were covered with her sister's fingerprints. Fingerprints that could lead the police not only to her sister but to Robin Hood as well if anyone was smart enough to put the clues together. "What if someone saw you?"

Crystal scowled. "You don't have to talk down to me. I'm not stupid. I looked around first to make sure nobody was watching. Besides, you said nobody would realize we were together."

Robin Hood's own words coming back to bite her in the ass.

"You're right," she said, forcing levity into her voice. "I'm just being paranoid." Really, what were the odds of anyone realizing her sisters had been in on the theft? Slim to none. The police were too busy to spend much time on a minor theft. They'd take a report from the victims and that would be it.

Right?

TWENTY-TWO
PISSED OFF

Megan

Two thirtyish women with stylish haircuts stormed toward me, their expressions so full of fury it wouldn't have surprised me to see flames shoot out of their nostrils.

"Our purses were stolen!" cried the first one to reach me, a tall woman with reddish-brown hair and a purplish bruise developing on her brow bone.

"And our rings!" added her darker-haired friend. "Our wedding rings and engagement rings!"

"Where did this happen?"

"The women's restroom," said the redhead. "Right over there!" She pointed to a door thirty yards away. "We were shoved up against the wall and held at gunpoint!"

Looked like the purse thief was not only back in business, but that she'd taken things up a notch.

I asked the women their names. The redhead was Lisa. The one with the dark curls was Dominique.

"Can you give me a description of the thief?" I asked,

readying my shoulder-mounted radio to send a BOLO, or be-on-the-lookout, alert.

"No," said Dominique, wrapping her arms around herself in an instinctive act of self-comfort. "They put dark pillowcases over our heads."

"Wait. *They?* There was more than one person?"

"Yes," said Lisa. "There were two of them."

The thief hadn't just taken things up a notch, she'd also recruited a helper—assuming, of course, that tonight's thief was the same one who'd snatched the purse last week. Though both crimes had taken place in a ladies' restroom, the difference in MO could mean that the incidents were unrelated and new criminals were at work here. Still, it seemed odd that so many female thieves would be working the rodeo when there were relatively few female robbers to begin with.

"I got a glimpse of the woman who attacked me," said Lisa. "She has short blond hair."

"How old?"

"Hard to say. Somewhere between eighteen and mid-twenties, I guess. I only got a quick look before she covered my head and all I could really see was her eyes. She was wearing a bandana over her nose and mouth like the train robbers in those old western shows."

"What about her build?"

"Medium all around, I think. Like I said, I only got a quick look."

"What was she wearing?" I asked.

She seemed even less sure about the thief's attire. "Jeans? And a dark-colored top. Black, maybe. Or navy blue?"

"Did you actually see their guns?" I asked, knowing in many cases criminals faked a weapon rather than be caught with one.

Lisa shook her head.

Dominique said, "No, but she stuck it right into my ribs. Right here."

She lifted her shirt to show me a red, circular spot on her side. The circumference of the bruise appeared a little on the small side for a gun barrel, but I couldn't definitively rule it out. Lisa lifted her shirt and showed me her spot, too. Again, it looked small for a gun, but I couldn't be certain.

I raised a finger to silence the women and pushed the button on my shoulder mic, turning my head to speak into it. "I have a report of a robbery. The suspects are two females in their twenties. One has short blond hair, jeans, and a dark shirt. They may be armed. Everyone keep an eye out." I pulled my notepad and pen from the breast pocket of my shirt and turned my attention back to the women. "Did you follow the thieves?"

"We tried," Dominique said, "but when we came out of the bathroom a woman got in the way and slowed us down."

"Got in the way? What do you mean?"

"We couldn't get around her until she hobbled aside," she explained. "She was on crutches."

Crutches?

A red flag popped up in my mind and began waving. "The woman on crutches. Was she alone?"

The two exchanged glances.

"I don't know," Lisa said. "I was so upset I really didn't pay that much attention. I was just trying to follow the thief."

"What did the woman on crutches look like?"

Dominique scrunched her shoulders. "Brown hair, average size." She looked to her friend. "I don't remember anything that stood out about her other than the crutches. Do you, Lisa?"

Lisa shook her head.

Dammit. I'd been keeping an eye out for a woman on crutches, just in case. Yet she'd somehow slipped by me. I probably shouldn't fault myself. After all, the stock show crowd was large and constantly in motion. The grounds were large, too. I couldn't be everywhere. But still, the thought that these thieves could commit a second theft right under my nose had me feeling as if I hadn't done my job.

Lisa put a hand to her tender brow. "Damn, this is starting to hurt!"

I got back on my radio. "Can someone bring a bag of ice to the ladies' room near the dance hall? I've got an injured victim here."

One of my fellow officers responded. "I'm on it."

"You want to see a medic?" I shined my penlight in Lisa's eyes, making sure her pupils responded.

"No. I think I'll be okay once I get some ice on it."

"All right, then." I waved a hand. "Follow me."

As we made our way to the restroom, Brigit lifted her nose in the air and twitched her nostrils as if searching for scented clues. Problem was, even if she smelled the thief, she wasn't trained like a search and rescue dog to pursue a specific person by scent. When she went after a fleeing subject, she simply knew to aim for the person who was running. When we searched in a building, woods, or neighborhood where someone might be hiding, she knew to scent for areas of the ground or structure that had been recently disturbed.

I stopped in front of the ladies' room door, noting a piece of transparent tape and the remnants of a white sheet of paper stuck to the door. "Was there a sign on the door when you went inside?"

"Not that I noticed," Lisa replied.

"Me, neither," said Dominique.

Hmm . . .

This was a different bathroom from where the purse

snatching had taken place last weekend. While the theft
the week before occurred in the building where the rodeo
was held, this one was in the building that housed the dance
hall. The strains of country music drifted from the open
doors down the corridor.

We stepped inside. My eyes scanned the floor, searching for any of the coins that had been dropped. I found three
pennies under the sink, two dimes near the floor drain, and
a nickel against the wall. I placed a paper towel next to each
of them, and used my keys to nudge them onto the towel
lest I disturb any fingerprints the thieves might have left.
When I'd collected all the coins, I folded up the towel and
stuck it in my pocket.

Whipping my baton from my belt I extended it with a
snap. Sticking it down into the trash can, I rummaged
around, looking to see if the purses had been dropped inside. *Nope. No sign of them.* Lisa and Dominique followed
me and Brigit as I stepped back out of the bathroom and
performed a quick peek into another trash can nearby.
Nope. Nothing. Just a bunch of food wrappers and soda
cups.

I unzipped my jacket and pulled my notepad, pen, and
a couple of business cards from the breast pocket of my
shirt. I handed the cards to the ladies, and readied my pad
and pen. "You first," I said, pointing my pen at Lisa. "Describe your purse and tell me what all was in it."

"It was a Louis Vuitton," she said. "The black Melrose
Avenue model. I just bought it two weeks ago." She rattled off the contents. Miscellaneous cosmetics. A comb.
A black leather wallet with her checkbook, debit card, and
several credit cards inside. "And a Starbucks gift card. One
that says 'Happy Birthday' on it. The office took up a collection and gave it to me three days ago. I hadn't even had
a chance to use it yet."

"Any drugs in your purse?"

She looked taken aback. "Drugs?"

"Prescriptions," I clarified. "Painkillers? Xanax? Ritalin? Anything like that?"

"No."

When Lisa finished, I turned to Dominique.

"My purse was a Giani Bernini. Black on the bottom with a strip of dark brown around the top." She listed the contents of her purse, which were similar to Lisa's. Miscellaneous cosmetics. A small hairbrush. A brown leather wallet with her debit card and credit cards inside. No checkbook. "I leave that at home. I hardly ever use it these days."

"What about you?" I asked. "Any medications or drugs in your purse?"

"Just aspirin," she said.

I pushed my baton closed and returned it to my belt. "Did the girl on crutches have a cast on her leg? Maybe a brace?"

"I don't remember seeing one," Dominique said. "Her one leg just hung limplike."

Same as the girl last week, who hadn't had a cast, either.

My eyes scanned the vicinity, searching for security cameras but finding none. "When she left the area, did you see which way she went?"

The two women looked at each other again.

"Left?" Lisa pointed tentatively toward the exit.

"I think you're right," Dominique said.

The fact that the girl on crutches had headed out of the building rather than turning right to go to the dance hall was further evidence that her presence at both purse snatchings was not likely coincidental. She'd probably been in on the heist, her job to impede the victims in their attempts to pursue the thief.

I pushed the mic on my radio again. "Look for a young woman on crutches, too. She's wearing . . ." I raised an inquisitive brow and looked to the women for details.

They both shrugged and shook their heads. This lack of details was exactly why it was so hard for law enforcement to track down these types of criminals. The victims were too upset to register details and retain information.

Dominique gave me an apologetic smile. "The only thing I remember were her boots."

"Me, too!" Lisa cried.

They were as bad as that woman last week. "Were the boots tan and pink?"

"No," Dominique said. "They were black on the foot part, and a bluish-green up the leg."

"Somewhere between turquoise and sea-foam green," Lisa clarified.

As if that description would mean anything to the male officers. "She's wearing boots," I said into my radio mic. "Black and light green." Close enough. No sense confusing them.

"Is that all she's wearing?" came Derek's voice. "Just boots? Hell, that calls for an APB."

Blurgh. The guy was such an ass.

"Just look for crutches, okay?" *Really, how many women on crutches are there likely to be out here hobbling around the stock show grounds?* Turning my attention back to the women, I asked, "Where were you just prior to going to the bathroom?"

"In the dance hall," Lisa said.

"Do you think the thief could have followed you from there?"

"It's possible," Lisa said. "We'd been in there for a while. Had a couple of beers. That's why we needed to visit the ladies' room."

Chances were the thief had watched the two of them drink those beers, knowing that as their cups emptied their bladders would fill.

"What about before that?" I asked, trying to gather as

much information as possible in an attempt to figure out the thief's MO.

Lisa looked up in thought. "We had dinner at Blue Mesa Grill on University."

"Then we drove here," Dominique continued. "We parked and headed straight for the dance hall. We don't come for the animals or the rides. We come for the bands."

Lisa's eyes snapped wide. "We didn't go straight to the dance hall. We stopped at the ATM, remember?"

Dominique's eyes went wide, too. "That's right!"

I summarized the obvious conclusion. "The thief had probably been watching the cash machine and followed you two after you made the withdrawals."

"Yikes." Dominique shuddered and cringed. "That makes me feel so . . . *violated*."

Another FWPD officer arrived then with a small blue ice pack. He handed it to Lisa.

"Thanks," she said.

I nodded in acknowledgment.

As he stepped away, I advised them to cancel their debit and credit cards as soon as possible. I jotted down their contact information and told them I'd file a report.

Lisa looked at me with hopeful eyes. "Do you think you'll catch them?"

"I can't promise you we'll catch them," I said. "But I can promise you we'll do our best." Always did. Brigit and I gave 110 percent. I knew 100 percent was the purported maximum, but if Sophie + Clint = ♥ then we were living in a world where math made no sense and I could tack on an extra 10 percent if I damn well wanted to.

"Is something going on?" called a familiar female voice from down the hall.

I turned to find Trish LeGrande, a television reporter from Dallas, trotting toward me, her cameraman hurrying along behind her. Trish was decked out in rodeo garb—jeans, a pair of tan boots embossed with magnolia flowers, and a fringed suede western-cut jacket in her trademark pink. A pink scarf encircled her neck, tied just so, the ends sticking out at jaunty angles. She'd worn her butterscotch-colored hair in a long braid and topped it off with a pink-banded cowboy hat.

Trish used to do strictly the upbeat human-interest stories for the station, reporting on chili cook-offs, child music prodigies, firefighters rescuing kittens from trees. She'd recently begun reporting on more serious matters, though she still handled the occasional fluff piece. Given her outfit, she'd probably come here simply to cover the event for the news, snag some sound bites from kids at the midway or couples scooting their boots in the dance hall. But it was clear from the intense look on her face that she'd be thrilled to get the scoop on a breaking story of greater magnitude.

"Well?" she demanded when she reached me. "Is there a story here?"

I stiffened. For one, street cops were supposed to refer all media to the police department's public relations office. For two, I didn't want news of the mugging to get out until I'd had time to discuss it with the supervisor on duty, maybe even the chief himself. The stock show and rodeo was a huge annual event, bringing lots of tourist dollars into the city. If word got out that the event wasn't safe, not only could it put a dent in the revenues, but it could also further damage the reputation of the Fort Worth Police Department, which had already suffered after the bombings and the domestic assault. Thanks to shows like *CSI,* the public assumed extensive forensic evidence existed at every crime scene and thought every case could be solved in an hour or less. In reality, many crime scenes provided few, if any, clues, and it could take months or years before a crime was solved, if ever. And thirdly, it was thanks to this woman that embarrassing footage of me after the mall bombing with tuna salad in my hair had been repeated ad nauseum on local news and gone viral on the Internet.

I forced a smile at Trish. My first inclination was to say *I've got a story for you. It starts with a dark and stormy night and ends with a house crushing you flat, you witch.* But instead I said, "Please c-contact our public relations office if you have questions. Thanks."

She tossed me a look that said *pfft!* and turned to Lisa and Dominique. "You two look upset. Is that a bruise on your forehead? Has something happened?"

Lisa threw her hands in the air, evidently reenergized by this new source of sympathy for her plight. "We were robbed at gunpoint! Two thieves stole our wedding rings and purses in this bathroom right here." She pointed at the door.

Trish raised a butterscotch brow and looked up, as if quickly thinking through what she might say for her lead-in. She turned to her cameraman. "Start rolling."

He lifted the camera to his shoulder and pushed a button. A red light came on to indicate the equipment was in use.

As Trish stepped up next to the women to begin her coverage, I seized the opportunity to sneak away, tugging on Brigit's leash to hurry her along. We exited the building and turned to head to the tower where the PD had its makeshift headquarters for the event. I spotted another trash can on the way, and stopped to poke through it with my baton to see if the thief might have dumped the purses there. Purse snatchers and pickpockets often ditched the purses and wallets they stole as quickly as possible to avoid being caught with the evidence. With any luck, I'd find one of the purses. Maybe the thief had eaten a greasy funnel cake before her crime spree and left clear fingerprints. Really, if you're going to wish for luck, you might as well go all the way, right?

Unfortunately, luck was not with me. There were no purses in this trash can, either.

As I continued to make my way toward the tower, another can caught my eye. Something was sticking out of the top. Something long made of wood and topped with padding.

A pair of crutches.

Looks like luck may be with me after all.

I hurried toward the can, but a trio of boys just old enough to be out on their own beat me to it. One of them pulled the crutches from the can, pulling some trash with them, the papers fluttering to the ground around the bin.

"Look at me!" the boy called, slipping the crutches under his armpits, crooking a leg up behind him, and lurching forward. "I'm Tiny Tim. God bless us, everyone!"

I raised my palm and ran up. "Stop!"

The boy took one look at me, noted my uniform, and reflexively lifted his hands over his head. The crutches slid out from under his arms and fell to the sides, hitting the asphalt with a clatter. "I didn't steal the crutches! I swear! I found them in the trash!"

I put my hand down. "It's okay," I told him. "I just need to take those crutches with me."

One of the other boys bent to pick them up for me.

"Don't touch them!" I cried.

The boys exchanged confused glances.

"They're evidence in a crime," I explained. "If you touch them it could wipe off any fingerprints."

I told the boys to have a good time and stay out of trouble, clipped Brigit's leash to my belt, then pulled a pair of latex gloves from my pants pocket. After slipping the gloves onto my hands, I gingerly picked up the crutches, grasping them near the rubber tips at the bottom where it was less likely there would be prints. I carried them upside down into the tower and down the hall to the temporary police station. Unfortunately, the shift supervisor desk was being manned by none other than the Big Dick.

Blurgh.

He leaned back in the chair, his feet propped up on the wooden desk as he played Doodle Jump on his cell phone. He looked up when he heard me approach and his phone gave off the slide-whistle sound of his long-nosed green avatar plummeting to his death. Derek's patronizing tone and disgusted expression let me know he considered me little more than a pain in his ass. "What is it now, Luz?"

Nice to see you, too. "I just took a report on a purse snatching. The victims said that a woman on crutches got in their way when they tried to chase the thief." I held up the crutches, one in each hand. "I found these discarded in the trash can. I think they might be evidence."

He stood and gave the waistband of his pants a firm, nut-juggling tug. He reached out. "Give 'em over. I'll have 'em dusted for prints."

No doubt he'd also claim credit for solving the crime if any prints lifted from the crutches matched someone in the criminal database. I knew how Derek operated. I also knew that, like me, he hoped to make detective someday.

"Nice of you to offer," I said, narrowing my eyes at him. "But I'll turn them over to the crime scene tech myself."

He shrugged, though the flash of anger in his eyes told me he wasn't pleased. "Do it your way, then." He plopped himself back down in the chair and resumed his game.

I radioed dispatch and requested a tech to come collect the evidence, then pulled a folding metal chair up to the other side of the desk. I motioned to Derek. "Let me use that laptop. I need to file a report." Might as well get it done now while the details were fresh in my mind.

He pushed the laptop across the desk and went back to playing games on his phone. As I entered the report, I told him about the theft the weekend before. "Given that the MO appears to be similar, I think the culprits may be the same in both crimes. Looks like we've got a serial *stealer* on our hands."

He looked up from his phone. "Have I told you how much I miss your puns since we stopped patrolling together?"

"No."

"Well, then, I'll tell you now how much I miss them." He shot me a sour look. *"Not at all."*

Fine with me. I didn't miss his sexist comments, sports radio shows, or excessive sweat, either. Seriously, the guy must have an undiagnosed glandular problem.

As I finished inputting my report, Derek placed a call on his phone. "Hey, Chief. Got some news."

It was no secret that Derek was Chief Garelik's golden boy. Within a year of Derek being assigned to the W1 Division, arrests had doubled and the crime rate had been cut in half. I suspected his heavy-handed interrogation techniques and intimidation tactics had led many repeat offenders to seek gainful employment or relocate elsewhere. Derek could always be counted on to volunteer for the most dangerous assignments, too. Drug busts. Serving arrest warrants on violent suspects. Handling risky domestic violence calls. Derek and Chief Garelik were also hunting buddies. The chief had gory photos of the two of them with their bloody kills on the bookshelf in his office. Still, it rankled that the Big Dick could exploit their personal relationship and go directly to the big cheese when the rest of us street officers had to obey the usual chain of command.

Derek's eyes met mine over the laptop's screen as he filled the chief in on the phone. "We've got someone robbing folks at the stock show. One last weekend and two more tonight." He paused a moment to listen to the chief.

"Officer Luz took the report. I'm on supervisor duty tonight. I wasn't out on patrol."

His words seem to imply that had he been out on patrol, his mere presence would have deterred the thieves from committing their crimes.

"Just a second. She's right here." Derek held his phone out to me. "The chief wants a word with you."

I held the phone to my ear. "Good evening, Chief."

"Good God A'mighty, Luz!" Chief Garelik barked, so loudly I had to pull the phone away a few inches lest he burst my eardrum. "I sent you and that dog over there to keep an eye on things. How could you let this happen?"

Anger boiled up in me and I felt my stomach tighten into an exasperated ball. For one, the chief had sent me and Brigit here for PR purposes. He'd said so himself. And I'd more than delivered. Brigit and I must have had our photos taken at least three dozen times in the past week. Secondly, no officer, no matter how diligent or observant, could prevent every crime, catch every criminal. Thirdly, *kiss my ass. And kiss Brigit's fluffy ass, too, while you're at it.*

"I didn't *let* anything happen, Chief," I replied. "I had no way of knowing whether the purse snatcher would come back."

I didn't think he could yell any louder, but I'd been wrong. His voice was as incredulous as it was furious. Evidently he wasn't used to back talk. "Are you arguing with me, Officer Luz?"

Obviously. "No, sir," I lied. Though I'd always been a quiet person due to my stutter, and had been unable to defend myself when I was young, I'd learned over the years that if I were going to take a chance on opening my mouth I might as well assert myself.

"This happened on *your* watch," the chief said. "The last thing I or the mayor need is some nosy reporter making our force look like a bunch of incompetent morons. You better figure out who's behind these crimes before the media catches wind of this."

Too late. Trish LeGrande had already caught wind of the thefts. "Sir, there was a reporter here tonight covering the stock show for TV and—"

"You didn't talk to her, did you?"

"Of course not. I know the protocol. But she spoke with the victims."

"Well, the shit's out of the bag now, isn't it!"

I didn't bother pointing out that he'd mixed his metaphors. As enraged as he was he'd probably fire me on the spot. Instead, I just remained quiet, trying not to flinch as he administered his verbal lashing.

Finally, he wrapped things up. "Catch this thief, Luz. *Pronto.*"

With a *click,* he was gone.

TWENTY-THREE
WHAT ARE PARTNERS FOR?

Brigit

As usual, Brigit could sense the tension between Megan and the male cop with the flat haircut. Megan didn't like the guy, that much was clear from the pheromones she secreted. Brigit decided she didn't like the guy, either. After all, what kind of partner would she be if she didn't support Megan?

Brigit knew humans didn't like it when she stuck her nose in their crotches. She'd done it enough times, been shoved back and heard enough squeals to know people didn't consider it to be the polite greeting it was among canines. As an act of solidarity with her partner, she quietly edged herself closer and closer to the male officer. He was lost again in the game he was playing on his cell phone, one that made irritating high-pitched noises, and was paying the dog no attention.

One.
Two.
Three.

She shoved her nose into his crotch with as much force as she could muster.

With a yelp of surprise and rage, he pushed back from the desk, falling over backward as his folding metal chair collapsed. As quickly as possible, Brigit scurried back to safety at Megan's side.

Purple-faced, the man stood and pointed a thick finger down at her. "You do that again, you damn dog!" he hollered. "It'll be the last time!"

Yeah, right. Brigit knew Megan would never let anyone hurt her. She waved her tail in an up-down wag. *Screw you, flathead.*

TWENTY-FOUR
EASY CREDIT

Robin Hood

She dropped her sisters off at their parents' trailer. She didn't bother walking them in. She also didn't bother stepping inside to say good night to her parents even though the flickering light coming through the window indicated her parents were still up, watching television in the living room. Instead, the instant her sisters had closed the car doors, she backed up and pulled away from the trailer as fast as she could, kicking up a cloud of dust illuminated by her taillights as the car sped off.

As she drove home, she thought about tonight's take. It wasn't bad, and pawning the jewelry would likely net her several hundred dollars more if not several thousand. But she wouldn't get rich pulling these small-time petty thefts. No, this was merely a stopgap measure until she came up with a better plan to assure her financial security.

Her mind pondered the newly acquired credit cards in her tote. Had the women had time to call their banks and cancel the cards? Maybe. Maybe not. Hell, one of the women had five different credit cards. MasterCard. Visa. American Express. Discover. Diners Club. Who needed so many cards?

She'd bet the woman wouldn't remember the Diners Club card. Unlike the MasterCard and Visa, the numbers on which were worn from use, the numbers on the Diners Club card looked as new as the day the card had been printed.

Do I dare to try it?

Hell, yeah, I dare!

She hadn't come this far to wimp out now. Still, it wouldn't be a bad idea to get some caffeine in her system. In case she had to run, the extra energy would come in handy.

She turned into the parking lot of a Whataburger across the street and half a block down from a Starbucks. She hadn't seen any security cameras on the coffeehouse as she'd driven by, but she knew sometimes they were hidden and she didn't want to take a chance on the camera picking up her license plate. She'd be using a stolen gift card here, one she'd taken at gunpoint. Well, lipstick point, anyway. She realized such precautions were probably unnecessary. The likelihood of the police following up on the gift card were extremely low. She and Heather hadn't hurt the women they'd taken the card from. There must be dozens of muggings like that every day in Fort Worth. The cops were too busy to invest any time in tracking her down. Right?

She climbed out of her car, crossed the street, and made her way through parking lots of an auto supply store, a gas station, and a Waffle House before heading inside Starbucks.

The place was warm and smelled like coffee, vanilla, and cinnamon. She suspected heaven might smell like this.

She wondered briefly if breaking the commandments

by stealing would keep her out of heaven years from now when she passed away. But then she remembered that the Ten Commandments had been essentially repealed by the subsequent enactment of the much broader, more malleable Golden Rule. *Do unto others as you would have them do unto you.* Surely the women she'd stolen from would want others to share with them. By forcing the women to share with *her,* she was only helping them do the right thing. Thus, her actions were totally justified. Hell, *righteous* even.

She stepped up to the counter, her heart again pounding in her chest. *Relax,* she told herself. *It's a cup of coffee. Not the crown jewels.*

The barista was a cute guy about her age. Hair just shaggy enough to look stylish, with a small tuft of beard on the bottom of his chin. He gave her a wide smile as he greeted her. "Hello, there. What are you in the mood for tonight?"

She bit her bottom lip in that beguiling way she'd practiced in her bathroom mirror. "I could tell you what I'm in the mood for, but you only provide coffee, right?"

He had a nice laugh. *Oh, how I wish I could be happy with someone like him.* But no. Not a chance. She was meant for bigger things.

"I'll have a Venti caramel latte," she said. "And can you make it half-caff?" She might need energy, but she didn't need to be up all night.

"For you, anything."

Such a charmer. After he rang her up, she handed him the gift card.

He took a look at the card and said, "Did you recently have a birthday?"

She smiled. "I'm having one right now."

He ran her card through the machine and returned it to her with a receipt. "Hope it's a good one."

She checked the paper tape. It showed $44.67 remaining on the card. That would keep her in lattes for a week or more. *Sweet!*

"Your name?" he asked, holding a pen aloft over the paper cup.

She gave him a grin. "Robin."

"Ah," he said, "like the bird."

"Not the bird," she said. "Like the guy who runs around Sherwood Forest in green tights."

"Stealing from the rich and giving to the poor?"

"Exactly. Though I prefer to think of it as equitable wealth redistribution."

He laughed again. "You should go into politics."

"That's not a bad idea." Maybe she should try to get an internship with a congressman. How many stories had she heard of them hooking up with their young aides and buying them lavish gifts? Seemed like there was a new one every week or two.

She stepped back and waited alongside two other customers for her drink. When the barista called her alias a minute or two later, she stepped back up to the counter. He handed the tall cup to her and she handed him three singles in return, spreading the wealth she'd accrued tonight just as a real-life Robin Hood should. "Here's a little something for the tip jar."

"Is this that wealth redistribution you were talking about?"

She answered with a wink.

"Thank you, milady." He doffed an invisible hat as she walked out.

A few minutes later, buzzing with both nervous energy and caffeine, she pulled into the parking lot of a Kroger grocery store. She'd decided not to stop at the one in her neighborhood where she normally shopped, but instead had searched locations on her phone and chosen one a few miles farther east. She parked at the far end of the lot where her car would be out of range of any security cameras that might be on the building.

As she glanced over at the store, something on the back-seat caught her eye. The always forgetful Heather had left her hoodie. She slipped out of her black sweater and into her sister's hoodie, pulling the top up to cover her hair and shade her face. She briefly debated putting her sunglasses on, but realized it would look odd for her to be wearing them at night and she might end up drawing the very attention she was trying to avoid. Steeling herself with a deep breath, she climbed out of her car and trekked across the parking lot.

Inside, she quickly rounded up some high-dollar items. Steaks. Shrimp. Razor blades. Teeth-whitening strips, the name-brand ones rather than the off-brand ones she normally bought. Though the holiday was still three weeks away, the store had already put out its Valentine's merchandise. Might as well treat herself to the biggest, fanciest heart-shaped box of chocolates, right? After all, it wasn't likely Prince Charming was going to ride up on his white steed before February 14 to whisk her off to his castle in Never-Neverland where they would live happily ever after, bluebirds cooking them breakfast and raccoons making their beds. Hell, she'd be lucky if she could score a date with Kevin Trang by then. He was proving to be a tough nut to crack, flirting but taking things no further.

As much as she would've liked to grab a few bottles of expensive wine, she'd have to forgo the liquor. If she bought any alcohol the cashier would ask for her ID to make sure she was of age. The cashier might notice that the name on her license didn't match the one on the credit card. *Damn.* But if she had to pass up the wine, she could at least stock up on vitamins and her over-the-counter allergy medication. Spring would be here before long, bringing all those pretty flowers and irritating pollen with it.

She pushed her cart up the checkout line, keeping her head ducked so the security camera mounted over the checkout lanes wouldn't get a good view of her. As she waited for the cashier to finish ringing up the man ahead of her in line, she ran her eyes over the magazines. Might as well get the latest *People*. Copies of *Vogue, Elle,* and *Cosmo* went into her cart, too. Forget *Better Homes and Gardens* and *House Beautiful.* Once she landed a husband and they bought a house, she'd hire a professional decorator.

The man in front of her grabbed his sack of tortilla chips and salsa in one hand, his six-pack of beer in the other, and headed out the door. Robin Hood moved forward and began unloading her cart.

"Hello, there." The grandmotherly woman manning the check stand tilted her head and smiled. "Find everything you came for?"

"I sure did," Robin Hood said, forcing a jovial tone into her voice.

After unloading her items onto the belt, she stepped over to the credit card machine to wait for the cashier to finish ringing up her items. A teenage boy stepped up to the end of the check stand to bag her groceries.

"Wow," the woman said when she picked up the oversized heart-shaped box. "Somebody could get a tummy ache eating all of this!"

Hell, Robin Hood was getting a tummy ache just standing here. *Can't this woman go any faster?*

When the cashier finished ringing the items up, she looked at her customer expectantly. "Do you have a Kroger card?"

Out of habit, Robin Hood almost said yes. Instead, she shook her head.

"The card doesn't cost you anything and you'll get some good discounts. Would you like to get one?" The woman pulled out an application. "I've got a form right here."

What I'd like is to get the hell out of the store as quickly as possible.

"Next time. I'm kind of in a hurry."

"But it only takes a second," the woman argued.

"I'll do it next time," Robin Hood repeated, more firmly this time.

"Whatever you say." The woman's quirked brows and superior tone said she thought the young woman was being ridiculous to throw her money away. Little did she know it wasn't the young woman's own money she was wasting.

Robin Hood slid the card through the slot on the machine and tried to breathe normally as it processed. Not an easy thing to do. Though she'd shoplifted dozens of times before, she'd normally taken only one item at a time and had made sure the value of the property she stole was under $50. If she'd have been caught, the offense would have constituted a mere Class C misdemeanor, punishable by a fine of up to $500 but no jail time. Tonight, however, she'd taken things to the next level. Not only was she using a stolen credit card, but the total of her purchases added up to $276.32, putting her in Class B range should she be apprehended. She could find herself facing jail time of up to six months. But nothing ventured, nothing gained, right?

My God, why was the machine taking so fucking long?!?

In hindsight, maybe the coffee had been a bad idea. She was jittery enough already without the extra stimulation of the caffeine.

A moment later, the signature screen popped up. She put the stylus to the screen and nearly signed her own name out of habit, yanking her hand back when she realized what she'd been about to do. *What was the name on the card again?*

As surreptitiously as she could, she glanced at the card in her hand. Dominique L. Petropoulos. *My God, could the name be any more complicated? Is it too much to ask for an Ann Smith or a Sue Jones?*

Quickly, she scribbled the name with the stylus. She'd probably left out a vowel or two, but with the barely legible writing who would be able to tell? She tapped the button to finalize the transaction. When a message popped up indicating the payment had been authorized relief surged through her. It was all she could do not to blurt out *Woohoo!*

The cash register belched out the receipt tape. When it stopped, the cashier reached out to tear the tape from the machine. *Rrrrip!*

"Here you go," the woman said, holding the receipt out. "You have a good night, hon."

"You, too!" Robin Hood called sweetly as she rounded up her bags.

Then forget you ever saw me.

TWENTY-FIVE
TO CATCH A THIEF

Megan

On Saturday, I was scheduled to work 3 P.M. to midnight at the stock show. That left my morning free. I took Brigit for a run, after which she rolled around gleefully on my stinky sweat socks. Why did dogs have to be so disgusting sometimes?

I ate a quick breakfast and grabbed the stash of quarters I kept in a plastic margarine tub in my kitchen junk drawer. I gathered up my laundry, found the bottle of detergent under the kitchen sink, and rounded up my dog. "C'mon, girl."

Brigit hopped down from where she lay shedding on my futon and followed me out the door. As I made my way to the steps, a piece of paper taped to the door of the apartment to the left caught my eye. NOTICE TO VACATE. Though it used more proper, legalistic terminology, the document basically informed the fiftyish hippie who lived there that he had three days to move both his property and sorry, deadbeat ass off the premises and that, if he failed to do so, the aforementioned property and/or sorry, deadbeat ass would be removed by force and sold to cover his past-due rent.

I couldn't say I'd be sorry to see him go. Present company excluded, the tenants here at Eastside Arms generally occupied the bottom rung of the social ladder. Exhibit A, the aforementioned drug-dealing Dwayne Donaldson. Exhibit B, my next-door neighbor. This particular resident had always given off an especially pervy vibe. His eyes would flick to my breasts when he spoke to me and the cheesy music audible through the thin wall separating our apartments sounded like a porn soundtrack. *Bow chicka bow-wow.*

Holding my heavy, overflowing basket to the side so I could see the steps, I made my way down the stairs and to the laundry room at the end of the first floor of Building A, stopping twice to pick up socks that had slid off the heap. *Blurgh.* The hippie sat on one of the two plastic lawn chairs inside the laundry room. He must have been trying to get a load or two in before packing up to move out. He wore cheap flip-flops, a thin T-shirt, and a pair of lounge pants under which he was clearly swinging free. I supposed I couldn't fault him too much. I was currently swinging free, too, having tossed my sweaty sports bra into the basket after my earlier run.

As usual, his eyes went to my chest before traveling up to my face. Again, couldn't fault him too much since my eyes had just been taking in his free-swinging man junk. Then again, my glimpse had been quick and unintentional and absolutely horrified while his lingered with purpose and seemed to bring him no end of pleasure.

"Hey," he said, the pervy grin spreading his lips.

"Morning," I said, purposely leaving off the "good" so that it was more an acknowledgment of the time of day than a wishful greeting. I turned to look at the washing machines. All four were in use, *chug-chug-chugging* away as they agitated their contents. *Damn*; now I was agitated, too.

Rather than carry my heavy basket back up the stairs, I slid it under the table used for folding clean clothes. "I'll come back in a little bit."

"I just started my loads," the hippie said. "Most weren't full. Why don't you throw yours in with mine?"

Oh. God. The mere thought of his underwear, assuming he owned any, swishing around with mine in the machine was enough to bring bile into my throat.

"Thanks for the offer," I said, "but I've got full loads."

Patting my thigh to round up Brigit, I all but ran back to my apartment, tempted to take another shower. *Yick.* I'd felt less disgusting after the run.

My cell phone bleeped with an incoming call. I checked the readout. The call came from FWPD. With any luck it would be the fingerprint tech telling me she had positively identified the person who'd been using the crutches and had a current address for her. Or maybe she'd been able to lift prints from the coins and had made a match. I'd round up the thieves, send them to the station for booking, and place a personal call to the chief to let him know that Megan Luz and her partner Brigit had singlehandedly solved the case. Well, singlehandedly and single*paw*edly.

I pushed the button to accept the call. "Megan Luz."

After identifying herself, the tech said, "Sorry. I was able to lift four different sets of prints from the crutches, but none matched anyone in the database."

"What about the coins?"

"No luck there. They'd been wiped clean."

It was time for my second *damn* of the day. "I appreciate your help. Thanks for calling."

I pushed the button to end the call. *What now?* The crutches were the only lead I had. I racked my brain but came up empty.

But two minds were better than one, weren't they? Maybe Detective Jackson could help.

Detective Audrey Jackson had been the lead investigator on the bombing case. After I'd told her about my aspirations to become a detective someday, she'd graciously taken me under her wing. Of course who wouldn't graciously accept the help of an ambitious street cop willing to put in unpaid overtime to help out?

Though the detectives' work could eventually take them all over the city, their caseloads involved crimes that originated within their district. Because the purse snatchings had not taken place in W1, Jackson would not have jurisdiction over the thefts. Nevertheless, it couldn't hurt to run things by her first, get her thoughts. Maybe she'd be willing to help me out, serve as a sounding board, give me some advice.

I pulled up her number on my cell phone's contacts list and placed the call. "Hi, Detective Jackson," I said when she answered. "I hope I'm not catching you at a bad time."

Fortunately, she was in the office, catching up on paperwork. When I told her I had something I wanted to run by her, she suggested I stop by so we could speak in person.

"Great! I'll be right there."

I slipped into my uniform, shoes, and belt, then dressed Brigit in her police vest and attached her leash to her collar. By the time we arrived at the W1 station, it was twenty past noon. I rapped on the door to the detective's office and she glanced up from the half-eaten sub sandwich on her desk.

Her mouth full, she waved me in and pointed to the spare chair pushed back against the wall. I grabbed one of the arms and pulled it closer to her desk.

She swallowed her bite and took a quick swig from a

plastic water bottle. "How are things with the guy from the bomb squad?"

Her question caught me off guard, and my cheeks heated with a blush. "How did you know about us?"

She let loose a chuckle. "I'm a detective, remember? I'm trained to look for clues, evaluate the evidence."

What clues? What evidence? My confusion must have been written on my face, because Jackson said, "After the bombs exploded at the country club. The two of you rode up together in his car."

"Oh. Right." We'd been at a museum in Dallas, on a date, when news came in about the explosions.

She arched a brow. "Is your relationship a secret or something?"

"No, that's not it. It's just . . ."

"Complicated?"

I mulled things over a moment. "Uncertain would probably be a more precise word."

"Precision is important for a detective." Jackson offered me a nod and an encouraging smile before her tone and demeanor became all business. "So, what's up, Megan?"

"I was hoping you could give me some guidance, Detective Jackson." I told her every detail I knew about the purse snatching and mugging. That one thief had blond hair and a bandana. About the presumed accomplice with the crutches and multiple pairs of cute boots. About Chief Garelik's demand for me to catch the thief, pronto.

She chuckled. "Megan, you've been a cop for what, a year? The chief would be thrilled if you caught the thief red-handed, but barring that he doesn't really expect you to investigate and solve the crime. With these kinds of small-time thefts sometimes the best the department can do is beef up patrols and hope it scares the thieves off."

"I get all that," I said. "Still, I'd like to catch the thieves if I can. I bet if I put some time into it I could figure things out."

"You're a smart cookie, Megan," Detective Jackson said. "But you may have more ambition than sense. You really want to spend your free time on this?"

"I do."

It might not make sense for me to take such relatively small crimes so seriously, but they had happened on my watch. I felt responsible for them, responsible to the victims. Besides, I wanted to test my moxie, prove myself, impress the chief.

I also feared the crimes would continue to escalate and that someone might get seriously hurt. The first purse snatching had involved no physical contact between the thief and victim, and the manner in which the criminal had taken the purse—snatching it off the hook where it hung—had been relatively impersonal and benign. This last incident was a much more serious mugging. Lisa's head had been bruised when the robber shoved her up against the wall. She was lucky she hadn't suffered a concussion. If the criminals weren't stopped, what might they do next?

Jackson gave me a pointed look. "You realize you're going to have to be careful not to cross a line here. If it looks like you're conducting an unauthorized, unofficial investigation, you might put some noses out of joint."

"Understood."

"All right then. I suppose if I can't dissuade you, the least I can do is help you." Jackson leaned back in her chair. "Tell me what you've come up with so far."

I pulled out my notebook, where I'd jotted down notes as I'd brainstormed. "I toyed briefly with the idea of trying to find out where the woman might have gotten the crutches. I figured she might have still had them around from some type of previous injury. I thought I could call some orthopedists in the area. But then I remembered that doctors can't give out confidential patient information, so it seemed like it would be a waste of time to contact them."

She nodded. "You got all that right. Go on."

"My next thought was that it seems like nearly everyone who has a garage sale has an old pair of crutches."

With five children to feed and clothe, my parents had had to cut corners and look for bargains wherever possible. As a child, I'd been dragged along by my mother to more yard sales than I could count. Most of our furniture and many of our toys had been secondhand. Heck, my first twirling baton had come from a garage sale. It had been a little dinged up, but I'd nonetheless been thrilled when my mother bought it for me. I'd been even more thrilled when she scraped together enough money to sign me up for twirling lessons.

Jackson eyed me intently as I continued. "I thought I could check the newspaper for garage sale ads and visit the people who'd held sales, see if they might have sold a pair of crutches, but I knew it would be a long shot."

The crutches would have been sold for cash, which left no paper trail. Besides, unless they'd sold the crutches to a friend or neighbor, the chances of the seller being able to identify who bought the crutches would be infinitesimally small. It would be like trying to find a needle in a haystack. Given all the time I'd spent at the rodeo recently, I knew just how big and prickly a haystack could be.

Jackson nodded. "If the crutches were a clue in a murder investigation, it would be a different story. You'd want to follow every lead, no matter how small the chances were of the lead paying off. But for a petty theft? It's not worth your time to go hopping down that bunny trail."

I nodded in agreement. "I've already searched the police reports for incidents that took place in bathrooms and involved female suspects and stolen purses. There were only two in which painkillers were stolen. The others involved stolen purses being discarded in bathrooms. None of them jumped out at me as being similar to these crimes."

"Put on your thinking cap," Jackson said. "Better yet, put on your think-like-a-criminal cap. Why are these young ladies working the stock show? Why did they choose these particular victims?"

"I guess they figure the stock show is a busy place and it's easy to disappear into a crowd and get away."

"Good. And?" She made little arcs in the air with her index finger as if telling me to connect the dots.

"They picked victims that were well dressed, carrying expensive purses. Ones that looked like they had money. The first victim wasn't drunk, but she smelled a little of wine. The other two had been drinking beers in the dance hall."

"So the thieves are targeting women who might be slightly inebriated and thus less aware of their surroundings or less able to put up a fight."

"Looks that way."

"You should follow up on any purse or jewelry thefts involving female suspects," she suggested, "whether or not the crime took place in a restroom. There may be something else that ties these crimes to others."

"Like maybe thefts that took place at large public events?"

"Yes, or at places where the victims would be drinking and could be more vulnerable, easier to rob. Bars and restaurants and nightclubs and such."

I made a few quick notes.

"Is that all you've got?" she asked.

I shrugged. "The only other clue is that the accomplice on the crutches wore cute boots. A tan and pink pair the first night and a black and turquoise pair last night. The victims seemed to pay more attention to the boots than the woman wearing them."

"Two pairs?" Jackson raised a brow and cocked her head, a gesture clearly intended as a nudge. "Sounds like she might have a boot fetish."

"The boots could be a key, couldn't they?" I thought aloud.

"Possibly," she said. "Of course a lot of girls wear those colorful boots, especially to the rodeo."

"But if I can figure out where she bought them, I might be able to identify her."

"It's a long shot," Detective Jackson said, "but you never know what might pan out."

I thanked her, rousted my napping partner, and stood to go, motivated by my newfound plan of action.

After meeting with Detective Jackson, I returned to my apartment. The first thing I did was go to the laundry room to wash the dirty clothes I'd slid under the table earlier in the day and promptly forgotten about.

As I riffled through the basket, I noticed all of my panties and bras were missing. "What the hell?"

Had the hippie taken them? There was probably a good chance of it. Frankly if his disgusting, slimy fingers had touched them I didn't want them back. I'd have to burn them.

I sorted the items that remained into the empty washing machines, scooped powdered detergent into the tubs, and inserted six quarters into each machine to get them started.

While my laundry churned in the machines, I returned to my apartment. I grabbed my laptop and sat down at the folding card table and single chair that served as my dinette set.

The first thing I did was search the police reports and criminal records for female purse and jewelry thieves. This time I left out the terms *drugs* and *bathroom,* which, of course, brought up even more records than last time. There were far too many to sift through.

I sat back in my chair to think. Lisa had guessed the thief to be anywhere from eighteen years old to her mid-twenties. Why not pare things down by eliminating any suspects over the age of thirty? Refining my search cut the number of reports by two-thirds. *Good.*

Next, I eliminated any records that were more than three years old. This decision was based more on practicality than logic. I simply didn't have time to go through several thousand records.

I was left with 354 records. A manageable number given that it took me only ten seconds or so per record to determine whether it seemed potentially relevant.

A great number of the police reports and convictions involved thefts occurring on the job, where a woman stole a coworker's purse or jewelry from a desk or locker. I quickly tossed those suspects out. The MO felt too different. Those thieves had targeted people they knew in relatively private places, whereas the thieves I sought targeted strangers in public places.

By the time I'd skimmed through dozens of reports, I'd found a couple of interest.

The first was a felony record involving two women named Cheyenne Wembley and Mackenzie Purdue. Cheyenne had been a waitress at a local sports bar until their arrests a year ago. According to the reports, she would distract the bar's female patrons with witty banter and free nachos while Mackenzie, an old high school buddy, would slip past the tables, snatching purses off the backs of chairs while the victims were distracted. The two had been caught when another customer noticed Mackenzie stealing a purse.

When Mackenzie was arrested, she'd squealed like a stuck pig, telling law enforcement that Cheyenne was in on it, too. Evidently, though she'd been literally caught holding the bag, she wasn't willing to go down alone, not when she'd shared the spoils with her friend. According to my research, though the two had received probated sentences, Mackenzie had recently been rearrested and was awaiting trial in Houston. Cheyenne, however, still lived in the area.

The second report that caught my eye involved a young woman named Mia Clarke who'd been arrested for stealing jewelry at a nail salon. The victim had taken off her wedding ring, engagement ring, and diamond tennis bracelet to get a hand massage and manicure. Mia had stepped over, feigning interest in the nail color the woman had chosen, and had scooped the woman's jewelry into her hand. The woman had immediately noticed that the jewelry was missing, chased the young woman onto the sidewalk, and tackled her. An unknown accomplice waiting at the curb in a getaway car had sped off. Unlike Mackenzie, Mia didn't squeal on her friend. Mia had served a month in jail and paid a $500 fine.

A glance at Cheyenne's and Mia's mug shots told me they were both blond, though Cheyenne's color appeared natural and Mia's appeared processed. Their driver's license data put Cheyenne at five five and 125 pounds, and Mia at five six and 130 pounds. Fairly average sizes. I printed out their mug shots and driver's license photos, and entered home addresses for them into my phone. I'd soon be paying each of them a visit.

When I finished reviewing the criminal records, I searched for boot and western-wear stores in the Fort Worth area. Of course there were dozens of places to buy boots in Fort Worth. The city was Cowtown, after all. But while most stores sold only a limited selection of basic styles, there were several that carried more extensive lines.

Luskey's. Maverick Fine Western Wear. M. L. Leddy's. The Justin Boots outlet store. Cavender's Boot City. Shepler's in the nearby city of Arlington.

Luckily, many of the stores showed photos of their inventory online. I used up an entire ream of paper and every ink cartridge I had on hand, but I was able to print out the pages depicting the boots. With any luck, these printouts would lead me to the thieves.

TWENTY-SIX
YOU STINK

Brigit

As Megan patrolled the stock show grounds, Brigit took advantage of the fact that her partner was distracted to snuffle around on the ground, grabbing up the occasional errant food scrap that someone at the event had dropped or tossed away. A small piece of beef gristle. The rounded end of a hot dog bun. A greasy, sugary bit of funnel cake. After making sure that neither her partner nor the child's parents were watching, she'd tugged a soggy salted pretzel out of the hands of a toddler who was sitting in a stroller, gumming it. Fortunately, the kid was too surprised to cry until after Brigit had eaten the evidence of her crime and moved on.

As they continued around the grounds, Brigit's nose detected a cacophony of competing scents. Her superior olfactory senses and advanced brain were able to distinguish them all. Her nose told her that Clint had ridden by on Jack not too long ago. She could scent both Clint's shaving cream and Jack's horsey smell. Near the midway, the smell of lemon-scented disinfectant attempted, unsuccessfully, to mask the stench of vomit expelled by someone who'd had no business getting on the Tilt-A-Whirl after eating a full platter of barbecue and potato salad. Her nostrils also discerned the faint notes of women's cologne, the same two scents she'd detected around the stock show's bathrooms last weekend and last night.

Whoever wore those scents had returned.

TWENTY-SEVEN
POTTY THEFT

Robin Hood

The evening news was on in her tiny apartment as she boiled some linguini noodles and sautéed the shrimp she'd bought at the grocery store last night. She wasn't much of a cook, but she figured if she tossed in some crushed garlic and lemon juice she could improvise a shrimp scampi. Besides, she needed to eat something other than chocolates. She'd opened the heart-shaped box at breakfast and made her way through a dozen pieces, including a milk-chocolate-covered caramel, a coconut crème, and a cherry cordial. If she wasn't careful, she'd end up with thick thighs and a fat ass and her chances of becoming a trophy wife would be over.

The small TV screen filled with an image of the big-busted reporter with Creamsicle-colored hair. What was her name again? Trish something-or-other? She was dressed in a stupid pink-banded cowboy hat, pink scarf, and pink fringed jacket, looking like a life-sized Barbie doll. Robin Hood didn't like this woman. She seemed pushy and full

of herself. Then again, Robin Hood was nothing if not tenacious, herself. Perhaps she had more in common with
the reporter than she'd like to admit. She'd never be caught
dead in such a tacky outfit, though.

She had just picked up the remote to change the channel when the camera panned back, showing the reporter
standing next to the two women whose purses and rings
she and Heather had taken last night.

Uh-oh . . .

"It was a busy night at the rodeo," Trish said to the camera. "And not just for cowboys and cowgirls. Thieves were
at work, too, catching unsuspecting victims with their pants
down."

Trish turned to the women next to her. "Can you tell
the viewers what happened here tonight?"

The tall, auburn-haired woman went first. "I'd just come
out of the bathroom stall when one of the thieves attacked
me. She pulled a pillowcase over my head, shoved me up
against the wall, and stuck a gun in my back. I was scared
to death! She grabbed my purse out of my hand and then
wiggled my wedding band and engagement ring off my
finger."

The other woman, the curly-haired one with the
impossible-to-pronounce last name, spoke next, telling virtually the same story. "I couldn't see out of the pillowcase.
It was like one of those thriller movies. I thought they might
shoot us and leave us for dead on the bathroom floor!"

Robin Hood rolled her eyes. The worst she and Heather
could have done with the lipstick tubes was give the women
a forced makeover.

Trish went on to say that one of the thieves appeared to
be a young woman with short blond hair. Apparently the
women must have gotten a glimpse of her before the pillowcases were secured. "We can only hope that Fort Worth

PD will catch this 'potty' thief." Trish grinned at the camera is if proud of her crappy pun.

Well, if the cops were looking for a short-haired blonde, they wouldn't find her tonight. Robin Hood dug through her closet until she found the Jessica Simpson brand clip-on hair extensions she'd bought a few weeks ago at the Sam Moon accessory store. The extensions were a color called chocolate copper. The dark color brought out the blue in her eyes. Not bad, even if the extensions were synthetic. She'd worn them on Halloween along with a belly dancer costume. She'd leave the costume and finger castanets at home tonight, though.

There had been no mention of the ATMs in the news report. Looked like the victims were not aware how she'd chosen them, that she'd followed them from the cash machine. *Good.*

Two hours later, pulling her peacoat tighter to combat the evening chill, she stepped up beside a tree where she could keep an eye on one of the outdoor ATMs. Her sisters, who had been trailing behind her, stopped at a nearby food stand and purchased churros and lemonade.

As Robin Hood eyed the cash machine, she spotted that dark-haired female cop and her furry dog. She'd seen them around the stock show grounds several times. Hard to miss a dog of that size. The damn thing was ginormous.

Tonight the cop and dog seemed on high alert. The officer scanned the surroundings as if looking for someone. *Is she looking for the thieves? Did she know that Robin Hood had followed her victims last night after they'd withdrawn money from one of the ATMs?*

Though she wore the dark hair extensions, she nonetheless felt her heart flutter in fear. If the cop came close enough, she might be able to tell the cheap things weren't real and realize the hair was a disguise.

Better get the hell away from the ATM.

She texted her sisters as she stepped away from the tree. *Nosy cop. Abort mission.*

She continued around the grounds, noting other police officers hanging around near the other money machines. *Damn!* A couple of them glanced her way as she passed, but none showed any signs of recognizing her.

As concerned as she was about the police presence, she hadn't come to the stock show tonight and paid the entry fee to go home empty-handed. She ducked down the alley between two of the cattle barns and placed a call to Crystal's phone. "The ATMs are all being watched," she said. "Change of plans."

A half hour before closing time, she tilted her head and smiled up at the scrawny, beady-eyed, hook-nosed guy she'd been dancing with for the past hour. "How about the two of us get out of here?" She punctuated her words with a teasing quirk of her brows.

She didn't have to ask him twice. He grabbed her hand and pulled her out the door, releasing his grip only to take a quick peek into his wallet, apparently checking to see if he had a condom. *Dumbass.* If this sleazeball thought she would sleep with him he needed to have his head examined. The only thing in his wallet that she was interested in were those bills she'd spotted when she'd been behind him in line at the bar earlier in the night.

They continued on, heading out to his pickup in the parking lot, her sisters coming along a hundred feet or so behind them. *Think Ryan Gosling,* she told herself as she backed up against the fender of the man's truck and reached out to pull him up tight against her. She put her mouth to his, fighting the urge to retch as the tip of the man's beer-coated tongue seemed to be taking an inventory of her teeth. *Upper molar. Lower molar. Two bicuspids . . .*

Ugh. *Ryan Gosling. Ryan Gosling. Ryan Gosling.* When the heartthrob no longer seemed to be enough, she added Bradley Cooper to the mix. *Ryan Gosling. Bradley Cooper. Ryan Gosling. Bradley Cooper.*

She wrapped her hands around the man's waist, then slid them down over where his ass would have been if he'd had one. Another *ugh.* She expanded the entourage to include Adam Levine now. *Ryan Gosling. Bradley Cooper. Adam Levine.* While one hand slid around to the front of his pants to cup his rock-hard, though unimpressively sized bulge, two pink-tipped fingers slipped into the back pocket of the man's loose-fitting jeans, emerging with the wallet pinned between them. Her mouth still pressed firmly to her victim's, she tossed the wallet to Heather as she and Crystal walked past the truck. Lustfully moaning into her mouth, the man had no idea he'd just been taken.

Anyone that dumb and horny deserves to be robbed.

Eleven *Ryan Goslings* later, her cell phone rang in her tote bag, belting out her ringtone, "Raise Your Glass" by Pink.

She pushed the man back and reached into her tote for her phone. "I better see who it is." She looked at the screen and faked a frown before punching the button to take the call. "Hi," she said. "Everything okay?"

On the other end of the line, Crystal snickered loudly. "Come quick, Li'l Sis!" she cried. "Zombies from outer space are invading the planet! Blah-blah-blah!"

Stupid Crystal. Didn't she realize the man was standing so close he might be able to hear what she said? Her sister didn't have the sense God gave a goose.

Still holding the phone to her ear, she quickly thumbed the button to turn down the volume, her sister's words now only a soft, "Blah-blah-blah! Blah-blah-blahbeddy-blah!"

"Oh, my God!" she cried into the phone. "I'll be there

as soon as I can!" She shoved her phone back into her purse. "I have to go! My mother's been in a car wreck!"

She supposed she should feel guilty for putting her mother through so many fictional traumas. But what her mother didn't know couldn't hurt her. Neither could the constant onslaught of make-believe cars, buses, trains, and garbage trucks. Maybe next time she should mix it up a bit, plow her mother down with a cement mixer.

As she scurried off, the man called, "Can I at least get your number?"

No concern at all about her mother's alleged car accident? *What an ass.* She wouldn't feel at all guilty when she spent this guy's money.

"Sorry!" she called over her shoulder. "No time!"

TWENTY-EIGHT
POCKET CHANGE

Megan

The night passed with no reports of a purse snatching or mugging. Though I would've loved to catch the thieves, the fact that no crimes had been committed tonight was an acceptable consolation prize. Sometimes you had to take what you could get.

As the show began to shut down for the night, Clint rode up on Jack. "Hey, there."

"Hi, Clint."

He swung down from the horse and gave Brigit a pat on the head before turning his eyes on me. "The radios were pretty quiet tonight."

It was true. Not only had there been no purse snatchings, there'd been only a few sporadic reports of shoving matches and lost children, with a single instance of public urination/public intoxication. All in all, a quiet night.

"Thank goodness." I stroked a hand down Jack's neck.

"You're off duty now, too, right? What say you and I go celebrate with a drink? Gotta spend my rodeo winnings somehow."

His dark eyes twinkled with possibilities. Possibilities that could become *probabilities*.

I found myself saying "Why not?"

Why not, indeed. Other than a single text—*just thought I'd say hi*—I hadn't heard from Seth all week. I supposed he might be working tonight, but for all I knew he could be out with another woman. Frankly, I was feeling frustrated. Our relationship had no parameters. I'd thought keeping things casual, having no obligations or expectations, would simplify things. Instead, this murky, squishy thing we shared felt undefined and unfulfilling. Of course the blame lay on me. I was the one who'd suggested the arrangement. He hadn't argued about it, though. That meant he hadn't wanted anything more from me, right?

"Hop on up into the saddle," Clint said. "No sense you walking when Jack can provide transportation."

I let out Brigit's leash a couple more feet, then grasped the saddle horn with both hands and put my left foot in the stirrup. In seconds, I was seated on Jack's back. The stirrups hung too low for my feet to reach them once I was settled, but the saddle horn gave me something to hold on to. Clint walked Jack over to a picnic table and stepped up onto the attached bench. He swung his leg over the horse's rump and took a seat behind the saddle, one hand crooked around me to hold the reins, the other resting on my hipbone in a gesture that felt simultaneously thrilling and overly intimate. But perhaps I was reading too much into it. His hand had to go somewhere, didn't it?

Clint squeezed the horse with his thighs, setting the big beast in motion. The rhythmic movement of the horse under us felt slightly erotic. Clint said nothing, though I could feel his soft breath on the back of my neck, the warmth of his body, which was separated from mine by mere inches.

We reached the exit and rode over to Clint's brown and tan pickup and horse trailer. Clint dismounted first, then held up a hand to help me down.

Just as my feet hit the ground, a skinny man in his forties came barreling up. He had beady eyes and a hooklike nose, giving him an odd, birdlike appearance. "I've just been robbed!" he cried in beer-scented syllables.

Clint and I exchanged glances. Looked like we'd planned our celebration too soon.

"What happened?" I asked.

"I'd been dancing with this girl the last hour or so, bought her a couple of beers. When the band announced the last song, she suggested we get out of there."

I would've thought he'd look a little sheepish admitting that he'd been hoping to snag an easy lay, but he seemed to have no such qualms.

He continued his enraged diatribe. "We got out here to the parking lot and went to my truck and, well, things started getting a little . . ." He waved his finger around as if the digit would fill in the blank for him.

"Go on," I said. Not that I really wanted to hear the dirty details, but those dirty details might help us nab the robber.

"Well, she backed up against the front fender and kinda pulled me to her, you know? Next thing I know, she was grabbing my ass. I just thought she was turned on . . ."

Standing behind the man, Clint looked him up and down and raised a dubious brow that said *No way would this man be able to turn a woman on.*

". . . but then she got a call on her cell phone," the man continued. "Some kind of emergency, she said, so she had to go. It wasn't until after I got into my truck that I realized my wallet was gone."

My eyes went to the seat of his pants. "You're certain your wallet was in your back pocket when the two of you left the dance hall?"

"I *know* it was," the man said. "I'd checked in it to make sure I had protection."

Behind the man, Clint grimaced in disgust. I nearly did the same.

My mind began to process the information. *Could the woman who robbed this man be the same one who snatched Catherine Quimby's purse from the hook in the bathroom stall last weekend? Or one of the two thieves who'd mugged the women last night? Had she realized the ATMs were under surveillance tonight and decided to develop a new MO?*

"The girl," I said, "how old was she?"

"Early twenties, I'd say."

Much too young for this creep. He didn't even have the sense to be ashamed of himself for trying to pick up a woman young enough to be his daughter. "Was she a blonde?"

He shook his head. "No. She was dark headed."

Hmm . . . Had the blonde maybe worn a disguise? Or is the brown-haired girl on crutches now starring in this show?

"Tall or short?" I asked.

He shrugged his skinny shoulders. "Average."

"Heavy or thin?"

Another shrug. Another *average*.

"Any distinguishing characteristics? A tattoo maybe? A scar? Maybe a mole or birthmark?"

"Can't remember noticing anything like that."

"Eye color?"

"Not sure. I remember she was wearing a red shirt, though."

No doubt the red shirt was cut low, exposing some cleavage and thereby explaining why the man had noticed virtually nothing about the young woman's face.

"Was anyone with her?" I asked. *Perhaps a woman with really cute boots?*

He shook his head again. "No. She was alone. She told me she'd come to the stock show with a friend, but that her friend had left with some guy."

My mind toyed again with the idea that the pickpocket could be the young woman who'd been on the crutches before. "What kind of shoes was the woman wearing?"

"Some kind of flat black ones," the guy said.

"Not boots?"

"No."

I pulled out my notepad and jotted down the man's name and contact information, a description of the thief, and a list of the contents of the man's wallet, including one Trojan-brand Ecstasy condom. *Ew. Ew. Ew.* This guy carried a rubber with him, as if he expected to get lucky? Who did he think he was, Ryan Gosling? Bradley Cooper? Not even close. This guy looked more like Steve Buscemi, who was a wonderfully talented actor but not exactly a sex symbol.

As the man stalked off, I turned to Clint. "I'm going to need a very large, very potent margarita to erase the image of that man naked from my b-brain."

"No shit," Clint said. "I might have to put a bullet in my head."

An hour later, the two of us had returned our cruisers to our respective divisions, changed into civilian clothes, and met up at the Fox and Hound. I'd dropped Brigit off at my apartment. I prayed she wasn't chewing up my shoes by now.

One of the pub's Perfect Patrón margaritas sat on the table in front of me. Normally I went for the 3-Citrus Skinny Margarita, but tonight called for something that didn't hold back. Clint had ordered a Corona with lime.

After taking a sip of my drink, I asked, "What do you think? Could the purse snatching and the mugging and the pickpocketing be related?"

Clint mulled things over for a moment. "Hard to say. It's unusual that all of these crimes were committed by women. Usually the bad guys are, well, *guys*."

"I had the same thought." I took another sip, the alcohol beginning to free up my brain for creative thinking. "Maybe we've got some k-kind of female gang activity on our hands. You know, like those cheerleaders who robbed the banks."

Clint held his beer bottle poised at his lips. "Wasn't that just in a movie?"

I raised my palms. "Fact or fiction, it could happen."

"True." He tipped his bottle for a long drink.

I, too, took another long sip of my drink, freeing my mind even further. "What kind of young women would do this kind of thing?"

"Ones looking for some quick cash to buy drugs."

Could be. Then again, people wanted cash for all kinds of reasons. To pay their bills. To cover an unexpected expense. To treat themselves to fancy jewelry or high-end electronics or cute boots.

"I talked to one of the detectives today," I said. "We think the accomplice's boots may be the key to solving this. The victims were able to describe them to me in good detail. They might be able to identify the boots if they saw them again."

He shook his head. "You women and your shoes. I've got black boots, brown boots, and a pair of tennis shoes. Three pairs of footwear. That does me."

It was *my* turn to shake *my* head. "You men and your lack of fashion sense."

Clint's mouth spread in a grin. "What exactly are you proposing? Putting a bunch of boots in a lineup and seeing if the victims can pick them out from the crowd?"

"Essentially." I realized it sounded a little silly, but it could work. I explained about the printouts. "I'm going to visit the victims and see if they might recognize the boots from the Web site photos. I've also found a couple of suspects that look promising. Young women who have records for stealing purses and jewelry."

"You're an exceptionally dedicated cop." He raised his beer in salute. "I'll give you that."

I raised my margarita glass and tapped it against his bottle. *Clink!*

Clint sat back in his chair. "That's enough shop talk. I know Megan Luz, the police officer. Now I want to know about Megan Luz, the woman. Your turn-ons. Turnoffs. Most sexy secret fantasy."

"Hmm . . . turn-ons. I'd have to say men who read. Who are kind to animals and kids and little old ladies. Who buy me top-shelf margaritas." *Whoa.* The drink hadn't just loosened my brain, it had loosened my mouth, as well.

Clint sent a fresh smile my way. "Go on."

"Turnoffs. Let's see." Another sip. "Guys with excessive egos. No goals or sense of direction. Men who pretend to be something they're not."

"Got it," Clint said. "Now for your most sexy secret fantasy. Does *that* involve a guy pretending to be something he's not? Some role-play, maybe? I've got a Lone Ranger outfit. I'd be willing to wear an Indian headdress and a loincloth, too. Or were you thinking more along the lines of a gorilla costume?"

I waved a finger. "Nuh-uh-uh. I'm not going to give it up that easily."

"Damn."

"And the gorilla costume? That's just disturbing."

He held up his hands. "Just feeling you out."

I swirled the straw in my margarita, mixing the alcohol back in with the parts that hadn't melted yet. "What about you?" I asked. "Turn-ons and turnoffs?"

"Turn-ons," he said. "Strong women that don't have to be coddled. The smell of cherry pie baking. Tight jeans or short skirts with high heels."

I rolled my eyes. "Gee. You're deep."

He smiled around his beer bottle. "Never claimed to be."

"Turnoffs?" I prodded.

"Clingy women. Turtlenecks. Earth shoes."

"Sexiest fantasy?"

He narrowed his eyes, casting me a look so hot it threatened to melt my margarita on the spot. "I could tell you, but you'd never be the same afterward."

A vibration in the outside pocket of my purse alerted me to a phone call. I pulled out my cell and checked the readout.

Seth.

Really? His timing sucked. Besides, one-thirty on a Saturday night? What could he possibly want at this hour, some type of drunken booty call? That was not on the table. Or maybe he'd just gotten off work. Firefighters worked odd hours. But calling this late was rude. Whatever it was could wait until tomorrow.

I punched the button to ignore the call and shoved my phone back into my purse. I looked up to find Clint eyeing me intently.

"Boy trouble?"

I closed my eyes and let out a long breath. I supposed I could explain about Seth, that we weren't serious, that we had a casual and open relationship, that I wasn't sure if I even wanted to pursue something with the guy. But frankly I didn't want to talk about it. "Yeah."

"Need me to kick someone's ass?"

"Thanks for the offer," I said, "but if there's an ass that needs kicking, I'll take care of it myself."

"I always admire a self-sufficient woman." Clint tilted his head. "You involved with someone?"

Good question. *Am I?* "I don't really know."

He raised a knowing brow. "One of those on-again, off-again things?"

I supposed that would be one way to describe it, but what was the term I'd used with Detective Jackson? Oh, yeah. "*Uncertain* would be a better term."

"Hm." He took a drink from his bottle. "Well, one thing that's certain is that you are here with me now and I am going to take full advantage of that." His brown eyes locked on mine in a look that was part challenge, part promise, part panty-melting sexual predation.

My phone gave off another wiggle, indicating Seth had left a voice mail, but I wasn't about to spoil this nice time I was having with Clint. This deputy made me feel interesting and worthwhile, attractive and desired. I'd listen to the message later.

After another round of drinks, the waitress came around to announce last call. "Bar's closing in fifteen minutes."

Clint nudged my foot under the table. "Let's go back to your place."

"It's awfully late."

"You working tomorrow?"

"No."

"Then sleep in."

"You're not going to try to get into my pants, are you?"

"Wouldn't dream of it. Fair warning, though. I might try to kiss you. Maybe nibble on your ear a little." He sent me such a hot look of seduction I was surprised I didn't turn to liquid and drip off my chair.

TWENTY-NINE
FREE LOVE

Brigit

Megan and Clint fell onto the futon, leaving Brigit with nowhere to go but her doggie bed in the corner and nothing to do but be a voyeur. She plopped down and watched as Clint tried to slide his hand up Megan's shirt. Megan pushed his hand away, but let him continue to kiss her neck.

Brigit was glad she wasn't a human. Their sexual relationships were far too complex. When dogs wanted to hump, they humped, pure and simple. No regrets afterward, no guilt, no tears if he didn't call. No walk of shame though, really, a dog didn't mind any kind of walk, shameful or otherwise. And if a dog wanted to hump another dog soon after, there were no hard feelings. Free love. A dog could even hump a blanket or a couch cushion if it wanted to.

Yeah, humans were ridiculous. But they could open cans. For that reason alone, Brigit figured it couldn't hurt to keep one around.

THIRTY
MEN ARE SO EASY

Robin Hood

Men are so easy, she thought as she drove home that night.

Getting that man all hot and bothered and taking his wallet had been a piece of cake. Hell, maybe she should've been targeting men from the beginning. She bet the guy wouldn't even be able to give the cops a good description of her. She'd purposely worn a tight, low-cut top and a padded push-up bra, knowing that with such distractions in place any potential victim wouldn't have his eyes on her face.

The only downside was that, since she'd had to hand the wallet off to Crystal and Heather, she hadn't been able to skim any funds off the top. They'd split the man's $97 three ways, with Crystal and Heather each taking $32 and Robin Hood getting an extra dollar for her efforts. Heather had taken the condom. She was the only one who currently had a boyfriend. Robin Hood hadn't gotten any since New Year's Eve when she and Ethan had hooked up for the last time.

Thirty-three dollars was hardly worth the planning and effort she'd put into tonight. And having that creep's tongue in her mouth? *Uck.* She wouldn't do anything like that again for anything less than a guaranteed grand.

She would definitely target a more attractive guy next time.

THIRTY-ONE
NO *KNOCK-KNOCK* JOKE HERE

Megan

With Clint's tongue in my ear, I barely heard the knock at my door.

Knock-knock.

I pushed him back. "Was that someone at the door?"

"Shhh," Clint said, nuzzling my neck. "If we're quiet maybe they'll go away."

Knock-knock.

I knew I couldn't ignore whoever was at the door. Chances were it was one of my neighbors stopping by to report that their hubcaps had been stolen or that they'd seen a suspicious person lurking about the property. But, hell, the most suspicious-looking people around here *were* the tenants.

I stood and stepped to the door. "Who is it?" I asked. Just because I was a cop didn't mean I wasn't going to take precautions, find out who was on the other side of the door before I opened it.

A male voice came through the door. "It's Seth."

Shit.

I glanced over at Clint, who raised a brow. "This have anything to do with your boy trouble?"

I nodded. "I'll be right back, okay?"

He didn't look real happy about it, but he raised a shoulder, grabbed the remote, and flipped on the television.

I slipped out the door and onto the walkway. Seth stood there, his shoulders slumped, exhaustion on his face. Something had happened. *Something bad.* I could tell.

When I tried to pull the door closed behind me, Brigit stuck her snout in the crack and forced it open, bounding out the door and down the stairs, heading straight for the dirt patch behind the Dumpster to pee.

Before I could get the door shut again, Seth cast a glance inside. When he spotted Clint, his posture went rigid. He gripped the rail as if choking it with his bare hand. "Looks like this isn't a good time."

"Not really." It wasn't, obviously. But I couldn't just turn Seth away, not with that look on his face. "Are you okay?"

"Not really," he said, echoing my words. "I tried to call you," he said softly. "When you didn't answer I left a voice mail. Didn't you get it?"

"I haven't listened to it yet."

He hesitated a moment before asking, "Why not?"

"I was on a date, Seth."

Finished now, Brigit trotted back up the steps, her tail wagging as she stood between us, looking from one of us to the other.

Seth opened his mouth as if to say something, then appeared to think better of it and closed his mouth again. Without another word, he turned and walked down the steps.

"Seth!" I called after him.

He raised a dismissive hand and kept right on walking.

I didn't know what to do. Should I run after Seth? Go back to Clint? The situation was beyond awkward.

I leaned over the railing as Seth made his way back to his car below me. "Let's talk in the morning, okay?"

His only response was to raise his hand again. Was the gesture meant to show agreement or refusal? I wasn't sure.

I opened the door to my apartment, let Brigit inside, and slipped in after her.

Clint waited on my futon. A repeat of the ten o'clock news played on the television.

I plunked down on the opposite side of my couch, picked up one of my cushions, and hugged it to my chest. Clint turned to look at me, his eyes searing into me as if trying to burn away my outer layer to reveal the truth that lay below.

On the TV screen, a male field reporter stood before a small wood-frame house that was engulfed in flames. "Tragedy struck tonight when a Christmas tree that had not yet been disposed of caught fire in this house in Arlington Heights. Three children had been left home alone when the fire broke out. While a twelve-year old was able to carry her two-year-old sibling outside to safety, she returned to the house, not realizing that her seven-year-old brother had escaped safely out the back door. Firefighters found the girl unconscious inside. She was taken to the hospital and is listed in critical condition. A neighbor caught this footage of a fireman carrying the girl from the home."

The screen switched to shaky video clearly filmed with a cell phone. The video showed a firefighter in a mask exiting the house with a girl's limp form in his arms. He carried her to a waiting ambulance, then appeared to break down, backing away and falling to a knee. Looking down at the ground, he pulled his mask from his face and ran his sleeve across his eyes.

Oh, my God. The firefighter on the screen is Seth.

"Oh, no!" I said on a gasp. "That's him!"

I leaped up from the couch, feeling like the most sorry excuse for a human being that had ever existed. Seth had come here seeking comfort, and what had I done? Turned my back on him at his time of need. The thought made me feel sick.

"It's *who*?" Clint asked, standing, too.

Instinctively I ran to the door and yanked it open to see if Seth had driven off yet. His car still sat in the lot below. I bolted outside, grabbed the railing, and ran down the stairs so fast I lost my footing, stumbled at the end, and fell onto my hands and knees on the asphalt. Forgetting all about Clint, I ran to the Nova's driver's window, splaying my scraped hands on it as I leaned in.

"I saw the news report!" I cried through the glass. "Are you okay?"

One look at Seth's shocked, sickened, and exhausted face told me he was anything but.

Clint had reached the bottom of the steps now. He raised a hand in good-bye, seeming to realize his presence was getting in the way of something far more serious and urgent. "We'll catch up later."

My eyes sought his and sent both a silent *thank you* and an *I'm sorry*.

I opened the door to Seth's car. "Come on up."

THIRTY-TWO
SIXTH SCENTS

Brigit

Brigit lay next to Seth on the couch, resting her head on his thigh and looking up at him as he ran his hand over and over and over her head. Although she appreciated being petted, she knew it was more for himself this time than it was for her, the repetitive motion calming his nerves, soothing him, giving him a way to work off the adrenaline she could smell on him.

But adrenaline wasn't the only thing she smelled. She also smelled smoke and water and charred flesh and sadness. Okay, so sadness didn't have a smell, but Brigit could sense it anyway, in the tone of his words, in his slumped posture, in the dullness in his eyes.

She offered a whine to let him know she was sad for him, too, and licked his hand to let him know she was there for him. She might be just a dog, but she was perceptive, and one thing was abundantly clear.

Seth needs someone.

THIRTY-THREE
A LONG, HARD LOOK

Robin Hood

After drying her face that night, she took a long, hard look at herself in her bathroom mirror.

She didn't like what she saw.

Her once-soft features seemed to have taken on a hard edge. Those blue eyes of hers seemed less warm summer sky and more frozen glacier. Her lips were red and raw from the rough scrubbing she'd given them, trying to remove the feel of that creep's mouth on hers. Hell, she'd brushed her teeth three times and could still taste his sour beer.

Is this who I've become? A desperate young woman, willing to lie, cheat, and steal to make a few lousy bucks? A woman who'd let herself be pawed by some lecherous old fart in return for a paltry amount of cash?

Hell, she was hardly better than a hooker. She shuddered in disgust and looked away.

No.

She forced herself to take another look in the mirror.

No, she wasn't some cheap, common whore, selling her body for money.

No, she wasn't some desperate, hopeless young loser with no prospects for the future.

No, she wasn't a career criminal who'd never rise above her unfortunate, unprivileged beginnings.

She was just tired, that's all, and feeling a little vulnerable. These little . . . *indiscretions* were merely part of a short-term plan, a little something to tide her over until she figured out what her next big move should be. And when she figured things out, there'd be no stopping her on her rise to the top. One day, she'd have everything she deserved.

She smiled at herself.

Ick. Better brush her teeth a fourth time.

THIRTY-FOUR
INTENSIVE CARE

Megan

Seth was a wreck.

At first he just sat on my couch, staring down at his knees and rubbing his hand along Brigit's head over and over and over again. Much more and the poor dog would end up with a bald spot. Not that she seemed to mind in the least. She lay there, enjoying the attention, occasionally tilting her head to lick Seth's hand.

I didn't know what to do, how to help him. I tended to work out my stresses and upsets by twirling my baton, but Seth didn't know how to twirl a baton and this matter was far too upsetting to be resolved so easily.

Finally, I simply reached over, took his free hand in both of mine, and held it to my cheek. He glanced my way and, when our gazes met, it was as if a floodgate of emotion broke open inside him.

"What if she dies?" He gripped my hand tightly, probably without even realizing it. His grip aggravated the scrapes on my palm, but I knew he wasn't aware of the discomfort he was causing me. I could endure a little pain for him. His body trembled as if he were shivering, the adrenaline processing out of his system. His voice was soft, strained. "What if that little girl doesn't make it? What if I didn't get to her in time?"

Surely Seth had seen people die before. After all, he'd spent eight years in the army as an explosive ordnance disposal specialist, and the last two years working as a firefighter and leading the fire department's bomb squad. But I supposed nobody ever got used to death. They wouldn't be human if they did.

And this little girl, what happened to her had been entirely preventable. All her parents had had to do was get rid of the dried-up tree. By now, the thing had become nothing more than a pile of kindling, fuel waiting for a spark. Why hadn't her father dragged the damn thing out into the backyard? It was the least he could have done to keep his children safe. Then again, having grown up in a large, busy family, I knew how easy it was to overlook these things, to focus on what had to be done right now, to put off these minor tasks for a tomorrow that never seemed to come.

I didn't know what to say to Seth. I supposed I could have said the obvious things. That he'd done his job. That he'd done all he could. That, if she died, her death wouldn't be his fault. But I knew he already knew all of that. Instead, I said, "If she dies it will be very sad. But she might live, Seth. Kids are amazingly resilient."

I should know. I'd seen my four younger siblings bounce back from some pretty harrowing injuries, including my brother Joey who'd suffered a major concussion after taking a header out the tree house window. *Lesson learned: if you're spying with binoculars on the cute girl next door, don't lean out too far.*

Seth's green eyes sought mine and held. "I hope you're right, Megan."

I gave his hand a final squeeze and released it.

He looked back down at his knees, then up at me again. "Do you ever wonder why we're even here? What's the point of all this?"

"Yes," I said, "sometimes." Not that my wondering had given me any concrete answers. How I wished I had answers for him. He seemed like he could really use some. "I don't know, Seth. I think maybe it's up to each of us to decide what the point of our own life will be."

"Have *you* decided?" he asked.

I nodded. "I want to stop p-people from victimizing each other." Victimization was at the heart of every crime, whether it be a murder, a rape, or a petty theft. *Or even the mere teasing of a young, defenseless girl who couldn't get her words to come out right.* "I want to make the world more just and fair."

"It must be nice to know that." He was quiet for a moment, his expression pensive.

It seemed that Seth was looking for affirmation. I hoped I could provide it. "Your life has purpose, Seth. You've saved untold numbers of people from being hurt or killed by explosives."

He waved a hand. "I just fell into that."

"What do you mean?"

He turned back to his knees and let out a slow breath. "I dropped out of high school my junior year to join the army. When the recruiter asked me what I wanted to do in the service, I told him I didn't know. So he asked me what I liked to do, and I told him I liked to blow things up." He turned to me again. "I must've sounded so stupid, huh?"

"No," I said. "Bombs are scientific. There's chemistry

involved, and physics, too. There's nothing stupid about that."

Seth snorted. "I didn't give a shit about all of that. I just liked to watch things explode. Watermelons and milk jugs and stuff like that."

He was being much too hard on himself. We'd all been goofy kids at one time, trying to figure the world out, trying to figure out where we fit into it.

I put a hand on his shoulder. "You were a kid, Seth. Playing is how kids learn."

"Oh, I learned all right. I learned not to put fireworks in the mailbox or my grandpa would take a wooden spoon to my ass."

I cringed. "Ouch."

Seth's mouth turned up in a smile. "It wasn't so bad. Every time he hit me with the spoon my grandmother would grab it from him and use it to make me chocolate chip cookies."

I didn't know whether to laugh or cry at that revelation. *Talk about dysfunctional.*

"Anyway," Seth continued, "the army assigned me to bomb detail. When I left the military, the only thing I knew how to do was dismantle bombs. The only place those skills are needed are on a bomb squad. That's how I ended up at the fire department." He offered a mirthless chuckle. "It was either become a fireman or flip burgers. It just sort of happened. It wasn't like I'd made any conscious decisions about my career."

"You might not have made all of those decisions consciously," I told him, "but something led you to all of this. That's how it happens for a lot of people. Serendipity. You've clearly got a gift, Seth. You're brave. Calm under pressure. Smart. Few people could do what you do. You ended up in a position where you can help a lot of people, where you can do a lot of good in the world."

"So what?" he said, looking into my eyes again now. "You think our lives are guided by fate? Some divine hand? God?"

I had no idea. After seeing some of the horrific things I'd witnessed on my job, I often had trouble believing in God, or at least the caring, compassionate, and merciful version proffered by most churches. The fire-and-brimstone God, the one who was always smiting people or turning them into pillars of salt or flooding the earth when he got pissed off? Maybe that one. I couldn't be sure what the truth was. But I knew that I *wanted* to believe in something more.

"I don't know about any of that, Seth." I stared at him, his face becoming blurry as tears welled up in my eyes. "The only thing I know for sure is that I am really glad you are here right now." With that, I wrapped my arms around him and held him tight.

Early Sunday afternoon, Seth swung by my apartment to pick me up. Though both of us were off duty, we'd worn shirts identifying us as members of the police and fire departments. We'd have an easier time gaining admittance at the hospital if we appeared to wield some authority.

Seth had brought Blast with him to keep Brigit company while we were out and about. As always, the two seemed thrilled to see each other. Leaping up and wagging their tails and play-wrestling on the floor. Sometimes I thought the two of them had a better relationship than me and Seth. They seemed to have no trouble communicating, and their feelings about each other were clear. They were in doggie love.

Seth and I had no idea what we might find out at the hospital but, hoping for the best, we didn't want to arrive empty-handed. On the drive to Cook Children's Medical Center, we stopped by a toy store.

Seth glanced around as we walked inside. "What should I get her?"

Twelve-year-old girls could be tricky, teetering as they were on the cusp between little girl and teenager. "Let's take a look around, see what catches our eye."

He stopped in front of a display of stuffed animals and reached out for a Dalmation wearing a red fire hat. "What do you think of this?"

"I think it's perfect."

I chose a Mad Libs and a jewelry-making kit with projects I hoped the girl could manage from a hospital bed.

As we made our way into the hospital, a dark and heavy sense of dread and horror enveloped me. It was only weeks ago that I'd visited one of the bombing victims in another nearby hospital. She'd lost an eye and three fingers, but had survived the ordeal and counted her blessings. I hoped this little girl would have some blessings to count, too.

As we walked into the hospital, we passed a newspaper machine outside. The headline was visible through the glass window on the front. "Purse Snatchers and Pickpockets: Is the Stock Show Safe?"

Damn. I realized the reporters needed a story and that the public had a right to know about crimes in their community, but did the story have to be plastered across the top of page one? Given that I'd been the officer to interview the victims and prepare the reports, the crimes felt especially close to me, the headline broadcasting to the world my failure to catch the culprits.

I stopped, put some coins into the machine, and purchased a paper. Might as well see what the journalists had reported.

As I pulled the paper from the machine, I noted that the bottom half of the front page featured a photo of the house where the fire had taken place last night. "12-year-old girl critically injured in fire." I folded the paper so Seth wouldn't see the headline. Futile, really, since he obviously already knew what had happened. After all, that's why we were here. But for those who read the headlines and the report, the story would be a sad but fleeting bit of news. For Seth, this story was much more personal.

We stopped at the nurse's station outside the intensive care ward. After Seth explained who he was and the reason for our visit, she asked us to wait at the station. Though I tried to read her expression, she was a professional, maintaining the stoic appearance of someone responsible for private information. She disappeared through the swinging doors marked AUTHORIZED VISITORS AND STAFF ONLY.

In a moment she returned with a dark-haired woman who appeared to be in her mid-thirties. The woman's eyes were pink and swollen from crying and lack of sleep, her makeup smeared and her clothes wrinkled, her hair a wild mess. Clutched tightly in her fists were at least a half-dozen wadded tissues.

The woman looked up at Seth, fresh tears rimming her lids. "The nurse said you're the one who rescued Savannah last night?"

Seth appeared almost sheepish, as if uncomfortable being referred to as a rescuer. "I found her on the floor and carried her out of the house."

The woman grabbed Seth in a bear hug so tight it wouldn't have surprised me to see his head swell up and pop like the balloons at the stock show midway. "Thank you!" she cried. "Thank you so much!"

Seth and I exchanged glances. Though the woman was obviously distraught, her use of the word *rescued* and her expressions of appreciation implied her daughter had survived the night, right? Then again, she might simply have been grateful that her daughter's body hadn't been left inside to burn up with the house. I was afraid to read anything into the woman's words, and I think Seth was, too.

Seth cleared his throat. "Is she . . . um . . ." He took a deep breath, or at least as deep as he could given that the woman held him as tight as a vise. "How is she doing?"

The mother released Seth and took a step back. As I stepped up to put a supportive hand on his shoulder, her eyes went from my face to the FWPD logo on my shirt, then returned to Seth's face. "They had her on a respirator last night but she's breathing on her own now. She has some burns on her feet and legs that will need treatment and skin grafts, but . . ." The woman burst into fresh sobs and dabbed her eyes with the tissues. "She's going to make it!"

Seth's eyes closed for a few seconds in relief. When he opened them again, he gave the woman a soft smile. "That's great news."

"Would you like to see her?" the mother asked. She turned to the nurse. "It's okay if they come back, right?"

The nurse glanced around, then whispered, "Make it quick. Some of the doctors are real sticklers about visitation."

We slipped quickly and quietly through the doors and followed Savannah's mother down the hall to the girl's room. The girl lay on a bed inside, her dark hair fanned out on the pillow around her face. Her feet and legs were wrapped in white gauze dressing. Though she was able to breathe on her own, the doctors had nonetheless kept an oxygen mask on her face. Her father sat on a chair he'd pulled up next to the bed, his head ducked and hands folded as if he were praying.

As we came in the door, the father crossed himself, looked up, and stood to greet us. Savannah slowly turned her head on the pillow to face us. Her woozy eyes brightened when she saw the stuffed Dalmation and toys in our hands.

Her mother turned to us. "They've got her on strong painkillers so she's a little out of it." After introducing us to her husband, the woman stepped to the side of the bed and looked down at her daughter. "Savannah, Mr. Rutledge is here to see you. He's the fireman who carried you out of the house last night."

Seth stepped forward and held out the dog. "I thought you might like this."

The girl smiled behind the clear mask and reached out her arms to take the dog. "Thank you," she said, the mask muffling her words.

Seth motioned for me to step up beside him. "My girlfriend brought you some things, too."

Girlfriend?

That was news, too. Maybe not front-page stuff, but nonetheless worthy of an inch or two on page seven next to an ad for a tire sale.

Is that how Seth thinks of me? As his girlfriend? I supposed it was possible. After all, he'd come to me last night when he'd needed emotional support, which was one of the assorted services a girlfriend provided.

My heart wriggled again, but this time like a happy kitten on its back in the sunshine streaming through a window. The wriggling stopped abruptly a moment later when I realized that calling me his girlfriend was probably just the simplest way of identifying me. I still had no real sense of what Seth wanted from me, where he wanted our relationship to go, or if he even wanted it to go anywhere at all. It seemed like he wanted me to be like a doctor on call, available if and when he needed or wanted me for companionship or support, but not on regular duty. Though that thought wasn't exactly flattering, I realized I wasn't exactly sure what I wanted from him, either. As much as I thought I could develop real feelings for the guy, I wouldn't be willing to agree to full-time status until—*and unless*—he let me know who Seth Rutledge really was and proved to me that he wasn't going to flake out again.

I handed the pad of Mad Libs and the jewelry-making kit to Savannah. She offered another smile behind the mask before her eyes blinked three times and slowly drifted closed. It was probably a good thing they'd doped her up. Maybe she could sleep through some of the pain.

"We should probably be going now," Seth said to both Savannah's parents and the nurse, who stood watch at the door. "She looks like she could use some sleep. Thanks for letting us see her."

"No, thank *you*!" said Savannah's mother, grabbing both of Seth's hands in hers and giving them a squeeze. "And I promise, we will never let our tree get so dry again. We're going to buy an artificial one next Christmas."

Though Seth was clearly relieved to see that the little girl he'd rescued would survive, it was obvious from his tight grip on his steering wheel that something still had him upset. He glanced my way a couple of times as if assessing me. "How about a late lunch?" he asked.

"Sounds good."

Seth had stayed at my place until after four in the morning. I'd let Brigit out to relieve herself when he left, so she'd been gracious enough to let me sleep in this morning. I'd dragged my butt out of bed around ten and had a bowl of granola, but it hadn't held me over long.

He drove to Spiral Diner, which was only a couple of miles from the hospital. The hostess seated us at a booth along the back wall. A waiter with a nose ring and the letters P-E-A-C-E tattooed across his knuckles swung by with brunch menus.

Seth continued to eye me over his menu, though he said nothing.

Finally, I could take it no longer and stared back at him for a moment. "Is there something you want to say to me?"

"No." He turned his gaze downward to his menu. An instant later, though, he tossed the menu onto the table and gave me a pointed look. "Who is he?"

My first instinct was to play it coy and say *Who? I don't know who you're talking about* But I'd never been one for games. "He's a deputy who's been working the stock show."

Seth's jaw flexed. "You've been seeing him?"

"We went for drinks after our shifts last night. That's the first time we've seen each other outside work."

The waiter came back to take our order. I ordered the Sunshine Sandwich. Seth went for the Lumberjack.

When the waiter had gone, Seth eyed me again. "You going to see him again?"

I shrugged. "I don't know. Maybe."

He looked past me, out the window, evidently looking at the lightpost on the sidewalk. "Don't."

"Why not?" *Is it simply because you're jealous? Or is it because you actually care for me?*

"'Cause it makes me want to punch something. Him, mostly."

A laugh escaped my mouth. I supposed Seth admitting that seeing me with another man made him want to punch something was an indirect admission that he had feelings for me. I supposed him being upset shouldn't have made me as happy as it did, but what can I say? It was nice to know he cared.

"What about our deal?" I said. "We're free to see other people, remember?"

"Maybe I want to renegotiate."

The conversation hung in the air, waiting for one of us to pick it up and continue. But I knew how negotiations worked. The first to speak often got the worst part of the bargain.

Finally, Seth broke the silence. "Have you kissed him yet?"

It wouldn't be fair to lie to Seth. I wouldn't want him lying to me. "Yes."

"He as good at it as me?"

"No."

Seth exhaled loudly and sat back against the booth. "So you're interested in him?"

"Maybe." I *was* interested in Clint, but more because he was a fun guy than because I thought he could be my soul mate. He was a little too flirty to take seriously, though he was a fun distraction. I sent an intent look Seth's way. "I'm more interested in you, though. By a three percent margin."

Once he'd processed my words, his shoulders relaxed. He grinned and cocked his head. "I'll take those odds. I bet I can work that number up to a hundred, push that deputy right out of the picture."

My cheeks warmed with a blush. It was nice to feel wanted, desired. And, perhaps it was wrong of me, but after the way he'd ended things before, I enjoyed having the upper hand on Seth for a change. And, now that he'd been properly motivated, I looked forward to seeing just how he planned to play those numbers.

THIRTY-FIVE
PARTNERS IN CRIME

Brigit

Blast had come over to play! Brigit was thrilled to see him. They sniffed each other's butts and naughty bits, shared a bowl of kibble, and wrangled on the carpet for fun.

When they ran out of things to do, Brigit led Blast to the closet. Megan had added a second sliding bolt to the door the day she'd come home with the sausage rolls and found the closet door ajar. Brigit hadn't yet gotten to any of the shoes, which was probably a good thing. She had a feeling Megan might not have given her a sausage roll if Brigit had chewed up another pair of shoes.

Still, those stilettos called to her like a siren, those boots beckoned. Such soft, supple leather. Really, how could she be expected to resist? You didn't leave meth with an addict, did you? It was pure common sense. Really, if anything happened to those shoes, Megan could only blame herself.

While Blast watched, his forehead crinkled in concentration, Brigit nudged the lower bolt upward with her nose, then over. It slid open with a click.

The other sliding bolt would be more problematic. Megan had placed it five feet high, near the top of the door. When she stood on her hind legs, Brigit's nose came just shy of it. She'd need Blast's help to get it open. With the two of them taking turns leaping at it, maybe, just maybe, they could get it open.

Then those shoes and boots will be all ours . . .

THIRTY-SIX
COLD COFFEE

Robin Hood

On her drive into work Monday morning, she made another stop for coffee. She parked in the lot of a business a full block down, well out of range of any security cameras the Starbucks store might have. The doughnut shop didn't appear to have any cameras, but even if it did she doubted anyone would take the time to view the footage in an attempt to track her down. The cops didn't have that kind of time, and, besides, they'd start with the closer businesses, the McDonald's and the dry cleaner and the tire store.

She waited in line a good ten minutes. Looked like everyone needed a little extra boost this Monday.

When it was her turn, she stepped up to the counter. "I'll have a Venti caramel latte."

"Name?" the young woman at the register asked, her marker poised over the cup.

"Kate," she said. It was the first name that came to mind, probably because she'd been reading all about Kate

Middleton's latest doings in *People* magazine last night. She handed the gift card to the clerk.

The clerk ran the card through the scanner and frowned. Pushing a button on her screen, she ran the card a second time. The frown deepened. She pushed the button once more and ran the card a third time. She looked up at Robin Hood. "I'm sorry. There's some kind of problem with this card."

"But it has over forty-five dollars left on it," she protested. "See?" She pulled the receipt from her last coffee purchase from her wallet and showed the cashier.

"Want me to call customer service?" the girl asked.

No, she did *not* want the girl to call customer service. Mainly because they'd probably tell the girl the card had been reported stolen and had thus been canceled, but also because she could feel the heated glares from the long line of people behind her who wanted their coffee *now.* "That's okay. I'll just pay cash."

Damn.

Coffee tastes so much better when someone else pays for it.

THIRTY-SEVEN
BOOT CALL

Megan

Though I officially had Monday off, I was at work none-theless, giving that aforementioned 110 percent.

At 1:30 in the afternoon, I met Lisa, the earlier purse-snatching victim, on the porch of a house in the Fairmount neighborhood. Lisa was a Realtor and had planned to meet a painting crew there to let them into the house.

While the painters tossed clear sheets of plastic over the furniture and floors in the living room and bedrooms, Lisa and I huddled at the kitchen table.

I pulled out Cheyenne's and Mia's mug shots and driver's license photos and laid them on the table in front of Lisa. "Could either of these women be the thief?"

Lisa leaned in and took a long look at the photos. She picked up the pages and eyed them from various angles. Her brow furrowed. "I wish I could say for sure, but I can't. Everything happened so fast."

"Take a look at this." I took the pages from her and ex-changed them for the printouts from the boot stores. I'd dog-eared pages depicting boots that fit the description Lisa and Dominique had given me. Black boots with a turquoise or light green upper. "Can you identify the boots the woman on crutches was wearing?"

"Maybe." She began to flip through the pages.

"Did the boots have pointed, square, or round toes?" I asked, attempting to narrow down the possibilities.

"I'm leaning toward square," she said, flipping another page.

Personally, I'd always thought boots with squared-off toes looked a little odd. You know, like maybe the wearer had their toes hacked off with an axe. Who the heck had toes that were all the same length?

After a few more pages, she stopped on a pair of Justin boots, a black soft calf model with green cowhide on the upper. She put a finger on the page and looked up at me. "I can't swear to it, but I'm pretty sure this was them."

I made a note on my pad.

She flipped to another page and pointed at another pair. "If it wasn't that first pair, this would be my second choice." She indicated a pair sold at Cavender's, a model identified as the Ariat Women's Black Deertan with Turquoise Top. "Or these." She turned back a few pages to a nearly identical pair, the only difference being the height of the shank.

"That gives me something to go on." I stood from the table. "Thanks."

She walked me to the door. "By the way, I got in touch with the woman at my office who handles the birthday collections. She was able to send me a photo of the receipt from when she bought the gift card. I called Starbucks to cancel it and get a replacement, but they told me part of it had already been used late Friday night at the store on I-35 and Western Center."

Another potential lead. If the boot trail ran cold, maybe the coffee lead would be hot.

"How much had been spent?" I asked.

"A little over five dollars."

Hmm. That figure was only enough to buy one large cup. What did that mean? That the girl with the crutches and cute boots wasn't in cahoots with the purse snatcher after all? You'd think the thief would at least buy her accomplices a coffee for their help. Then again, was there any honor among thieves? Maybe the thief had decided the gift card should be all hers and to hell with her aiders and abettors.

"Can you send the photo to my phone?" I pulled out my cell and rattled off the number so Lisa could text it to me. A few seconds later my phone bleeped with the incoming photo. "Got it."

Lisa walked me to the door.

"As soon as I know anything," I told her, "I'll be in touch."

Before visiting Dominique, I headed north of the city to the Starbucks. I explained the reason for my visit to the manager. He waved me back into his small office and offered me a seat. I showed him the photo of the gift card receipt, which included the gift card's identifying number.

"I can use the gift card number to trace the transaction," the manager said, turning to his computer to input the data.

"Any chance she used the drive-through?"

If so, all I'd have to do was take a look at the video surveillance recording, get her license plate, and bring down the hammer. *BAM!*

His eyes scanned the data on the screen. "Looks like she came into the store. She bought her drink at register two at the counter."

So much for bringing down the hammer. Still, the lead wasn't dead yet. "Can you tell who helped her at the counter? Which employee?"

He took another glance at the screen. "Looks like Jason was working the register that night." He consulted the schedule. "He'll be back in on Wednesday. He's scheduled to work the two-thirty to eleven-thirty shift."

"Great." I'd come back then and see if Jason remembered anything about the young woman who'd used the card. "Any chance I can take a look at the surveillance tapes?"

"Store managers aren't authorized to show security videos without getting clearance from the corporate office first." The manager reached into a drawer and pulled out a form. "You have to fill this out and send it to our legal department. They decide whether or not to allow it."

If my request were denied, I supposed I could try to get a search warrant and force the issue. But then my superiors would realize I was conducting an unofficial investigation. They might not like that. Hell, I was probably exceeding my authority simply by filling out the form. But sometimes it was easier to ask forgiveness than permission. Besides, surely they'd be happy with me for catching these criminals, right?

On the other hand, here I was, on my day off, talking to witnesses and trying to track down clues. Why was I doing this? Was I trying to prove something to my superiors at the police department? To those kids in school who'd made me feel small and stupid and ashamed? To myself? Maybe all of the above?

Whatever my motivations, and regardless of whether they were healthy, I'd come this far. No sense stopping now.

I handed the completed form back to the manager and thanked him for his time. As I left the store, I bought a cinnamon dolce latte with soy. No sense leaving without a warm drink, either.

* * *

Dominique waved me back to her office at the insurance agency and closed the door behind us. The space was decorated in pastels, pretty watercolors of lilies and poppies and irises gracing her walls. I found myself wondering how I'd decorate my office once I made detective and was assigned a space of my own. Should I go for something bright and cheerful, maybe some white bookcases and colorful printed throw pillows on the chairs? Or should I go for something more traditional and businesslike, perhaps chairs covered in faux-leather upholstery with brass studs? Oh, well. No need to decide today. I had at least three more years before office décor would be an issue.

I handed the printout to Dominique. "I'd like you to take a look. See if you can pick out the boots you saw."

While she carefully looked over the pages, I sat in her comfy wing chair and helped myself to one of the foil-wrapped Lindt truffles on her desk. Between the sugary, high-calorie coffee and now this chocolate, I'd really fallen off the wagon today. Tomorrow I'd eat nothing but organic kale raised by fair-trade farmers.

Wanting to see if she chose the same boots as Lisa, I didn't tell her which ones her friend had picked out. But when Dominique finished, she'd chosen the first two pairs that Lisa had. "These two look about right."

No harm in telling her now. "Those are the same two Lisa picked out." Not surprising, really. Although there were several other pairs with dark chocolate and turquoise or green, the ones they chose were the only models with black lowers. Clearly, the two were firm on that.

Since she hadn't gotten a look at the thieves, there was no point in showing her the photos of Cheyenne and Mia. I thanked her for her time and told her I'd be in touch if my investigation went anywhere.

"I appreciate you going the extra mile," she said as she walked me to the front door of her office. "Everyone told

me the police don't usually have time to follow up on these
types of things."

"Unfortunately, that's true." Limited manpower, limited
budgets. "But I had a little extra time today so I figured
I'd see what I could do."

I stepped out of the building and headed to my car.

She waved her hand and called after me. "Good luck!"

On Tuesday morning, I visited Catherine Quimby, the purse
snatcher's first victim. She was far less helpful. Then again,
there were a much greater number of boots in pink-and-
tan styles.

"Oh, honey." She shook her blond head as she turned
page after page after page. "I just don't know. They all start
looking alike after a while."

"Were the toes pointed, rounded, or square?" I asked.

"Round maybe? Or pointed?" The inflection in her voice
made it seem as if she were asking me the questions. "I
don't think they were square."

"Do you recall how tall the shank was? Did they come
all the way up below the knee or were they those lower
ankle-type?"

Again, she wasn't much help. "Maybe somewhere in between?"

When it was clear she had nothing else to offer, I gathered up the printout. "Thanks, Catherine. If I have any
news, I'll let you know."

I stopped by both Cheyenne's and Mia's homes on Tuesday and Wednesday morning but nobody answered the
door. The two were probably at work, assuming they'd been
able to find gainful employment given their criminal his-
tory. Likewise, there was no sign of Clint at the stock show
on Tuesday or Wednesday. Curious, I inquired with one of

the other deputies, a stumpy guy with a patchy mustache.
He appeared to be suffering some form of mange.

He gave me a knowing look, amusement in his eyes.
"Why is it all of the ladies are looking for Clint and none
are looking for me?"

"Do you see my uniform?" I asked, an edge in my voice.

"Sure I do. And I bet it has nothing to do with your reasons for wanting to find Clint."

The jerk was right, of course. Nevertheless, it put a little
twist in my panties. "If you happen to see him, tell him
Officer Luz has some information about the robberies."

The guy rocked back on his heels, his thumbs in the
front pocket of his pants. "Oh, I doubt I'll see him. He's
been sent up to the north side. Lots of folks in town for
the stock show are staying at the hotels up that way."

The north side was home to a number of tourist attrac-
tions. The White Elephant Saloon, where various scenes
from the television show *Walker, Texas Ranger* had been
filmed. A vintage steam train that traveled between Fort
Worth and the city of Grapevine, which lay a half hour to
the east. The Cowtown Cattlepen Maze, once featured on
the *Amazing Race* television show. And, of course, Billy
Bob's, touted as the world's largest honky-tonk. Numerous
shops and restaurants were situated up that way, too. There
was also a twice-daily cattle drive down the main street,
a show put on for tourists in which a half-dozen longhorn
cattle were herded along for a few blocks while spectators
watched from behind wooden sawhorses erected for their
safety. The cattle plodded along without protest, the looks
of boredom on their face saying *Damn, this is getting old.
Why don't you take down those sawhorses and let us chase
after these people like our buddies in Pamplona get to do?*

I was disappointed to learn that Clint wouldn't be at the
stock show. Things between us had been hanging since

Clint left my apartment Saturday night. I hoped he didn't think I'd been rude. On the other hand, if I tracked Clint down, he might read something into it. The last thing I wanted to do was lead him on, especially now that Seth finally seemed to be acknowledging he had feelings for me. On the other hand, if I wasn't yet ready or willing to devote myself only to Seth, why pass up the chance to have some fun with Clint in the meantime? I deserved to have a good time, right?

Blurgh. Why are relationships so confusing?

My cell phone rang then, giving me an easy out of the conversation. I pushed the button to accept the call and stepped away. "This is Officer Megan Luz."

The caller identified herself as Dominique. "I checked my Diners Club account online today. It showed charges of nearly three hundred dollars at a Kroger grocery store last Friday. I'd nearly forgotten I even had that darn card. I never use it. That thief must've made the charges."

I advised her to pursue a claim through the credit card company's fraud department, and asked her to e-mail me a copy of the account information. "I'll follow up with the store," I told her. "See if they can tell me anything."

She thanked me for my efforts. "I hope y'all find that girl," she said. "Thanks to her I had to stand in line for three and a half hours at the DMV today to get a new driver's license. That's how criminals should be punished, I tell you."

Not a bad idea.

After the stock show closed down at ten, I drove up I-35 and exited on Western Center Boulevard. I left Brigit in the squad car. I didn't expect to be here long. Besides, she'd fallen asleep on the way over and had been snoring happily until I'd stopped the car. She'd probably rather go back to her dreams than be dragged into the store. I had no idea why I was worried about her comfort, though. The damn dog had managed to circumvent the slide bolts I'd put on my closet last weekend and chew up a pair of cute ankle boots I'd bought at an after-Christmas sale. She'd even shared them with Blast. I'd since moved all of my shoes to the top shelf of my closet and replaced the levered handle with a round one that locked. If the dog was smart enough to figure out how to get into the closet and get the shoes off the shelf, she'd deserve to have them.

"Be a good girl," I told her as I climbed out of the car. "I'll be back real quick."

She yawned then settled her head onto her paws.

I went inside and found a shaggy-haired guy working the register. His chin sported a small tuft of hair, not enough to constitute a beard but enough to prove that he was actively producing testosterone.

"Hi," I said. "I'm Officer Megan Luz. Might you be Jason?"

"Yeah. That's me. My boss said you'd be coming by." He motioned with his head for another employee to cover the cash register while he and I took seats at one of the small round tables.

Knowing he'd need to get back to work as soon as possible, I got right to the heart of the matter. "I'm trying to find the person who used a gift card," I told him. "It was a fifty-dollar card with the words *happy birthday* printed on it. The person used it shortly before the store closed up for the night last Friday."

"I remember," he said. "It was a girl about my age. A blonde."

"Attractive?"

"I probably wouldn't remember her if she wasn't."

Men. Sheesh. Of course the same could be said for women. We tended to remember the attractive men more than the plain ones. So, to be fair, *Women. Sheesh.*

"Was her hair short?"

"No," he said. "It was long."

Hmm. That didn't fit the description Dominique had given me. Of course the woman could have had her hair pinned up in a barrette or clip or elastic band earlier in the night.

"How long?" I asked.

He turned sideways and put a finger to his back, just under his shoulder blade.

I pulled my notepad from my breast pocket to take notes. "Was it curly or straight?"

He circled a finger in the air. "She had those big curls. The kind they make with that pointed wand thing."

My surprise at his insight must have been clear because he added, "I've got a sister. She wears her hair the same way. I've burned myself three times on her curling iron. She leaves it on the bathroom counter right next to the toothpaste."

My siblings and I had similar problems growing up. I couldn't get in the shower without first having to round up the Barbie dolls and plastic boats from the drain. Our living room was a minefield of Lego blocks and green army men. Walk through it barefoot and you'd be hopping and howling by the time you reached the other side.

"Do you remember what the girl was wearing?"

"Jeans," he said. "Some kind of black jacket or sweater."

"What else can you tell me about her? Eye color, maybe? Any moles, scars, tattoos, birthmarks?"

"I'm pretty sure her eyes were blue. No scars or tattoos or moles that I noticed. No birthmarks, either."

I supposed it was too much to ask that she have something easily distinguishable, like a Tinker Bell tattoo in the middle of her forehead or a mole shaped like Mickey Mouse on the tip of her nose.

"How big was she?" I asked. "Can you estimate her height and weight?"

"She was medium," he said. "About like you. How much do you weigh?"

I gave him a pointed look. "I'll just write the number down on my pad."

Back at the counter, the barista on duty called out, "I've got a skinny soy latte for Jemma!"

A girl who'd been texting on her phone stepped forward and took the cup without even looking up.

I turned back to Jason. "Her name. Did she give it to you when she ordered?"

"Yeah," he said. "I remember because we joked about it. It's Robin. I said it was like the bird, and she said it was like the guy in green tights who stole from the rich to give to the poor."

"Robin Hood?"

"Yeah. She said something about how Robin Hood re-distributed wealth. Then she gave me a three-dollar tip."

Interesting . . .

What did it say about the thief that she'd been gener-ous with the barista? And could her tip even be called generous when it was paid with someone else's money? I wasn't sure what to make of that, but I made a note of it. *Three-dollar tip.* I also wrote down the name she'd given. *Robin.* Surely it was made up, but it might mean something.

I found myself wondering what fake name I might use in such a situation. Maybe Aphrodite. She'd had numer-ous lovers, both gods and mortal men. Or perhaps Phoebe, just 'cause it kind of rhymed. I just knew it wouldn't be Apple. Really, what had Gwyneth Paltrow and her husband been thinking? Had they lost a bet? And was the kid named after the fruit or the computer company? Either way, it was ridiculous.

I looked back up at Jason. "Any chance you saw what kind of car she was driving?"

He shook his head. "No. I started cleaning up right after she left the counter."

Looked like I'd squeezed all I could out of this kid. "Thanks for your help." I pulled one of my business cards out of my breast pocket as I slid the notepad back in. I held it out to Jason. "If she comes in again, give me a call immediately. Okay?"

"Yeah. Sure."

As we stood, the manager I'd spoken with when I'd stopped by the store a few days ago stepped out of a back room and spotted me. He waved me over. "I got word from legal that I can show you the video. Would you like to see it now?"

"Absolutely."

He took me back to his office and offered me his chair. Bending forward next to me, he pulled up the video feed but paused it. "I assume you'll want a copy of this?"

"That would be great."

He slid a thumb drive into the computer and instructed the machine to copy the feed as it ran.

I leaned in and watched closely. Jason and another employee stood behind the counter, helping customers, making drinks, wiping down the equipment, snapping towels at each other's butts. Approximately thirty seconds into the feed, a pretty young blonde woman stepped up to the counter. Though the tape had no audio, it was apparent that Jason asked for her order. The girl bit her lip in a sensual, flirtatious way and said something back to Jason, no doubt her drink order. He punched buttons on the register, told her the total, and she handed him the stolen gift card. He looked down at the card then back up at the woman, his mouth moving again. She smiled and said something back to him. He ran the gift card through the machine and returned it to her, then picked up a paper cup and a Sharpie, holding the pen aloft. His lips moved again as he asked her name.

Her mouth formed *Robin*. But surely that was a made-up name, right? Perhaps her comment about Robin Hood was a clue, a hint about her motives for committing the thefts. *Is she some type of ultra left-wing socialist? Or just a young woman with an overdeveloped sense of entitlement?*

The woman stepped back from the counter to wait for her drink. When it was ready, she took it and handed the three singles to Jason. He doffed a nonexistent hat in gratitude and she left.

Everything on the video jibed with what Jason had told me. And, unfortunately, it told me nothing new.

The manager stopped the feed, pulled the thumb drive out of the USB port, and handed it to me.

"Thanks," I told him. "You've been very helpful."

I stepped out of his office and made my way back through the store.

As I passed the counter, I raised a hand in good-bye to Jason.

"Want a doughnut to take with you?" he called.

"Why? 'Cause I'm a cop?"

"No. Because I'm about to throw out the ones that didn't sell."

"In that case," I said. "I'll take two."

THIRTY-EIGHT
NOT HER FIRST RODEO

Brigit

On Thursday, Megan and Brigit had lunch with Seth and Blast at a deli near the fire station. Megan ordered her partner a platter of sliced lunch meat. Not bad, but Brigit would have preferred the entire roll of salami she saw in the refrigerated deli case.

Brigit could tell that seeing Seth made Megan happy. Her partner had showed her teeth a lot on the drive to the deli, and even more on the way after. Brigit liked it when Megan was happy. Her partner tended to be more generous with food scraps and more forgiving of Brigit's bad behavior when she was in a good mood.

Friday night, she and Megan were back at the rodeo. The deputy whom Megan had brought to the apartment last weekend was at it again, riding bareback on a horse that looked damn pissed off about it. As the horse spun and bucked, Clint hung on, his legs moving up and down in his fringed chaps. Brigit felt for the horse. It was like the poor thing had an enormous flea on its back and couldn't quite reach to scratch it. *Been there, done that.*

As they set back out on patrol, Brigit got back to work, putting her nose to the air to scent for anything out of the ordinary. She smelled the usual food smells, the usual smells of the livestock. She even smelled the two colognes from those three women who seemed to be here every weekend. But her nose caught something else, too . . . a vaguely familiar scent . . . an odor that triggered a suppressed recollection from deep down in her memory banks . . .

Beer-scented sweat.

The ramen noodles and frozen pizzas the guy seemed to subsist on.

The dope he always had in his front pocket.

If Brigit had been capable of laughter, she would've broken down in guffaws. *Watch out, asshole. You're about to get some long overdue payback.*

She tugged on her leash, pulling Megan into the crowd and after the scrawny guy and his friends. At first, Megan tried to hold her back. But when her partner realized that Brigit had scented drugs and was following the trail, she let Brigit take the lead, trotting after the dog as she weaved in and out of the crowd.

The stench grew suddenly stronger as she broke out of the horde.

There he is. Stepping into line at the corn dog stand.

Brigit bolted forward, ran around to the front of the guy, and sat, giving her passive alert signal. Her thoughts then were uniquely canine, but if translated to English would read: *Jig's up, numb-nuts!*

"Holy fuck!" the guy said, bending down to get a good look at Brigit. "Is that you, Shithead?"

Megan stepped up next to Brigit and held up a palm.

"Sir, my dog has alerted to drugs on your person. I'm going to need you to stand still and raise your arms while I pat you down."

His eyes flashed in alarm and his mouth fell open. "Uhhh . . ."

It was the most intelligent thing Brigit had ever heard him say.

"Raise your arms," Megan repeated, her voice more stern this time.

But the numb-nuts didn't raise his arms. Instead, he turned and took off running, as numb-nuts are wont to do.

Megan unclipped Brigit's leash and gave her the signal to take the guy down.

Gladly.

Six seconds later, the guy fell face-first onto the ground with Brigit on top of him. He squirmed under her, trying his best to throw her, just like the horses and bulls in the rodeo tried to throw their riders. But he had far less luck than the rough stock. Brigit was enjoying some sweet revenge and wasn't about to be thrown. *It's not fun to have something heavy on your back, is it?*

Megan stepped up beside them. "Stop resisting my dog!"

Again, the shithead didn't listen.

"I told you to stop resisting my dog!" Brigit heard the snap of Megan extending her baton, the *swish-whap* as it came down on the guy's thigh.

The guy hurled a string of obscenities that had mothers covering their children's ears. "Fucking cunt cop! Get your dumbass dog off me! This is fucking police brutality!"

Another *swish*. Another *whap*. Cell phones were pulled from purses and pockets and record buttons were pressed.

Brigit sensed Megan stiffen, her resolve to give this ass the beating he deserved lost in the face of a potential brutality charge. But Brigit had no such qualms. She knew how she could cool this guy down really quick.

Her teeth still firmly clenching his collar, Brigit copped a squat on the guy's back and released her urinary sphincter.

"Aaaagh!" the guy shrieked. "Your dog's pissing on me!"

Though Brigit's former handler would have likely put a stop to the dog's bad behavior, Megan made no effort to pull Brigit off the guy's back, letting her completely empty her bladder.

Partnering with another bitch definitely had its benefits.

THIRTY-NINE
SHOCKING

Robin Hood

The balding man at the pawnshop held the gold diamond ring up to the light and scrutinized it through one of those little eyepiece things. *What are they called again?* Oh, yeah. A loupe.

He set the loupe on the counter. "This is a nice ring. High-quality diamond."

"I know," she said. "So I'll expect a good price."

He chuckled before leaning in and giving her a scrutinizing look. "Is it hot?"

Robin Hood felt her face blaze. *How dare he accuse me of trying to pawn stolen property! What do I look like, a common thief?*

Of course she *had* stolen the ring. But that was beside the point. She'd only taken it because fate had been unfair to her and someone had to even the score, right? Once fate got off her lazy ass and started giving Robin Hood what she was entitled to, there'd be no more of these petty crimes. Really, that kind of thing was beneath her.

"Of course it's not hot," she spat. "I got divorced and I don't want the rings anymore, that's all."

His brows quirked in skepticism. "You look awfully young to be getting divorced already. Didn't give your marriage much of a shot, did you?"

She glared at the man. "My private life is none of your business. Now how much will you give me?"

He stood up straight. "Two hundred for the set."

She sputtered. "That's nothing!"

"The price reflects the risk I'm taking here. You don't have a receipt for these. How do I know they're not stolen?"

She grabbed the rings back out of his hand. "You just lost a good deal here, buddy!"

She'd sell the damn things on eBay or Craigslist. She'd probably get more for them anyway and at least she wouldn't have to put up with some asshole treating her like a derelict.

She'd chosen her quarry well tonight. A middle-aged cattle rancher who reeked of both prosperity and the spicy classic Calvin Klein Obsession for Men cologne. She'd caught his eye from across the room in the dance hall and gave him that practiced come-hither smile. A minute later, he'd successfully ditched his rancher friends and their wives and taken a seat at the table next to hers, close enough that he could chat her up, see if she might be interested, but not so close as to appear lecherous.

Her eyes cut to his left hand. No band on his ring finger, no telltale ring of pasty skin where a ring had recently been removed, and thus presumably no worries that someone would snitch to a wife back home. He probably just had the sense to realize his friends' wives would call him a dirty old man for hitting on a girl half his age. Of course his friends would placate their wives by agreeing with them, all the while thinking how they'd love to trade places with their rancher friend and bang a sweet young thing like her until their eyes crossed and their balls fell off.

Ha.

"Enjoying yourself?" he asked as he took a sip of his beer.

"I was until my friend ditched me," she said. "She hooked up with some cowboy."

"Rodeo groupie?"

"The worst kind." She rolled her eyes dramatically. "All it takes is a pair of chaps and spurs and her panties come off."

The man offered a soft chuckle and cut an intent glance her way, a glance that said he was wondering what it would take to make Robin Hood's panties come off.

Shame he'd never find out. He was attractive enough, and appeared to be successful enough, too, but the gold Robin was digging for would preferably come with a more sophisticated type of man. A younger one, too. She knew that riding a man's coattails would also mean riding his cock, and she'd prefer that cock to be perky and spry.

A waitress with a round tray came by their tables. "Can I get y'all anything?"

The man raised his bottle and looked in Robin's direction, lifting his chin in question.

"Coors Light for me," she told the waitress. She didn't normally drink beer, of course, especially not the everyday brands sold at convenience stores and gas stations. But she needed to do her best to blend into this crowd and drinking beer seemed to be a good way to do it.

The woman scurried off to round up their drinks.

The man turned back to her. "May I ask your name?"

You may. But you're not going to get it. "Robin," she said without hesitation. She might not have a red breast, but the name worked just as well for a spunky redhead, which she was tonight thanks to another Jessica Simpson hairpiece.

"Robin," the man repeated, as if committing her name to memory. "I'm Sloane."

She fought a laugh. She'd pegged him as a Bill or a Bob or maybe even an Earl. Sloane sounded like a character from a soap opera or an action movie. "It's nice to meet you, Sloane."

His lip twitched. "The pleasure is all mine."

Yeah, she thought. *It is.*

They made small talk for a few minutes, and she learned he was a widower from the small town of Kermit out in west Texas. Oil country.

"What about you?" he asked.

"My friend and I drove down from Norman," she said, referencing the city that was home to the University of Oklahoma.

"You a Sooner?"

"Sure am."

"What are you studying up there?"

"Business."

The part about attending college was a lie, of course, but Robin did consider herself a business student of sorts. To her life was a business, the ultimate goal to acquire more income and assets while investing the least amount of time and effort. Why give a hundred percent when you could find a sugar daddy to do it for you? Of course Sloane would *not* be that sugar daddy. She had no intention of playing grandma to a bunch of sticky-fingered children, and no way in hell would she move out to the sticks, especially not to west Texas where the air reeked of petrochemicals and dust storms were common. There was also no way would she live in a town that shared its name with what was assuredly a homosexual frog puppet. Why Miss Piggy kept chasing

Kermit she would never know. Didn't that "Rainbow
Connection" song he loved to sing give the pig a clue? If
Robin lived on Sesame Street, she'd set her sights on the
Count. He might talk with a goofy accent, but he did have
a castle.

The waitress returned with their drinks. Sloane paid for
them, then asked if he could join her at her table, evidently
sensing that his odds with Robin Hood were good enough
that he no longer cared much what his friends' wives might
say.

"Of course." She put her foot to the edge of the seat
across from her and pushed it back in invitation.

Ten minutes later, Sloane was leading her around the
dance floor. Two more beers and one hour later, and he was
leading her out to his vehicle in the parking lot. Crystal
and Heather trailed behind, keeping a dozen yards between them so it wouldn't be obvious they were together.

Robin Hood and Sloan reached his truck. She noted that
it was one of those king-cab super-duty Lariat models that
ran around fifty grand. Not too shabby. Still, it was a pickup.
She'd much rather ride in Kevin Trang's Porsche. Besides,
the infant car seat in the back was a total turnoff. *No doubt
about it now. This guy was someone's granddaddy.*

As the man went to open the passenger door for her, she
grabbed his arm and looked up at him with bedroom eyes.
"There's something I've been wanting to do since I spotted you across the dance floor."

His eyes flashed with desire. "And just what might that
be?"

She stepped toward him, pushing herself up against him.
"This." She angled her head back and stood on tiptoe to
kiss him.

This guy wasn't nearly as repulsive as the man she'd
ripped off last night. Tonight she'd be able to engage in a
little parking lot make-out session with help from Ryan

Gosling alone. No need for Bradley Cooper and Adam Levine. They could have the night off.

Sloane pulled back for a moment. "That was nice."

"Then why stop?" She stretched up for another kiss, opening her mouth to him.

The two had been going at it for a full minute when Robin slid her hands down from the man's neck to his chest. Her left hand kept going, down to his hip, which she cupped to pull him tighter against her. She could tell he was aroused from the bulge in the front of his pants, but she was much more interested in the bulge in his back pocket.

Moaning erotically to distract him, she slipped two fingers into the back pocket of his jeans and slowly eased his wallet out. Heather and Crystal stepped up to the front of the truck, ready to catch the wallet when she tossed it their way. *Yeah, men are so easy.*

Bam! The back of her head hit against the passenger window as the man forced her back and grabbed her wrist so tightly her hand was immobilized. His wallet hung limply from her fingers.

Shit! Caught in the act!

Her frantic heartbeat roared in her ears and Sloane's voice roared along with it. "What the hell do you think you're doing?"

What the hell do I think I'm doing? The better question is what the hell does he think he is doing? Manhandling her like this, as if she were some common hooker? How dare he!

He'll pay for this.

And he'll pay good.

She tried to push him back with her right hand, but had little luck. His grip was like a tight manacle, holding her in place. *So much for making him pay.*

She turned to her sisters. "Help me!" she shrieked. "Get him!"

But the two just stood there, frozen, mouths agape. Much longer and they'd catch flies. *Dammit, those two are useless!*

Panic set her mind racing as fast as her heart.

Ohmigod-ohmigod-ohmigod! What should I do?

"Look," the man said, "just drop my wallet and I'll let you go. Okay? No harm. No foul."

No harm, no foul meant *no cash,* either.

No deal. She hadn't spent all that time with this guy earlier, coaxing him with her feminine wiles, to end up empty-handed.

With a primal cry, she brought her knee up, hard and fast, giving him a blow to the balls sure to put him out of commission for months.

The man crumpled and stepped back, but managed to hang on to her wrist so tight it felt like her bones would snap. "You nasty little bitch!"

She swung her purse at him, hitting him upside the head, but when she tried again he batted it away.

I need to get free!

I need to run!

I need a better weapon!

As they wrangled, her eyes searched for anything she could use to free herself from this man's relentless grip. Something stuck up from the bed of his pickup, some kind of metal or plastic handle attached to a rod. She had no idea what the thing might be, but whatever it was would have to do. She dropped her purse to the ground, seized the handle, and swung the stick, hitting the man smartly upside the head. *Whack!*

While the strike dazed him temporarily and left a welt along his temple and cheek, he still hadn't let go of her wrist.

Damn! This rancher is as tenacious as the bulls he raises.

She pulled the stick back and hit him with it again.

Whack! If he were a piñata, his head would've split open then, spilling out candy and gum. But given that he was made of thick flesh and sturdy bones rather than papier-mâché, his head was still intact.

As she pulled the stick back for a third hit, she realized exactly what she held in her hands.

A cattle prod.

He threw up an open palm, fingers splayed, apparently expecting her to come at him again from the side, but she surprised him by coming in from below. She shoved the two tips up under the man's chin with all the force she could muster. Hell, she half expected the thing to punch through his skin and come out of his opposite cheek. Would serve him right if it did.

She pressed the button to activate the prod.

Zzzzzt!

The man cried out, performed some involuntary and graceless twerk moves, and let go of her wrist.

Ha!

"No!" Crystal screamed, running toward them. "Stop!"

"Shut up, Crystal!" Robin Hood spat. Couldn't her sister see this force was necessary? If she didn't get free from this man, they'd all be up shit creek—without a paddle, a boat, or even a snorkel. The cops would figure out they'd been the ones to steal the purses and rings last weekend and the wallet last night. They'd end up in the county jail.

She pressed the button again. *Zzzzzt!*

The man made no sound this time. Instead, he just flopped his arms and legs around like a marionette with an untrained puppeteer, then crumpled to the ground.

She dropped the cattle prod and retrieved her purse. She turned to her sisters, who continued to gape like wide-mouth bass. "Run!"

FORTY
NOSFERATU VISITS FORT WORTH

Megan

The Big Dick, Brigit, and I stood over the man, who lay on the ground, rolling side to side and groaning. His neck bore two small round marks.

Derek chuckled. "Looks like we've got us a vampire."

I rolled my eyes. "More likely that cattle prod lying next to him had something to do with this." Rather than pick up the prod, I left it in place for the crime scene techs to handle.

Derek looked down at the man. "I feel for ya', buddy. More than you will ever know."

The Big Dick sent a knowing look my way, a look with such an edge I instinctively stepped back to avoid decapitation. Yeah, thanks to yours truly Tasering him in the groin, Derek knew what it was like to be electrocuted.

A twinge of guilt cramped my gut. My former partner might be an oversexed, offensive boor with a body odor problem and poor manners, a rude and obnoxious jerk, an overly aggressive, sexist pig . . . *Wait, where am I going with this?* Oh, yeah. Despite Derek's many, many, *MANY* faults, he *had* been the one to find me when I'd been tied to the carousel with the bomb strapped to my chest. I wouldn't have been standing here today if it weren't for him.

"What if I give your truck nuts back?" I'd won them fair and square in our bet, but frankly I'd be more than happy to return them to Derek. The pendulous rubber things were hideous, and they were severely hampering my gas mileage. Besides, I was tired of people pulling up next to me at stoplights and giving me weird looks. "Could we call it even if I return them?"

He yanked on his waistband and juggled his junk. "It would be a start."

"Consider it done."

The man stopped rolling and looked up at us.

"An ambulance is on the way, sir," I told him. Luckily for him, paramedics were already on site for the rodeo. He wouldn't have long to wait. Also lucky for him was the couple who'd happened upon him writhing on the ground and immediately dialed 911. "Are you up to answering some questions?"

He managed to push himself into a sitting position. "That little bitch! That little redheaded bitch from the dance hall! She took my wallet and hit me with my own cattle prod!"

A redhead now? My goodness, how many women were involved in these thefts?

I pulled my notepad and pen from my pocket and knelt down to his level. "Tell me what happened. From the beginning."

The man, whose name was Sloane Gallatin—a soap opera name if ever I'd heard one—said he'd been in the dance hall with some associates from the earlier cattle auction when he'd spotted the redhead eyeing him from across the way. He'd gone over and bought her a beer. "She told me she was a student at OU and that her name was Robin."

Robin? The blond thief who'd stolen the purses and rings in the ladies' room had given that same name to the barista at Starbucks. Surely it wasn't coincidence. Tonight's cattle-prod-wielding redhead had to be the same woman.

I was certain she'd lied about both her name and her college attendance, but nevertheless I jotted them down. If nothing else, it meant I could rule out any girl named Robin who was a student at OU as a potential suspect. That left only approximately 13.5 million other females between the ages of eighteen and twenty-five in the U.S. who could possibly be the guilty party. My odds of finding this young woman were approximately the same as winning the Powerball. Then again, I had something the megalottery did not. A nimble brain that could assess clues, follow leads, and narrow down the list of potential suspects.

Sloane continued his story. "After a couple of beers and some dancing, we decided to leave. We came out here and the next thing I knew she was all over me like a bitch in heat."

The Big Dick snorted. "You lucky dog."

"Lucky?" The man cut him an incredulous look. "I got fried with a cattle prod, remember?"

"Oh, right," Derek said. "That was a kick in the nuts, huh?"

"No," the man said, angling bladed hands to indicate his groin. "The kick in the nuts was the kick in the nuts."

"Uh-uh-uh." I waved a hand between them to break up their conversation. This was *my* interview. Besides, I didn't want to hear any more about anyone's groin. *Yick.* "Go on," I told the man.

"When I felt her take my wallet out of my back pocket I grabbed her wrist. She fought me for a few seconds, kneed me in the testicles, then grabbed the cattle prod out of the back of my truck. She hit me with it first, then zapped me with it. Twice!" He put a hand to the marks on his neck. "Damned prod burned right through my skin!"

It was a good thing the guy didn't have a heart condition or we might have a corpse on our hands. I'd faced a lot of things in my days as a cop, but so far had been fortunate enough to avoid a murder scene.

"Anything else you can tell us?" I asked. "What she was wearing? Any distinguishing marks?"

"She was wearing jeans and a light blue sweater." He made an X mark over his chest. "The kind that crosses in the front."

And thus reveals a lot of cleavage. This thief was no idiot.

"Did you notice her eye color?" I asked. "Moles or scars? Tattoos? Birthmarks?"

"Didn't notice any of that. But she had two other girls with her. Kinda plain girls with brown hair."

He definitely had my attention now.

"These other two girls you mentioned. Were they with Robin in the dance hall?"

"No," he said. "She was alone then. But once she grabbed my wallet, they came up out of nowhere and watched the whole thing. One of them yelled at Robin to stop when she hit me with the prod. She hollered back at them. She called one of them Crystal."

Crystal, huh?
Finally!
A solid lead!

I wrote the name Crystal in all caps on my pad and underlined it three times for good measure. "Did you see what these other two girls were wearing? Crystal and the other one?"

"Jeans, I guess," the man said. "I only got a quick look before Robin zapped me. The one called Crystal was wearing boots. Purple ones."

A *third* pair of colorful boots? It was clear what Crystal was spending her share of the take on. Talk about a shoe whore.

"When you say purple," I asked the man, "what exactly do you mean?"

The man chuffed. "When I say *purple,* I mean *purple.* What kind of question is that?"

"I understand you're upset, Mr. Gallatin," I said, "but—"

"I'm not just upset!" he yelled. "My balls are bruised and I've got holes in my neck! I drove halfway across the state of Texas to come to this godforsaken stock show and this is what I get?"

I held up a palm. "I'm very sorry for what you've gone through, sir. But keep in mind that I'm trying to help you here. What I meant by my earlier question is do you mean the boots were a plum color? Or a lighter color, like lavender? Or more of a pink-type purple? These details could be important."

"Hell, I don't know. Lavender, I guess."

"Were the boots solid purple?"

"No. Just the upper part."

Derek punched the mic for his radio. "Everyone keep an eye out for a hot redhead in jeans and a low-cut light blue sweater. Also for a couple of fuglies, one with purple boots."

"He didn't say the women were ugly," I admonished Derek.

The Big Dick rolled his eyes this time. "He said they were *plain.* That's guy-speak for fugly."

"Point taken." Things would be a lot easier if men and women would use the same language. I stood. "I'll be right back," I said, looking down at the victim. "Stay here."

"Jesus Christ," he muttered. "Where do you think I'd go in this condition?"

Leaving Derek in charge of the victim, I jogged over to

my cruiser, Brigit running along beside me, her tags jingling like a Christmas sleigh. When I reached the patrol car, I unlocked it and pulled the printouts from the boot stores out of my bag. After locking the cruiser back up, I hurried back to Gallatin.

I held the documents out to him. "Look through this. See if you spot those boots."

Before Gallatin could take the papers from me, Derek snatched them out of my hand. He paged through them then eyed me suspiciously as he held up the documents. "What's this?"

I had to tell him the truth. For one, it would help him do his job as a cop. For two, he had a direct line to Chief Garelik. If I wasn't up front with Derek, he could sic the chief on my ass. "Everyone who's been robbed here has reported a potential accomplice with colorful boots."

Derek's eyes narrowed. "Why didn't you tell the rest of us?"

"I did. Remember when I told everyone to look out for a girl wearing black and green boots? You asked if that was all she was wearing. Suggested we put out an APB."

Derek's expression turned sour. He couldn't deny it.

"Besides," I added. "All of those details were in my reports. I left copies along with a summary memo in the office here. It read *urgent* across the top in twenty-four-point type. Didn't you read it?"

He didn't bother answering me verbally, responding only with a snort.

I snatched the printout back out of his hands and passed it to Gallatin. "Take a look."

The man glanced down at the pages. "It's too dark. I can hardly tell what I'm looking at here."

I activated the flashlight app on my phone and shined the illuminated screen down on the pages. He flipped through them, stopping on a pair of boots identified as the

Tan Arizona model. He jabbed a finger at the picture. "That's what they looked like."

The boots were sold at the Justin Boots outlet store, just like some of the pairs the female victims had identified. I dared not let myself get too excited. Yes, this tidbit helped me narrow down which boot store to hit first, but the lead wouldn't necessarily pan out. The store could have sold dozens of these types of boots, maybe even hundreds. This Crystal woman might have paid for them in cash, which would be untraceable. Heck, for all I knew she'd borrowed the boots from a friend. Or she could be from out of town. Maybe she was just in town for the rodeo and had ordered the boots online. I'd had a similar lead in the bombing case and it had gone nowhere. Nevertheless, I was glad to have some direction.

The paramedics arrived then. I let them tend to Mr. Gallatin. I figured I'd gotten pretty much all I could from him.

Chief Garelik came riding up on one of the courtesy golf carts, jumping off before the stock show staff member driving the cart could bring it to a full stop.

"What the hell is going on?" he barked.

Derek crossed his arms over his chest and looked at me expectantly, as if I were responsible for this crime and therefore should be the one to explain it to the chief.

I gestured to the man sitting on the gurney and being poked and prodded by the paramedics. "This is Sloane Gallatin, sir. He came out to his truck with a young woman he met in the dance hall. When he realized she had taken his wallet out of his back pocket, he grabbed her wrist to stop her. She responded by kneeing him in the groin and then hitting and shocking him with a cattle prod she'd pulled from the bed of his truck."

"So now we've got actual injuries?" The chief turned and kicked the back tire of the golf cart, taking his frustrations out on the vehicle, startling the driver. "I tell you what!" the chief bellowed. "This godforsaken stock show can't end soon enough for me. It's been a cluster fuck of epic proportions!"

With that he put a hand on Derek's shoulder. "Let's go get a goddamn beer."

The two of them climbed into the golf cart and the driver took off. Having loaded Gallatin into the ambulance, the paramedics climbed into the cab and drove off, too.

I waited for the crime scene tech to arrive, directing people not to walk between Gallatin's truck and the one parked next to it. "Protected area!" I called, motioning with my hand for them to circle around the other side of the vehicles. "Go around that way, please."

The crime scene tech arrived and used tongs to pick up the cattle prod and place it in a large plastic evidence bag. While he carefully scanned the ground for any overlooked pieces of evidence—a piece of the woman's jewelry, a button from her jacket, maybe a cell phone dropped in the struggle—I shined my large flashlight over his shoulder and under Gallatin's pickup and the one next to it.

"I don't see anything," he said from his prone position between the trucks. "Other than some cigarette butts, a plastic straw, and some goat droppings." With that he pushed himself to his knees and began to gather his things.

The *clop-clop-clopping* of horse hooves on asphalt drew my attention to the right. Clint rode up on Jack. He'd traded his chaps and spurs for his deputy uniform. Back on duty, evidently.

He pulled his horse to a stop in front of me. "Hey."

I looked up at him. "Hey yourself."

The tech raised a silent hand in good-bye. I gave him a nod of acknowledgment before returning my attention to my favorite deputy.

Clint pulled a new blue ribbon from his pocket. "Another one for the trophy case."

"Congratulations," I told him. "Looks like this was a lucky night for you."

"Luck, nothin'. Blue ribbons are earned with talent. And skill. And balls."

"Well, I suppose you're lucky to have that talent and skill."

"Don't forget the balls."

I pursed my lips. "Of course. How could I?"

"I just hope I'll be wearing a new championship belt buckle come next Saturday night."

The night would mark the final rounds of the rodeo events and the end of the stock show. Frankly, the night couldn't come soon enough for me, either. I was tired of patrolling outside in the cold. Tired of the evasive purse snatchers and pickpockets. The only thing I wasn't tired of was Clint and his gorgeous brown eyes.

He cocked his head. "Heard you were asking about me."

My face warmed with a blush. "Just wondering where you'd gone."

"Did you miss me?"

I put a hand on Jack's velvety nose. "I missed your horse."

Clint pulled his foot from the stirrup and nudged my butt with his boot. "Come on. You missed me a little bit, too. Admit it."

I slapped his foot away. "Okay. I did miss you. But *only* a little bit." No sense giving this guy a bigger head than he already had at the moment. Besides, men never wanted a woman they didn't have to work for. Not for long, anyway. I'd watched enough romantic comedies to know that. I supposed I wouldn't want a guy I didn't have to work for, either.

Clint stared down me for a moment. "How are things with 'boy trouble'? Still uncertain?"

Things with Seth were more certain than they'd been a week ago, but I wasn't ready to commit just yet. I was still getting to know Seth, still trying to figure him out, what made him tick, still wondering whether I could fully trust him, whether he was relationship material. He'd come to me the night of the fire seeking solace, which spoke volumes about how he looked at me now. Still, no sense in investing all of myself in one man until I was sure about things. Diversifying my portfolio would pose less risk, right? Nonetheless, a sense of guilt settled on my shoulders. I might not be ready to commit to Seth, but I didn't want to lead him on. I didn't want to lead Clint on, either, though given that he was aware of Seth he seemed to be walking into whatever this was with his eyes wide open.

I ran a hand over Jack's shoulder, trying to decide how to respond.

A man of action, Clint didn't wait. He nudged me again with his boot. "Nothing wrong with you and me having a drink, is there?"

I looked up at him. "I suppose not."

"Well, well, well." His brown eyes lit with a spark. "Looks like this is my lucky night, after all."

FORTY-ONE
PAWING AND PETTING

Brigit

Megan left Brigit at her apartment and set off with Clint. She didn't even give Brigit a chew toy or dry dog biscuit to keep the dog occupied before she left.

How rude. Stupid, too. Had Megan learned nothing?

Well, Brigit would show her. Just as soon as she figured out how to open the closet door. Megan had removed the lever-style handle and replaced it with a round type that would be much harder for Brigit to open. *Damn my lack of opposable thumbs!* What's more, the handle had a lock on it. A lock that required a key. Not that Brigit fully understood what the jagged hole in the center of the knob meant. She only knew that after an hour of trying, she still couldn't get the darn door open.

Well, if I can't pull the door open, I'll just have to go through it, won't I?

She put her paws to the door and began scratching her way through.

* * *

When Megan returned with Clint, Brigit could tell she was furious. The floor was covered with splintered wood and the soggy, bite-marked remains of a tennis shoe and a fuzzy green slipper. Not exactly gourmet fare, but Brigit had worked her way through Megan's footwear over the past few weeks and pickings had become slim. Besides, she'd had to take what she could manage to grab. Megan had moved her shoes to the top shelf of the closet. They hadn't been easy to reach.

Megan glared down at the dog. "Wish I had that cattle prod right now."

Brigit wasn't sure exactly what Megan's words meant, but by their tone she could tell Megan was enraged. She also knew if the words contained a threat it was an idle one.

Megan might be a tough cop, but when it came to her furry partner she was all bark and no bite.

FORTY-TWO
SOLE PROPRIETOR

Robin Hood

Could her sisters have been any less helpful when that man had grabbed her wrist last night? For God's sake, they'd just stood there screaming, like a couple of little girls who'd seen a mouse. As usual, Robin Hood had had to do all of the heavy lifting.

Despite the fight the man put up, she had nonetheless managed to get away with his wallet. That cattle prod sure had come in handy. Of course she couldn't count on being so lucky again next time should one of her targets try to restrain her. No, she'd have to make sure she could defend herself. She'd sign up for karate lessons later this week, become a female Chuck Norris. *Hi-yah!* The classes would be a good workout, too, keep her in shape until she could land a husband and become the trophy wife she'd always dreamed of being. But, until she became proficient in martial arts, she needed a means of defense. That's why she was on her way to a pawnshop to buy a gun. Of course it wouldn't be the same pawnshop where she'd tried to sell the rings.

The man's wallet had held three hundred dollars in cash. Well worth the sore, bruised wrist she suffered today. He'd wrenched it good before she'd taken him down with a knee to the nuts. Still, she couldn't help but feel that all of that cash should have been hers. Her sisters had done nothing to earn their hundred-dollar shares. If anything, they'd jeopardized the operation, what with their shrieking drawing unnecessary attention.

Amateurs.

That's why she'd decided she'd work alone from now on. Well, that and the fact that her sisters had told her in no uncertain terms that they were out, that the risks were too great, that taking someone's money was one thing but hurting people was going too far. They thought she should've given the man his wallet back when he'd asked for it. Robin Hood snorted. A little bit of violence and they couldn't handle it. *Chickenshits.* Good riddance as far as she was concerned. She would get along just fine without them. Besides, she'd replace them with two new assistants. Who needs Merry Men when you've got Smith and Wesson?

The pawnshop contained the expected assortment of sketchy characters, some tooling around on the guitars, others looking over the electronics, one working sales at the gun counter. As much as the thought of a used gun repulsed her, she'd rather save her funds for clothing and accessories.

As she approached the counter, the clerk leered, revealing teeth upon which algae appeared to be growing. His hair looked like something you'd pull out of a dryer's lint trap.

"I want to buy a gun," she said.

"You looking for protection?" He leaned over the counter and looked her up and down suggestively. "Maybe you should just get yourself a man."

"A man? Sure. You know one?"

Cowed, the guy stepped back, casting her a furious look before getting down to business. "What kinda gun you want?"

"Something small and lightweight that will fit in my purse. One that's easy to use."

Without a word the clerk reached down and pulled a small black handgun out of the case. He laid it on the counter in front of her. "Beretta nine-millimeter Nano. You'd pay four hundred new. Our price is one twenty-five. Can't beat that with a stick."

She laughed and cut him a look. "Oh, you'd be surprised what I might beat with a stick."

The guy had the sense to look downright concerned now.

She picked up the gun. It was lighter than she had expected, easy to grip. She held it up and pretended to take aim at a framed *Iron Man* movie poster. *Bang!* she thought. *Bang! Bang! Bang!* Take that, you stupid superhero.

Satisfied, she turned her attention back to the clerk. "I'll take it. Give me some ammo, too."

In less than ten minutes, she was armed and out the door. So easy. *God bless Texas.*

FORTY-THREE
HOUSE CALLS

Megan

Given that the thieves had now caused serious bodily injury to a victim, Chief Garelik officially assigned a detective to the case. The detective phoned me early Saturday morning and arranged for me to meet him that evening at the stock show. Of course I'd then immediately phoned my mentor, Detective Jackson, to ask for a heads-up about the guy.

"Who got the case?" she asked.

"Detective Hector Bustamente," I said. "Do y-you know him?"

"Oh, yeah," she said. "Me and old Bust-a-move were in the academy together back in the day. Heck, we were just kids then."

When I asked for information about the detective, Jackson warned me not to judge a book by its cover. "He's a clever guy, though you wouldn't know it to look at him. He can be very disarming, charm a confession out of the tightest lips. He has an innate ability to understand criminals, to figure out their motivations and reasoning. Watch him closely, see how he handles things. You could learn a lot."

Exactly what I'd hoped for. Another potential mentor.

Given that I was already up, I figured I might as well make a run by Cheyenne's and Mia's residences to see if I might catch them today. With it being the weekend now, maybe I'd have better luck.

I dressed in my uniform, rounded up Brigit, and snagged our patrol car from the W1 lot. Fifteen minutes later I pulled up in front of Mia's duplex. An older-model pickup with a camper shell was backed up to the open garage door. Inside the garage, Mia and a stocky, dark-haired man moved large cardboard boxes around. The boxes were imprinted with the names of sport shoe brands. Nike. Adidas. New Balance. Reebok. Fila. Not exactly the type of thing one would expect to find in a residential garage. If I had to hazard a guess, I'd say these two had ripped off the inventory from a delivery truck or a store's stockroom.

Looks like Mia's brush with the law hadn't scared her straight.

Shame.

The man picked up one of the boxes, turned to slide it into his truck, and froze when he spotted me and Brigit standing at the end of the driveway.

"Hello, there!" I called. "Want to tell me what you're doing with those boxes of shoes?"

He glanced back at Mia.

She raised a hand as she stepped toward him. "Don't say anything!"

If I hadn't known before that they were up to no good, I certainly did now.

"You have receipts for that merchandise?" I asked, moving up the drive toward them.

Mia sidled toward the door at the side of the garage that led into the house. "We don't have to tell you anything!"

She pushed the button to lower the garage door, leaving the bewildered guy standing outside on the driveway, still holding the box of stolen goods.

As the door came down, I stepped forward, whisked my baton from my belt, and extended it. I swung my baton underneath the door. The sensor registered the movement and the door changed direction, heading back up now.

I pushed the button on my shoulder mic and requested backup. "I've got two suspects in possession of stolen property." I gave dispatch the address.

"Stay right here!" I ordered the man, pointing my baton at him. "Don't move or you will be very sorry!"

I unclipped Brigit's leash and went to the door inside the garage. I turned the knob to find that Mia had locked it behind her. Running back out of the garage, I tried the front door. It, too, was locked.

The sound of feet scrambling on wood out back drew me to the gate of the six-foot privacy fence that surrounded the backyard.

"Dammit!" The gate was locked, too. These people sure did love their locks.

With Brigit running loose by my side, I darted back, past the man in the driveway, and dashed to the end of the block. In the distance, Mia ran full speed across the road and down another side street. She was damn fast. She must be a runner herself.

Knowing I'd never catch Mia with the lead she had on me, I checked for cars and, seeing none, gave Brigit the signal to take Mia down. Brigit's nails scrabbled on the asphalt as she took off after her quarry.

I ran after my partner, lagging half a block behind, then three quarters of a block, then a full block. Ahead, Brigit gained on Mia by leaps and bounds. Mia turned her head just as the dog launched herself into the air. The impact of one hundred pounds of furry beast sent Mia sprawling forward on the sidewalk, her shrieks shrill in the winter-morning air. *"Aaah! Aaah!"*

Knowing Mia was under Brigit's control now, I stopped running and walked the rest of the way, trying to catch my breath.

When I reached Mia, I pulled out my handcuffs and bent down next to her. I grabbed her left hand and cuffed it around the wrist. Calling Brigit off her, I waited for the dog to move, then cuffed her right wrist. "Up to your old tricks, are you?"

"I have no idea what you're talking about," Mia spat.

"Stealing jewelry? At the stock show?"

"I haven't been to the stupid stock show," she snarled. "That's for hicks."

I stood and nudged her with my foot until she turned over. She had a bloody scrape on her chin and cheek, and a look in her eyes that could cut through metal.

"Where were you last night?" I demanded.

"At the movies with friends. Then we went to Chili's for a late dinner."

"Can you prove it?"

"Yeah. I can prove it."

"What about last Friday?"

"Stars game," she said.

"Can you prove that, too?"

She snorted indignantly. "Got the ticket stub and program."

I yanked her to her feet and Brigit and I escorted her back to her house. She produced a movie ticket stub and receipt from Chili's indicating she'd eaten a burger and fries late last night, along with a margarita. The time stamp on the food receipt was right around the time we found Sloane Gallatin writhing in the parking lot. The Stars ticket checked out, too.

"Told you," she snapped.

So Mia was not one of the stock show thieves. She was, however, selling stolen tennis shoes, thus earning herself a ride to the lockup.

I stopped by Cheyenne's apartment next. A young woman with brown hair answered the door. I wondered whether she might be one of the accomplices.

"Hi," I said. "Are you Crystal?"

She shook her head. "No. There's no Crystal here. Sorry."

"Actually, I'm l-looking for Cheyenne Wembley. She around?"

"She's at work."

"Where's that?"

"Dairy Queen on Montgomery."

"Thanks."

I hopped back in the car and drove to the Dairy Queen. Brigit and I went inside and stepped up to the counter. Might as well get my partner some lunch while we were here. "Two plain burgers," I told the lanky boy working the counter, "hold everything."

I handed him my debit card and he ran it through the machine. As he handed me my card and receipt, I asked, "Is Cheyenne Wembley available? I need to speak with her."

He stepped back a few feet and called into the food prep area. "Cheyenne! There's a cop here wants to talk to you."

Cheyenne's face popped up over the soda machine, her eyes alight with anxiety. Her reaction could mean she was guilty. Then again, people tended to get nervous around cops, even if they were innocent.

"I'll be right there," she said.

She finished Brigit's burgers, wrapped them, and handed them to the counter clerk, who in turn handed them to me. When Cheyenne came around the counter, I gestured to an empty booth in the far corner where we could have some privacy. "Let's sit over there."

Cheyenne took a seat on one side of the booth, while Brigit and I slid into the other. Knowing Brigit would wolf down the burgers whole if left on her own, I tore her lunch into smaller, digestible bites and fed them to her one by one, forcing her to pace herself.

"I know about your criminal record," I told Cheyenne, keeping my voice low. "That you and a friend stole purses from customers at the sports bar where you worked."

Across the store, a middle-aged woman stepped up behind the counter, wiping down plastic trays and eyeing us.

Cheyenne cast a worried glance in her manager's direction. "That was a mistake," she said. "They know about it here. That's why I have to work the grill and fryer. They won't let me near a cash register. But why are you asking about that?"

"Someone's been mugging women at the stock show," I said. "Taking their purses and jewelry. You know anything about that?"

"No." Her eyes widened. "You don't think I did it, do you?"

"I'm here, aren't I?" Again with the bluster.

"I didn't do it! I swear!" She made an *X* over the left side of her chest with her finger. "Cross my heart and hope to die!"

What is this, junior high? "Where were you last Friday night?"

Her eyes went up as if she were thinking back. "Here," she said. "I worked the late shift that night."

"Can you prove it?"

"We have to punch in when we get here and when we leave. My manager can show you my time card."

She stood, scurried up to the counter, and spoke with the manager. The woman nodded, put down the tray she was drying, and disappeared into the employee-only area at the rear of the restaurant. A minute or so later, she reappeared with a slip of paper in her hand and handed it to Cheyenne.

"See," Cheyenne said, handing me the time card when she returned to the table. "That shows I was here last Friday from five in the evening until two in the morning."

Indeed it did. Looked like Cheyenne wasn't the stock show thief. Her crossed heart would continue to beat indefinitely.

"Thanks for clearing that up," I told her as I stood to go.

"So we're good?" Cheyenne asked.

"We're good." I rounded up Brigit's leash and gave the manager a nod and a friendly wave as we headed out the door.

FORTY-FOUR
WELL DONE

Brigit

Warm burgers for lunch? What a great day!

Her partner had finally learned to leave off the pickles and onions and lettuce and tomatoes. It had taken weeks of training, of Brigit spitting out the vegetables in the cruiser and on the floor of Megan's apartment, but her partner had finally figured things out.

Now if Brigit could just convince her to move to a bigger place . . .

FORTY-FIVE
NEW STOMPING GROUNDS

Robin Hood

She didn't return to the stock show Saturday night, concerned that Sloane what's-his-name-and-who-really-gives-a-crap-anyway had given a description to the police and that she might be recognized. Of course the description he'd given would have been of a redhead. The sleazeball from the weekend before would have described her as a brunette. The two women who'd tried to chase her after she'd snatched their purses from the bathroom had told the police the thief was a blonde. Probably the police had no real idea who to keep an eye out for. She could be anyone.

Still, she'd be a fool to return to the event. She could tell that both the Fort Worth PD and the Tarrant County Sheriff's Department had beefed up patrols after the purse snatchings, and surely they'd added even more officers after what went down last night. The police chief had said as much when he'd been interviewed on television earlier today. He'd assured viewers that the stock show was safe, that additional officers had been deployed, and that it was only a matter of time before the person or persons behind the rash of robberies would be caught.

Yeah, right.

They'd never catch her. Just as the sheriff of Nottingham had been helpless to stop the fictional Robin Hood, law enforcement would never catch up with her. She'd stay one step ahead of them, changing her MO to knock them off track, keep them guessing. After all, there was no sense taking unnecessary chances. Tonight she'd forgo the stock show and instead head up to the north side. There would be plenty of out-of-towners up there she could set her sights on.

She'd dressed in stilettos, jeans, and another tight, low-cut top, this one in a shimmery black fabric. She parked in a paid lot, sliding a ten-dollar bill into the automated machine and punching in her parking space number. She stepped onto the sidewalk and aimed directly for the White Elephant Saloon.

A Fort Worth legend, the White Elephant Saloon was purportedly the site of a gunfight between a corrupt lawman and the bar's owner way back when. The place was always brimming with tourists impressed by the fact that scenes from *Walker, Texas Ranger* had been filmed there.

She paid the five-dollar cover charge and stepped inside. It was against the law for her to be carrying a gun into a bar, but who would know? Besides, after what had happened the night before, she wouldn't have felt safe without it.

She took a look around. The place contained the usual dark wood found in many such bars, with the standard neon beer signs gracing the walls. The wide-horned head of a black-and-white steer was mounted on the wall over the bar, the beast appearing to be keeping watch over the crowd. Cowboy hats in a variety of colors adorned the upper part of the walls and continued across the ceiling.

She had arrived early enough to snag a seat at the bar,

giving her a good vantage point from which to watch both the men coming in and those stepping up to order a drink, as well as giving her a bead on the band, which had just begun to set up on stage. She ordered a frozen margarita, then turned on her barstool, facing into the room, resting a crooked elbow on the bar behind her and angling herself in a backward lean so that her breasts would appear bigger and perkier. Having practiced in the mirror at home, she knew exactly how she looked.

Unattached.

Sexy.

Inviting.

With any luck, a man with a wallet full of cash would soon accept that invitation. *Répondez s'il vous plaît.* She chuckled inwardly. Sure, she might be an uppity snob, but her two sisters were nothing but stupid white trash.

Though a few men passed by with their wives or dates, their eyes responding to her invitation with sincere and lascivious regrets, it was a mere half hour later when the subtle summons she'd sent out was accepted. A bulky, thirtyish guy who'd been eyeing her from across the way sneaked up and grabbed the seat next to her when the woman who'd been sitting there paid her tab and moseyed.

"Hello, there." He had sandy hair, friendly blue eyes, and a sociable demeanor. No cheap beer for this guy. He held a cocktail glass filled with dark liquid. Scotch, probably. Or maybe bourbon. But, more importantly, the hand that held the glass sported a gold nugget pinky ring. A shiny, expensive-looking TAG Heuer watch encircled his thick wrist. His boots also looked expensive. Instead of the usual leather, they were made of some type of exotic hide, ostrich, if she wasn't mistaken.

This could be my luckiest night yet. If she could somehow manage to get the jewelry off this guy, she could sell it on eBay or Craigslist, too.

Her visual inventory complete, she returned his greeting. "Hi."

She'd left her hair natural tonight. His gaze traveled down the blond locks cascading over her shoulders, traversed her pushed-up breasts, then made its way back up, lingering for a moment on her glossy lips as if he were imagining what things those glossy lips could do.

"I'm Sam Gunderson," he said, extending his hand.

She took her hand in his. "Robin." She glanced down at his feet. "Nice boots."

"They're Luccheses," he said. "Ostrich. Set me back eleven hundred dollars."

He was obviously trying to impress her. *And impress her he had.* For God's sake, the guy might as well have said *If you're looking for some rich fool to rob tonight, look no further!* She tossed him a coy smile and a *tsk-tsk.* "You poor thing."

He chuckled, took a sip from his glass, then slid her an assessing glance. "You alone?"

She lifted a shoulder. "I was supposed to meet a friend, but she texted me a little while ago and said she's not feeling well." Robin Hood was as hard on this fictional friend as she was on her mother. "I'd already driven all this way and paid my cover charge. Figured I might as well stay and listen to the band."

Sam raised his glass in a toast. "I'm glad you did."

Their conversation was interrupted when the band's lead singer stepped to the stationary microphone and performed a sound check. "Testing. One, two, three. Testing." An irritating squeal of feedback followed.

"Come here a lot?" Sam asked, turning back to her.

"On occasion," she lied. She'd been to the White Elephant only once before. She much preferred the more sophisticated, trendier nightclubs in the neighboring city of Dallas. "How about you?"

"First time," he said. "I'm from Macon, Georgia. Came to town for the stock show."

She took a sip of her margarita. "You a cattle rancher?"

"Pig farmer."

Uck. Not exactly one of those careers a woman fantasizes her Mr. Right will have. An architect would do. Or a pilot. Any kind of doctor, of course. But a *pig farmer*? Still, there must be a lot of money in swine or he wouldn't be dressed the way he was. "You must do well," she said, casting a meaningful glance at his watch.

"Shoot." He snorted. "There's no money in pigs. I made my money in real estate."

Real estate, huh? If this guy owned valuable realty, maybe she would forgo trying to get that gold nugget ring off *his* finger and see if he'd put a ring on *her* finger instead. She hadn't yet given up on becoming a trophy wife and, pigs aside, this guy was reasonably attractive and age appropriate. Perhaps she should expand her range of acceptable candidates. And, hell, it's not like she'd have to stay married to him forever. A year or two should be enough to give her a sizable divorce settlement, right? If she decided to pursue this avenue, she could easily explain that she'd given him a fake name for protection. "You own property?"

"Some. When my father passed away, he left me fifteen acres in Rabun County, up near Dick's Knob."

She choked on her margarita. "Did you just say *Dick's Knob*?" What kind of ridiculous, hillbilly name was that?

Sam chuckled. "It's a mountain."

She blinked twice. "Good to know."

Sam went on. "Dad used to take me hunting up there when I was little. We'd stay in this little shack he'd built himself. No electricity, no running water. Boy, we'd smell ripe when we got back home after those weekends."

How charming.

He shook his head but smiled at the memory. "A

developer approached me a few months back and offered
me a shitload for six of the acres. They're going to build a
resort and spa up there."

The remaining adjacent property would only go up in
value. This pig farmer could be sitting on a gold mine.

She raised her glass in a toast. "Congratulations on your
windfall."

He tapped his glass to hers and took another drink.
"What do you do?" He leaned toward her, offering a flirtatious smile and a look that fell just short of a leer. "I'll
bet you're a supermodel, aren't you?"

Could he be any more obvious? "How'd you guess?"

What she did was none of his business. Besides, what
she did was what she had to do to get by until her ship came
in. She was beginning to wonder if the guy on the stool
next to her just might be that ship. She could almost hear
the foghorn.

Wee-ohh.

FORTY-SIX
A NEW MENTOR

Megan

I began my shift and strolled about the stock show grounds, twirling my baton as Brigit and I patrolled. *Swish-swish-swish.*

Today, a local *ballet folklorico* group was performing on the outdoor stage. I stopped to watch them, enjoying the festive music, the colorful dresses of the performers, their graceful dance maneuvers.

When they finished, I joined in the applause and set back out to patrol. *Swish-swish-swish.* As I walked I tossed the baton into the air and caught it behind my back.

A woman wearing one of the stock show staff shirts rode up on her golf cart. "You sure are good with that baton."

"Thanks. I twirled in high school."

"We could use someone to fill in time on closing night," she said, "while the judges are adding up the scores at the rodeo. Would you be interested? Or willing?"

It had been a long time since I'd performed in front of

a crowd, and back then I'd been surrounded by a couple hundred members of the marching band. Still, it could be fun.

"So long as my supervisor okays it, I'd be happy to," I told her. "I've got fire batons. You think the crowd would like to see me twirl those?"

"Heck, yeah! These rodeo crowds love anything that smacks of danger."

Fire certainly was dangerous. Nobody knew that better than Seth and Savannah.

The woman told me where to check in and at what time. She raised a hand before setting off. "Thanks again! You'll be a big hit!"

I hoped so. I wasn't sure my performance could compare with bull- and bronc-riders who had an apparent death wish, but I'd do my best. Give that 110 percent. Maybe I'd even go for 111 percent this time.

It was straight up nine P.M. when I took a seat across the desk from Detective Bustamente in the temporary police station in the Will Rogers Tower. Bustamente was a portly man with thick lips, round cheeks, and dark, crazy brows in dire need of a trim. His argyle sweater and slacks were just ill-fitting and wrinkled enough to make him seem ignorant and unimpressive. But given Jackson's warning, I knew better than to underestimate this guy.

Derek hovered in the office, pretending to be checking work-related e-mail on his phone, but it was more likely he simply wanted to listen in on my conversation with the detective, butt his way into the case.

Bustamente must've had the same suspicions, or so I thought.

"Officer Mackey," he said, "please close the door behind you as you leave."

The Big Dick's ears flamed red, but he left the room

without argument. He did slam the door behind him, though. *Bam!*

"Don't want him listening in?" I asked.

"Don't want him on my planet."

Detective Bustamente and I are going to get along great.

Though he had read through my reports, as well as the urgent memo ignored by my fellow patrol officers, the detective asked me to go through everything again. "Sometimes when I'm talking to an officer, a detail will come out that's not in the reports. Some itsy-bitsy teenie-weenie factoid that can make all the difference."

I gave him a rundown of everything that had happened at the stock show and rodeo, beginning with Catherine Quimby's snatched purse and ending with Sloane Gallatin's punctured neck and bruised balls. He took only a note or two while I spoke.

"I pulled up the criminal records for women with similar robbery and theft convictions who live in the area. I visited a couple that looked promising, but both had alibis for the nights in question. I also talked this over with Detective Audrey Jackson a few days ago. She helped me realize the boots could be a lead." I pushed the criminal record reports and Internet printout across the desk. "I printed out images of the women's boot inventory at local stores online and showed it to the victims to see if they could identify the boots worn by the accomplice, Crystal. Given what they told me, I think it's most likely that Crystal bought her boots at the Justin outlet here in town."

Bustamente took a quick look at the document, noting the pairs of boots the victims had identified, and nodded. "Got anything else?"

I handed him the thumb drive that contained the video feed from Starbucks and explained what it was. "Unfortunately, I couldn't glean anything new from the footage."

"That's a bummer." He slid the thumb drive into his pocket.

I pulled my notepad from my pocket and ripped off the page on which I'd written the name and phone number of the head of security at the Kroger store where Dominique's credit card had been used, as well as the store's address. "I made an appointment with store security for Monday morning at nine. They've arranged for the cashier who handled the transaction to be there, too."

The detective eyed me intently for a moment. "You've put quite a bit of thought and time into this."

I shrugged. "Just doing my job."

"No," he said. "You've been doing *my* job. Gunning for a detective position, aren't you?"

"Is it that obvious?"

"To a detective it is." He chuckled. "Actually, Detective Jackson called me earlier to put in a good word for you. She said you're a dedicated cop and a hard worker with good instincts. Lord knows we can always use more of those."

"If there's any way I can help in your investigation," I told him, "I'd be happy to."

"Let's do this," he said. "I'll meet you at the grocery store Monday morning, then we'll scoot from there over to the boot place. That work for you?"

That worked just fine. "Yes, sir!"

Brigit and I set back out on patrol. Seemed every minute or two we'd pass another cop. With so much law enforcement on duty, the thieves would have to be fools to pull anything here tonight.

Evidently, the thieves were no fools.

The event closed down with no purses having been snatched, no pockets having been picked, and no cattle ranchers having been kneed in the groin or prodded.

Frankly, it was a damn boring night.

FORTY-SEVEN
DULL PATROL

Brigit

She and Megan walked around the stock show grounds yet again. Brigit saw the same sights. Heard the same sounds. Sniffed the same odors. Well, the same odors minus the two colognes she'd smelled so often recently. Whoever wore those scents wasn't here tonight.

Nobody accidentally dropped their hot dog and let Brigit eat it. None of the pigs or goats ventured close enough to the bars of their enclosures for Brigit to take a nip at them. They didn't even see Jack the horse or the guy who rode him.

Frankly, it was a damn boring night.

FORTY-EIGHT
PILLOW TALK

Robin Hood

When her glass emptied, Sam signaled the bartender for another round, tossing his triple bourbon back in six seconds flat when it arrived.

She offered a flirtatious giggle when he slammed his glass down on the bar. "You are obviously a man who knows how to have a good time."

"Hoo-hoo! You know it!" With a lift of his chin, Sam signaled the bartender for yet another drink.

They made small talk for an hour or so, during which time Sam plowed through three more triple bourbons. She asked him what Macon was like. He complimented her on her shoes. She asked what kind of pigs he raised. He complimented her on the way her jeans showed off her legs. She asked him where he was staying. He offered—in slurred, bourbon-scented words—to take her back to his room and show her.

"Why not?" She gathered her jacket and purse. By that point, she'd given up on the idea of becoming a pig farmer's trophy wife. The guy was a sloppy drunk with an irritating pet phrase, too boorish for her refined tastes no matter how much valuable real estate he might own. But he might have more jewelry back at his hotel room that she could snatch. As many drinks as he'd had she could probably steal it right from under his nose.

Sam asked the bartender for the tab, signed the paper slip, and slid his credit card back into his wallet, which bore a Hugo Boss logo. The guy might be a pig farmer, but he had good taste.

Sam stood from his barstool, weaving dangerously on his feet as he made his way through the saloon, bumping into people and tables like a ball in a pinball machine. He stumbled on his way out the door, but she was able to catch his arm and prevent him from falling.

The bouncer working the door stepped in front of them and put a hand on Sam's chest. "You're not driving, are you?"

"Nope!" Sam said, much too loudly. "I'm the designated drunk tonight! Hoo-hoo!"

Passersby cast them various glances, some amused, others disgusted. She didn't mind the amusement, but being looked down upon did not sit well with her.

Sam draped his arm over her shoulders, nearly bringing her down when he put too much weight on her.

"You got 'im?" the bouncer asked her. "Sure you're okay here?"

"Yes, thanks," she said, mustering all the muscle she could to right the two of them. "I'll take care of him."

I'll take care of him, all right.

In thirty-seven wobbly steps they were inside the Stockyards Hotel, which sat directly across the street from the White Elephant Saloon. The hotel lobby was painted a terra-cotta color and featured rustic Western décor, much of it either antiques or reproductions. She'd heard that country-western stars Garth Brooks, Vince Gil, and Tri-sha Yearwood had stayed at the hotel, as well as actors Jim Belushi, Dan Aykroyd, and John Leguizamo. She was proud to be included among the hotel's esteemed guests, though she planned to stay only long enough to relieve Sam of his valuables.

As they made their way through the lobby to the elevator, she ducked her head to prevent any security cameras from getting a good look at her. She doubted anyone could identify her from the grainy videos those cameras seemed to produce, but she wasn't going to take any chances.

It took Sam three tries to hit the right button inside the elevator, but eventually his fingertip made contact and up they went. Sam's room was on the third floor. When he got the door unlocked, he threw it open, the door slamming back against the wall with a loud bang.

"Careful!" she told him. If he continued to make this kind of racket, someone would call hotel security. The last thing she needed was some rent-a-cop banging on the door.

Though only a standard room, the king-sized bed and Western décor were anything but shabby. She estimated that Sam was dropping around three hundred a night for the space. It was the nicest hotel room she'd ever been in by far. The only vacations her family had ever taken were camping trips. She'd been forced to use a common shower and toilet and sleep on the ground, protected only by a cheap nylon tent.

This was *much* better.

This is what I deserve.

Inside the room, Sam headed straight for the phone, scooped it up, and called room service, asking them in slurred, halting words to send up a bottle of champagne. "I met the prettiesht girl . . . anyone'sh ever . . . laid eyesh on," he said into the phone, casting a grin in her direction.

"If that ain't cause for . . . celebration I don't know . . . what ish."

When he finished placing the order, he attempted to drop the receiver back into the cradle but missed by a good six inches, the receiver falling to the carpet. He bent to pick it up, but ended up first stumbling forward into the wall, then falling back onto his ass. "Hoo-hoo!" he hollered from the ground, apparently entertained by himself. "Who put this floor here?"

She turned his way. "You sure more liquor is a good idea?"

Sam's mouth gaped with incredulity. "Hell, honey! More liquor ish alwaysh a good idea. Hoo-hoo!"

He struggled to a stand, returned the phone to the cradle, and careened into the bathroom, leaving the door wide open as he ambled to the toilet and unzipped his pants *Zzzip*. He put one hand on the wall to brace himself. "Youshud comoutta . . . Georgiasometime," he called out in run-together, barely coherent speech as he filled the toilet, and the floor around it, with hundred-proof urine. "Peashtrees are . . . purtywhen tharbloomin'."

Talking to me while he takes a piss? She felt her gut clench in revulsion and rage. His behavior was too familiar and offensive. What kind of woman did he think she was? Some common tramp?

While Sam did his business, she discreetly cased the room, pretending to admire the Western art on the walls and the view from the window while actually making a mental inventory. *An iPad on the nightstand. A silver horseshoe-shaped ring with diamonds on the dresser. A black leather camera bag with the Canon logo.*

She'd bet the camera was top-of-the-line, just like his boots, watch, and wallet. As she looked around she was careful not to touch anything. She didn't want to leave any fingerprints the cops could use to identify her.

She glanced into the bathroom, where Sam was washing his hands. If he hadn't left the bathroom door open, she would've shoved everything into her purse and been on her way immediately. But given that he'd have a clear view of her sneaking out, and that room service was coming, she figured she better not chance it.

Sam came out of the bathroom, unbuttoning his shirt along the way. He plopped down onto the bed, and pulled off his boots, releasing both a sigh and the faint odor of sweaty feet. After tossing his boots aside, he backed up against the pillows, settling in. He grabbed the remote from the night table and turned the TV on, clumsily punching the buttons, inadvertently turning the volume up to a near deafening level until he finally managed to hit the channel change button and find ESPN.

"Could you turn that down?" she called over the din.

"Could I *what*?" he hollered.

Drunken idiot. Irritated, she darted to the bed, grabbed the remote out of his hand, and jabbed the volume button until it had been lowered to a reasonable level. She then turned away from him and used the hem of her sweater to rub the remote free of any prints.

He patted the bed next to him. "Have a . . . seat, Rhonda. Let'sh watch . . . Sportshcenter."

She wasn't sure which offended her more. The fact that the jerk couldn't even remember the fake name she'd given him or that he'd rather watch some dumb sports show than try to get into her pants right away. It was just as well, she supposed. She had no intention of sleeping with the guy. If absolutely necessary she'd give him a hand job to satisfy him, then once he nodded off she'd round up the goodies and be on her way.

Wait. Could the cops dust his dick for fingerprints?

She wasn't sure. But there was no way in hell she'd leave a potential saliva sample instead.

She sat gingerly on the edge of the bed, casting a glance back at him. His drooping, unfocused eyes and deep breathing told her there was probably not much harm in climbing onto the bed with him. As drunk as he was, it was doubtful he'd even be able to participate in the limited sexual activity she'd had in mind. He'd probably fall asleep in a minute or two. It took everything in her not to shout *Hip! Hip! Hooray!* If she could get out of here without having to touch him she'd be thrilled.

She pushed herself backward and positioned herself up against the pillows on the other side of the bed. Just as she settled in, a knock sounded at the door. The room service had arrived. When Sam went to stand, he went totally off-kilter, falling sideways into the dresser.

She raised her hand. "Sit down, Sam. I'll take care of this."

He turned and dove back onto the bed, sending the mattress sliding until it lay cockeyed on the box spring.

She answered the door, but averted her face, hoping to prevent the waiter from getting a good look at her. The room service staff wheeled in a small cart loaded with a bottle of champagne in an ice bucket and two champagne flutes. The man looked from her to Sam, apparently waiting for a tip.

"Tip?" she asked, turning to Sam.

"Tip?" Sam repeated, a dopey, drunken smile on his face. "Hell, honey, I'll give you the whole thing! Hoo-hoo!"

This pig farmer is the worst kind of swine. Huffing, she grabbed his wallet from the dresser and pulled out a ten-dollar bill. Keeping her head down, she handed it to the waiter. "Thank you."

"My pleasure," he said with a slight dip of his head. "Enjoy."

"Bring me that bottle, Rachel!" Sam hollered as the door closed.

"Keep your voice down!" she hissed. Wrapping her hand in a cloth napkin, she pulled the champagne from the ice and carried the dripping bottle across the room to the bed. She thrust the bottle at him. "Here."

"Hoo-hoo!" Sam called again, wiping at the drops that had fallen to his white undershirt. "That's chilly!"

He yanked the bottle from her hands and clawed at the foil wrap at the top until he managed to remove it. He put the bottle between his thighs to hold it still, put his thumbs on the plastic cork, and pushed with his fingertips. Twice the bottle slipped out from between his legs, but she made no move to help him. She wasn't about to leave her prints on that bottle. Eventually, Sam managed to get the bottle open with a resounding pop.

He raised the bottle and eyed her with pupils that couldn't quite seem to focus. "Here'sh to pretty ladiesh!" he slurred, putting the bottle to his lips, tipping it up and taking a huge swig. He ran the back of his hand across his mouth and held the bottle out to her. "Here! Have a drink."

Ew. Like she'd drink from his slobber-covered bottle. Still, she needed to keep up the pretense. She put her thumb over the hole and pretended to turn it up to her lips. When she pulled the bottle away, she gave him a forced smile. "Good stuff."

"Don't hog it!" he hollered, grabbing the bottle back out of her hands. "Hoo-hoo!"

She made a mental note to wipe the bottle clean once Sam was done with it.

He continued to chug the champagne as if it were Kool-Aid and he were a kid at summer camp. She briefly feared for his liver. Then she realized his liver wasn't her problem.

When Sam patted the bed again, she slid onto it once more, keeping a couple feet between them.

He eased across the space and wrapped an arm over her

shoulders, nearly bending her in two with the weight of his meaty limb. He nuzzled her neck. "Time to say my bedtime prayers! *Now I lay you down to shcrew . . .* hoo-hoo!"

Dear Lord. Could this guy be a bigger ass?

He continued to drink as *Sportscenter* went on. When the bottle was empty, he went to set it on the night table but missed and instead dropped it to the floor. He reached over and fumbled to pick it back up but had no luck, eventually emitting a "bah!" and waving a dismissive hand.

He slumped lower and lower against the pillows, his head angling back, his mouth falling open. Just as the show wrapped up, he emitted a loud snort then segued into a snore that resembled a chain saw. *Hraaaaaaaaar. Hraaaaaaaaaaar.*

Robin Hood's lips curled up in a smile.

He's made this so easy.

She eased his arm off her and sat up.

Hraaaaaar. Hraaaaaaaar.

For God's sake. Does he have to be so damn loud? She pulled the pillow from behind her and positioned it over his face, fighting the urge to push down on it and smother him.

Though it didn't eliminate the sound entirely, the pillow helped to drown out the snores while she scurried about, packing his camera, ring, and iPad into her purse. Using a washcloth from the bathroom as an improvised glove, she opened his luggage locks as quietly as she could. She found a pair of jeans inside, along with three pairs of socks, four pairs of underpants, and a sweatshirt bearing the Atlanta Braves logo. Nothing of any value to her.

She stepped back to the bed and looked down at Sam's hand. *Dare I try to remove the nugget ring and watch? Hmmm . . .*

Hraaaaaar. Hraaaaaaaar.

Yes, she dared. This guy was dead to the world.

She reached down and pinched the pinky ring between her thumb and index finger, wiggling it back and forth, back and forth, as she eased it off his finger. She tucked the ring into the front pocket of her jeans.

Now for the watch. She reached down and put a finger on the clasp, forcing it open. Sam shifted a little as the watch slid down his hand, but continued to snore. *Hraaaaaar. Hraaaaaaaar.* As much liquor as the guy had drunk, he'd be sleeping off his booze for the next week. She grasped the loose fabric on his sleeve to gently lift his arm and grabbed the watch with her other hand as it slipped down and off his fingers. She tucked the watch into her other front pocket.

As easy as this had been, she felt a little silly for buying the gun and bringing it with her tonight. Thankfully, the weapon had been unnecessary. Good thing since she wasn't entirely sure she knew how to use it. She should probably find a gun range and get in some practice.

Gathering her purse, she took one last look around the room, satisfying herself that she'd touched nothing from which prints could be lifted. There was no evidence to prove she'd been here. For the first time in her life, she was glad to be a nobody.

"See ya', Sam," she called softly as she opened the door. "Sweet dreams."

FORTY-NINE
PHOTO BOMB

Megan

On Sunday morning, I drove to my parents' house in Arlington Heights. The place was a single-story three-bedroom, two-bath wood frame house with faded yellow paint, peeling trim, and virtually no landscaping. My busy parents had had little time for home maintenance while they were raising young children, and they continued to neglect the place out of habit.

I'd worn a long-sleeved FWPD tee and brought Brigit with me in her police vest. After the way she'd shredded my closet door, I didn't dare leave her at home for extended periods of time. She might eat through the drywall and into the apartment next door. I'd rented the crappy place because it was cheap and would free up some extra funds for repaying my student loans. I was beginning to think it would be worth a few hundred dollars more a month in rent to get a house. Maybe if Brigit had a yard to run around in she'd work off her excess energy chasing squirrels and stop taking it out on my shoes.

I parked at the curb and led my partner inside, having my usual fight with the front door, which had hung slightly askew for years and tended to stick in the frame. "Good morning!" I called as I stepped inside.

Though I saw no one, various greetings carried from the kitchen and bedrooms down the hall.

"Hey, Megan!" from Gabby.

"Yo, big sis!" from Joey.

"See if you can find my keys!" This came from my mother and was of no surprise as we went through this same routine every Sunday I came by.

My first human sighting was when my tall, dark-haired father stuck his head out of the master bedroom door, pulled the foam-covered toothbrush from his mouth, and waved it at me in greeting.

Brigit and I aimed for the kitchen, enduring a cat-caphony of hisses and yowls as we passed my mother's three orange tabby tomcats in the living room. When we reached the kitchen, Brigit promptly set to work cleaning out their food bowl. *Crunch-crunch-crunch.* I set about finding my mother's keys, looking under errant dishtowels, poking around behind the toaster, checking among the piles of mail and advertising circulars on the countertop. After a minute or two I finally located them under Gabby's algebra textbook.

"Found 'em, Mom!"

"Thanks!" She rushed into the kitchen like an auburn-haired whirlwind and grabbed the keys out of my hand. "Come on, everybody!" she yelled. "We're late!"

Ten minutes later we pulled up to the church, took the last two available spots at the far end of the lot, and ran up the stairs and into the foyer. We dipped our fingers in the holy water and crossed ourselves, putting our fingers to hearts pounding from exertion. When I'd completed my "Father, Son, and Holy Spirit" and returned my arm to my side, Brigit lifted her head and licked the remaining drops of holy water from my fingertips. I half expected a heavenly glow to erupt from her anus.

My parents, Gabby, Joey, and I slipped into the back row, with Brigit hopping up onto the pew next to me. We'd arrived just in time. The altar boys began their procession down the aisle.

After murmurs of "Thanks be to God" and various other Catholic rituals, it was time for communion. I led Brigit down the aisle with me when I went up to the altar. I knew better than to share my wafer with her, though. Last time she'd choked on it and horked it up in the pew. I'd feared I'd be smitten down by the Almighty or at the very least excommunicated.

When we returned to the pew, she lay down at my feet by the kneeler rather than sitting on the bench. She had more space down there and could stretch out to take a nap. A few minutes later my brother Joey nudged me with his elbow and pointed downward. *Holy crap!* The darn dog had chewed through the padding on the kneeler, the stuffing in tufts on the floor, the vinyl cover in shreds. I couldn't take her anywhere.

I put my hands together, closed my eyes, and prayed for forgiveness on Brigit's behalf.

Clint called me early Sunday afternoon, not long after I'd returned to my apartment. "I want to take you to dinner."

"And I want to let you take me to dinner." I'd had lunch at my parents' house. My mother had made her infamous lasagna, which Joey referred to as "las-agony." Parts of it were undercooked and the rest had burned and stuck to the pan. She'd set the dirty casserole dish on the floor and let Brigit have at the burnt remnants. A good strategy. That dog could lick anything clean. It saved a human from having to scrub the pan and it kept the dog occupied. But, needless to say, the meal had been less than satisfying. A nice dinner would be welcome.

"How's six o'clock?" Clint asked.

"Great. See you then."

Seth phoned an hour later. "Let's get together for dinner tonight."

"Sorry," I told him. "I can't."

Seth was quiet for a moment. "You having dinner with your family?"

"No."

He was quiet another moment. "You having dinner with Deputy Dawg?"

"Yes."

He wasn't quiet this time. This time he was loud. "What the hell, Megan? What's it going to take for you not to see him?"

"It's going to take . . . *time.*"

He made a sound that was very similar to Brigit's growl. "For God's sake. I told you I screwed up. Can't you just get over it?"

Just get over it? Did he have no idea how badly he'd hurt me? How shitty he'd made me feel? And did he not realize that the reason I couldn't get over it right away was because I'd had serious feelings for him and his rejection had scarred me to my core? Of course I supposed he was feeling rejected now, too.

"Let's talk later," I said. "Okay?"

"I'll think about it." With a click, he was gone.

I fumed for a few seconds. *Who the hell does Seth think he is, getting mad at me for going out with another guy? He's the one who called things off before. He's the reason I'm going out with Clint. He's getting a taste of his own medicine here. Screw him!*

But when the anger left me I felt empty and grief-stricken instead.

*Why does dating Seth seem as dangerous and chaotic
and crazy as riding a bull in a rodeo?*

Clint picked me up at six and we went to dinner at a casual place in Sundance Square. Over our meal, Clint mentioned a suspicious death he'd heard about at the Stockyards
Hotel.

"It's a possible homicide," he said. "The maid found the
guy this afternoon. He was dead in the bed with a pillow
over his face. All of his valuables were gone. Wallet. Watch.
Rings. Electronics."

"So he was robbed? And s-smothered?"

Clint fished a French fry off the pile on his plate. "Looks
like it."

*Who would do such a horrible thing? Kill someone just
for their belongings?* It was sad and sick and selfish. "Any
suspects?"

"Haven't heard. Far as I know they're still interviewing potential witnesses."

I guessed I was lucky the thief at the stock show had
resorted to violence only after a victim had tried to restrain
her and that she hadn't inflicted fatal wounds. I wasn't ready
to deal with a cold-blooded killer.

"What's going on with the stock show robberies?" Clint
asked. "Any progress?"

I told him about Detective Bustamente and our plans
to visit the Kroger store and the Justin Boots outlet.

"You like that part of police work?" he asked. "The
mental part? Questioning witnesses? Figuring out the
clues?"

"Definitely." Frankly, it was the only part of police work
I did like. The other parts were either boring or frightening.

"Not me," Clint said. "I like the physical part best. Chasing people. Cracking skulls. Kicking ass."

"You're such a *guy*."

"That I am," he said unapologetically, ripping a fry in half with his teeth like a rabid wolverine.

I had to laugh. But then I wanted to cry. *Why can't things be this easy with Seth?*

After dinner, Clint took me back to his place, a two-bedroom condo situated on the brink of where the city gave way to the western suburbs. His décor was manly and spare. Lots of oversized pieces in earth tones with few decorator accents.

We settled in on his couch to watch a movie. Just two minutes in and his mouth was on my neck, nuzzling behind my ear, causing certain parts of me to throb with want. His lips moved, trailing kisses just under my jawbone until he captured my mouth with his. He put his chest against mine, a hand on my back, and gently eased me down until we were lying side by side on the couch.

He ran his hand up my side, his thumb lingering just below the swell of my breast. I was aware of every pulse of my heart, felt the blood move in my veins, heard it flow past my ears.

His hand slid down to the hem of my sweater and up under it, his fingers splaying across my rib cage. *So close.* I felt my nipples pucker into painful peaks.

He pulled his mouth from mine and put it to my ear. "Let me touch you, Megan."

God, how I want to hear those words. God how I want to be touched. But I wanted to hear those words spoken in Seth's voice, to be touched by Seth's hands. As screwed up as our relationship was, and as attracted as I was to Clint, I realized Seth was the man I really wanted to be with.

I wiggled myself back into a sitting position. "I'm sorry, Clint. But I'm not ready for this."

I realized, too, that my hesitation wasn't solely because of Seth. Clint and I had only been out three times. We hardly knew each other. Regardless of Seth, it was too soon for things to get physical.

Clint groaned. "I get it. But you can't blame a guy for trying."

We sat up and watched the rest of the movie. When he drove me back to my place, he gave me only a chaste closed-mouth kiss on the lips. It felt horribly unsatisfying, yet I knew it was the right thing to do.

Damn you, Seth.

Monday morning, I met Detective Bustamente at the Kroger store where Dominique's Diners Club card had been used to purchase groceries. Frankly, I was rethinking my agreement to help out on the investigation. I had enough to do without taking on extra work. I'd tossed and turned all night thinking about Clint and Seth, wondering what I should do about both of them, and had woken up tired and grumpy. But I'd promised to be here, and I wasn't about to risk my reputation by failing to follow through.

Today Bustamente wore a pair of khaki pants that were three inches too short, along with white crew socks and black dress shoes. His cotton shirt had a mismatched button a third of the way down. I had to remind myself what Detective Jackson had said. Not to judge this book by its cover.

Given that I was playing detective today rather than street cop, I'd chosen to wear business clothes, too. Loafers. A pair of black slacks. A gray cableknit sweater. I'd left my hair down rather than twisting it up in its usual bun, though I had secured it in back with a silver barrette. I'd brought Brigit along with me. Didn't want the dog getting bored at home and eating my couch.

The head of store security was a man named Kirk, a former marine who was built as stout and sturdy as the amphibious assault vehicles he'd once commanded. He led us into the administrative offices on the second floor of the store and took us back to a small conference room with a built-in television screen.

After the detective and I took seats at the table, Kirk pushed the button on the remote to run the security video. "That's her," he said, pointing to a young woman whose head was mostly obscured by a hoodie.

The woman approached the checkout counter and unloaded various items onto the belt. From this distance it was difficult to tell exactly what her items were, but we knew from the copy of the receipt Kirk had provided to us that the woman had purchased several high-dollar items, including shrimp, teeth-whitening strips, vitamins, and allergy medication. She'd purchased a variety of gossip and fashion magazines. She'd even bought the most expensive heart-shaped box of chocolates the store sold.

When the video had run its course and showed the young woman leaving the store, Kirk let the cashier into the room. The woman, whom we'd seen in the video, was in her early sixties. She had salt-and-pepper hair that was heavy on the salt, and the soft, fleshy figure of a grandmother who liked to bake cookies for her grandkids and sample the dough.

Bustamente and I shook hands with her and introduced ourselves.

"I'm Loretta Sneed," she said. "Pleased to meet you."

She took a seat across the table.

"We appreciate you coming in to talk with us," Bustamente said. "We'll try to be brief."

He asked Kirk to run the video again for the woman, then proceeded to ask her a series of questions.

"What, if anything, did you two discuss while you rang up the young woman's groceries?"

"The only thing we talked about was the box of chocolates," Loretta replied. "I said something to the effect of a person getting sick if they ate the whole thing. She didn't really respond. Just kind of scowled at me."

"Mm-hm," Bustamente said, nodding. "And what about the paper you held out to her? What was that all about?"

"Oh, right," Loretta said. "I asked did she have a Kroger card and she said no. Well, I hated for her to miss out on the sale prices. I mean, there's no sense in somebody spending more money than they have to, right? Especially a young woman like her who's probably not been on her own long. I told her that all it takes is a few seconds to fill out the form to get the card and the discounts, but she refused. Said she was in a hurry and she'd get a card the next time she came in."

"Did she say why she was in a hurry?" the detective asked. "Did she mention somewhere she might be headed to?"

"No," Loretta said. "She was a little short with me about the card so I didn't try to engage her in small talk after that."

"Did the woman say anything that might provide a clue regarding who she was or where she lived?"

Loretta shook her head. "Not that I can remember."

"Have you seen her in the store again?"

"No. Not since that night."

"Do you recall having seen her in the store before that night?"

Again Loretta responded in the negative.

"Was there anything about her that was distinctive?" Bustamente asked. "Did she have any piercings, scars, birthmarks? Maybe a tattoo? A gap between her teeth? A lisp or accent? Anything like that?"

Loretta shrugged. "She was just your typical pretty blue-eyed blonde."

Bustamente opened his briefcase and pulled out a stack of photographs, handing the first to Loretta after holding it up to show me. "Take a look at these pictures and tell me if any of these could be the young woman you rang up."

Loretta looked down at the first photo. "This definitely isn't her. This woman looks like she hasn't washed her hair in a week."

"Try to see past that kind of thing," Bustamente told her. "I need you to focus more on her facial features. The shape of her eyes and lips. Bone structure. Brows. Nose."

Loretta took a second look at the photo. "I still don't think this is her."

"Okeydoke," the detective said. "Set that one aside and take a look at this one." He handed her a second photo.

"No," Loretta said. "This isn't her, either. This woman looks like she's got some type of disease. The girl who came in the store looked healthy. Like she took good care of herself."

The two continued through the stack. Loretta set a couple of the photographs aside as possibilities, but even so she seemed to think they were slim possibilities. Most of the photos depicted women who were emaciated from drug use or showed other signs of hard living. Dark circles under their eyes. Bruises on their cheeks. Broken teeth. Scars. I found myself wondering what crimes each of them had committed. I also found myself wondering why. I also found myself hoping that these women would be able to turn their lives around. None of them looked like they'd ever had it easy.

When he reached the end of the stack, Bustamente made a note of the photos Loretta had picked out and gathered all of them up. He returned them to his briefcase and stood. "Thanks for your time." He held out his hand to shake hers again.

I gave her a nod and shook her hand again, too.

The detective, my partner, and I headed out to the parking lot.

"What do you think?" I asked.

"I think this thief is a new kid on the block," he said. "I showed these same photographs to the other victims yesterday and nobody could make a positive ID. They said pretty much the same thing as Loretta did in there. That the girl looked well. Her last victim, the one she injured, speculated that she came from money. Said she seemed well dressed and well mannered. At least up until she put her knee in his howdy-doodies."

FIFTY
WHAT? NO DOG TREATS?

Brigit

Brigit had no idea what type of cruel trick Megan was trying to pull. She leads Brigit into a grocery store, but then
fails to take her to the pet food aisle to pick out a treat?
Why had Megan teased her like that? It was downright
mean.

Brigit would have to come up with a revenge plot. She'd
already ripped through the closet door and chewed up the
last of Megan's shoes, so that wasn't an option. The only
food Megan kept in the apartment was tofu, soy milk, and
vegetables. Eating any of that would be more of a punish-
ment for Brigit than Megan. She supposed she could pass
gas in the cruiser, but she'd already pooped this morning
and couldn't muster up a respectable toot.

*Wait. Is Megan pulling into the drive through of the
burger place?*

She was!

Megan talked into the speaker and pulled up to the window. She handed some money to the lady, and the lady in

turn passed a white bag to Megan. Brigit's partner pulled
the burger from the bag, unwrapped it, and tore it into
smaller chunks, shoving them through the small gap at the
top of Brigit's metal enclosure. The burger pieces fell to
the platform at the dog's feet.

Lunch!
Do I have the best partner ever or what?

FIFTY-ONE
NEVER SAY DIE

Robin Hood

She had brought a frozen Lean Cuisine for lunch today, and headed into the employee break room to heat it up in the microwave. She didn't even mind that her lunch would be cheap and tasteless. After days of her flirting and dropping hints, Kevin Trang had finally asked her out for Friday night. He'd even suggested they have dinner at Reata, one of the city's fanciest steakhouses. Things were definitely looking up.

I'm finally getting what I deserve.

She slid the meal into the microwave and punched the buttons to nuke it. *Beep. Beep-beep. Beep.* While the food warmed in the oven, she stepped over to the television to catch snippets of the noon news.

A male reporter stood in front of the Stockyards Hotel. Behind him, paramedics could be seen wheeling out a body completely covered in a white sheet. *What the hell?*

The reporter angled himself toward the ambulance. "As you can see, folks, the body of Sam Gunderson is just now being taken to the medical examiner's office for an autopsy. Hotel housekeeping found Mr. Gunderson dead in his third-floor room yesterday afternoon. Sources say a pillow had been placed over his face and that all valuables had been removed from the room. Police suspect foul play. Anyone with information is asked to contact the Fort Worth Police Department."

The room spun around her. Robin Hood—no, *Amber Lynn Hood*—had to reach out and grab the table to keep from falling.

Ohmigod-ohmigod-ohmigod!

One of the older ladies who worked as a secretary on the first floor looked up from her table. "You okay? You look like you've seen a ghost."

She might not have seen one.

But she might have *made* one.

Amber Lynn forced herself to look at the woman. "Just having a dizzy spell. That's all."

Just found out she was a killer was more like it. Had she accidentally smothered Sam when she'd put the pillow over his head?

No! It can't be! She hadn't pushed the pillow down or anything. She'd just laid it across his face. She did the same thing herself when she had a hangover and too much light was coming through the bedroom window. Besides, he'd been snoring when she left the room, hadn't he?

Yes! Yes, he had! Of course the snoring had been softer, weaker.

Had he slowly been suffocating?

Had Amber Lynn ended his life?

Am I a murderer?

FIFTY-TWO
SHOTGUN WEDDING

Megan

Detective Bustamente and I pulled into the parking lot of the Justin Boots outlet store on west Vickery and parked. I cracked the windows on the cruiser so Brigit could get air, and left her in the vehicle. After all the shoes that damn dog had chewed up, there was no way I could trust her in a boot store. She might go berserk and destroy the entire inventory. I wasn't sure the FWPD insurance would cover that and, even if it did, the chief would can my ass. He wasn't exactly my biggest fan.

I had the printout of the boot selection in my purse, ready to show to the manager on duty. It was probably a long shot, but we had to see whether he or she could help us track down those customers who had purchased the particular models of boots the victims had ID'd as belonging to the crutch-wielding accomplice.

The detective held the door for me and I stepped inside the store. The place smelled like leather and boot polish. No big surprise there. My nose also detected faint undertones of rubber from the work boots, and a few hints of a floral cologne.

I glanced around as I followed Bustamente to the counter. So many cute styles. I'd never been much into western wear, but I had to admit that these boots were fun and fashionable, much more chic than the cowgirl boots of yesteryear. I was still checking out the footwear when I heard a female voice ask, "How can I help you?"

Bustamente put a hand on my back and guided me forward. "My wife here would like to try on some boots."

His *wife? Whuh?*

My gaze met his. I saw something in his eyes, a warning perhaps? I turned to the clerk. She was a woman about my age. Plain, with mousy brown hair.

Again, *whuh?*

A glance at the name spelled out on her plastic badge answered my question.

CRYSTAL.

Whoa.

All of the sudden it made sense why she had so many pairs of boots. She worked in a boot store!

Obviously, Bustamente was role-playing for some reason, pretending I was here as his wife rather than in an official capacity. I wasn't sure what his reasons were, but I knew I had to play along.

I forced a smile at the woman I would've much rather throttled. Thanks to her and whoever her two cohorts were, the chief had jumped down my throat. This woman and her coconspirators had not only ripped off and physically injured their victims, they'd made Fort Worth PD look bad and hampered sales of tickets to the stock show and rodeo. They'd cost a lot of people a lot of money and caused untold amounts of frustration and heartache.

Crystal stepped out from behind the counter. "Were you looking for any particular style?"

"Something with a pointed toe," I said. *You know, the kind that would be good for putting in someone's ass. Yours, perhaps?* "Maybe with a shorter shank?"

"Got just what you're looking for." She led me to a display.

I picked up a pair in tan and ivory. "These are cute."

"What size do you wear?"

"Eight and a half."

Bustamente and I waited on the sales floor while Crystal retrieved the boots from the stockroom.

"What would you like me to cook for dinner tonight?" I asked my new husband as I tried to get into my role.

"Enchiladas," he replied. "Rice and beans. Flan."

"Okay. I'll have it ready when you get home."

When Crystal returned with the box, I sat down on a bench, removed my loafers, and slid my feet into the boots. I stood and took a few steps in them, pretending to admire them in the mirror.

"What do you think, honey?" I asked the detective, hoping I sounded wifelike.

"Meh." He angled a bladed hand in a so-so motion. "I can take 'em or leave 'em. You know I prefer you in spike heels and fishnets."

He'd delivered those words so convincingly there must have been some truth to them.

"Well, *I* like these boots," I said. "But I'm not sure we should spend the money right now." I turned to Crystal. "I think I need a night or two to think on them."

"No problem," she said, sliding the boots back into their box. "Y'all have a nice day."

Bustamente and I left the store and walked back to our cars.

"Just FYI," he said, "no wife asks her husband what he wants for dinner. She just makes it and sets it in front of him and tells him to shut up and eat it."

"Duly noted," I said. *Make. Set. Shut up. Eat.*

Now that we were a safe distance from the building, he told me that we needed to run the license plates on every car in the lot and see if any of them were registered to a Crystal.

"That way we can get her full name and address," he said.

"Why don't you just arrest her now?"

"Because if I did she'd get a defense attorney and refuse to talk. We might not ever find out who she was working with. She'd probably get off, too. You saw what a hard time that cashier had identifying the thief. The witnesses who saw Crystal only remember her boots. None of them would be able to give a positive ID. Better to do some digging first, some surveillance of her house, see where she goes and who she goes with. Maybe she'll meet up with the other two women involved in these robberies. If she doesn't, we can always come back and put the screws to her, see if she'll talk then."

What the detective said made sense. A bird in the hand wasn't always worth more than two in the bush, especially if the bird in the bush was the bird you wanted most to get. Nevertheless, my eagerness to put the thieves behind bars had me feeling impatient and frustrated and wanting to do something *now*.

Bustamente motioned for me to get into his unmarked cruiser. Once we were seated, he handed me his laptop. As he rattled off the license plate numbers of the vehicles in the lot, I ran them through the system. The first three cars were registered to a John Fremont, a Mary Anne Murdock, and a Yusef Diswali, respectively. The fourth, a 1997 Buick LeSabre, was registered to a Crystal Dawn Hood.

"Bingo." I angled the laptop screen so Bustamente could see the information.

"See where that address is located."

I input the address into my cell phone's GPS app and consulted the map. "Looks like it's in a trailer park north of town."

Bustamante nodded as he appeared to be processing the information. "Okay. Here's what I've come up with. The main thief is someone who grew up poor, didn't like it, and thinks the world owes her something. She has expensive tastes, delusions of grandeur, and a sense of entitlement."

"How'd you reach these conclusions?"

He jerked his head to indicate the store. "That woman in there? Crystal? She lives in a trailer and works as a retail sales clerk. Most of her acquaintances, including the thief, are likely to be from similar backgrounds. The fact that the thief bought those gossip rags and fashion magazines at Kroger says she's fixated on celebrities and the wealthy and their lifestyles. She wants to live like they do. That's what these robberies have been all about."

Wow. Detective Jackson was right. Bustamante was sharp.

Would *I* ever be that clever?

FIFTY-THREE
THE SHOES BLUES

Brigit

The dog put her nose to the small opening at the top of the window and sniffed. She could smell leather. And lots of it.

Mmmmm . . .

Brigit would've loved to go into the store and go to town on that leather, but Megan didn't take her inside. What a party pooper.

Disappointed, Brigit nestled back against the enclosure. As she sat there, a slight breeze carried other scents her way.

The acrid smell of gasoline.

The faint smell of a burning cigarette.

The same floral cologne I smelled at the stock show.

Whoever had been wearing it that night was here now, at the store. Brigit wished that whoever it was would bring a leather boot out to the car for her to enjoy. It was the least she deserved after all those nights patrolling through rowdy crowds at the stock show, wasn't it?

FIFTY-FOUR
DESTROYING THE EVIDENCE

Amber Lynn Hood

Holy shit! Holy shit! Holy shit!

Amber Lynn still had the dead guy's wallet, and camera, and iPad, and jewelry in the trunk of her car. If she were caught with his things she could go to prison for the rest of her life. She might even get the death penalty!

Oh, God!

Did they still zap people in the electric chair? Or were they killed by firing squads? No, all of those methods were outdated. Now they used lethal injections, putting people down just like they did stray dogs from the streets.

Amber Lynn didn't want to die like a stray dog. *She didn't want to die at all!*

She left her Lean Cuisine rotating in the microwave and all but ran to her cubicle. She grabbed her purse and headed to the exit. She didn't bother checking in with her supervisor in person, instead opting to call her boss from her cell phone as she rushed through the parking lot.

"I had to leave," Amber Lynn said, faking a cough. "I

suddenly started feeling really bad." *That part is true.* "I think I've got the flu." *That part isn't.*

"Don't you worry," her supervisor said. "I'll get one of the other girls to cover for you. You just go on home and stay in bed until you feel better."

"Thanks."

Go on home and stay in bed. Amber Lynn had no intention whatsoever of doing either of those things. At least not until she'd gotten rid of Sam's things.

She dashed to her car, barely noticing the cold temperature despite the fact that she'd left her coat in her cube and wore only a thin blouse and skirt. She climbed into her car, her tires screeching as she pulled out of the lot. She checked her gas gauge. Thanks to the cash she'd pilfered from Sam, she had a nearly full tank. She could drive far away from Fort Worth and back without having to stop anywhere.

She headed north on Interstate 35 and drove and drove and drove, her panic continuing to build, until she passed over the state line into Oklahoma. She pulled into the parking lot of the first convenience store she saw, driving around back to the Dumpsters where she wouldn't be spotted disposing of Sam's things. She braked to a stop, but left the engine running in case she needed to make a quick getaway.

After a quick glance around to make sure nobody could see her, she gathered Sam's camera and iPad from the backseat, and retrieved his wallet from the glove compartment. She shook so badly that she immediately dropped his wallet. The credit cards and other contents spilled out over her floorboards. Sam's driver's license sat on top, his face looking up at her from the photo, his expression seeming to say *Why, Robin? Why did you kill me?*

Now he remembers her alias!

"Oh, God!" She felt as if she were going to be sick.

She scooped up all of the items, including the wallet it-self, and crammed them into the camera bag. She leaped from the car and ran up to the Dumpster, hurling the bag and iPad over the top.

"Hey! No dumping allowed!"

She turned to see a man storming out the back door of the store.

SHIT!

He continued toward her, his face contorted in anger. "That garbage bin is for store use only!"

"I'm sorry!" she cried. "It was just a couple of small things. That's all!"

"I don't care!" the man spat. "People keep leaving mattresses and washing machines and all kinds of shit out here that I have to deal with." He stepped up onto a wooden crate next to the Dumpster, reached in, and pulled out the camera bag. Stomping over to Amber Lynn, he forced the bag back into her arms. "Take this back. Throw it in your own damn garbage."

"Okay! Okay!" Amber Lynn cried, on the verge of hysteria. She climbed back into her car and set the camera bag on the passenger seat. She shifted the car into drive and took off once again with screeching tires.

"Hey!" the man called after her, holding up Sam's tablet. "Do you realize you just threw away an iPad?"

FIFTY-FIVE
TALK IS CHEAP

Megan

When I wasn't working the stock show that week, I played spy in one of the unmarked squad cars that Bustamente had arranged for me. I followed Crystal to work in the mornings, followed her home to her trailer in the evenings, and watched from the parking lot of a small country church to see if she went anywhere at night.

She didn't.

This woman really needed to get a life. All she seemed to do was work and go home to watch TV on the couch. She needed some motivation. A purpose. A swift kick in the rear.

The crime scene techs had been able to lift prints from the cattle prod the thief had used on Sloane, which was good news. The bad news was that the prints didn't match anyone in the criminal fingerprint databases. Looked like Bustamente was right. The primary thief was a first-time offender.

I'd heard through the grapevine that the forensics team

had also lifted a partial print from a champagne bottle found under the bed in the dead man's room at the Stockyards Hotel. That print likewise had no match.

Score: Bad guys 2. Law enforcement 0.

Seth called me on Thursday. "We need to talk."

"No kidding."

"When can I see you?"

Again, we had trouble finding a time that worked for both of us. I was scheduled to work the later shifts at the stock show through closing night on Saturday, and would be spending my mornings keeping an eye on Crystal. Seth was on round-the-clock duty starting midday on Friday until midday on Saturday.

"Sunday, then," he said. "I'll come to your place first thing in the morning."

"Give me till ten," I said, more to assert myself than for any valid reason. It wasn't like Brigit would let me sleep in. "I'm performing at the closing ceremonies of the rodeo Saturday night and I won't get home until late."

He let out an irritated huff. "All right. Ten o'clock."

A few minutes after four on Friday, as Brigit and I were patrolling the livestock barns, Detective Bustamente called my cell.

"Big news," he said.

"What is it?"

"The print on the cattle prod didn't match anyone in the system," he said, "and the print on that champagne bottle from the Stockyards Hotel didn't match anyone in the system, either."

"Right." I knew all of this, already. This wasn't *big* news. This was *yesterday's* news.

"Here's the thing," he said. *"The prints matched each other."*

It took me a moment to process this data. "The same woman who robbed the people at the stock show is the one who robbed the guy at the hotel? And smothered him with the pillow?"

"The robberies appear to have been committed by the same person, yes," Bustamente said. "But the medical examiner just released her report on Sam Gunderson. Turns out he died of alcohol poisoning. We suspect he started drinking before he headed over to the White Elephant. He had a few drinks there, too, then the champagne when he returned to his room."

"Oh." I wasn't sure how I felt about this bit of news. On one hand, it was nice to know there was one less killer among us than we'd suspected. On the other hand, a person drinking himself to death seemed like such a waste of a perfectly good life.

"Keep the information about the alcohol poisoning to yourself," he said. "That's not public information. As far as everyone else knows, Sam Gunderson's death is still a potential murder investigation."

"Why?" I asked.

"Because we're going to use his death to flush out our thief. We can't wait any longer. We've got to force the issue. Meet me at the outlet store ASAP."

I checked in with the on-site supervisor, who deferred to Bustamente and allowed me to leave the rodeo grounds.

Fifteen minutes later, I met up with the detective in the parking lot of the boot shop. We headed inside. I'd decided to bring Brigit with me this time in case Crystal tried to flee, though I kept my partner on a very short leash.

I followed Bustamente down a row. Crystal stood near the end, straightening a display of boots. Twice I had to use my hand to push Brigit's muzzle away from boots. She looked up at me with angry eyes and gave a boot a long lick with her tongue as if to let me know I wasn't the boss of her. Sometimes my partner was a real pain in the butt. Still, she was more mature than Derek had been.

Crystal looked up as we approached, but didn't seem to recognize us from our previous interaction. Of course I looked much different in uniform than I did in civilian clothes, and she probably saw hundreds of customers or more each week.

"Hi," she said tentatively. "Can I help you find some boots?"

"Nope." Bustamente flashed his badge. "We're here to talk to you."

Crystal's eyes grew wide. "What . . . um . . . what's this about?"

She had the same insincere tone of incredulity I'd heard dozens of times, usually coming out of the mouths of people I'd caught speeding.

Speeder: *Why did you pull me over, Officer?*

Me: *Really, dipshit? You were doing eighty miles per hour in a thirty-mile zone. If you weren't aware of that you're even more stupid than you look. Trust me, that's saying a lot.*

Okay, so I'd never put it quite that way. But that's how it sounded in my head.

Bustamente took a step closer to Crystal and leaned in as if to share a secret. "Miss Hood, we believe you may have witnessed a crime."

Witnessed? Crystal had gone much further than being a mere witness. I realized then that Bustamente was using that disarming technique Detective Jackson had mentioned. It was the same tactic Columbo had used in those TV reruns I watched as a kid. It had been quite effective, too. Play dumb and the criminals don't fear you, let down their guard, slip up.

"A crime?" Crystal said. "What crime? Where?"

"At the stock show?" the detective prodded. "A thief snatched some purses in the ladies' room. She took wallets from a couple of men, too."

Crystal's eyes blinked rapidly in bewilderment. She clearly didn't know how to respond to Detective Bustamente. I could practically read her thoughts. *How much does this guy really know? Should I rat on myself and hope the cops will show me some mercy? Or should I remain silent, exercise my rights?* Her eyes flicked down to Brigit. *No sense trying to run. That oversized dog would catch me. Dammit!*

A thirtyish man in a starched shirt and chinos stopped at the end of the aisle, spotted us, and headed our way. "I'm the store manager. Everything okay here?"

Bustamente raised a palm. "Everything's fine, sir. We just need to speak to Miss Hood about a crime she might have seen taking place. Mind if we take her out front so we can talk privately? See what she knows?"

"Be my guest," the man said. "I hope Crystal can help you out."

Bustamente tossed him a thick-lipped grin. "Oh, I'm sure she'll be a big help."

Seconds later, the four of us were standing next to the building in the cold and dwindling daylight. Brigit snuffled along the bottom of the building as we talked.

Bustamente cut right to the chase. "Miss Hood, we believe you might have seen the person responsible for the thefts at the stock show. Two of the women whose purses were snatched remembered you from the bathroom. They noticed your boots. They said you were on crutches?"

Crystal shook her head vehemently. "I don't know what you're talking about!"

Nonplussed, Bustamente raised his hands. "Look, Miss Hood. You're not in trouble here. We know you had nothing to do with these thefts." *Yeah, right.* "We're just trying to find out if you might have gotten a good look at the thief."

Crystal stopped arguing and stood there, chewing her

lip, her arms crossed over her body as if to shield herself from the truth. She stared at Bustamente, a look of fear on her face, like he knew her most shameful secret and was about to share it around the supper table at summer camp.

Bustamente lifted both his round shoulders and his palms. "We have absolutely no idea who this woman is."

Crystal's posture relaxed, her spirits evidently buoyed by the detective's admission that law enforcement was clueless.

"The woman who took the purses," Bustamente continued, "she got away with a nice chunk of cash." He pulled a notepad from his pocket and rattled off the amounts that were reported stolen. "Let's see. She got fifty dollars the first night, over two hundred the next time."

Crystal's eyes narrowed. Bustamente had evidently struck a nerve. I surmised from the woman's reaction that the thief hadn't given Crystal her full due.

Bustamente returned the pad to his pocket. "Here's the problem," he said. "We don't know who the woman is, but it's awfully important that we find her. Now I'm going to share some inside police information with you, and I need you to keep this to yourself. Okay, hon?"

Crystal nodded. "Okay."

"This thief?" the detective said. "Her fingerprints were lifted from a cattle prod that she used to fry one of her victims in the stock show parking lot. Those same fingerprints were discovered on a bottle of champagne found under the bed in a hotel room on the north side."

Crystal's expression became perplexed. "I don't understand. She was at a hotel? Did she rob someone at the hotel, too?"

Bustamente let out a long sigh. "Yes, she did. Robbed a man blind, Miss Hood. Every valuable he owned taken." He leaned even closer to Crystal. "The man she robbed?

He was found dead in the room. *With a pillow over his face.*"

It wasn't a lie, though the implication was misleading. But we had to mislead Crystal so that she would lead us to the thief.

Bustamente let his words hang in the air for a moment, giving Crystal a chance to process them. Once she had, she gasped and her eyes went crazy, darting about. She didn't seem to know what to do with her hands, either, putting them first to her shirt collar, then crossing them over her chest again, then wringing them.

"She killed the man?" Crystal asked. "Murdered him?"

Bustamente didn't exactly confirm Crystal's words, but he didn't exactly contradict them, either. "He's dead as a doornail."

"Oh, my God!" Crystal expelled on a hysterical breath. "Oh, my God!"

The detective raised one of his wild brows. "This woman, this blonde, she's in some mighty big trouble."

"No!" Crystal cried. "She couldn't—" She put a hand to her mouth as if to hold her words back.

Bustamente cocked his head. "She couldn't *what,* Miss Hood?"

She gulped, as if forcing down emotions, and removed her trembling hand from her lips. When she spoke, her voice quavered, too. "I was just going to say that . . . um . . . I don't see how someone could do something like that. Something so . . . *terrible.*"

"Do you remember seeing the woman?" the detective asked.

"No," Crystal said. "I mean, the stock show is crowded, and there's lots of people going in and out of the restrooms."

"That's true," Bustamente said, pulling out his cell phone. "Maybe these video clips will jog your memory." He retrieved the video files from Starbucks and Kroger, held up his phone, and played them for Crystal, along with a third video clip that showed the thief and Sam Gunderson stumbling into the Stockyards Hotel. The detective paused the video and pointed to the thief. "This is her. The woman we're looking for. Do you recognize her?"

Crystal shook her head, but it seemed as much a nervous tic as an indication of denial. Still, I had to give her credit for not ratting out her friend.

"All right," Bustamente said, sliding the phone back into his pocket and retrieving his business card. He held the card out to Crystal. "If you happen to think of something, please give me a call. Okay, hon?"

Nodding, she took the card between two fingers as if she were touching something radioactive.

FIFTY-SIX
THE CHASE IS ON

Brigit

Brigit could sense Megan's tension, smell the adrenaline her glands seemed to be producing by the gallon. They sat in the cruiser, waiting on a dark side street. Brigit only wished she knew what they were waiting for. Still, she knew it was at tense moments like this when her special skills would be needed. She might chew up her partner's shoes, but she'd never let her partner down on the job. Brigit kept her ears pricked for sounds, her nose wriggling for scents, and her eyes on the dark street around them.

After a few minutes, a voice came over the radio. It was a man's voice. The voice of the man who'd been with them at the boot store a half hour ago.

Megan started the cruiser and slowly pulled away from the curb.

Brigit stood on her platform in the back of the squad car. *Looks like the chase is on.*

FIFTY-SEVEN
FINGERPRINTS AND FINGER-POINTING

Amber Lynn

Bam-bam-bam!

The frantic knock on the door of her apartment sent Amber Lynn virtually jumping out of her skin. She'd been on edge since she'd heard of Sam Gunderson's death, had been debating what to do.

Should I go to the police, confess my crimes, explain that I hadn't meant to kill Sam? Oh, hell no. This was America, where she was innocent until proven guilty. If the cops wanted Amber Lynn, they'd have to build their own case against her. She'd never had anything handed to her. Why should she hand this case to them?

Should I run? There seemed to be little reason to flee. Even though the police suspected foul play, she'd been careful not to leave any fingerprints at the scene. She doubted anyone could positively identify her. She wasn't a regular at the White Elephant Saloon and she'd paid cash for her margarita. In fact, suddenly running off without explanation could raise suspicions. She'd decided she was better off staying put.

After the convenience store clerk had shooed her away, she'd tossed Sam's things out at a trash can at a rest stop. She had also gotten rid of the designer purses she'd taken from the women at the rodeo, putting them in a trash bag along with food scraps and throwing them out in a garbage can at a city park. She'd been sorry to see the nice bags go, but if things worked out with Kevin he'd be able to buy her all the designer purses she could ever want.

And speaking of Kevin, could this be him? If so, he was an hour early for their date. *Not likely.* Who was it then?

Her heart seizing up in her chest, she stepped to the door and looked out the peephole. She hadn't turned on the porch light, so all she could see was the movement of an unidentifiable head. *Damn! What should I do?* If she turned on the light, whoever was out there would know she was home. What if it was a cop on her porch? She'd rather them think she was out.

"Amber Lynn!" came Crystal's voice through the door. "Open up! Right now! It's an emergency!"

Thank God! It's only my sister. Amber Lynn turned the knob and opened the door. "What do you want? I've got a date coming over."

Crystal pushed past then whirled on her. "You killed a man!" she shrieked. "Smothered him with a pillow!" She burst into terrified sobs. "How could you do that? How could you?"

The better question was how did Crystal know about Sam? Her pulse rocketing into power drive, Amber Lynn grabbed her sister by the shoulders. "How did you hear about this? Tell me now!"

"The cops!" Crystal cried. "They came to the store today. Just a little while ago. They know I was in the bathroom when you stole those purses. They asked if I knew who you were!"

Sheer terror welled up in Amber Lynn, making her feel foggy and frantic. As stupid as her sister was, she might have told the police something they could use to positively ID Amber Lynn. As it was, the police were far too close for comfort. *How the hell had they tracked down Crystal?*

"What did you say, Crystal?" She dug her nails into her sister's shoulders and gave her a firm shake. "What did you tell them?"

"Nothing! I told them I didn't know who you were. But they've got videos! They've got you at Starbucks and at Kroger and at the hotel!"

Holy fuck.

Amber Lynn released Crystal and turned, pacing back and forth across the room. "How was the film? Was it clear? Could you tell who I was?"

"I don't know!" Crystal grabbed a paper towel from the kitchen counter to wipe her eyes, then took a seat on the edge of the couch. She waved the paper towel around. "I mean, I recognized you, but maybe it's only because I know you. I think other people would have a hard time telling that it was you on the video."

Okay, okay, okay, thought Amber Lynn. *Calm down! The jig isn't up yet.*

Bam-bam-bam! A fresh knock sounded at her door, followed by a male voice. "Fort Worth Police! Open this door! Now!"

The jig appeared to be up.

Panic seized Amber Lynn in an iron grip. But just as quickly, she forced the panic aside.

No.

Not yet.

This jig was just getting started and Amber Lynn was putting on her dancing shoes.

FIFTY-EIGHT
I DON'T DO WINDOWS

Megan

Bam-bam-bam!

"We said open up!" hollered Detective Bustamente.

Still the door remained closed, the porch dark. My heart twirled in my chest like a baton completing 5,000 rpms. I pulled my nightstick from my belt and flicked my wrist to extend it. *Snap!* I readied my heavy-duty flashlight, too, turning it on but aiming the beam down for now.

Brigit sat quivering next to me, unleashed, ready to spring into action on my command.

When still no one opened the door, Bustamente raised a beefy leg and went to kick the door in. Just as his foot was about to make contact, the door whipped open and he ended up falling forward, knocking Crystal back onto her ass on the carpet.

Brigit and I squeezed past them into a small living room. My eyes scanned the space, looking for the blonde.

"Where is she?" I demanded of Crystal. "Where's your sister?"

When Crystal had entered the apartment a short time ago, Detective Bustamente and I matched the unit number to the corresponding number painted on the assigned parking spaces, finding Amber Lynn Hood's yellow Chevy Spark in the spot. Another quick search of the vital statistics records confirmed that Amber Lynn and Crystal had the same parents.

Sisters in crime.

I was shocked to realize it was the same car I'd seen driving away from my apartment complex all those days ago, but suddenly things made sense. Amber Lynn had probably sold Catherine Quimby's Vicodin to Dwayne Donaldson.

On the floor, Crystal burst into sobs and gestured toward the bedroom. "She went in there."

I dashed into the bedroom to find one of the two windows wide open, the screen knocked out. I gave Brigit the signal to follow the woman's trail out the window, while I ran back through the living room, out the front door, and onto the sidewalk.

The sounds of Brigit's toenails clicking on the cement along with the pounding of her paws told me the woman had run off to the left. I ran through the dimly lit parking lot, holding my flashlight up to illuminate my way. I swung the light around but saw nothing. No thief. No dog.

I yelled as loud as I could, issuing the order for Brigit to bark so I could locate her.

Woof! Woof-woof!

Sounded like they were off to my right now.

I took off running in that direction, passing several tenants who'd evidently just arrived home from work. They stepped back as I ran past, their heads turning to track my progress.

Woof! Woof-woof!

Brigit's barks grew louder and louder. I was getting close.

I rounded a brick wall and found myself in an alley with multiple Dumpsters. Brigit had the woman backed up against the wall between two of them. The woman had a gun in her hands.

A gun that is aimed at Brigit.

"Nooo!" I shrieked, hurling my baton at her forearms just as she squeezed the trigger.

Bang! A bright muzzle flash lit up the night and Brigit dropped to the ground.

"Nooo!" I shrieked again, a madwoman now, hurling myself at the shooter this time.

The force of my body impacting hers knocked her to the ground. I landed on top of her. The gun slid out of her hand and under the Dumpster, out of her reach. I grabbed my baton from the asphalt and leaped to my feet, ready to beat this woman to death for killing my partner.

To my surprise, Brigit leaped to her feet, too. I supposed when she dropped to the ground she'd merely been cowering from the gunshot noise. *Thank God!* Perhaps that holy water she'd licked from my fingers had given her some divine protection.

The woman rolled onto her belly and tried to push herself to a stand, but there would be none of that. I put my foot on her ass and sent her tumbling forward on the gritty asphalt, then ordered Brigit to keep her down.

A few seconds later, Bustamente and Crystal ran up beside me.

"You got her!" Bustamente said, pumping a victorious fist.

"You got her!" Crystal wailed, falling to her knees on the ground beside her prone sister.

I called Brigit off the woman, and Bustamente and I bent down to cuff her.

"Help!" she screamed, flailing about on the ground. "Police brutality!"

"Be still!" I ordered, grabbing for her arm.

She was still struggling, still fighting, but between the two of us Bustamente and I finally managed to get her shackled.

"On your feet," the detective said.

She responded by turning onto her back and kicking out at him.

Swish, whap! One stroke of encouragement from my baton was all it took to settle her down.

"Okay! Okay!" she cried. "I'll do what you say!"

We dragged her to her feet. She cursed the entire way as we led her back to her apartment, directing some of the slurs at us, others at the world in general.

Back in her apartment, I pointed my baton at the couch. "Sit down. And don't move or my dog will tear you to bits."

As if to add credence to my threat, Brigit offered a growl and bared her teeth.

Bustamente put his hands on his knees and bent down to look Amber Lynn in the face. "You want to talk? Tell us where you hid the jewelry and stuff?"

She responded only with a glare.

Detective Bustamente and I left Amber Lynn Hood sitting on her couch with Brigit keeping watch as we searched her unit, starting with the bedroom.

"You take the closet," Bustamente said. "I'll start on the dresser."

I opened the closet and began pulling boxes of accessories off the shelves to look through them.

Back in the breakfast nook, Crystal had totally given up by then, willing to accept whatever fate might have in store for her. She simply sat at the dinette table and cried, wiping her eyes with a paper towel. "Why'd you do it, Li'l

Sis?" she said finally. "Why'd you kill that man? Why'd you drag me and Heather into all of this?"

Bustamente and I exchanged glances.

He stepped to the bedroom door and looked out at Crystal. "Who's Heather?"

"Our other sister," she responded between sobs.

He pulled his radio from his belt. "She the other one who used the pillowcase to rob those two women?"

Crystal nodded.

"Where is she now?" he asked.

"At home. At our parents' house."

"She have her gun with her?"

Crystal shook her head. "She never had a gun. They used lipstick."

So I'd been right to think the circular bruises on Lisa and Dominique had been too small for a gun barrel.

Bustamente radioed dispatch and asked them to send officers out to the trailer to arrest Heather.

We continued our search, painstakingly going through clothing, shoes, suitcases, and bedding, looking for the stolen jewelry or cash. Although we found nothing that belonged to Sam Gunderson, Bustamente found the stolen marquise diamond ring taped inside an A/C vent. Looked like Amber Lynn had decided to keep that piece for herself.

We'd just finished our search and called for another officer to transport Amber Lynn Hood to police headquarters for booking, when a knock sounded on the door to the apartment.

"I'll get it." I flipped on the porch light and opened the door to find an attractive Asian guy standing there, a bouquet of pink roses in his hand.

While Amber Lynn had stoically seethed since we'd nabbed her, on seeing the guy with the flowers she broke down with an ungodly wail, tears streaming down her face, her shoulders shaking with emotion.

"Uhhh . . ." said the guy, looking from me, to Detective Bustamente, to Brigit, to Amber Lynn. "Is this a bad time?"

FIFTY-NINE
THIS DOG DONE GOOD

Brigit

Brigit could tell that Megan was pleased with her performance. Her partner fed her seven liver treats. Totally worth that loud noise that still had her ears ringing.

Following the woman who'd escaped out her window had been easy. Her flowery cologne marked her trail for Brigit like spotlights would for a human.

Yep, Brigit was pleased with herself, pleased with the way things had gone here tonight. She'd be happier, though, if it hadn't been so long since she'd seen Blast.

She laid her head on her paws and sighed.

I miss that dog.

SIXTY
DRESSED TO THE NINES

Amber Lynn

She was booked, stripped, and deloused, though it hardly seemed fair to call it a delousing when there were no louses present in the first place.

A seasoned, white-haired female guard handed Amber Lynn an orange jumpsuit. At least it was new rather than secondhand. Amber Lynn decided that maybe she should start being happy for small favors.

Amber Lynn slid into the jumpsuit.

"Look at you," the guard said, "dressed to the nines."

Actually, according to the number on the chest of her uniform, Amber Lynn was dressed to the 9384652s.

After Kevin Trang had left Amber Lynn's apartment, the detective had told her that Sam Gunderson had died of alcohol poisoning, not suffocation. The pillow she'd put over his face had nothing to do with his death. Amber Lynn found herself feeling something far beyond mere relief. She found herself realizing that fate had given her another chance.

Maybe fate isn't so unfair, after all.

The defense attorney she'd been assigned gave her more reason to hope.

"Your sisters will only get probation," he assured her. "You'll get some time for the thefts, but the knee to the groin and the cattle prod? We can claim self-defense there."

He'd made sure that the photographer on duty took pictures of the yellowish-green bruise that encircled Amber Lynn's wrist.

She'd never liked secondhand clothes, but she did like second chances. She planned to make the most of this one she'd been given. As she sat in the holding cell, waiting for the police to transport her to the county jail, she thought things over. Maybe she'd look into going to college, after all. She was only twenty-one. It wasn't too late. Heck, she'd always been a good speller. Maybe she'd major in English, write a book someday. She had no idea what she might write about, but she knew it wouldn't feature a woman just sitting around, waiting for her Prince Charming. She also knew the story would have a happy ending.

SIXTY-ONE
OLD FLAMES

Megan

Bustamente had nailed Amber Lynn Hood to a T. She was exactly what he'd predicted. A girl who'd grown up poor and had a chip on her shoulder. I could only hope that someday I'd be as adept as he was at analyzing clues and profiling suspects. He'd suggested some books on criminal psychology for me to read, and I'd immediately hopped online to order them.

After Amber Lynn had been taken to the station, I continued on to the stock show grounds to complete my shift. As Brigit and I patrolled, I spotted Clint sitting on Jack outside one of the barns, chatting up yet another rodeo groupie, this one a tall brunette in leather pants. He smiled down at her, laughed at something she said, nudged her in the butt with his toe.

Been there, done that.

Though I supposed I should've felt jealous, I didn't this time. I guess I'd known on some level that Clint and I would be nothing more than a passing thing, a bit of fun to enjoy for a while before moving on.

Not like me and Seth.

For better or worse, Seth and I seemed to have some type of necessary connection, loose as it might be. And given how upset he'd become over me seeing Clint, I figured he might be more attached to me than he wanted to admit, to me or even to himself. We just needed to figure out how to make things work between us.

Saturday night, I was back at the rodeo with Brigit, standing at the gate, waiting for Clint to take his ride. Assorted groupies hung nearby, some of them the same young women and men I'd seen before, while others were new faces.

As I watched a bareback rider do his best to stay on his horse, Brigit stood up next to me and turned around, her tail whipping back and forth in excitement. She barked, too, an excited *arf-arf-arf!* that could barely be heard above the din of the cheering crowd.

I turned to see what had her so worked up.

Blast. He wore his vest identifying him as a member of the Fort Worth Fire Department. No doubt the vest had gotten the dog into the event, but it had also probably freaked out a portion of the attendees who realized he was an explosive-sniffing dog. Oh, well. It was the last night of the stock show and rodeo. All of the tickets that were going to be sold had been already.

The bareback rider was thrown from his horse and the crowd quieted down as they waited for the next rider to get ready. According to the schedule in my hand, that rider would be Clint.

Blast trotted up the ramp on the end of a leash grasped in Seth's hand.

My eyes traveled upward from the dog to meet Seth's gaze. He appeared unsure but hopeful, a half smile on his mouth as he seemed to wait to see what kind of reception he'd get from me.

"Hey," I said, as he stepped up. I looked into his green eyes. "It's good to see you."

The half smile doubled to a full. "I figured I'd come out and see your performance. You doing some tricks with Brigit?"

I was flattered that he remembered I'd be performing tonight. "Nope. I'll be twirling my fire batons."

His eyes sparkled. "Seriously? Are you going to wear a skimpy costume?"

I'd debated that very thing, but when I tried on my majorette uniform from high school I feared if I wore it I would split the seams. I'd filled out a bit since then. The last thing I needed was a Janet Jackson–style wardrobe malfunction in front of this crowd. "No. No costume. Just my police uniform."

"Okay if I visualize you in something that barely covers your ass?"

Seth was as bad as Bustamente and his fishnets and stilettos. "Have at it. All I ask is that it have black sequins."

"Done."

He squeezed into the space next to me and the announcer's voice came over the loudspeaker.

"Ladies and gentlemen, next up is everyone's favorite deputy, Clint McCutcheon!"

The crowd roared, and several of the groupies around us squealed and jumped up and down, clapping their hands.

Seth cut a glance my way. "Is this your guy?" he called over the din.

"No." I nudged him in the ribs. "*This* is my guy."

A fresh smile tugged at his lips.

We turned our attention to the arena as the gate flew open with a resounding clang.

The gray horse Clint rode burst out of the chute, bucking like the ground was on fire. The crowd cheered Clint on as he spurred, one hand moving up and back over his head in a surprisingly graceful motion. He got his eight seconds, and swung himself off the horse, landing on his feet in the soft dirt of the arena floor, sending up a poof of dust as he circled his hat over his head.

"He sure knows how to ride a pony," Seth said. "I'll give him that."

We watched until the event was nearly over. "Can you watch Brigit for me?" I asked. "I need to get my batons and warm up."

Seth agreed to babysit my dog. I scurried to the police office in the tower, retrieved my batons, then hurried to the area where the contestants and performers waited for their turn in the arena.

Clint strode around the space like a peacock, giving and receiving high fives and butt slaps from the other riders. When he spotted me practicing at the far end of the space, he ambled over.

"Holy cow!" His face tilted upward as his eyes followed one of my spinning batons forty feet into the air. "If it's this impressive now, I can only imagine what this will be like when they're on fire."

"You're about to find out."

The show manager rounded me up and put me in line near the entrance behind a teenage girl who rode a trick horse. "You're on after them."

I watched from the shadows. The trick horse was impressive, performing a sideways grapevine maneuver, walking several steps on its hind legs, even putting one leg out in front of itself to take a bow at the end.

When the applause settled down, the announcer introduced me. "Folks, we've got a first tonight here at the Stock
Show and Rodeo. Let's give a warm welcome to tonight's
hottest act, Fort Worth police officer Megan Luz and her
flaming fire batons!"

I waved the three batons over my head and trotted out
to the center of the arena. Using a cheap plastic lighter, I
set the ends of each baton aflame. The lighter safely in my
pocket, I signaled the sound crew to cue up "Deep in the
Heart of Texas," a song I'd performed to years ago with
the band.

I started slow, twirling one baton, then amped things
up, twirling faster. I added in the second and third batons,
twirling them for a moment as one, and again increased
the speed of rotation. As the song launched into its first
refrain—*"The stars at night, are big and bright!"*—I sent
the first of the batons sailing high into the air. The crowd
cheered and clapped and sang along with the music. *"Deep
in the heart of Texas!"*

I continued on, performing an aerial, spinning around
in the dust, dropping to one knee and bouncing up again,
all the while twirling my batons and sending them into the
air like oversized sparklers. As I turned first one way, then
the other, I spotted Clint watching me from the entrance,
with Seth positioned directly across from him on the other
side of the arena.

When the song wrapped up, I grabbed my batons out
of the air, held them up together one last time like the
Olympic torch, then blew out the flames with a flourish.
After a curtsy to each side of the stadium, I waved good-
bye to the crowd and returned to the backstage area.

Clint waited in the doorway, leaning sideways against
the wall, his arms crossed loosely over his chest. "That was
rockin'!"

"Thanks. I'm just glad none of my batons landed in the hay." That would've been a disaster.

As I went to round up the cases for my batons, Clint followed me.

"Guess what?" he said, his face beaming.

I looked up into his brown eyes, which sparkled with excitement. "You're the champ?"

He threw a victorious fist in the air. "Hell, yeah! Three hundred and thirty-three points on four rides. Can you believe it?"

I offered him a smile. "Congratulations."

His grin faded and his face grew serious for a moment. "I've decided I'm going out on the circuit. It's like they say. You only live once."

"That's true."

"I'm off to Utah next week. Already put in my resignation at the sheriff's department."

"What about Jack?"

"Shoot, that horse is my best friend. He'll come with me, of course." Clint eyed me for a moment, his gaze assessing me. "I'm going to miss you, Officer Luz. When the rodeo comes through town, I just might look you up. If you decide to give boy trouble the boot, maybe we can go out and have some fun."

I reached out a hand to take his and gave it an affectionate squeeze. "I wish you all the best, Clint."

He gave me a squeeze in return. "You, too, Megan." He released my hand, tipped his hat to me one last time, and turned away.

I returned to Seth's side and together we watched as Clint was awarded his championship belt buckle. Seth even clapped for Clint, though his enthusiasm was less than mine, naturally.

Seth and Blast hung around while the show's staff

packed everything up and closed down. Finally, at two A.M., the last barn was locked and my shift was over.

The four of us headed out to the parking lot, stopping next to my cruiser.

"So we'll talk in the morning?" Seth said. "Sort things out?"

"Sure. Ten o'clock." I stepped closer to him, put a hand on his chest, and looked up into his eyes. "But what about now?"

"Now," he said, "we do this."

With a soft smile, he put his mouth to mine.

"Diane Kelly's writing is smart and
laugh-out-loud funny."
—Kristan Higgins, *New York Times* bestselling author

Don't miss the next novel in Diane Kelly's
Paw Enforcement series

LAYING DOWN THE PAW

Coming in August 2015 from St. Martin's Paperbacks